Copyright © 2023 by Ken Lozito

All rights reserved.

No part of this book may be reproduced in any form or by any electronic or mechanical means, including information storage and retrieval systems, without written permission from the author, except for the use of brief quotations in a book review.

Published by Acoustical Books, LLC

KenLozito.com

Cover design by Tom Edwards

IF YOU WOULD LIKE TO BE NOTIFIED WHEN MY NEXT BOOK IS RELEASED VISIT

WWW.KENLOZITO.COM

Paperback ISBN: 978-1-945223-60-0

Hardback ISBN: 978-1-945223-62-4

SPACE RAIDERS
FORGOTTEN EMPIRE

KEN LOZITO

CHAPTER 1

The thing I'd learned after traveling with aliens was that they could be a conspiring bunch to work with. The only thing they had in common was that they all thought they knew best, which was how I wound up on this boring planet, fulfilling a salvage contract for not that much money.

Another icon flashed on the holoscreen, and I glanced at it for a second before peering ahead through the semi-translucent screen at the grassy fields that went on for miles.

I slumped in the chair and sulked.

A comlink chimed, and Kaz turned toward me with an arched, thick eyebrow. I stared back at him for a moment, ignoring the chime. Then I straightened, and suppressing a yawn, I declined the request.

He grinned a little and shook his head. "You don't really think that's going to work, do you?"

I inhaled deeply and sighed. "Sometimes it's the little things."

Kaz Durgen is an Akacian, a race that looked like a cross

between a Komodo dragon and a wolf, and he's my friend. As he adjusted the flight controls and angled the recon skiff toward the new waypoint, his white hair frilled into the air like a lion's mane. His face was all sharp angles, with eyes that remained fixed ahead.

I was the captain of the *Spacehog*, but I shared ownership with two other people. We'd been abducted from Earth over six months ago, and we not only survived an encounter with a cutthroat alien by the name of Kael Torsin, but we fulfilled a huge service to some very rich aliens. Instead of just taking the money and running away, I convinced the others to invest in a ship to explore the galaxy.

I glanced at the atmospheric readings, which I'd configured to show a simplified output because I really didn't care what the actual composition of the atmosphere was on this planet. I cared whether I could breathe and whether the temperature was too hot or cold. While I preferred a practical approach to exploration, Ben, one of my partners, was well on his way to becoming a brilliant scientist. He would probably have set the maximum data output for sensor readings.

Another comlink chimed, and after a few seconds, my gaze slid toward it.

"Want me to get it?" Kaz asked, not looking at me.

I straightened in my seat and acknowledged the comlink request.

"I'm sorry. Nathan Briggs can't answer the phone right now because he's died of boredom."

A soft chuckle came over the comlink. "Still pouting, are we?" Serena asked.

"Are you kidding? No way! This place is amazing. I mean look at these rolling hills off to the right," I said.

Serena was my other business partner and the daughter of a

friend who'd been killed by Kael Torsin. She was in her mid-twenties, very attractive, and way more practical than I was.

The *Spacehog's* hauler flew in the distance, and he imagined Serena looking out the ship's window toward him. The hauler was meant for transporting cargo. It had a large storage crate attached to the body of a ship, but otherwise had smooth lines. Without the obnoxiously huge storage container attached, the hauler flew just fine in an atmosphere, but they needed to use the extra-large cargo container because the client had requested that functioning parts of the wreckage also be recovered. The cargo container made the hauler fly like it was dragging its ass, appearing as if it had lost the will to live.

"Well, suck it up, Nate. We won't be here that long."

I snorted. "This *is* me sucking it up," I said, waving toward the other ship.

Kaz cleared his throat.

I rolled my eyes. "I'll be happier when we get paid."

"That's the spirit," Serena said.

Her voice sounded like she was smiling sweetly, and she probably enjoyed poking fun at my sour mood.

I glided my thumb over the drop button, flirting with the thought of disconnecting it, but shook my head. "The crash site looks like it extends for another mile or so. We're going to make a sweep of the area."

"Okay. Oh, Kierenbot sent a message asking whether you transferred our permits to the Minoa Star System Authority."

I frowned. Kierenbot was on the *Spacehog*. I remembered him mentioning that I needed to okay the permits to be sent, but I couldn't remember if I'd actually done it.

"Yeah, I think so," I said and winced.

"You think so!"

Serena was very much a by-the-book sort of person. She

liked to play nice and didn't share my view on salvage permits being a form of legalized extortion for some fat bureaucrat skimming off our hard work.

I considered my reply for a few seconds and then just disconnected the comlink. I closed my eyes for a second. "I'm going to pay for that."

Kaz chuckled. "Oh, you can count on it."

I shrugged. "Well then, add it to the list."

Kaz eyed me for a second. "Do you mean for Serena or the rest of us?"

"Take your pick. Did anyone ever tell you that your old job was a thankless one sometimes?"

Kaz gave me a look that seemed to imply I'd done this to myself. I also knew he'd switch places with me in a heartbeat if he had the chance.

"Where to, Captain?"

I blew out a breath. "Now *you're* going to start on me?"

"I was merely asking which direction you wanted to go. It's a big decision, I know."

In the six months that we'd been traveling around the galaxy aboard the *Spacehog*, Kaz had taken great amusement in teaching us about the ship and how to traverse the galaxy. I'd rather "fail while daring greatly," as the saying goes.

I gestured ahead of us. "Go that way really fast."

Kaz thrust the throttle forward, and the inertia dampeners took milliseconds to compensate. I still felt like the hand of God had swooped out of the sky to push us ahead.

"Excellent," I grinned.

The grasslands weren't all flat. There were quite a few hills in the area. I studied them in the distance and felt my brows push forward into a thoughtful frown.

"How many of these types of contracts did you have to take while you were captain?"

Kaz thought about it for a few seconds. "Not enough. I lost the ship, remember?"

I didn't know it when I'd first met Kaz, but he'd been drowning in debt and was on the verge of losing everything. He'd gotten a second chance, but in order to wipe the slate clean, he'd lost the ship.

"Well?"

"More than a few. Serena is right. Taking these kinds of contracts helps to fill the gaps between riskier endeavors."

I'd made a deal with Serena and the others that we'd treat the ship like an enterprise. We'd amassed a small fortune by being caught up in an alien succession plot. One chance encounter had changed our lives forever. We could've returned to Earth, but where was the fun in that? We had a spaceship, and we could go anywhere we wanted.

And we'd chosen to come here.

The ground moved beneath us as if a giant gust of wind had attempted to flatten the landscape. I looked down and saw thousands of floating, tannish-colored creatures. They bobbed as they rode the airwaves, and the blowholes on top of their heads expelled some kind of dusty particles.

Some of them rose a few feet into the air, but I couldn't spot any wings.

"What are those things?"

Kaz shook his head. "I'm not sure. Use the console if you want to see if there is any data on them."

"Take us in for a closer look," I replied.

I brought up a sub window on the holoscreen and ran a search using the video feed as the source.

As we flew toward the ground, I saw that the creatures had

two appendages sticking out the sides of their short, stubby bodies, and I thought I could see dark eyes in their sockets. They had blackened snouts, and four hairy legs hung limply beneath them.

"How the heck are those things flying? They don't have any wings," I said, frowning for a few seconds. "They look like giant sheep bugs."

"Sheep?" Kaz asked.

"A sheep without the hair. I knew this girl that sheared sheep on the weekends to collect their wool. She was a little out there."

"Fascinating," Kaz said and brought up a data window. "Looks like they're not native to this world. They were brought in for some reason."

I peered at the screen. "Does it say how they're floating in the air?"

"Some kind of internal process," Kaz replied as he read the data. "Oh, they're filtering the atmosphere. I bet this was some kind of long-term terraforming project."

"They dump these things here and wait a few decades for the atmosphere to be to their liking?"

Kaz nodded. "Yes. Low effort, and it doesn't require maintenance."

Tens of thousands of those creatures floated along the countryside, occasionally bobbing down to eat something off the ground.

"Who left them here?"

Kaz shrugged. "Doesn't say. Multiple colonial efforts use this method. This could've been slated for use a century ago."

"Aren't they worried someone else would come and set up shop here?"

"Evidently not."

I stared at him. Several of the sheep glanced up at us.

"If they were, the holders of the territory would file a grievance with whoever manages the sector."

I pressed my lips together. "Seems kinda…bureaucratic. I mean, I invest in putting these creatures here to help terraform the atmosphere to my liking and someone else decides to take this place for their own? We call it squatting, and it's complete bullshit."

Kaz regarded me for a second. "Such a peculiar way of looking at things. There are conflicts, but it's better if they are worked out locally rather than involving sector authorities."

I snorted. "Cheaper, too."

Kaz dipped his chin in agreement.

"So what happens to all these creatures when the settlers arrive?"

"They're recycled."

I blinked. "They just kill them all?"

Kaz nodded. "Their biomasses are used for other things. Don't look so shocked. They're engineered for this, Nate. Think of them as biological machines."

I looked at Kaz, trying to decide if he was just toying with me. He looked serious.

"They survive purely on a few basic instincts encoded into their DNA. Honestly, they don't have much going on in their brains," he said, tapping the side of his head.

I imagined hordes of animal rights activists screaming in protest, but I'd come to understand that many advanced alien species viewed the galaxy from a more practical standpoint. No one gave a thought to replacing a broken blender, but I wondered if I should feel differently about this. It wasn't as if there were thousands of lonely puppies running around, looking for someone to play with. I guessed I needed to digest the concept a little bit more before forming an opinion about it. My wisdom knew no bounds this morning.

"How many sheep do they send here?"

"Not many. They're actually grown here. A small seed ship arrives with a mobile lab. It samples the environment and alters the DNA as necessary. Then they're grown and released."

"All of these things are grown in a lab?"

Kaz shook his head. "No, of course not. Just enough to get the population going. Then they procreate."

My gaze narrowed, considering.

Kaz gestured toward the holoscreen. "According to this, they do it quite a lot, actually."

I cleared my throat. "Let's hope we didn't come during their busy season."

Something flashed to my side, and I turned toward it. "We might have some company after all."

I gestured toward the right as something metallic flew low to the ground, and the space sheep bobbed out of the way. Some didn't move fast enough, and something puffed in the air as the sheep's bodies split apart. The result of that wasn't blood but something else that reminded me of a bunch of pollen floating in the air. The space sheep deflated and fell to the ground like expelled balloons.

"That's brutal."

"They're drones," Kaz replied.

I nodded and sent a message to Serena and the others. The drones were heading toward the crash site, but not all of them.

"Looks like they came from over there. Let's go check it out."

Kaz swung the recon skiff around. "And you thought this was going to be another boring salvage run."

I grinned, unable to contain myself. "Now the fun begins."

CHAPTER 2

Kaz followed the drones as they continued their run through the space sheep. The dumb creatures hardly seemed to notice, but they did try to move out of the way when they did.

The recon skiff didn't have any weapons. The only thing we had was speed, and lots of it. We easily caught up to the drones, and they didn't react to our presence at all.

"No comms signals detected," I said.

"They're autonomous then."

The drones were oval-shaped and the size of a small car. They flew in a phalanx formation, but they suddenly split apart in pairs. Kaz flew us higher for a better vantage point to see where they were going.

I peered ahead along their flight path. "There's something down there."

Kaz looked in the direction I pointed. "Doesn't look like anything to me."

"The landscape changes. Looks like there are a few chasms. Maybe some of the wreckage found its way all the way out here."

Kaz considered and didn't reply.

"We should split up," I said.

"You've been looking for any excuse to use that flight gear for your combat suit."

I shrugged. "Hey, I did the training, and we can't be in two places at once."

I tapped the collar of my combat suit and my helmet extended from the storage unit just below the base of my neck. The faceplate became translucent so Kaz could see me.

Kaz sighed. "I knew you were going to say that."

I smiled. "Great minds think alike. Ready?"

The recon skiff used a shield canopy to isolate us from the planet's atmosphere. It wouldn't stop anyone from shooting at us, but that hadn't happened for over six months. Today was going to be a good day.

Kaz engaged his own helmet and disabled the skiff's shield. Wind rushed by, and I pushed off the seat, leaping into the air. The recon skiff angled away from me, and I activated the flight system for my combat suit. Thrusters hidden in my heels came online, and I pushed my arms back to compensate for the thrusters in my hands. Twin boosters came from a small pack on my back. I hovered for a few seconds, getting my bearings. Then, I lunged through the air, ignoring the speed on my HUD as I flew like Iron Man.

Handles like a dream.

I just had to focus on the direction I wanted to fly, and the combat suit computers managed the flight system to get me there. Changing directions took very little effort but required more of a delicate approach. I'd crashed in the simulator more times than I could count while qualifying to use the system, but that hardly happened anymore.

Kaz was right. I couldn't wait to use the suit. Who wouldn't? How many people dreamed of soaring through the sky? I know I did, and now I could. It was better than I could've imagined. Serena thought I was crazy, but I'd caught her sneaking into the simulator to give it a try. This wasn't the simulator, and I was pretty sure I could fly faster than Iron Man, but I didn't have much in the way of armament other than the hand blasters on each of my wrists. I'd much rather explore than fight a war anyway.

I tracked the drones as they flew over the hills and scanned ahead into the distance. Something about the landscape seemed artificial. Over the years, before aliens had decided to pluck me off Earth, I'd flown in more than a few survey flights using LIDAR scans to find artificial anomalies on the ground that might indicate hidden ruins beneath the surface. My combat suit had similar capabilities, and a scan overlay of the ground appeared on my HUD.

I scanned ahead, willing what my gut was telling me about this place to be true—that it was more than what it seemed. Finding remnants of ancient civilizations wasn't unheard of in the galaxy, which I found profoundly reassuring. I couldn't remember when I'd become interested in these things. It was sometime between early childhood and my mid-twenties, wondering if this was really all there is. We couldn't have discovered all there is to know about Earth, and I still believed that, but now I'd expanded that viewpoint to the galaxy as well. The universe was, after all, a very old and unusual place. Nothing I'd seen had convinced me otherwise.

As a rule, I'm wary of anyone who believes they've figured

everything out. Chances are they haven't stretched their imaginations enough to fill a pickle jar, much less understand everything life has to offer.

There must have been something almost universal that occurred with structures that had been reclaimed by nature. Perhaps this place hadn't always been rolling green hills. What separated natural landscapes like hills, forests, and mountains from something else? When did hills become mounds built by an ancient civilization? I didn't expect to find anything like Stonehenge, but there was a pattern to the landscape below that was reminiscent of a grid. It would be like finding Manhattan had existed tens of thousands of years ago, and over the years the entire surrounding landscape had changed.

I flew higher into the sky, and the combat suit computer attempted to predict the layout of the city hidden beneath the ground. It was a grid but lay within a huge oval that went on for miles. All my instincts were screaming that there was something beneath the ground—some subterranean vault from the distant past that must have remained undisturbed for who knew how long. At this point, I knew better than to venture a guess. I needed to take a closer look.

The hills gave way to a deep ravine, and I flew toward it. The ravine was almost jagged, as if whatever had been underneath had collapsed.

A comlink from Kaz registered with my suit and I accepted the call.

"The drones are doing a standard grid search. I think they're just surveying the area and are not interested in the salvage claim."

"Same here."

"Good. Do you want meet up, or would you rather fly back to the hauler?"

"Actually, there's something I want to check out."

Silence consumed the comlink for almost a minute.

"Nate, what are you doing?"

I grinned. "I'm not doing anything."

Kaz sighed. "There's no wreckage out here, and since the permits weren't actually registered for this claim, we should get out of here before anyone notices us."

I glanced around the almost nondescript landscape. "Who's going to notice us here?"

"That wrecked ship sent a distress signal, which is how we got the contract. Someone could come searching for it. And someone sent the drones here."

"Yeah, but if they were interested in the salvage claim, they'd already be at the crash site. Kaz, I'm going to check something out. I'll send you my coordinates, or you can just meet me back with the others."

I knew he wouldn't leave me here, but I thought it was best to put the option out there.

"You know I'm not going to do that. Can you at least wait for me to catch up to you before going in?"

I laughed, and Kaz sighed.

"Fine. I'll be there as soon as I can."

"Great. Sending coordinates now," I said and paused for a second. "Oh, and Kaz, I've got a feeling about this place."

"Is it the same feeling you've had before?"

I'd chased a few red herrings in my short time exploring the galaxy, but as mentioned, I'd rather fail at something while daring greatly.

"Hey Kaz," I said, waiting for a few seconds before severing the connection.

There were few things that annoyed my first mate more than the lack of a response.

I spun in the air, getting another survey of the area. Then I leaned forward, jutting my chin out and shooting ahead like a bullet leaving the barrel of gun.

God, I loved flying like Iron Man!

CHAPTER 3

There was a phrase that got spoken when trying to hit a target or navigate a challenging trek, no matter the mode of transportation. As I blazed a path toward the fissure, I became aware of a couple of things. One, threading the needle is a lot harder than someone might think. Two, a more rational side of my brain advised me to slow down. It was a defining moment, and sometimes I liked to wave at those moments as they sailed by me.

The fissure was a relatively small opening, perhaps thirty feet long and a dozen feet wide. Ben had tried to get me to start using the metric system—something about it being the language of science and how the future was heading that way. I guess I'm a holdout for what works for me, and since I was part owner of a spaceship, I figured I could see the world as I pleased. It also helped that my preferences used on the *Spacehog* carried over to the equipment I liked to use. I didn't know how Kaz referred to measurements in his own language, and the computer systems helped bridge the gap between language barriers for the different species.

A warning about my speed flashed on the HUD as I flew toward the fissure. Even the suit computer thought I was crazy.

The combat suit I wore could withstand quite a beating, something I had experienced firsthand and could speak confidently to when the situation called for it. I eased off my suit thrusters, and smaller maneuvering thrusters helped slow my descent to a more manageable speed. It was still quite fast, bordering on suicidal, but I'd practiced this maneuver many times in the simulator. How different could it be?

I was about to find out.

The fissure was locked dead center in my HUD. I approached the target at a steep descent while maintaining an angle. Scans indicated a large open space past the fissure. I was counting on it; otherwise, I was going to be like a bug on the windshield of a car.

I tightened my arms to my sides and felt the suit thrusters alter my course a little. I was through the opening in less than a second, and alarms flashed across my HUD because the ground was much closer than I'd anticipated.

Gritting my teeth, I jerked my hands out in front of me, maximizing my thruster output and rapidly slowed down, but not enough to keep me from walloping the ground.

In terms of crashes, I barely kissed the ground. I was sure there wasn't going to be a crater, but I felt the jolt as I bounced off the ground. My arms flailed as the suit's maneuvering thrusters quickly stabilized me for a few seconds in the air. Then, I sank toward the ground.

"Woohoo! Yeah, baby! That's what I like," I said, pumping my fist into the air. I might have done a little hip shaking in celebration of what I would tell the others was a perfect landing, although any landing I could walk away from was good enough for me.

I blew out a breath and glanced above me. Sunlight shone on the ground nearby in a pool of yellow light, penetrating various cracks through the ceiling of overgrowth above me. My HUD compensated for the lower light, and I could see my surroundings.

At first glance, I was surrounded by some kind of hardened dirt. It might have been a road, and what had been a straight path was now curvy. I could walk it, but why walk when I could fly?

I flew at a leisurely pace and noticed that the ground sloped, moving me farther away from the surface. I spotted the remnants of several buildings that had collapsed, confirming my instinct that I'd stumbled upon some kind of ancient ruin. The path became wider, and shafts of sunlight streamed in from high above. I came in for a soft landing and stopped. There was a feeling of perpetual quietness, reminding me of old churches and cathedrals in the middle of the night.

Water rushed through the remnants of buildings nearby. They hadn't been made from stone but some kind of darkened metal that sometimes reflected the light, giving the area a sparkly brilliance.

I walked along an old road that was still fairly smooth, and puddles of water had pooled from a recent storm. I just wanted to take in the ambiance of the place, allowing my imagination to wander. I couldn't make any sense of the buildings, other than knowing that someone had built them. I wondered what purpose they'd served, but I doubted the combat suit computer could reconstruct a version of what these buildings might've looked like. Too much time had passed, and who knew what had transpired here? Maybe Kierenbot could do something with the data back on the ship.

A high-pitched squeal pierced the silence, echoing nearby. This was followed by a chorus of squeals. I narrowed my gaze and tilted my head, more out of habit rather than any practicality of hearing it better. It almost sounded like shrieks of delight by something comically small and full of mischief.

The sounds were coming from the other side of a fallen building. Rust-colored vines grew among the debris in a tightly knit formation that only smaller bugs now called home. I crept forward, trying to move as quietly as possible. As I came around the edge, I saw a wide chasm. I peered at it and realized that I wasn't standing on the ground; I was standing atop an ancient city, and judging by the depth of the chasm, whoever had lived here had built their own versions of skyscrapers.

The chasm was over a hundred yards wide. Small, brown, furry creatures scurried along the edge, peering downward like meerkats. There were hundreds of them, and they weren't being quiet about it. They must have been communicating with one another, but I couldn't figure out what had gotten them so excited.

I moved toward the edge unnoticed, and the feed on my HUD zoomed in closer so I could get a better look at the creatures. They had folds of extra fur and looked as if they stood about three feet tall. I zoomed out and saw one of them push his neighbor over the side into the chasm. It happened so quickly that I did a double take. The creature let out a long, high-pitched squeal as it fell, while the others seem to chitter with mischievous laughter.

I leaned forward and saw that the creature had spread its arms wide, and the folds of fur spread out into a thin layer of skin, enough for it to glide. It swooped around as it made its descent. Several other creatures were knocked off, and I spotted others climbing back up the chasm walls.

They were enjoying this.

Grinning a little, I watched the little furballs continue to play their game. When I eventually stepped closer to the edge, a group of creatures moved toward me. I wasn't sure where they'd been hiding. They approached me with a bit of caution, moving slowly and deliberately.

I calmly watched them approach. Two of them darted ahead and began to tumble right toward me. They bounced off my legs and were sprawled onto their backs. The others watched with meerkat fascination, and then several more tried to knock me off the edge.

I laughed. "It's going to take a lot more of you than that."

I spread my arms wide, and the creatures flinched back. Their skittering screech language went high in alarm for a few seconds before they settled down. Another creature leaped high into the air, aiming for my chest, and I caught him. He squirmed in my hands, staring at me in utter shock. The others watched me with intense curiosity. Dark patches surrounded their eyes like goggles. The one I held blinked a few times and tilted his head to the side, looking adorable, his eyes sincere. I smiled and tossed the creature over the edge, watching as he twisted in the air and spread his wings to glide toward the other side.

The creatures nearest me squealed in delight and began bouncing up and down in front of me like children demanding a ride. I held out my hands, and one of them leaped right into them.

"I guess you want to go for a ride, little buddy."

I tossed him even farther than the last, and my new furry companions chittered uproariously. I joined in with a hearty laugh. This was the highlight of my day. It was fun, and they seemed to be having a good time. I started up the video recorder so I could show the others what I'd found.

Several more creatures lined up near me, eager for me to toss them into the air. The higher I threw them, the louder they squealed in delight. They even started using the palm of my hands as a springboard.

ND of them from the other side began making their way over to me while several groups of enterprising creatures climbed higher so they could glide over to me. I had to wonder who had taught them this game. Had they come up with it on their own, or had someone else been here to play with them?

It was a refreshing change to be among creatures that knew how to have a good time. Most of the other planets I'd been to offered a quick education on just how vicious the galactic animal kingdom could be. They varied in how intelligent they were, and there was an ongoing bounty paid by Zerian Enterprises for newly discovered species. They were always on the search for any species that had a chance of developing higher forms of intelligence. They wanted to do something small, like categorize the entire galaxy. It would only take them a million years to visit every star system in the Milky Way.

I didn't mind sending them data and getting paid a small stipend for something that didn't take a lot of effort.

The creatures clustered around me and were becoming so loud that I had to turn down the volume inside my helmet. I stepped toward the edge and a wave of excitement swept over my furry companions, as if they anticipated a great show.

I made a production of glancing over the edge into the depths below. Then I shrugged and leaped over the side.

My suit thrusters came online, and I hovered in the air for a moment. Then, I spun and swooped to the other side before returning toward the middle. The creatures leaped up and down in anticipation of another show. I was waving at them when a bright flash came from below me, along with a loud boom that shook the area.

The creatures scattered, quickly running away and disappearing into whatever crevice they used to travel through the ruins. I stared down below. It looked like the ground was several hundred feet down. I glanced toward the edges of the chasm to find that I was completely alone. They were probably much smarter than I was because I was going down there to see what had caused all that noise.

I began a slow descent into the chasm. I'm not an overly violent person, but I did put a priority on knowing how to defend myself. Ignoring how to use weapons didn't prevent anyone from using them on me, so I learned what I could. After the whole alien abduction part of my life, I found that I didn't know nearly enough. The more advanced species had been at it for a lot longer than Humans, but some of the principles were the same. It was with that in mind that I engaged both my hand cannons.

I'd modified the weapon I'd taken from Kaz. The hand cannons had a stub barrel that could elongate, depending on whether I was shooting a target far away from me. That hadn't happened very often. The stub barrel was about three inches long, appearing over my wrists, and a metallic handle extended across my inner palm so I could squeeze the trigger. The ammunition was set for plasma discharge, which should be protection enough if I needed it. If it wasn't, I wasn't above running away.

I continued my descent until I reached the ground. A large tunnel appeared to my right, and I saw small flashes of light that looked like someone was using some kind of arc welder in the distance. I leaned forward and flew down the tunnel.

Nothing moved on the ground. In fact, there seemed to be

some kind of ancient wreckage along the way. Rocky mounds were strewn along the ground with such regularity that it made their formation seem like anything but a natural occurrence.

I flew toward the source of the flashing and saw the remnants of one of the drones I'd seen earlier. It looked different. When it had been flying through the air, it had a capsule shape, but here on the ground it unfolded and looked like some kind of robot—tall and humanoid, with long, thick arms and legs. Its broad-shaped head reminded me of a hammerhead shark. One of the stalactites from the ceiling had speared through its chest, and blue liquid splattered the ground nearby. I glanced above and saw hundreds of stone sickles just waiting for an excuse to skewer yours truly.

I regarded the drone for a second. "Tough break, buddy."

The drone had been cutting into a small mound. It must have had some kind of plasma cutting tool, because it had made a lot of progress. I ran a scan of my own and detected a trace heat signature deep inside. Could this place still have power, or was it something from the drone that had fallen into the hole?

I landed next to the drone and peered into the small tunnel. It sloped downward a good distance and then opened up more than wide enough for me to climb through. I took a quick look around to see if there were any other robots in the vicinity. Seeing none, I ducked into the tunnel.

I bent over and quickly made my way through, emerging into an inner chamber that had several solid-looking, floor-to-ceiling pillars, along with a central altar. I couldn't be sure if it was an actual altar. If I'd found this place on Earth, then I'd say it was an altar of some kind, but out in the galaxy it could be anything. I'd learned to keep an open mind about the things I'd seen. Chances were good it was some kind of workstation, but I wasn't sure what it did. It was tall, looking as if it would come up to my chin. Water trickled in from several places on the far walls. According to my sensors, the air was cool and a bit humid. I was already several hundred feet below the ground above, but perhaps this chamber was even more subterranean than that.

I peered at the walls, allowing my camera feed to record what I saw. I brought up my omnitool and increased the sensitivity of my scanners, then slowly panned around the room. A very faint impression of complex shapes decorated the walls. What had once been a very elaborate artwork was mostly covered. I walked toward one of the walls and used my hand to wipe away some of the dirt that had accumulated over time. Not much came off, so I banged my fists on it, which caused it to break off, exposing more of the artwork.

I couldn't make any sense of what I was seeing, so I decided to move on, walking toward the altar on the far side of the room. As I crossed the middle of the chamber, I heard a hissing sound near the base of the altar. The lights on my helmet lit up the entire room, but some kind of large shadow moved toward me. There were two of them that seemed to materialize near the altar and moved right for me. I could only see vague outlines, as if they were partially covered by some kind of camouflage that blotted them out. They moved like a specter, seeming to stalk toward me.

The two creatures suddenly howled, moving on all fours like giant wolves.

I thrust my hand cannons in front of me and fired. Plasma bolts slammed into the creatures, lighting them up in orange bursts. They still shifted toward me, and I gripped the trigger, firing at full auto while stepping backward. Some of the plasma bolts passed through the creatures while others knocked them back. The floor blackened where the creatures had been, but they just disappeared as if they didn't have the energy to keep fighting.

"That's enough weird for me," I said, backing up toward the tunnel, eager to get out of there.

A hissing vapor rose from the ground where the two specters had died, but all evidence was quickly fading, as if it had never happened. I raised my gaze toward the altar and only just realized that I'd broken it apart in my assault on those things.

A shiver went down my spine, but I couldn't take my eyes off the altar. I peered inside and saw the intricate workings of some kind of console. This wasn't an altar but was a kind of workstation.

I glanced back at the tunnel and sighed. I hadn't come all this way *not* to take a closer look. That was the difference between success and failure, sometimes between life and death too, but the danger was minimal, at least for now.

I strode across the chamber, keeping my hand cannons raised just in case something else popped out to attack. The crunch of my footsteps was the only sound in the room as I closed in on the workstation. My plasma bolts had melted the inside, destroying whatever had been there. I circled around and saw that something had been dumped out. It was an octagonal sphere about a foot in diameter. I knelt down, watching the sphere. It was dark and gritty, with tiny flecks of something shiny as it caught the light from my helmet. It reminded me of quartz. As I peered at it, I noticed that there were countless layers of gray colors that formed a gradient from top to bottom.

I stared at it, waiting to see if it was going to do something. Hundreds of horror movies had taught me that a little bit of patience went a long way toward surviving. When nothing burst from the gray sphere and there was no warning glow that something had activated, I reached out gingerly, leaning away just in case this was the egg of a Xenomorph, and tapped the top of the sphere. It was solid. Nothing happened.

Pressing my lips together, I poked it harder. It was heavy and solid. That was something. I placed my palm on it and left it there.

The sphere disintegrated. My eyes widened and I snatched my hand back.

"What the," I said, staring at it, wide-eyed and a little disappointed.

The gray sphere was now a pile of very fine grains that shimmered a little. I was sure that if I'd taken my helmet off and blown on it, it would have billowed into the air until it disappeared.

"Way to go, Nate. You're now the owner of an ancient pile of dust."

A pyramid of sorts formed in the middle of the dust, and I reached down, feeling something solid under my fingertips. I lifted it up and saw it was a black metallic frame—a collapsible octagon. I expected it to fall apart in my hands, but it didn't. I watched it for a second, wondering what I'd just found. First, there'd been weird specters and now this. I glanced around the chamber for a few seconds and then put what I'd found into the storage compartment on my hip. I'd check it out later.

I looked down at the remains of the metallic sphere. It was almost gone. It had disbursed quicker than I thought.

Starting to feel like I should get out of this chamber as quickly as possible, I hastened back toward the tunnel and climbed through.

As I emerged from the tunnel, four robots were standing over their fallen comrade, and then four hammerheads turned toward me. Their pale metallic chassis reflected the light, making them appear to glow a little bit. A red slash covered their heads and parts of their bodies. They each lifted one of their hands and pointed a hand cannon at me.

I raised my hands. "Take it easy. I didn't hurt your friend."

I stepped toward them, and one of the robots fired his weapon. A plasma bolt blackened the ground in front of my feet.

A warning flashed on my HUD. The weapon's intensity was enough to penetrate my combat suit. These things weren't messing around. They'd fired a warning shot, and I was sure the next one wouldn't be. I stared at them, trying to think of something I could do to get away. My flight system was ready, but I was pretty sure they could take me out as I tried to escape. What I needed was a distraction.

I raised my eyes at the stalactites high above us, and an idea formed in my head. It might not be the smartest idea I could come up with, but it would do in a pinch.

"Identify," a robot said. His voice was deep and machine-like.

I kept my hands raised.

"No problem. I'm—"

I fired my hand cannons at the ceiling, then leaped to the side, making sure I hit enough of the sharp pointy objects above as I could.

CHAPTER 4

Heavy spikes dropped from the ceiling, and the robots scattered out of the way. I leaped into the air and sped off. My barrage of plasma bolts caused a cascade of destruction that nipped at my heels as I raced to get clear of it. I didn't know if it had been a one-in-a-million shot or if I'd caused enough damage to destroy the proverbial lynchpin holding the tunnel together, but it was coming down like an avalanche.

I glanced at the rear camera feed and saw that two of the robots were following me, having changed forms back into a large capsule. Good to know for sure that the drones from earlier were these attack bots.

I left the long tunnel behind and raced toward the upper levels. The furry creatures scampered up the sides of the chasm and I wished I could do something for them, but they were on their own. I hoped they'd make it to safety.

I flew toward the roof, but there was nowhere for me to get through. The cracks weren't large enough. I thrust my fist in front of me and increased the power output to my hand cannon.

The shot primed and then barfed out of the weapon, racing ahead. It hit the roof at an angle, blowing a hole out the top. A large shaft of sunlight hit the ground and was soon joined by more shafts as a spiderweb of cracks formed in the roof.

I locked onto the central opening and maximized the thrust for my flight system. It took all my strength to lock my arms at my sides, and I darted ahead, bursting through the roof into open air.

I shot into the sky and leveled off while I got my bearings.

A flash of blue light blotted out my HUD, and my combat suit went offline. I felt myself begin to fall toward the ground.

Cursing, I poked blindly at where my omnitool should be. It didn't work. For a few painstaking seconds I was blind to the outside world, and I knew I was within moments of crashing. Then my HUD came back online, and my combat suit took control only seconds from hitting the ground. I shoved my hands in front of my body and the thrusters maximized output. My velocity slowed, but it wasn't enough. I twisted around and slammed onto the ground. I might've bounced a few times before tumbling the rest of the way. This was what my clothes must have felt like in the dryer.

Gritting my teeth, I squeezed my eyes shut until I finally stopped moving.

My head kept spinning, but nothing was broken, which meant my combat suit was still operational. I stood up—tried to stand up—and stumbled to the side as if the entire world had suddenly tilted. I stuck out my hand to prevent me from falling completely flat on my face, got my feet under me, and swayed back and forth.

A ship flew overhead and landed nearby. It had a white hull and wasn't much bigger than the recon skiff I'd flown in earlier. I didn't recognize it. The loading ramp opened at the bottom, and someone strode down it. He carried a rifle and wore a matching set of armor. His faceplate was clear, and I saw the dark green skin and white hair of an Akacian. His face showed signs of age, but he moved like he was strong and definitely had the upper hand.

"You've got something that belongs to me, stranger," he said.

I stepped forward and pointed a finger at him. "Did you shoot me?"

The Akacian slowed a bit. "You didn't comply with my broadcast."

"Bullshit. There was no broadcast."

He stopped about ten feet from me and pointed the end of his rifle at me.

I activated my hand cannon. "Yeah I've got them too," I said and charged.

The Akacian moved to the side while firing his weapon, but he couldn't get a clear shot because I was already returning fire.

One thing I'd learned from traveling on the fringe was that I had to protect myself, and anyone who shot me out of the sky wasn't my friend. I closed the distance, and using my suit thrusters to assist my movements, I slammed my fist into center mass and knocked the Akacian off his feet.

"How do you like it?!"

His rifle flung out of his hands as he rolled on the ground. He didn't get back up; instead, he had his omnitool out.

I fired a warning shot at the ground next to him, and a small crater appeared. "Get up. Hands where I can see them."

I transmitted my location to the skiff. Kaz should've been there by now.

The Akacian stood up and regarded me with a bit of wry amusement.

"You always shoot people you don't know? I haven't taken anything from here."

Akacians were sometimes smug. I'd seen that knowing expression on Kaz's face a bunch of times while he showed me the ins and outs of the *Spacehog*. My prisoner had a similar expression, and I didn't appreciate it.

"Perhaps introductions should be made."

I smiled. "Great. You go first."

He frowned and looked a little surprised. "You don't recognize me?"

I blinked a few times. "It's a big galaxy."

He blew out a breath. "I'm Griff Tarken."

He'd spoken it like it was some kind of grand pronouncement—nothing like a self-important ass who believed he was a legend.

I chuckled. "I bet that sounded a lot more impressive in your own mind than it did aloud."

Griff Tarken glared at me.

I was about to reply when I saw the recon skiff flying toward us. I waved toward it and Griff frowned toward me.

Kaz landed the skiff nearby and exited the vehicle.

"About time," I said, but Kaz ignored me.

He stared at Griff, and the two recognized each other.

"Kaz Durgen, is that you?" Griff said.

Kaz's mouth hung open, and he glanced at Griff's shuttle before looking at him. "Tarken…Griff Tarken. Gabris, I thought you were…" Kaz said and didn't finish.

I cleared my throat, and Kaz tore his eyes away from Griff to look at me. "Remember me? Who *is* this guy? He shot at me."

"As I said earlier, you have something that belongs to me," Griff said.

I shook my head. "Like I already told you, I don't know what you're talking about."

"Then allow me to refresh your memory," Griff said and brought up his omnitool.

Drones raced toward them, slamming into the ground, and the same robots I'd faced earlier stood up. Dozens more of them landed nearby, including a couple of the dirt-covered robots I'd seen earlier.

"Oh, so these belong to you. Well, *they* shot at me too, so you might be short a couple," I said.

Kaz turned toward me. "Is this true? Did you take something?"

I shook my head. "No, all I did was explore the area a little bit underground. Found a really interesting chamber, but there was nothing inside."

"Chamber!" Griff said. "That's what I sent my bots in to search for."

I glared at him. "Good for you."

"Nate!" Kaz hissed and shook his head.

"What?" I growled.

Several bots walked toward us, and I raised my hand cannons. "Hey Griff, call off your dogs or I'm going to start shooting."

"He doesn't mean that," Kaz said and spun toward me.

He looked at me as if I was the crazy one.

"Who's your companion?" Griff asked.

"Gabris, this is Nathan Briggs."

Griff regarded me, unimpressed. "Never heard of you."

I chuckled. "The feeling is mutual," I said and glared at Kaz. "What the hell is wrong with you? You're swooning like some starstruck fanboy. Get it together."

Kaz winced and looked at Griff, smiling sheepishly.

Sheepishly!

I looked at the approaching battlebots. The one thing I could say about aliens was that they build things tough and big. I was liking our odds of escaping even less the more time passed.

"Please excuse us. We're here fulfilling a salvage claim for a wrecked ship nearby," Kaz said.

Griff considered this for a few seconds. "There weren't any permits granted for that salvage. I know because I checked before I came out here."

"What are you doing out here then?" I asked.

"Searching for the ruins you were at earlier."

I stepped toward Kaz. "Well, you have fun with that, but it's time for us to go."

Griff laughed. "I don't think so," he said and frowned, looking at Kaz. "What species is he?"

"Human."

Griff pursed his lips for a second. "I really have been gone for a long time. Last I heard about Humans they'd barely left their own planet."

I smirked. "Well, times are a'changin'," I said and grabbed Kaz's arm, shooting my hand cannon at Griff's feet and catching everyone by surprise. Then I engaged my flight system, hauling Kaz into the air. We landed in the recon skiff amid a tirade of curses from Kaz. I ignored him as I engaged the skiff's engines and slammed the throttle all the way down.

The skiff lurched forward, and I flew right toward Griff Tarken, who, along with his small army of battle bots, scrambled out of the way.

CHAPTER 5

After sparing a second to memorize the view of Griff Tarken and his battlebots scrambling for cover with no small amount of satisfaction, I put us on course with the crashed ship site. I chuckled a little, and Kaz gave me an incredulous look.

I frowned at him. "What the hell is the matter with you?"

"Me?" Kaz sneered.

"Yeah, you. Was he your uncle or something? You were all like, 'Oh, oh, Griff Tarken, I'll do anything you want.'"

Kaz showed me his teeth for a second and then shook his head. He sighed. "Do you ever think that maybe, just maybe, you take things too far?"

I glanced into the distance at the crash site, hoping Serena was almost done reclaiming the storage containers.

I looked at Kaz and shook my head. "Not really, no."

Kaz blinked.

"Geez Kaz, what's wrong with you? That guy was a bully. He's got a gang of battlebots getting ready to tear us apart, and you're occupied with whether I took things too far. That asshole shot at me. Disabled my suit. I'm lucky I survived."

"You don't know who that was."

I shrugged. "I really don't care who he was."

Kaz gave me a sidelong look. "Did you do it?"

"Do what?"

"Take something from the ruins?"

"He doesn't own the land, Kaz. He's got no rights to anything there."

Kaz lifted his hand palms up in a there-you-go gesture.

"And his bots attacked me. I've got a recording of the whole damn thing."

Kaz stared at me. I hated it when he did that.

"What?"

"He's going to figure it out. Then he's going to come after you."

I shrugged. "So what? He can get in line."

Kaz blew out a breath. "You don't get it."

"All I get is that you were fanboying him when you should've had my back. I had to save us back there."

Kaz grimaced. "Save us? *Save us!*"

He drew in a breath to launch into what I was sure was going to be a long tirade that I just didn't want to hear right then. Instead, I opened the communications system to the others, and he became quiet.

"Yeah, Nate. Did you find more wreckage?" Serena asked.

Kaz clamped his mouth shut and exhaled explosively through his nose.

"No, we didn't. Are you guys almost done?"

"No, not by a long shot. In fact, we could really use a hand. Are you on your way here?"

I winced.

Kaz actually looked smug as he regarded me. "Finally figured it out, did you?"

"Shut up."

"What?" Serena asked.

There were few things that could get a woman madder for extended periods of time than telling her to shut up. Although, I think I could top it off if I said something about making sandwiches. (That had been an ongoing joke with one of my uncles.)

"Sorry, not you" I said. Sometimes it was just best to get the apology out of the way. "Kaz is upset."

"Why? What did you do?"

"Judge much?" Right away she had concluded that I'd done something to make Kaz upset.

Kaz brought up a window on the holoscreen showing current scanner detections. A scatterplot of icons had taken over the plot behind us. We still had a significant lead, but I had to do something.

"Never mind that. How much time do you need?"

Serena sighed, losing her patience. "A few hours, Nate. What happened? What's going on? You sound on edge."

I muttered a curse.

Another comlink registered. It had an unknown signature.

"Nate?" Serena asked.

"One second, I have another call," I said and switched over to the other channel.

"By now you've no doubt detected my bots coming after you," Griff said.

His voice reminded me of an early James Bond villain. *(No Mr. Briggs, I expect you to die.)*

I shook my head.

"Something tells me they're not going to be fast enough," I replied.

I muted the comlink and looked at Kaz. "Send a message to Kierenbot. We need to get out of here."

I altered course so we were heading away from the crash site.

Kaz nodded grudgingly and brought up a data window.

"Perhaps," Griff said, "but they really don't need to catch you at all."

"Good, so you'll call them off then and we can go our separate ways."

Griff laughed. It sounded purposefully irritating, as if we were playing cards and he had all the good ones.

"No, I don't think I will," he said. He let out a grunt as if he were climbing or had just jumped down from something. "I think I'll send them to that crash site."

The icons on the scanner changed course. They were heading toward Serena and the others. If I didn't warn them, they would be blindsided.

"Return what you've stolen, and I'll recall them," Griff said.

I knew that was complete bullshit. He was trying to call my bluff. Admitting to him that I'd recovered that dinky little artifact wasn't going to change anything and would probably make things worse.

"Amateur," Griff growled. "You all learn the same way."

"Who are you calling amateur?"

A small group of battlebots separated from the main group and were coming for them.

I grinned. "Now you made it interesting. Hey Griff. Griff Tarken. That's your name, right?"

"Yes," Griff drew out a reply that was partially a growl.

"Good, I didn't want there to be any misunderstandings. I've just got one thing left to say to you."

Kaz looked at me and frowned. I held up my hand, gesturing for him to be quiet.

The edges of my lips lifted in anticipation.

"On the contrary, you're going to say quite a few things to me," Griff said.

I chuckled. "You'll have to buy me a few drinks first, but for right now, this is what I've—"

I severed the comlink with a satisfied smirk.

Barely a second passed before another comlink chimed.

It was Griff.

I grinned and ignored it by swiping it off the holoscreen.

"Dammit Nate, you don't know who you're dealing with."

I shrugged. "Neither does he. That conversation was getting old anyway."

I looked at Serena's comms channel. She was still waiting for him to reply.

I sighed. "Time to deliver the bad news."

"She's going be furious."

I bit my lower lip and nodded.

"I know, maybe you should try that comlink trick with *her*."

"Now you're just trying to get me killed," I said and opened Serena's comms channel.

CHAPTER 6

"Are you kidding me!" Serena shrieked.

I winced. "I'm afraid not. We've got to get out of here."

"Nate, stop screwing around. Kaz, is he messing with me?"

"No, Serena. He's not. We've…" he paused as he regarded me for a second, "…found some unexpected company. They're hostile."

"And they're heading for the crash site," I said. "You need to pack it up, now. Recall the others to the hauler and get back to the *Spacehog*."

Serena didn't reply right away, but I heard her breathing through the comlink. I could only imagine the look on her face.

Yeah, I was going to pay for this.

"Fine," she said.

"We'll try to draw them away from you."

"How? The skiff doesn't have any weapons."

"I'll come up with something."

"No, Nate. Just get back to the ship. We'll be fine," she said and severed the comlink.

There was *that* word again.

Fine.

Things weren't fine.

They were anything but fine.

"She's right," Kaz said.

"Why don't we have weapons on our ships?"

Kaz blinked, not expecting my response. "You're the captain."

"Right, so it's my fault. I'm using your old equipment. Why didn't you ever equip the ships with weapons?"

"It's expensive, and when the people I owed credits to wanted to be paid, I had to make sacrifices."

Kaz's money issues were how I had come to be part owner of the *Spacehog* and everything inside it.

I knew blaming Kaz for our current predicament wasn't right, though I hadn't really blamed him…maybe just implied a little.

"Never mind that now. We'll talk about it later. After we make it out of here."

Kaz nodded. "What are you going to do?"

I slowly let out a breath, trying to think of something.

A text message appeared on Kaz's holoscreen. "Kierenbot says the ship will be ready."

"Good," I replied.

I put the skiff back on course toward the hauler, hoping Serena and the others could get everything stowed in time. T'Chura was there. I'd seen him take on an entire platoon of Mesakloren soldiers, who were as tough as they came, but T'Chura had gotten hurt, too. I wasn't going to let that happen again.

We'd lost a few seconds while trying to lure the battlebots away, and the hauler was still on the ground as the battlebots flew toward it.

"Why are they still folded up in a capsule?" I asked.

"They can probably fly faster that way."

The small group heading toward the skiff was also in capsule form. They hadn't fired any weapons.

I smiled. "They can't fire on us like that."

Kaz frowned for a moment and then nodded. "You might be right."

"I *am* right. If they could, then they would've by now."

The crash site was strewn with the bones of the cargo ship's remains. Several large storage containers were intact, and that was where Serena had concentrated her recovery efforts.

The hauler still had its loading ramp down. A large, hulking figure stood there, firing his rifle. The battlebots quickly scattered, using the remains of the wrecked cargo ship as cover.

T'Chura started to retreat up the loading ramp but kept his weapon ready.

The battlebots moved fast. They quickly flew around the scattered remains of the ship and started firing their weapons on the hauler.

The battlebots formed a phalanx, which neutralized any effective fire T'Chura could return. Without cover, focusing on a target would leave him open to the other bots.

I pushed the flight controls forward and the recon skiff plunged down.

"What are you doing?"

"Evening the odds."

The recon skiff dove toward the ground, heading right for a huge piece of bulkhead that the battlebots were using for cover.

Once we were low enough, I jerked the lateral controls to the side. The skiff's engines swung around, and I blasted the bots and the bulkhead, sending all of them flying.

Thankfully, whoever was piloting the hauler seized the opportunity to launch straight up into the atmosphere. We followed and soon reached the upper atmosphere.

I kept watching the scanner, waiting for the bots to pursue, but they didn't.

"He must've called them off," I said.

Kaz nodded.

I left the atmosphere of the planet behind and rendezvoused with the *Spacehog*.

As the ship's white hull gleamed in front of us, the large hangar bay doors retracted, and the hauler flew in first. I followed, flying the skiff to the side and bringing it in for a very soft landing—probably one of my best so far.

I looked at Kaz, eyebrows raised.

He nodded after a second. "You stuck the landing."

I grinned. "Damn right, I did."

We climbed out of the skiff and walked over to the hauler. There were a few dozen scorch marks from where it had taken fire. It looked like some of those hits had penetrated a bit and would need to be patched.

The hauler's loading ramp lowered a little and stopped short. It must have taken damage. The ramp rose up and then back down, then slammed onto the ground. I added it to the list of things that needed to be fixed.

Ben gave us a small wave as he walked down the ramp. He was followed by T'Chura, our resident and honorable Sasquatch. He was nine feet tall, had lots of hair, and brown eyes the size of coffee mugs.

Raylin followed. The pale-skinned alien walked down the ramp with a dancer's grace and an envirosuit that hugged her body in all the right ways.

She looked at me with pursed lips. "Well, that was an experience."

I glanced up the loading ramp at what they'd been able to recover. "Sorry, couldn't be helped. Is this all you were able to get?"

The hauler wasn't even a third of the way full.

Serena stuck her head out from behind one of the metallic storage crates and narrowed her gaze at me.

A tactical retreat wasn't an option, so I walked up the ramp.

"Yes, this is all we got," Serena said.

"What were you doing all this time?"

"We were cataloging the wreckage so we could get the most valuable items loaded first."

I tried not to look at the emptiness of the hauler, but Serena wasn't fooled.

She stormed up to me. "What did you do? Why were we attacked?"

I almost told her to calm down, but yeah, that would've gone over well.

"There's not much to it. Someone else showed up and chased us off."

Serena blinked several times and glanced at Kaz. "That's ridiculous. We've got a legal right to reclaim the cargo from this wreckage."

I winced. "Yeah, about that."

Serena stabbed daggers at me with her eyes.

A comlink chimed on my omnitool. It was Kierenbot.

I accepted it. "Go ahead."

"Nate, I've detected several new ships entering the star system. They're on an intercept course."

I sighed. "Understood. That's our cue to leave. Set a course and get us out of here."

"They're hailing us. They're local enforcers saying we're conducting salvage operations without a permit."

"That's absurd," Serena said. "Just send them our permits and they'll leave us alone."

I looked away from her for a second and winced. She stared at me expectantly.

"I forgot to transmit the permit application and fees."

Serena sneered. "You *forgot?* Nate, how many times did you tell me you'd get that done. How many times?"

I raised my hand in front of my chest. "Calm down." Whoops. "It's an honest mistake."

"But now we're here illegally."

"Kierenbot, get us out of here. Now," I said and closed the comlink. I looked at Serena. "It's only illegal if we get caught."

Serena's mouth hung open for a few seconds. "You're unbelievable."

I smiled a little and shrugged. "Sometimes it doesn't pay to play by the rules. If you don't believe me, ask Kaz."

Serena swung her gaze toward Kaz. He stood at the bottom of the loading ramp where he'd been speaking with Raylin.

"I'm not one to agree with someone just for the sake of it," Kaz said. No one else had seen him gushing over Griff Tarken, but I knew better than to mention it right then. "But Nate is right. We're better off avoiding the authorities until we can get this sorted out."

Serena considered it for a few seconds and looked at me. Some of the frustration had gone.

"I'm sorry. I know you wanted this to go smoothly," I said.

Serena ignored me and looked at Kaz. "Thanks."

She started walking away and I caught up to her.

"I'll get this sorted out. I promise. We'll take what we've got to the contract holder and come back for the rest."

Serena rested her hands on her hips, staring at the floor for a second before lifting her gaze toward mine. "I hope you can."

I found those simple words to be more chilling than facing Griff Tarken and his legion of battlebots.

"I know you didn't want to come here. This kind of work is boring to you."

"It's not that," I said, to which she arched an eyebrow. "Okay, yes. I wasn't as enthusiastic about this contract, but I didn't sabotage it either."

She regarded me for a few seconds, peering at me with those big brown eyes of hers. Serena was an attractive woman, there was no denying it. When she stared at me, sometimes it felt like I was swathed in a blanket, but this wasn't one of those times. This felt more like I was about to be boiled. "I believe you, Nate. I really do. Maybe you didn't intentionally sabotage this, but that doesn't convince me you were fully committed in the first place. We've got to do better. We've got to be able to count on one another."

Sometimes she reminded me of her father, a man who certainly had his flaws, but he'd taught me a few things over the years he'd taken me under his wing.

"We can," I said.

We walked down the loading ramp and Serena looked at me, pursing her full lips in thought. "Well, are you going to tell me about it?"

I frowned. "About what?"

She stared at me, waiting for me to get on with it.

"I found some ruins near the crash site."

"What kind of ruins?"

"I'm not sure. They were subterranean and looked old. I have some recordings of it, and I even found this," I said and opened the storage compartment to pull out the octagonal, dark-metal relic.

She peered at it for a second. "What is it?"

"I don't know. It was hidden inside some kind of metallic globe thing."

The others gathered around.

"That's all you found?" Ben asked. "Looks brittle."

He reached toward it, but I kept it beyond his reach. "Easy there, tiger. If it *is* brittle, I don't want you breaking it."

Ben held his hands in front of his chest in a placating gesture.

Kaz gave me a dubious look. "This is what you wouldn't hand over?"

"It's the principle of the thing."

"Hand over to whom?" Serena asked.

I stared at Kaz. "Do you want to tell them, or should I?"

The others looked at him.

"Who was it, Kaz?" Raylin asked.

T'Chura leaned in and waited for him to reply.

Kaz sighed. "It was Griff Tarken. My Gabris."

Raylin frowned. "Really? Your mentor?"

"He wouldn't explain it to me, but you should've seen him. He was in rare form. You would've thought his childhood hero had arrived," I said.

Raylin smiled. "That's not surprising. Kaz was apprenticed to him during his formative cycles."

"An apprentice," I said and looked at Kaz. "Does that include hero worship? The kind where you just roll over and show him your belly, waiting for a treat?"

Kaz glared at me. "That's enough."

I'd definitely struck a nerve.

Raylin glanced at me. "There is usually a strong bond, akin to that of a familial kind. The behavior patterns are well established, and sometimes they're difficult to overcome."

"It's not that," Kaz said.

I waited for him to continue but he didn't. "Don't leave us hanging. Out with it already."

He sighed. "Griff Tarken was a renowned explorer until he was disgraced in the eyes of the Akacian Hegemony," Kaz said and pressed his lips together, not making eye contact with anyone, as if the memory of it still made him feel ashamed. "He'd been taking credit for others' exploits across the galaxy. Since then, he's been determined to restore his reputation by seeking out every conceivable mystery in the galaxy. He'd once been held up as an example of the best of us. It was an honor to be his apprentice."

The others were quiet for a few seconds.

"Until it wasn't, but this shouldn't have reflected on you," I said. "You shouldn't have been caught up in his mistakes."

Kaz shrugged. It looked like he was trying to cast off the weight of something that he just couldn't let go. "His reputation was smeared, and that also extended to whoever was with him."

"Sounds like it happened a long time ago."

Kaz nodded. "It did."

"Then it…"

Kaz shook his head. "It's fine. I just need some time," he said and hastened away from us.

We watched him go.

Ben cleared his throat and I looked at him. "You should let

Crim take a look at what you found. Maybe he can figure out what it is."

I nodded and then looked at Serena. "Want to come along?"

"I'll pass."

Yeah, things were going to be a little cool between us for a while.

CHAPTER 7

Red-and-pink neon lights reflected off the chrome panels along the ceiling of Crim Cormin's workshop. It was a small hangar bay that served as the place where all things got fixed on the ship. I didn't know what the nautical term was for it on a ship back home. "Workshop" was the umbrella for everything that was required to keep the *Spacehog* space worthy.

Beyond the reception area, a half-wall functioned as a natural barrier to the rest of the shop. I heard the clickety-clack of Crim's many feet coming from one of the storage rooms off to the side.

Crim Cormin was an alien in the truest sense of the word. He was some kind of insect-humanoid hybrid with six legs and the upper torso of something that vaguely resembled a humanoid form.

"Nate, is that you?" Crim called out from the storage room.

"Yeah."

"Ben sent me a message that you were coming."

I glanced next to me at Ben. He shrugged.

"Just makes things easier if he knows you're coming," Ben said.

Crim was territorial about his workshop, which put him right in line with just about every mechanic I'd ever met.

Crim emerged from the storage room, and his split-pupil, lizard-like eyes locked onto me. He had a dome-shaped head the color of desert sand, two arms, and hands with four long, thick fingers on each.

He moved gingerly, holding one of his feet in the air. Each foot had three long, thick toes about half the length of my arm. They spread wide when he stood and formed a kind of fleshy tripod. A thick black claw was at the end of each toe, the source of the clicking sound when he walked. The leg he was favoring had a gray bandage wrapped around one of the toes.

"What happened?" I asked.

Crim tilted his head to the side, and the foot-long tentacles that hung from his chin shifted a little. Sometimes they moved like a cat's tail. "That's nothing," he replied, gesturing toward his leg. "My claws renew every year or so, and sometimes the irritation gets…" he looked away for a second and mumbled something.

I raised my eyebrows. "What?"

He lifted his gaze toward me. "An infection."

I stared at this bandaged toe, giving in to an instinctual and sometimes morbid curiosity that demanded to know what the claw looked like.

"Is it bad? It must be since you're walking funny. Is this something the autodoc can cure?"

Crim shifted on his five remaining good feet. He was a borderline hermit at times and completely amicable at other times. I'd saved his life once, so he gave me a little more latitude than he did some of the others.

Ben cleared his throat. "I've got something to check on over there," he said, gesturing toward a workbench on the far side of the hangar.

Ben didn't quite run, but I was sure that if I wanted to catch up to him, I'd have to sprint to do it.

I turned back toward Crim. "Come on. What's going on here? What am I missing?"

Crim considered me for a second and then sighed. "The claw isn't right."

I frowned. "Huh?"

"It's not coming in right."

It was like pulling teeth to get answers out of him. It had been suggested by some that when it came to being sensitive about subjects requiring a certain amount of understanding, I had a gap a mile wide, especially when it came to the uptake of the situation. This I acknowledged by reminding them that people and aliens alike were prone to being overly dramatic. This kind of insensitive response wasn't appreciated.

I rested my hands on my hips. "So, do you need surgery to correct it?"

Crim blew out a slow breath that was paired with a sneer—though not at me, so I hadn't mishandled what could be a very serious problem with a member of my crew.

"The autodoc advised that the defective claw would need to be removed."

I pressed my lips together a little. "Doesn't sound so bad. Won't you grow another one eventually?"

Crim raised his gaze. "You don't understand."

"I'm trying to understand, Crim. You're not making it easy for me."

Crim regarded me thoughtfully for a few seconds. "Think of it like losing some of your teeth when you get older."

"Okay, but they get caps or something else to fill their place," I said and frowned. "This isn't entirely about the claw. You're getting older, and this is a reminder."

"I am old. But this," he said, gesturing toward his foot, "implies a lack of preventive care and hygiene."

I blinked. Crim was worried about appearances. "So, what are you going to do? I can't have you hobbling around. I'm assuming it'll just get worse as time goes on."

"It's not that simple. It'll throw everything off. I won't be able to walk properly."

I hadn't thought of that. "What about a prosthetic claw?"

Crim narrowed his gaze, and I held up my hands. "I'm sorry, Crim. I'm not up on Ustral physiology. I'll back off if you want."

"Yes, that's exactly what I want."

I looked away, shaking my head a little. I could almost hear Serena admonishing me for not being more supportive. I turned back toward Crim.

"Look, I'm not your father, or whatever it is that Ustrals have for parents, but I am your friend, Crim. I don't want you to suffer. If there's something I can do to help, then say the word, and I'll do whatever I can."

Crim sank onto his haunches, which made him shorter than me. He looked oddly vulnerable like that. He wasn't. I'd seen him fight before. Crim was extremely deadly when the situation called for it.

"I don't know what that thing is going to do to you. I do know that for us," I said, pointing at my chest, "when something gets infected, that can spread and cause all kinds of problems down the line. Things that can be avoided. If you want, I'm sure you've got some kind of cutting tool in this shop of yours. We can take care of that claw right now. What do you say?"

A few moments passed and Crim chuckled. "That would be a negative."

"Okay, do you need a special doctor or something then?"

He shook his head. "The autodoc can do it. I'll need some time to heal."

"I could get T'Chura to carry you if you need."

Crim drew himself up quickly. "That will not be necessary."

I eyed him for a second and then nodded.

"Ben said you've got something for me to look at."

I nodded and showed him the relic I'd found.

Crim peered at it and then brought up his omnitool. He scanned it. "Where did you find it?"

"Tucked away in a chamber underground. Looked like it was in some kind of workstation," I said and showed him the video feed I'd captured.

The camera work was shaky except for those rare moments where I'd panned the room. I skipped ahead to the sphere. "Any idea what it is?"

Crim considered it for a few moments. "Nope. It looks like some kind of matrix."

I frowned. "For what?"

"That's the part I'm not sure of. It's some kind of alloy, but I'd need to do a thorough examination of it to find out what it is. Can you leave it with me for a while?"

I glanced at the dark-metal object.

"I promise not to damage it."

Sighing, I handed it to him.

Crim flinched. "I don't want to touch it."

I would touch it. I still wore my combat suit and my hands were covered, so I hadn't actually touched it. I disabled the armor over my hands and felt the metal.

"Are you crazy? You don't know anything about it."

The metal felt cold, much colder than the room. The surface was gritty, like fine-grit sandpaper under my fingertips.

I smiled at him. "I'm pretty sure it's not going to explode."

I held out the relic to him.

"Stop it. Here, just put it in the container. Good, now give it here," Crim said.

He held a container and activated some kind of field that surrounded the relic, but I could still see it.

"There," Crim said. "Now it's sealed up."

He regarded the relic as if it was something that was going to attack. I wasn't beyond using a certain amount of caution, but if the relic was dangerous, I thought something would've happened by now.

"All right, I'll leave you to it. I need to get changed. Let me know what you find out and be careful with that thing."

"I'll give it the respect it deserves, Captain, which is more than I can say about you."

I grinned. "That's why I keep you around."

Crim waved off the comment. "Get out of here. You'll stink up the place."

I laughed and left the workshop.

I stopped by the armory to disarm and recharge my combat suit. Then I took a quick shower and put on some clean clothes. I stopped in the commons area to grab a roast beef sandwich with melted Swiss cheese and carried the tray of food to the bridge.

I saw Kierenbot standing next to a workstation. The robot was made of a dark-gray metal in a humanoid shape, with a bar of red light where eyes should have been. A brighter orb moved back and forth inside it.

The artificial intelligence inside was convinced that he was some kind of ascended being who'd given up his physical form to live out the remainder of his life as a robot. No amount of convincing on my part would change his mind.

Kierenbot turned at my approach and his eyes brightened. "Captain," he said by way of greeting.

I set the tray down. "Hello, Kierenbot," I said and then took a bite of my sandwich.

The food fabricator had even warmed the beef. It was packed with salty, juicy goodness that made me happy.

"We should make the Nerad Star System quite soon."

I nodded. "Good. Oh, and thanks for getting us underway so quickly."

"You're quite welcome. The local authorities from Minoa weren't happy about it."

I shrugged and stopped eating long enough to take a swig of water. I eyed him for a second. "Did you know I'd forgotten about the permits?"

"Of course, but you told me that you'd take care of it. I can replay the actual interaction if you're having trouble remembering. You told me to go find something useful to do."

I winced and nearly choked on my food. "That won't be necessary."

Kierenbot peered at me. "Has my performance been lacking?"

Interacting with AIs wasn't as straightforward as it seemed. Sometimes they took liberal interpretations with your orders, especially when it came to providing information. They often chose a course of action that led to the most permanent way to educate a person. I'd found this out the hard way.

I couldn't fault him for not reminding me about the permits. "Why is it that I have to apply for the permits?"

"You're the captain."

"Is this how it's done on other ships?"

"I'm not sure."

"Is this how Kaz did it?"

Kierenbot considered this, and I was positive that he was pretending. He could process information much faster than anyone on the ship. "It was."

"So, I don't need to do it in the future. I could have someone else do it. It'll have to be someone responsible so something like this doesn't happen again."

"I would volunteer to do this for you. It's the most efficient way to get it done in the future and would avoid mishaps like this."

I regarded the robot for a few seconds. "I don't know if that's a good idea."

Kierenbot turned toward me. "Why not? Haven't I proven the reliability of my services in the past?"

I shook my head. "No, not really."

He tilted his head to the side, and the bar of red light became a bright sphere in the middle as he peered at me. "If you're referring to the story I told you about aquatics having inferior intelligence, that was purely for entertainment."

He was referring to when we'd first come aboard the ship.

"Entertainment? You ill-advised us about a subgroup of species that are actually quite capable."

"Yes, but this was before you became the captain. I would never do that now."

I finished my sandwich and my water, set the cup on the tray, and sighed. "What assurances do I have that if I assign this duty to you, it will be done?"

"I could inform you when the task is completed."

"What if I'm sleeping? Would you wake me up?"

He shook his head. "No, you've been quite assertive on how important sleep is to you. Honestly, you should consider uploading your consciousness like I did. You'll never have to sleep again. Hunger is a thing of the past. It's quite the way to live, I assure you."

"It's not for me," I said, and not wanting to insult him, I quickly added, "at least for now. Maybe some other time. You know, like you. You didn't upload until you were so old that your body was going to expire."

"Understood. If you don't want me to wake you, then I could send a message to your omnitool."

"That's better, but what if I miss it? What if my omnitool breaks?"

Kierenbot considered this for a second. "I could send the entire crew a status update that includes the relevant information."

I slapped the workstation and pointed my finger at him. "That's a heck of an idea. I think that'll work, but there is just one thing."

"What's that?"

"Sometimes requesting permits for anything, really, should only be done at the appropriate time. Sometimes people monitor that kind of activity and could cause trouble for us," I said.

"I think I understand, so I would still need direction as to when the permits are requested."

"It'll depend, but we should all be involved."

"By 'we' do you mean the entire crew?"

"Yes, but if you don't think that's appropriate, then myself, Serena, and Kaz. One of us will be able to figure out what's best."

"I understand now."

I really hoped he did; otherwise…sometimes Kierenbot could be extremely creative in his actions.

"There is something else I'd like to discuss with you, Captain."

"Okay, what is it?"

"I'd like to join you on missions."

"Missions? We're not the military."

"Indeed not, but you do designate away teams. And I'm not even considered for those. Why is that?"

"I've told you before that I need you on the ship."

"You have indicated that in the past, but it's not appropriate in every instance. For example, when we get to Pica Station, I'm to stay with the ship again. Do I have to request shore leave?"

Since Serena, Ben, and I had taken ownership of the *Spacehog*, Kierenbot had adopted more Human nomenclatures than we expected given his previous speech.

"Why do you want to leave the ship?"

"Because I can be of use to you out in the field."

"I know that, but sometimes we go into dangerous places. I'd hate for anything to happen to you."

When Kaz had been captain, he'd allowed Kierenbot to go with him off the ship, but that had usually been for space stations and low-risk missions. For instance, he'd brought him to Earth when they'd abducted me.

"I should be able to accept the risk that all of you do. It is my right to do so."

This was one peculiarity of the AI that believed it was a sentient being.

"Okay. You can come along if you want. When we reach Pica Station you can go ashore."

"Thank you, Captain."

"No problem," I replied. I stood and picked up my tray.

"We'll be at the station in forty minutes."

"Understood. Please arrange for pickup of the salvage we were able to recover."

"Will do, Captain."

I left the bridge and brought my tray back to the commons area. It was empty. I had a cup of coffee and thought about the ancient ruins I'd found. Someone was terraforming a world that had had a civilization on it at some point in time. I wondered how much time had to pass from when a civilization perished before another could colonize the planet.

I headed toward the docking area and picked up a portable life-support system. It was just a small pack that attached to my long coat.

I went near the airlock and waited. Through the window I saw Serena standing with Kaz, T'Chura, and Raylin. Ben ran up behind me and joined me in the airlock.

"How's Crim?" I asked.

"He's preoccupied with that relic you found."

"I'm glad he's looking into it. Sometimes he gets preoccupied with other things."

Ben nodded. "Well, I think he appreciated what you said to him."

I frowned. "What did I say?"

Ben chuckled. "I don't know. I figured you guys needed some privacy, so I didn't listen in."

Ben was a good kid. He worked hard at anything he took on and wasn't oblivious to discretion.

I shrugged. "Sometimes the good guys win."

He laughed and we went through the airlock.

Kaz, T'Chura, and Raylin walked away from Serena.

Ben glanced at me. "I'm going to catch up with them."

"Sure, leave me to fend for myself then."

He'd already hastened ahead, tossing a wave over his shoulder. Gone were the days when he'd stand there full of indecision.

I walked over to Serena. She was staring at the holoscreen above her omnitool.

"Look at him go," I said.

Serena frowned and looked up from her holoscreen. She saw Ben catch up to the others and begin speaking to T'Chura. The edges of her lips lifted a little, but then she looked at me. "Kaz is upset."

I rolled my eyes. "Let me guess. He's all shook up because he met his Gabis or whatever."

"You know they don't need your approval to have something bother them."

I shrugged. "The world would be a much easier-going place if they did."

She stared at me for a second, and I cracked a smile. I was joking.

She smiled and shook her head. "Nate, sometimes."

"I know." We shared a quiet moment and then I asked. "What's the damage?"

Serena was about to reply when an aircar landed nearby. It bore some kind of official Pica Station emblem, and several Akacians climbed out.

They gestured toward us, and we walked over to them.

"Are you Nathan Briggs?"

"Yes."

"My name is Naviks, and I'm with Pica Station Affairs. This is a compliance summons in connection with failing to obtain the proper salvage permits in the Minoa Star System."

He made a passing motion and my omnitool alerted me to the receipt of the document.

I opened it and read, my eyes widening. "You've got to be joking. These fines are outrageous." Naviks didn't say anything. "Who reported this?"

"Local Minoan authorities spotted your ship failing to comply with their requests for communication."

"We received no such requests."

"Be that as it may, you were reported for recovering the salvage associated with an open contract with Veslon Industries. The permits were not submitted, and you are therefore liable for the fees incurred."

I knew a bureaucrat when I saw one. Nothing I said or did was going to get me out of paying the fines.

"Is there an appeals process?"

Naviks looked amused. He really seemed to enjoy his job, and this must have been the highlight of his pathetic day. "Of course. It'll take approximately forty days to process your request, but I must inform you that docking fees for your ship will incur during that time."

I chuckled bitterly. "Quite the process you have here for extorting credits from people."

"Compliance is assured."

I stepped toward him, and his two goons started to intercept.

Serena grabbed my arm. "We'll pay the fees."

Naviks looked at her for a moment and then nodded. "I wait for payment."

I muttered more than a few curses under my breath, then brought up my omnitool and transferred the funds. "There you go. Another checkbox in the old 'To Do' list. Now get lost."

Naviks returned to his aircar and left.

I sighed. "I hate bureaucrats."

"Really? I hadn't noticed."

I looked at Serena. "How bad is it?"

"Oh, it's bad. This trip ended up costing us."

So much for running this venture like a business. I chewed on my bottom lip and exhaled through my nose.

"Maybe you need to learn to play by the rules instead of finding ways to circumvent them."

"Where's the fun in that?"

She shook her head. "I got a message from Kierenbot about what you guys discussed. I think it's a good idea."

"You think?"

"Honest mistake, right?"

It was an olive branch. I accepted it and nodded.

"So, what was so special about these ruins you found?"

"Let's go get a drink and I'll tell you all about it."

CHAPTER 8

Ben twisted around in his chair, taking in all the sights of the entertainment pad—at least, that was how the aliens referred to it, but for anyone else it would be a bar, even if the "pad" was the size of a sports arena.

"It's unbelievable how many different species are in here and how many are similar to us," Ben said excitedly.

The other aliens were carbon based and breathed oxygen, so we didn't need our own individual life support.

T'Chura's hulking form sat across from me and dominated most of my view. A reinforced stool supported him. I leaned to the side to try to see what Ben was looking at, and T'Chura tipped his head to the side.

"Is something wrong, Nate?" he asked.

I grinned and looked at Serena. She sat next to the Sasquatch and was staring at something I couldn't see.

I lifted my gaze to T'Chura. "They don't make them small where you come from."

He gripped the oversized handle of his clear mug and raised

it to his mouth. The mug was bigger than a gallon of milk and was filled with some kind of green liquid. He paused right before his lips and inhaled deeply. Then he took a hearty swallow and closed his eyes contentedly. He sighed, and I could hear a subsonic moan coming from his broad chest. "It's a shame that your digestive systems are much too delicate to handle a true drink from my homeworld. Then you could know true peace."

"Is that before or after it melts away my insides?" I asked.

T'Chura was about nine feet tall and had evolved on a world with lots of heavy metals. It would kill me to consume anything designed for T'Chura's tastes.

My gaze sank to my cup. It was filled with a pale blue liquid that the serving bot had assured me could be safely consumed by Humans. He'd taken a sample of our DNA by having us place our palms on a pad that he carried. He then brought each of us a different kind of drink, along with a promise of "quite the experience," whatever that meant.

Serena had black liquid in her cup, and I'd joked about it being her witch's brew. Ben had pink liquid that reminded me of strawberry Nestle Quik. None of us had dared sip our drinks yet.

Ben turned back toward our elevated table and rested his hands on the metallic top. The middle was solid but had the appearance of a swirling dark mass of clouds. "This is amazing." He looked up at T'Chura. "What do they call this place again?"

"It's an entertainment pad for terrestrial beings. The name is Infinity."

I frowned, and Ben noticed. "He means beings like us."

I knew what he meant. "Thanks for the insight, kid."

I had alien DNA in me, as did Serena and Ben. A species called Nasarian had changed all of us, but me most of all. I was able to decipher alien languages better than most translators, but sometimes certain words or expressions confused me... or puzzled the Nasarian part of me. Thank god it didn't change my body at all. I don't think I could've handled that very well. The others had experienced changes as well, but my exposure to it had been more than the others, so I'd won the prize.

Serena chuckled a little as she glided her fingertips along the handle of her glass.

I raised my glass and said, "How about we all go at the same time?"

Ben nodded and lifted his glass. That wasn't a surprise. He'd rarely be first but would join in if others were participating.

Serena sighed and did the same.

T'Chura watched us, amused.

"What are we celebrating?" Ben asked.

We hadn't earned any credits. Quite the opposite. This trip had cost us.

Serena eyed me for a moment and lifted her glass a little higher. "Let's just enjoy the moment. Something...someone I used to know toasted by raising his glass and saying '*buona salute,*' which means good health."

We shared a look. She'd been pulled into serving organized crime, and I knew where she'd learned that expression.

"Ciao bella," I said in my best Italian accent.

Serena snorted a grin in the back of her throat.

Ben frowned at me. "What does that mean?"

"It means 'Hello beautiful.'"

He glanced at Serena for a second and tipped his head forward with a smile.

"It's the language of love, kid. You should learn a little bit of it."

Ben's gaze sank a little and his expression sobered.

Serena shook her head. "Yes, and it's often put forth as a cheap pickup line in a bar."

I smiled and kept my eyes on her. "I guess that depends on who you're saying it to."

She grinned, grudgingly at first.

T'Chura clapped and heaved his bulk forward. "I love this about your species—this camaraderie among friends. Not every species does this. Shall we drink?"

He lifted his mug and watched us expectantly.

We drank.

And that's when things got strange.

The pale blue liquid passed across my tongue. It was warm and smooth, igniting all the taste receptors in my mouth. It went down easily, and I felt my muscles relax as if I'd spent an hour in the sauna. An explosion of colors painted halos around everything I looked at. I expected to feel dizzy, but I didn't. It was as if all my senses had been heightened but were also perfectly balanced and isolated, unless I focused on them.

Serena had one hand braced on the edge of the table, holding herself up. There was a flush to her cheeks. Our gazes locked and I sucked in a breath. Heat spread across my chest and arms. Serena was a strikingly beautiful woman and the daughter of my old friend. My gaze slid down from her eyes to focus on the shape of her full, pink lip. The edges curved slightly, and I swallowed hard.

The thumping of the music resonated through me, and I wanted to believe the hungry look in her eyes was filled with desire for me. What man didn't want a beautiful woman to be attracted to them? My vision blurred and I blinked as I tore my gaze away from hers. My glass sat empty on the table.

Had I really downed all of it?

The serving bot had promised an experience, and he hadn't lied. I felt like I was riding a rollercoaster without a seat belt. I looked at Serena, except she wasn't sitting across from me. She'd stood and begun to slowly shake her hips, which drew my attention to the exclusion of all else. Every instinct inside me screamed to throw myself across the table and take her in my arms. I was filled with a primal urge that hadn't been fulfilled in entirely too long.

She turned toward me, her arms wrapped caressingly around her body, and our eyes locked. I exhaled a hot breath past my teeth and grabbed the edge of the table, ready to fly. The music had become muffled, dissolving into the background noise until it suddenly changed. The lighting became brighter, and I blinked. It was like being doused by a bucket of cold water. One second I was watching Serena dancing alone with some secret feminine grace that made men lose their minds, and next she sat directly in front of me, her mouth agape as if seeing me for the first time.

T'Chura slapped the table, letting out a hearty laugh, and we flinched. I remembered to breathe, and I blinked, shaking my head to clear it.

He blew out a breath. "The sexual energy coming from you both was enough to be felt by every empath in the area."

I glanced at Serena, but she'd turned away from me, letting her hair fall across her face like a curtain.

I still felt as if my mind was emerging from a fog, and I gestured toward my glass. "What the hell was in that drink?" I said, my voice sounding a little hoarse.

"I'm not sure," T'Chura said.

I looked over at Ben. He was slumped back in his chair with a dazed expression.

"Hey kid, are you all right?" I asked and slapped my palm down on the table a few times. It wasn't as shocking as when T'Chura slapped his dinner-plate-sized palm down, but Ben did snap out of it.

"The effects will quickly wear off," T'Chura assured.

Ben leaned forward and groaned. He rubbed his head, and I thought he was going to throw up. He took several deep breaths and sat up. Had he experienced the same thing I did?

"I don't know if I can drink that again."

I nodded. "Same here."

At the same time, Serena said. "Me, too."

T'Chura waved away the comments. "Nonsense. They have other kinds of drinks and food here."

Ben heaved a sigh. "I don't think I can eat anything right now. I need to get some air."

He stood up and swayed on his feet for a second.

I wasn't sure I could stand just yet either, and I looked at T'Chura. "Can you keep an eye on him?"

The Sasquatch downed his drink and stood up. He put a companionable hand on Ben's back, and they walked toward the exit.

I blew out a long breath and Serena did the same. I don't know who started laughing first, but we couldn't stop for almost a full five minutes, during which time the serving bot came back to our table and offered us another drink.

"Not right now. Just bring us some water," I said.

Now that T'Chura was no longer blocking my view, I saw Kaz's head poking above a large group of aliens. He looked as if he was speaking intently, as if he had an audience around him. The crowd shifted and he disappeared from view.

I looked at Serena. "We don't have to talk about what we saw, right?"

She eyed me for a moment, considering. "Nate..."

I swallowed hard. I'm as Human as the next guy, and it's not like I hadn't noticed Serena *that* way, but I hadn't pushed for anything more than some harmless flirting.

A memory flashed of her standing there, alluring, staring at me as if we were alone instead of in a crowded room.

The serving bot came back with food for all of us, interrupting whatever she'd been about to say.

I wasn't sure if T'Chura and Ben would be back.

Serena looked at the plates of food and said, "I'm starving."

We'd both ordered filet mignon with sautéed onions and mushrooms—definitely not the typical alien fare, but once I'd uploaded the data from the ship, they'd been able to accommodate us.

Whatever T'Chura had ordered was inside a large pot with the lid firmly attached.

We ate in silence, each of us enjoying the perfectly cooked steak. It was full of the salty goodness I loved.

"The only thing missing is a glass of Pinot Noir," Serena said.

"If you say so. I'd be fine with a beer."

The edges of her lips slid upward, and she shook her head. "Expand your palate, Nate. A good red will complement the flavor of the steak. Trust me."

I smiled and regarded her for a moment. "I do trust you," I said, using my napkin to wipe the edges of my mouth. "Pinot isn't a bad choice, maybe a Cabernet if you want to play it safe. There's Zinfandel if you prefer something sweeter. But you could just have an Old Fashioned."

She pursed her lips for a second, rounding her high cheek bones. "I had no idea you were so refined."

I snorted. "I'm like an onion. I've got layers."

She giggled and I eyed my empty plate for a second.

She looked away as if deciding something, then lifted her hand, palm up, and said, "I might have been a little too hard on you about the permits."

I leaned back, eyes wide. She rolled her eyes. "Apology accepted." I leaned forward. "It won't happen again."

"It better not."

I grinned. "Not a chance." She pursed her lips thoughtfully and there was something lingering in her gaze. I cleared my throat. "Kierenbot is going to handle it by keeping us all in the loop. So, unless none of us are available, this should never happen again."

She bobbed her head once. "You didn't waste any time."

"I hate wasting time."

"So, what did you find on that planet? Tell me about the ruins."

I did. I told her about the creatures I'd encountered and even showed her a video of me tossing them into the air.

"Listen to them all!" she said.

I nodded. "I was their newest plaything. It was, uh, fun."

She looked down at her nearly empty plate and used her fork to push a mushroom around. "I wish I'd been there."

There was something in her tone that made me stare at her. She looked at me and I shrugged. "Next time, although you might not have enjoyed the…" I wasn't sure how to describe the beings I'd encountered.

She frowned. "What?"

"I saw something in the chamber the drones were trying to reach. I can't really explain what it was without sounding crazy."

She shifted on the stool, leaning forward. "Did you record it?"

I nodded and brought up the video on my omnitool. When I got to the part with the wolf specters, some kind of interference warped the recording. I stared at it and tried to replay it.

"I don't know what happened."

She peered at the recording for a few moments more and then shook her head. "I can't see anything."

The recording didn't clear up until after I'd left the chamber. "I'll see if Kierenbot can clean it up," I said and shrugged. "It was spooky."

She held up her hand, gesturing toward our surroundings. "A few months ago, we'd have found *this* spooky."

I looked over at the cluster of aliens surrounding some kind of long table, once again catching a glimpse of Kaz speaking animatedly to a smaller group as if he was some kind of ringleader.

"If I squint, I could be anywhere back home, I guess. These are just people going about their business. Look at them. They look like they're betting on something."

Serena glanced toward the large group of aliens on the far side of the section that bordered another. Then she turned back toward me.

"How do you do it?"

I frowned, not knowing what she meant. "Do what?"

"You just…just make your own fun. I've seen you serious before. I'm not saying you're goofy or anything, but you manage to squeeze every ounce of fun out of almost any situation. I feel like I'm the one who's always serious. I didn't used to be this way."

I knew a little bit about her past. She'd seen some terrible things that she only hinted at sometimes.

"I wasn't always like this either," I replied.

She gave me a doubtful look.

I leaned forward. "Serena, we're all works in progress. You're wound up a little tight sometimes, but you do keep us in line."

"I wish I didn't have to."

"You don't. No one's making you do it."

She shook her head. "Yeah, but if I don't, we'll never make this work."

So many things came to my mind that I wondered which she was referring to. She caught my hesitation and frowned.

"We've only been at this a few months. Give it time," I said and paused.

I heard the large group of aliens howl with laughter. It sounded like a chorus of the damned.

She looked at me and I asked, "Do you want to go back to Earth?"

She considered this for a few moments, her fork clanging against the plate, and wiped her hand on the napkin. She shrugged.

"Okay, you want to know how I do it? This is how," I said, resting my elbows on the table. "Are you ready?"

She nodded.

"Don't sweat the small stuff. I can't do anything about the past. I just try to focus my attention on today, sitting here at some orbital installation, sharing a meal with a friend. I don't think about almost getting killed."

"A friend," she said and stared at me. "But what comes next for you, Nate?"

"What do you mean 'next'?"

"Do you just plan to roam around the galaxy on a spaceship and that's going to be your life?"

She looked so serious, I felt like whatever my answer was going to be might come back to haunt me. "It's as good a plan as any. I get bored easily."

She blew out a breath, and her eyebrows knitted together.

"Do you always need a plan?"

She blinked. "I've always *had* a plan."

"So now you have a new plan. Be a leaf on the wind that

involves aliens and a spaceship and seeing things other people only dream about."

She didn't look convinced.

I was still mulling over the 'friend' comment she'd made.

"Sometimes just go with it, and then think about what you want next. You don't have to decide anything right now."

She pressed her lips together for a second. "You make it sound so easy."

"That's because it is."

"Not for everyone."

"Serena, you're here. You're doing it. We all are."

She sighed. "I'm not sure how well Ben is doing."

I frowned. I'd thought Ben was doing just fine. "What do you mean?"

"I think he's a little lonely."

"Lonely… He's never alone. He's always working with Crim, learning all kinds of things."

She gave me an impatient look. "Not that kind of lonely."

I blinked a few times, finally understanding, and sighed. "Oh."

I drank the rest of my water.

"He's not the only one."

I nearly choked as the water decided to assault my lungs. I coughed a few times and stared at her.

"Come on, Nate. Tell me you haven't felt the same."

I set my cup down on the table. "I've been wondering when you were going to visit my room in the middle of the night for some casual tension relief."

Sometimes my mouth worked before my brain caught up, or maybe it was the look she gave me. She wasn't offended, so my suggestion hadn't put her off. Instead, her expression was challenging.

"What if I was waiting for you to come to my room, Casanova?"

I grinned, and she waited for me to reply. "This is what comes of a lack of options."

She narrowed her gaze, and I raised my hands in a placating gesture. "This isn't a slight on anyone. I think you're beautiful, but would whatever we're doing here be the same if there were more options?"

"Didn't you just tell me that I should live in the moment?"

I hadn't expected my words to be thrown in my face quite so quickly.

"It's complicated," I said.

"Flynn is gone, Nate. I don't need you to take his place."

I blinked and shook my head. "I'm not."

I'd watched Flynn die, and his dying wish had been for me to protect his daughter, not sleep with her. That didn't mean I hadn't thought of it, and clearly I wasn't the only one.

"I thought we were talking about Ben."

She shook her head. "Nice deflection."

I guess I wasn't manning up enough for her. I inhaled a deep breath and my chest puffed out a little. "As farfetched as it might sound, there is the possibility that you might reject me."

"Somehow I don't see that stopping a man like you."

"You're right about that."

"So, what's the problem?"

"Do you want me to pluck you out of that stool and set you on my lap?"

She laughed, and I joined in. "Maybe."

Suddenly, it was like I'd had another drink of that alien aphrodisiac. What had she experienced?

She arched an eyebrow, waiting for me to reply.

I could call her bluff and pick her up out of the chair. I

wanted to, unless she wasn't bluffing, which would introduce her to a shipwreck that is one Nathan Briggs.

I eyed her. "What is this? What are we doing here?"

She arched an eyebrow. "I don't know, Nate. What are *we* doing?"

I stood and walked around the table, leaning toward her. She didn't blink or push me away. "Is this what you want?"

The edges of her lips lifted, and they pursed a little. "Maybe you should buy me another drink," she said, giving my chest a gentle push back.

I smiled and tipped my head to the side. Then I walked toward the bar.

As I approached the bar, a holoscreen appeared. I pressed the call button for the serving bot. Its upper torso was shaped like Kierenbot, with dark metal and a red eye that moved along a bar across its face. Its lower body rolled atop a sphere, making it appear as if it floated up and down the serving line.

The bot rolled to a stop in front of me and waited for me to speak.

I ordered two beers, which involved me sending a small data packet from my omnitool to the serving bot. He spun around and opened a holoscreen. I watched him navigate the interface for a few seconds. Then I looked over to where Kaz had been. I'd only been off Earth for a few months, and I had no idea how many different species there were. Most of the ones in the bar breathed oxygen, and the ones that didn't wore some kind of environmental suit. They came in all shapes and sizes. Some aliens had multiple legs and body shapes that I would've assumed existed only in some people's vivid imaginations. There were short, stubby aliens that looked like a squat, thick bear without hair. I tried to remember what their species was called, but I couldn't. I remembered Kaz telling me that they came from a large planet that had significantly higher gravity than Earth. They were easily offended and incredibly strong.

The bot placed the two beers in front of me and I transferred the credits over to him.

I turned away from the bar and looked across the room to where our table was. Serena raised her chin and smiled. I held up the beers and wondered if both of us were going to regret what might happen.

Who was I kidding? This tension between us had been building for six months. I should've trusted my first instinct and done something about it already.

Kaz shouted nearby, and I looked over at him.

The crowd of aliens pulled back, and I saw Kaz swaying on his feet, looking beyond drunk. He glared at an alien cyclops.

"Say that again," he said.

The cyclops was shorter than Kaz but made up for it in width and muscle. "I said your Gabris is a discredit to your species. Akacians haven't done anything worth recording."

Kaz growled, snatched a plateful of alien gruel, and flung it at the cyclops. Bellowing, Kaz threw himself at the offending creature and his companions. Kaz was never one to go halfway when he committed to an action.

I glanced back at Serena. Her eyes were wide.

I set our beers down on the bar and saw Kaz stumble to the ground nearby. He frowned up at me, blinking several times.

I smiled down at him. "Want some help?"

He stood up and leaned against the bar. "Nah, I'm just getting started."

He grabbed a stool and charged back into the fray.

I'd been in a few bar fights and maybe even caused some of them. Once I was in them, I had to go full tilt and then get out as quickly as possible. Kaz was a formidable fighter. I should know, because he'd tossed me around the bridge of the *Spacehog* the very first time I'd met him. He'd had a few advantages over me at the time. Not anymore.

I grabbed a beer and downed it in a few gulps. I looked at Serena and she gave me a don't-you-dare look as she shook her head.

Several of the cyclops were holding Kaz above their heads, and one of the shorter hairless bears had its fingers around his neck as it dangled off the ground. Kaz gasped for breath and his gaze found mine. I took that as my signal to go save his drunk ass. I looked down at the second beer.

Kaz twisted and jerked his body, trying to get free.

"Anytime, Nate!" he shouted.

I abandoned my beer—Serena's beer—and ran toward the fray. The best kinds of tackles were when I threw my whole body into them. I had to be careful to move my head to the side so I didn't slam it into anything. Years of football had drilled that into me.

Several cyclops toppled, dropping Kaz to the ground.

Then the fight really began.

The other thing about bar fights was that we couldn't really remember everything that happened after it was all over. There were times when Kaz and I were back-to-back, facing our attackers. Other times, we were separated.

It wasn't long before the orbital station security enforcers showed up and rounded up the lot of us.

They lined us up outside the entertainment pad, and I leaned against the wall. Kaz slumped next to me. He kept muttering something under his breath.

He was still out of it.

No one had died, which was a good thing, and no one knew how the fight started. I found that a bit of a stretch, and I expected someone to point their alien tentacles at Kaz at any moment, but no one did.

I learned a couple of things about orbital security that day. They regularly dealt with this sort of thing. They slapped us with yet more fines for us to pay, along with orders to leave the station immediately.

We were released into Serena's custody.

She gave me a wry look. "Was that going with the flow?" she asked innocently.

I had a healthy set of bruises that were going to show their colors anytime now. I stood up and helped Kaz to his feet, slipping his arm around my shoulder to keep him standing. Then I looked at her and shook my head. "No, that was making sure your idiot friend didn't get himself killed."

Serena went to Kaz's other side and took that arm. Then, we led him back to the ship.

CHAPTER 9

Kaz was no lightweight. We had to rest every so often until we found a transport terminal. I'd sent a message to T'Chura, but he hadn't responded.

I leaned Kaz against the wall. He had more or less passed out. Serena and I stood there, catching our breath.

"I don't know how much farther I can carry him," Serena said.

I nodded and glanced down at him. "He's a lot heavier than he looks."

"I've never seen him like this. What do you think set him off?"

"Seeing his mentor—his Gabris or something."

She frowned and glanced at Kaz, considering.

I could see the questions stacking in her brain. "He just needed to blow off some steam."

We shared a look and grinned. Then a comlink chimed from my omnitool. It was Kierenbot.

"Captain, there is a problem that requires your attention."

"We're on our way back. It would go a lot quicker if we didn't have to carry Kaz the whole way. I've tried to contact T'Chura, but he hasn't replied."

"T'Chura is back on the ship. So is Ben."

"Are they all right?"

I heard some shouting coming through the comlink.

"Just get back as quickly as you can. It's not safe to discuss over an unsecured comlink."

"All right, we'll be back as soon as we can."

I looked at Serena as I leaned down to pick Kaz up. "Just think of all the calories we're burning."

She sighed and then did the same. "Oh yay. Feel the burn."

We heaved Kaz to his feet and half-carried, half-dragged him to the transport terminal to rent a taxi—or as Ben liked to refer to it, Uber in space.

The aircar dropped us off outside the *Spacehog* where T'Chura was waiting for us.

Serena and I climbed out of the aircar, and T'Chura leaned in to pick Kaz up. He hoisted his body over his shoulder as if he were throwing a bath towel over it.

"Sorry I wasn't able to take your comms request. Ben and I… found something. Come on, you'll see soon enough."

He walked ahead of us into the airlock. There was a brief pause as the atmosphere cycled, along with a bright flash of light that was part of the decontamination process.

Soon it was finished, and we were back aboard the ship. Our home.

I heard Ben's elevated voice coming from inside the hangar bay.

"You don't know anything about this?" Ben asked. He was red-faced, chest heaving, and wore an expression akin to a cornered animal.

I craned my neck and saw that he was speaking to Raylin.

They stood in the hangar bay. Ben stood next to the recon skiff. I saw someone huddled on the floor within the shadow of the skiff.

"Of course, I don't know about this," Raylin said.

Crim stood nearby and waved us over. "You better see this."

We hastened over to them. Behind Ben was a young girl, her arms wrapped tightly around her knees as if she was afraid to let them go. She had Nordic blonde hair, the kind that appeared almost white. Her skin was so pale that I wondered if she'd ever been in sunlight. But most importantly, she was Human. Not humanoid, or human-like, but an honest to goodness girl that looked no older than Ben was.

"What happened? Where did you find her?" I asked.

Ben looked at me and visibly relaxed a little. "On the station. She was walking as if in some kind of daze."

I blinked a few times and glanced at Serena, then looked at Ben. "Come on, give it to me straight."

He sighed. "T'Chura and I followed her for a little while. She noticed us and I walked over to introduce myself. She didn't understand me at first, but then her translator must've started working," he said and paused for a second. "Look at her. She's Human."

I nodded, but she wouldn't look at me. "How did you end up here?" I asked Ben.

"I asked her if she was alone, and that's when things got strange. She told me that the masters would be upset because I didn't have my beacon turned on."

I blew out a breath, rubbing the back of my neck. "That's new."

"I told her I didn't have a beacon and she started to get upset. To calm her down, I told her that my beacon was on the ship. I just needed to go get it and then I could come with her to find the masters. We came back to the ship, and when she saw Raylin, she hid behind me and collapsed to the floor, crying."

I looked at the girl, but she stared fixedly at the floor.

Serena knelt on the floor so she was eye level with the girl. "Hello, I'm Serena. Can you tell me your name?"

She wouldn't answer.

"You're safe here. No one is going to hurt you."

The girl stared at her for a moment and then frowned.

Ben cleared his throat. "Her name is Lanaya." He swallowed hard and looked at me. "I, I think she was some kind of slave." He said the last in a voice just above a whisper.

I rubbed my chin for a second. "Okay," I said and looked at Raylin. "Do you know anything about this?"

Raylin shook her head. "I don't."

Crim cleared his throat, and I looked at him. "The Tamerrons are involved in all kinds of things."

"So are a lot of species," Raylin replied frostily.

I snapped my fingers twice and they looked at me.

"Nate," Serena said, gesturing for me to come closer, "we should get her to sickbay and let the autodoc examine her. She might have been abused."

I stared at her for a long moment, willing myself not to stare at Lanaya. Serena had been an inner-city ER nurse for years. She'd seen a lot.

I nodded. "I don't think I'll be much help with this."

Serena bobbed her head once and then looked at the others. "Maybe give us some space."

I nodded and moved away from them. I called Ben over and Crim followed.

Raylin stayed. I raised my eyebrows, and she gave me a challenging look. "She might respond to me, especially if she's already familiar with my species."

Ben started to say something, and I raised a finger toward him. "Just calm down for a minute. Let Serena try to help her."

Ben stared at me and then glanced at the others. "Nate, you didn't see how she reacted to Raylin."

I reached out and gently pulled him around so he was facing me. "Yeah, but you know Raylin. She's not going to hurt her."

Serena began to speak softly to her. Raylin joined them and Lanaya flinched. I heard Serena reassure her that Raylin was a friend.

I could tell that Ben was seconds away from interrupting them. "You did okay, Ben." He raised his gaze toward mine. "Bringing her here was the right thing to do, but you've got to let Serena take over, okay. I have a feeling she's done something like this before."

Ben frowned. "No, she hasn't. How could she have? We're so far from home. No one else like us is supposed to be out here. What if there are more of them? We have to find them."

"Slow down, kid. I get what you're saying. We'll figure this out, but give Serena some time."

"But she can't know how to help her."

"And you do?"

Ben frowned and looked away from me.

I leaned toward him and spoke softly. "She's in shock."

Ben licked his lips and frowned.

"Of all of us here, Serena is the best one to help her. She's helped people in shock before."

Ben sighed and nodded. "Haven't you dealt with someone in shock before?"

"I just cover them with a blanket and bring them to a doctor.

Since we don't have a doctor aboard the ship, Serena is the best we've got. And it's better than looking for outside help."

Ben considered it for a few moments and nodded. "Thanks, Nate."

"No problem, kid. Like I said before, you did good."

He smiled.

I looked at Crim. "Maybe we're not the first abductees from Earth. Are you able to do some digging around to find out?"

"Where do you suggest I start?" Crim asked.

"I figured you'd have a couple of ideas about that."

"The trouble is that it could invite unwanted attention. Someone is bound to miss her before long."

Ben's eyes widened. "The beacon. She's transmitting her location."

Crim shook his head. "I blocked the signal."

Ben nodded. "We should be able to trace it."

"Now you're learning," Crim said.

"We need to be careful," I said, and they looked at me. "Don't look so surprised. I want to find out who the 'masters' are, but we shouldn't advertise the fact that we're looking."

"She was right out in the open. No one seemed to care about that," Ben said.

"It's a crowded space station, or maybe someone wanted *you* to see her."

"Devious," Crim said.

"I've dealt with some devious people before."

Ben frowned. "Yeah, but who would do that?"

"Someone who wanted us to search for the 'masters.' I don't know. It just seems suspicious to me."

I looked over at Serena. Lanaya was standing.

"We're going to sickbay," Serena said.

Lanaya looked at Ben as if she was going to say something to him.

"Can I come with you?" Ben asked.

Serena nodded, and Ben hastened toward them.

I watched them go for a few seconds, and Crim cleared his throat.

"I need to show you something in my workshop. There's a problem."

I sighed and gave him a long look. "When it rains, it pours."

CHAPTER 10

We went to Crim's workshop.

I knew the ship pretty well now and it wasn't that difficult to navigate once I'd understood the layout, along with some of the other peculiarities about it. Ben was more preoccupied with learning all about the technology used on the ship, while I was just concerned that it functioned.

We walked the gray corridors outside the hangar bay. The corridors were different colors on each deck and sections, so it was easier to determine our location on the ship.

Crim glanced over at me but didn't say anything.

"Have you noticed if Ben is having trouble with life on the ship?" I asked.

We reached the elevator and the doors dissipated, allowing us to go aboard. Crim selected the level where his workshop was located and looked at me, surprised by the question.

"I don't know what you mean."

I leaned against the wall and saw that there were several

splotches on my shirt from the bar fight. Maybe it was dried blood, but it wasn't all mine.

"Serena mentioned that Ben might be feeling lonely."

The moment I said it I felt foolish. I didn't normally get wrapped up in people's feelings. Ben looked fine to me, but I did try to look out for him. I thought about Kaz and our encounter with his old mentor. He'd let it wreck him. Was Ben going to self-destruct next?

"Perhaps," Crim said as we left the elevator and walked down the corridor. "It might be better to ask T'Chura or Raylin about it."

"Why?"

"Because they're more sensitive to things like that, especially Raylin."

I thought about it for a few seconds. "I guess it goes with her being a shapeshifter." I shrugged. "The kid is twenty, and probably needs…"

"Intimate companionship," Crim supplied. "I might be old, but I haven't forgotten what it was like to be a new hatchling." I chuckled, and he continued. "You're a social species."

I shook my head. "So, you're telling me I just need to suggest he bring a friend on the ship or take a vacation?"

Crim shrugged. "Don't *you* know? You're not *that* far from his age. What would you have done back on Earth?"

I blinked, trying to remember. My mind was blank. "Yeah, I've got nothing."

Crim chuckled. "In my experience, there are times when people simply don't adjust to ship life. They try it for a time and just prefer to have solid ground under their feet."

"We're not so different. He might have just been feeling a little nostalgic about something and Serena misinterpreted it."

Crim eyed me for a moment. "Think of this as a probationary period, and the likelihood of it changing is pretty great. You might find that you'll be the sole proprietor of the ship one day."

My lips pressed together. I hadn't considered that, but now that Crim had mentioned it, I had to wonder if he was right. Serena had hinted at not knowing if this was the life for her. What if Ben was considering the same thing?

I'd barely given it any thought at all. This was still so new, and aside from the latest debacle, it was a lot of fun. Why couldn't everyone just enjoy the moment?

I looked at Crim. "We'll see. You could be right, but then again, who knows?"

Crim nodded and we walked down the corridor in silence for a few minutes. "You've traveled quite a bit, haven't you—before we showed up, that is."

I nodded. "Yeah, I'm just a rolling stone, so this life suits me just fine."

"Well then, I'm sure you'll be fine."

I wasn't sure what he meant by that. Of course, I'd be fine. Why wouldn't I be fine?

I'd had enough of this conversation and decided to switch the subject. "What kind of problem did you find?"

Crim palmed the access panel for his workshop and the door dematerialized—a process where a seemingly solid door dissolved into thousands of tiny pieces, giving us access to the workshop. After we walked through, the door rematerialized. I'd gotten so used to it that I hardly noticed it much notice anymore.

He led me around the half-wall that divided the entrance area and the rest of the shop. There were several vehicles parked nearby in the converted hangar. I looked over at the battlewagon. Technically, it was an Ustral XG8 Javelin assault vehicle, but that was too much of a mouthful. Crim had given up on trying to get me to call his precious assault vehicle anything but a battlewagon. I knew things had changed between us when he'd started to refer to it by that name as well.

"Looks like you've installed the new armored plating," I said, gesturing toward the battlewagon.

It was Crim's most prized possession. After the previous battlewagon had been scrapped, he'd decided on a newer model that had some additional features. I didn't know the entire list of those new features, but Crim assured me that if we were to take on a platoon of Mesakloren soldiers, they'd be the ones running for cover. I liked how he addressed the issue of inadequate fire power by getting even more fire power.

"Only just this morning. The, uh, curing process takes a long time."

I frowned. "Curing process?"

"Nate, this isn't really your expertise."

"So."

He sighed and then began a lengthy explanation on the process of preparing some kind of hardened alloy into the size of panels that fit over the existing battlewagon frame. He kept mentioning things like matrix alignment. About the only thing I understood was that it didn't add much additional weight and had better stopping power than the standard armorplast that came with the vehicle. It also had some kind of special shield webbing to disperse the energy of more powerful weapons fired on it. Apparently, Crim expected that I would be taking on an army at some point.

He'd stopped speaking and I looked at him. "So, it talks, right?"

Crim blinked a few times and then rolled his eyes, muttering a few curses.

A grin bubbled out of my chest, and I pointed at him.

He crossed his arms. "Sometimes, Nate, I think you enjoy pushing my buttons entirely too much."

"Keeps things interesting."

"But did you understand everything I just told you about the new plating?"

"Yes, it stoppy, more boom, boom." I mimed shooting a rifle.

Crim blew out a breath. "Sometimes I can't believe your partners allow you to captain the ship."

I laughed, and eventually Crim chuckled. "Really, I understood most of it. Doesn't mean I could replace you, Crim. No one could do that, but I understand just how impressive your work is, while at the same time I can't wait to take it out on a test run."

Crim had been nodding until that last part when he did a double take. "No, absolutely not!"

Sometimes, I really should try to show some restraint, but with Crim it was too much fun.

"You're joking again," he said, and looked away with a thoughtful frown.

"Want me to stop?"

He considered for a few seconds and shook his head. "No, I need to learn not to be so possessive of…" he looked at the battlewagon and didn't finish.

I nodded and didn't comment. We'd almost died in the last battlewagon while trying to rescue Ben and Serena. Crim had always been a bit standoffish with the crew, but Kaz kept him around because he was exceptional when it came to engineering and maintaining the ship's critical systems. I'd pulled Crim out of the wreckage and a bond had been forged.

In light of the previous conversation, maybe Ben wasn't the only person aboard the ship who needed more in the way of companionship.

"Okay, what's this problem you need me to see?"

Crim activated a holoscreen showing the ship—a smaller version of the ship status that was on the bridge. "There have been environmental anomalies detected throughout the ship."

More than a dozen icons appeared on the ship's schematic. They all had different timestamps and weren't concentrated in any part of the ship.

"When did it start?"

"After you came back from the planet. I had Kierenbot run diagnostics on some of the sensors in these areas near environmental, but they're functioning within specs. So I had him go inspect them, and there's nothing wrong with the sensors."

"Do we need to inspect all the sensors?"

"There are automated checks for the ship's systems, but we haven't checked the other sensors. The ones that were physically inspected didn't indicate that they were defective, so I doubt the others will be."

I crossed my arms in front of my chest and rubbed the stubble on my chin. "What are the anomalies? What's being detected?"

"It's strange, but it seems like the atmosphere in those areas is shifting. Most of them show that temperatures have dropped by a significant margin. It only lasts from a few seconds to a few minutes. Sometimes less than that, but I can't explain why."

"Has it caused any damage to those areas?"

Crim shook his head. "Not yet."

I frowned. "What do you mean not yet?"

"It could be the randomness of the occurrences, and they haven't occurred in a critical system."

I considered this for a few moments. I reached out and manipulated the schematic of the ship, zooming in on one of the icons. A three-dimensional view of the area appeared, showing the exact location of the anomaly. It was almost in the middle of the corridor.

I switched back to a high-level view of the ship and took a closer look at a couple of the other locations. Some were in various rooms, but they seemed to mainly reside in corridors.

"That can't be by accident," I said.

Crim frowned. "What do you mean?"

"I mean that they don't occur inside a wall or something else. They're happening in an open area. Are there any video feeds in the corridors during one of these events?"

Crim reached toward the holoscreen and stopped. "Kierenbot would be better at that."

"Why?"

"Because he's an AI and this kind of analysis is part of his repertoire." Crim eyed me for a moment. "Is there something you don't like about Kierenbot?"

"No, it's just that his judgement seems a little off sometimes, so I've been restricting him to tasks that I know he can handle."

"Well, he can handle this," Crim said and opened a video comlink to the bridge.

Kierenbot answered almost immediately.

Crim cleared his throat and nodded toward me.

"We need your help," I said.

The red orb of Kierenbot's eye flashed. "What can I do?"

"Crim told me about the environmental anomalies detected with the sensors. I wanted to know whether we detected anything with the camera feeds," I said.

A few seconds later a large window appeared on our holoscreen. It was split into six sub-screens.

"We don't have constant surveillance with video, but I managed to put this together based on sensor feeds. It's a video representation of the event," Kierenbot said.

Crim nodded approvingly, and I played the first screen.

It showed an empty corridor. Something flickered for half a second and it was gone. I watched the others, and they were no better. I couldn't get a good look at whatever had caused the interference.

I looked at Kierenbot. "Can you slow it down so we can at least see what it is?"

The sub windows all updated at the same time at precisely the moment the flicker occurred. Kierenbot looped the image in slow motion. It helped but I still couldn't tell what it was.

"I'm afraid that's the best I can do. It does have a peculiar energy signature that happens right before each occurrence," Kierenbot said.

"What's different about it?" I asked.

Kierenbot looked at me, considering. He was probably coming up with a way to best explain it to me. "Usually there is evidence of a trigger for an energy disruption. Even with a disturbance in spacetime, it can be detected with our sensors, but there is usually some kind of trigger that's detected beforehand."

I considered his response for a few moments. "I'm with you so far."

"Excellent. With these occurrences, the event and the trigger appear to happen at the exact same time."

Kierenbot was an artificial intelligence capable of precise calculations that I had no hope of ever understanding, so when he said the events and triggers were happening at the same time, he meant it with a precision that was as accurate as possible.

"So, we can't predict them."

"I'm afraid not. I've tried thousands of models to come up with a solution, but they all fail."

I frowned. "You did this while speaking to us?"

"Of course. My perception of time is different," Kierenbot said.

Crim cleared his throat. "Let's avoid getting lost in the technical weeds." I looked at him, eyebrows raised. "Fine, quick version. Kierenbot can think faster than any of us. Speed of thought goes hand in hand with his perception of time. His thoughts and computational abilities go so fast that he has to slow himself down in order to interact with the rest of us."

I raked my teeth over my lower lip for a second and smiled. "Wow, that's pretty cool."

Kierenbot leaned toward the camera a little. "This is why some of my interactions with you appear to be off kilter, as I've heard you describe it."

I nodded once. "I'll keep it in mind."

"We still need to figure out why this is happening," Crim said.

"You're right about that. This is going to take some coordination."

Crim frowned. "What do you mean?"

"It means we're going to have to search the ship."

"What good will that do?"

I chuckled. "It beats waiting around for it to happen again."

"I still don't see how searching the ship is going to help us," Crim said.

I glanced at Kierenbot and he remained silent. "You tried to rely on the ship's sensors to find whatever this thing is. Well, we've all got senses of our own. Maybe we'll figure out what this thing is and, with a little luck, be at the right place at the right time."

"And do what if you find it?"

"I think this is a good idea," Kierenbot said. We turned toward him. "If we can generate a response from this thing, then we could get more data to aid in our analysis of what's happening."

I smiled, and then looked at Crim. "It means you're going to have to leave the workshop."

He rolled his eyes.

"Where do you want me to meet you?" Kierenbot asked.

I pursed my lips in thought for a second. "Actually, I want you to stay on the bridge. You'll help with coordinating the search. Also, I have something else for you to do. I'll tell you about it when I get to the bridge."

"Yes, Captain," Kierenbot replied and closed the comlink.

Crim stared at me for a moment. "I look forward to hearing your plan."

I shrugged, heading toward the door. "It's simple. Observe. We don't know what we're dealing with. I think a little bit of caution is in order."

Crim narrowed his gaze. "Why do I suspect that you know something you're not telling me?"

I smiled with half my mouth. "I'll meet you on the bridge."

"Where are you going?"

"I need to change my clothes and get some help. Bring whatever you think will help with the search."

"Who else is going to search with us?"

I palmed the door controls and backed out into the corridor. "Ben and T'Chura for sure. I'm going to revive Kaz, even if I have to drag him from his bed. Serena and Raylin are helping our guest, so they'll be otherwise occupied."

Crim nodded. "I'll see you on the bridge, Captain."

CHAPTER 11

I went to the commons area where our rooms were located. If I was going to use Earth naval nomenclature, they'd be called bunks or some such, but our rooms were better than the suites I'd stayed at in some of the finer resorts around the world. I went to my room and threw my shirt into the recycler for cleaning. I put on a fresh set of clothes and washed my face, doing the sniff test of my underarms. I was borderline needing a shower, but I just didn't have the time.

I walked out of my room and crossed the commons area to Kaz's room. T'Chura would have brought him there. I banged on Kaz's door and didn't get a reply. After waiting a few seconds, I banged again.

"Wake up!"

Still no answer. I palmed the door controls and used my credentials to override the lock. The door dissolved and I walked inside.

There was soft amber lighting in the room that was bright enough for me to see the various pieces of furniture. Kaz was sprawled out, face down on his bed. I glanced at his bathroom and considered tossing a bucket of water on him, except I didn't have a bucket.

I walked over and shook him. "Time to wake up."

Kaz groaned something I couldn't quite make out. It was probably better that way.

"On your feet, Nabris!" I shouted using my best Griff Tarken impression.

Kaz sputtered something and rolled onto his side. He looked at me and sank onto his back.

"The next thing I've got is a stunner. I hear it's quite a jolt to the system," I said, bringing up my hand blaster. I changed the settings, and an almost undetectable, high-pitched whine sounded from it.

Kaz sat up on his elbows. "Leave me alone," he moaned.

"Can't. I need you. We've got to search the ship."

He raised his gaze to me. "Why?"

"Because something might be on it with us."

"Just use the sensors and find out where it is. Then send T'Chura to deal with it."

I grinned and shook my head. "It's that kind of effort that lost you this ship in the first place. Now, are you going to get up, or am I gonna have to make you?"

Kaz slumped forward, looking pathetic. "Storage container by the wall."

I frowned and looked around his room. "What?"

Kaz blew out a breath, sounding irritated. "Container by the wall. Go over there and get something for me."

"Get it yourself. What do I look like?"

Kaz raised his fist into the air and then let it flop down into his lap. "Do you want my help or not?"

I peered at him. "You can't stand up and get it yourself?"

He tipped his head to the side and gave me a baleful glare. "I can't. All right. *I can't,*" he said through gritted teeth, still using a whiny tone.

"Gee whiz, Kaz. Did you overdo it *just* a little bit?" I said holding up my hand, keeping my finger and thumb apart by an inch.

He stared at the floor. "I hate you."

I grinned. "I'm actually enjoying myself," I said and wandered over to the nearest wall. I found the room's environmental controls and increased the lighting in the room.

Kaz clamped a palm over his eyes, cursing. "Damn it, Nate!"

"Where's that container again? Is it here?"

Kaz peeked through his fingers and meant to shake his head, but it was more of a total body shake.

"Well, where is it then?"

A burp came from him, and he groaned.

"If you're going to be sick, at least get to the bathroom first."

He gritted his teeth and slammed his fist onto the bed. "I won't be sick if you do what I tell you!"

I stared at him for a few seconds. "I'm waiting."

"It's by the door."

I walked across the room and found a small refrigeration unit. I opened it and saw several shelves full of vials. I frowned. What did Kaz need with all of these? I made a mental note to ask him about it later.

"Which one do you need?"

"The pale green one."

"What? I didn't quite catch that. Did you say this blue one?" I asked, grabbing the vial he'd asked for.

"No. No!" he shouted, then in a much calmer voice, "I said the pale green one. Dammit, you're such…I'm going to…" He rubbed his face and whatever threat he was about to make was muffled.

His whiny tone reminded me of a toddler at the end of their rope. I wondered if he'd roll around on the floor in full-on tantrum mode. I'd definitely record that. Maybe Kierenbot could make it part of his system login process.

Kaz slumped his shoulders and I could just about see his eyes through the break in his fingers covering his face.

Smiling, I made as if I were tossing him the vial. "Catch!"

Kaz flinched and his hand snatched at the air for the vial I hadn't thrown. He took several long blinks and looked at me dumbfounded.

I dangled the vial in front of him, and he took it from my hands.

"I'll give you a few minutes to pull yourself together," I said, walking toward the door with a spring in my step. I paused in the doorway. Using my best 'dad' voice I said, "Don't make me come back in here."

Kaz muttered something and I closed the door.

My omnitool buzzed with an incoming comlink.

"Captain, Delos Nadeau is waiting to speak with you," Kierenbot said.

Delos was the newest Zerian Omega board member. We'd helped legitimize his claim to the highly sought after board seat by delivering Quickening's legacy. The process had nearly killed us, and it was also the reason I had alien DNA as a permanent part of me.

The commons area was empty, and I went over to the nearest table and sat.

"Put him through."

A holoscreen became active in front of me and a video comlink came online. Delos Nadeau was a Nasarian. They were a species that lived over a thousand years. He had pale skin with a grayish hue. He was in a dimly lit room, and I thought he might have been alone.

"Hello, Delos. I'm surprised to hear from you."

Delos tilted his head to the side. "I've sent messages to your ship. Didn't you receive them?"

I thought about my inbox filled with messages that I deleted without reading on a regular basis.

"They probably made it, but…" I said and paused.

Delos leaned toward the camera, looking slightly amused. "You don't enjoy the deluge of offers that come into your inbox."

I chuckled, appreciating his understanding. "Something like that."

Delos had helped facilitate our compensation for being abducted and swept up into a corporate succession plot. However, appreciation aside, I knew the personality type, and I didn't want to become an extension of the struggles of the galaxy's elite grandmasters, as it were.

"I see. I heard you had some problems recently."

And he was keeping tabs on me. Good to know.

I arched an eyebrow. "Are you spying on me?"

Delos grinned. "You performed a great service, so yes, I do make it a point to keep an eye on you. You're still finding your way, and I'd hate for something unfortunate to happen to you."

Despite Delos's young appearance, he was nearly a century old.

"I appreciate it," I said, not wanting to insult him. "As far as problems go, it's nothing we can't handle."

Delos leaned back and nodded. "Understood and point taken. I'll back off."

"It's nothing personal."

"Understood. Since we're talking, I do have an opportunity for you to consider."

When people came to you offering "opportunities," they usually had strings attached, and my guard went up immediately.

"Oh," I said.

"Would you consider doing the occasional investigative contract for me?"

I tipped my head to the side. "You personally? You, the Zerian Board, or is it something else?"

Delos smiled. "Not me personally and not the board. This is for Wonfiner Limited. It's an independent company that checks on exploration efforts in various galactic sectors."

"So you want me to spy on someone else. Is that what you're asking?"

"It's not as covert as you make it sound, Nathan. It's just doing some observation work and reporting your findings through secure channels." He paused for a second and raised his hands, stalling my reply. "I don't want an answer right now. I doubt I'd like it. I just want you to consider it. I will send a few sample contracts for you to take a look at and evaluate for yourself."

I considered this for a few moments. Depending on the type of contracts, it could be a slippery slope. "All right, I'll take a look at them when I have time."

Delos nodded. "I also feel I should add that the compensation for these contracts is quite generous."

I chewed on my lower lip for a second, allowing my teeth to rake over it a little. "You must have an abundance of contractors that are better able to take on this kind of work. Why come to me with this?"

Delos regarded me for a few seconds. "I recognize talent when I see it, and I prefer to put it to use if I can."

He had a certain charisma that made me want to consider his offer. He knew how to establish rapport, and I had no doubt that he was just as adept in a boardroom as he was at dealing with me. Delos wasn't the most powerful being on the Zerian Board, but I had no doubts that as time went on he would become a force to be reckoned with. The question was whether I wanted to allow him to have his hooks in me.

"Delos, I have to be honest with you. I don't want to be an employee for you or anyone else. I just want to take the contracts that I want and be left alone to pursue other interesting things."

"I know that, Nathan. It's why my offer is on a contractual basis. It gives us both the freedom to choose when and how we work together."

I nodded. "I'll consider it."

"That's all I can ask. Now, I'll let you get to it."

The holoscreen turned off and I saw Kaz standing just outside his door. He looked way more alert than he'd been before, as if he'd had a full night's sleep and perhaps a shower.

"What was in that vial?" I asked as I stood up.

He narrowed his gaze for half a second and the flash of irritation was gone. He'd brought it on himself. Some people might call it the bro-code, but I never liked that expression. Males, no matter the species, had a particular way of interacting, much to the perplexity of others.

"It's a purifying agent that helps rid my system of poisons and reduces the time it would normally take to restore my equilibrium."

"All that from a little blue vial," I said with a grin. I knew which vial he'd used.

He sighed, not rising to the bait. "Was that Delos?"

"It was."

"What did he want?"

"To offer me a job."

Kaz considered this for a moment. "Are you going to take it?"

I shrugged. "Not sure, really. It's an offer for some contract work. Investigative type stuff. I don't know if I want to get involved."

Kaz nodded. "Why not? Could be worth it from someone like Delos."

"It's almost like picking a side. I like my independence."

Kaz chuckled. "I can find no fault with that logic."

I eyed him for a second, giving him a quick once-over to be sure he was ready to resume his duties. "No hard feelings?"

He blinked and then shook his head. "It's my own fault. But I do look forward to returning the favor one day."

I laughed. "That's how the game is played. Come on, we need to do a sweep of the ship."

We met up with T'Chura outside the commons area where I brought them up to speed about the anomalies that had been detected.

"You just want us to observe it? What if it attacks us?" Kaz asked.

"Shoot first and ask questions later. Just don't hit anything important. This isn't a free-for-all," I said.

I'd lost count of how many movies and TV shows I'd watched where the mysterious encounter resulted in a person's death because they weren't told to defend themselves. I couldn't see T'Chura, Kaz, Crim, or anyone doing anything that foolish.

"We should first try to communicate with it," T'Chura said.

"Agreed," I said. Kaz looked doubtful. I couldn't see Crim because he was still in his workshop, listening in via comlink. "The events recorded only occur for a few seconds, less than that in some instances. Kierenbot is going to help coordinate our efforts by monitoring the ship's systems. Keep the comlink open."

"Isn't Ben joining us?" Crim asked.

"No, they need him in sickbay. It's the four of us," I said, and then quickly added, "Five of us. I didn't forget you, Kierenbot."

"Thank you, Captain. I will monitor and advise accordingly."

We split up after that, dividing the ship into sections to explore. I wore a small earpiece that projected a HUD only I could see. It was similar to wearing a helmet, but it allowed me to receive data from the ship's sensors and see what Kierenbot highlighted if the anomaly occurred nearby. It also saved time for conveying important information.

I'd explored the ship quite a bit in the months we'd been aboard. Nothing was unfamiliar, but I still moved at a steady pace. I didn't want to rush into anything.

For the next hour we moved through our assigned sections, and no anomalies occurred. If they followed the established pattern, one should have happened somewhere.

I walked inside one of the storage modules in the belly of the ship, or midships, if I was being technical. The lighting immediately became brighter as I walked inside. Empty racks lined the area, but along the wall there were storage units in standby mode. We weren't carrying that much in the way of cargo but had the ability to accommodate a large variety of requests.

I walked through the storage modules without noticing anything out of the ordinary. Once I was in the corridor, I went toward the environmental section.

"All clear over here. I'm going to head back now," T'Chura said.

"Understood," I replied.

"Yeah, Nate, not that I don't appreciate the exercise, but I haven't noticed anything," Kaz said.

"My area is clear, too," Crim said. "I'm going back to my shop."

Crim dropped out of the comms channel.

Kaz cleared his throat.

I sighed. "Yes."

"Isn't it great being in charge?" he asked, and before I could respond he dropped out of the comms channel as well.

Why was it that people came to me to solve a problem and then just complained when I tried to work said problem?

I stood in the long corridor between environmental and the storage modules. Underneath me was the main hangar bay. I had started to turn around when several targets flashed on my HUD.

"Captain!" Kierenbot said. "Don't move! I've detected the strange energy readings all around you."

I looked around, trying to see anything out of the ordinary.

"The corridor is clear. I'm the only one here."

More targets flashed on my HUD in a blinding succession that was more disruptive than useful.

Then I saw vapors of my breath rising in front of my face. The temperature had dropped. I gasped and spun around, looking for the cause. The temperature was so cold that my face started to hurt. I hastened back down the corridor, but it was the same. I covered my face with my hands and breathed into them, and my face warmed a little.

"Kierenbot, talk to me. Is this thing following me?" I asked as I went farther down the corridor.

He didn't respond. The comlink was dead. I tried to contact him again, but my omnitool wouldn't work. The earpiece began screeching so loudly that I tore it off, letting it drop to the floor. A layer of frost formed over it.

Frost began covering the walls nearby and quickly spread

down the corridor. It went up to the middle of the wall in concentric patterns. Some disappeared as quickly as they formed.

I stretched my eyes wide. They looked familiar. The patterns were the same as what I'd seen in the ruins. I was sure of it.

I activated my hand cannons, and they powered up immediately. I held them out in front of me, ready to fire on anything that attacked. Then I remembered T'Chura suggesting that we try to communicate with it.

Feeling more than a little foolish, I lowered my weapons. "Hello," I said. "I don't want to hurt you, but could you stop freezing me out?"

The frost patterns on the walls spread to the floor and ceiling as it moved toward me. It was a thin layer. It wasn't like I was in the Arctic surrounded by a glacier, but I did back up a little.

The corridor was very quiet, and I realized I couldn't hear the life-support systems cycling the ship's atmosphere. It reminded me of that first snowfall in the middle of the night when everything was so peaceful and serene.

I considered saying my "we come in peace" message again but dismissed it. "All right, now what? Do you understand me?"

I didn't get any kind of reply. I looked down and saw frost particles on my pants detach and float away from me to become a swirling mass hovering just above the floor. The frost in the area drew toward it and the temperature increased. I watched as the particles merged into a small antique bronze color that had a soft glow around it. The swirling mass slowed to take on a shape that was about three feet tall. It had a triangle-shaped head and feline body. The folds of skin reminded me of the alien meerkats I'd encountered in the ruins. With each passing moment, it became more defined, but when it moved it kind of dissolved, as if whatever force was holding it together was barely doing so.

The meerkat sat on its hind legs and stared up at me expectantly.

My mouth hung open as I stared at it, unable to move and with no idea what to do. This…thing had literally formed out of thin air and was looking at me. It stared at me curiously, as if waiting for me to do something.

I squatted down, maintaining eye contact. "Hi there," I said, hoping this didn't become a scene from a space horror movie where my eyes were sucked out of my skull.

I love being a spacer.

CHAPTER 12

The alien meerkat tilted its head to the side, lifting one ear as if it was trying to understand me.

I decided to go full tilt and really put myself out there. I retracted the hand cannon and sat on the floor.

"So, I guess you're what's causing all this disruption."

The creature moved its head in what could loosely be described as a nod. It opened its mouth, but no sound came out.

I frowned. It only resembled the creatures I'd encountered in the ruins. This was something else. I thought that if I touched the bronze material it might disintegrate, or at the very least it would be cold to the touch. Worse case, he might think I was attacking him, and then the monster would come out. I wasn't going to try it because I really wasn't sure how much I wanted to push this little alien encounter.

I cleared my throat. "You know, your buddies thought it was great when I threw them out into the abyss so they could glide down the chasm."

The creature peered at me, and I didn't think he could understand me. I looked down at my wrist and saw that my omnitool was now working. I brought up the video from the ruins and showed it to the creature. He watched it for a few moments, his eyes tracking it like a cat follows a laser pointer.

I let him watch it for a few minutes and then stopped.

"Don't suppose you have a name?" I asked.

The creature moved closer to me and sat less than a foot away. It didn't make any noise. I lifted my hand about halfway toward it. After a few seconds it mimicked the gesture with one of its paws.

Swallowing hard, I moved my hand closer.

The creature did the same.

We touched, and there was a tingling sensation like the air was alive with electricity, but it was also cold—not Arctic cold but cooler than the normal temperature.

I grinned. At least it hadn't hurt, and the creature hadn't morphed into a monster ready to bite my head off.

"Do you plan to stick around? Because if you do, I have to call you something."

I really had no idea what I was doing. I hoped that by now, Kierenbot had alerted the others and they were on their way here. All I was really doing now was stalling, because if this creature turned into anything like the others that had attacked me, I'd have less than a second to react.

I stared at the creature with my lips pressed together. "Since I don't know your name, I'll call you Larry. How's that sound?"

The creature stood up and then spun around. As he moved, his body shifted as if he was just barely holding himself together. He shook himself like a dog that had just gone swimming. Then he leaped around excitedly, and I laughed.

"I guess you like the name. All right, Larry it is," I said.

"What are you doing?" Kierenbot said, his voice coming over a nearby speaker.

I glanced up at it and waved. "I found the source of the disturbance."

"You did? Where is it?"

I frowned and gestured in front of me. "He's right there."

Larry stared up at me curiously.

"I'm not able to see anything on the camera feeds. Sensors show you're alone in the corridor."

I stood up. "Like hell I am. It's standing right there."

Larry walked toward the side of the corridor and, for a second, disappeared entirely. Then he reappeared near the wall. He turned toward me, and his eyes widened as if he had just realized I was there.

I heard others coming down the corridor.

"Nate!" Kaz called out as he ran toward me.

T'Chura followed him.

I looked at them. "Hey guys."

Kaz looked at me and then down the corridor. "What happened? Kierenbot said there was a huge anomaly detected here."

I nodded. "There was, but it's stopped." I gestured toward where I'd seen Larry. He was walking slowly down the hall. "Do you see that?"

Kaz peered down the corridor and shook his head.

"There's nothing there," T'Chura said.

I blinked. They couldn't see it.

Kaz narrowed his gaze. "This isn't funny, Nate. We thought something happened to you. The temperatures plunged to below freezing."

"I know, I was here. I'm not trying to be funny."

Kaz's shoulders slumped a little and he glanced at T'Chura. "I swear, if this is some kind of joke…"

"It's not. I'm telling you that there is something here in the corridor right now, and I'm the only one who can see it," I said.

Kaz frowned, looking as if he wasn't sure whether to believe me.

"Larry, can you show yourself to my friends here?" I asked.

Larry twisted his head around to look at me. Then he trotted over toward me. He looked up at T'Chura and Kaz, but they didn't see him.

"He's right there. You'd step on him if you weren't careful."

Kaz peered down at the floor and shook his head. "I don't see anything, and nothing is showing on the sensors."

"I think we should take him to sickbay. Let the autodoc examine him," T'Chura said.

"I'm fine. Nothing is wrong with me, and I don't need to see the autodoc." I eyed them both suspiciously. "You seriously don't see him? Three feet tall, looks like one of the creatures from that planet I told you about?"

Kaz shook his head. "Come on, Nate. You're seeing things. You might have picked up a parasitic organism that's affecting your brain."

I rolled my eyes. "No, I haven't. The decontamination field would've eliminated it."

"Maybe, but we won't know for sure until the autodoc runs its analysis. As your executive officer, I must insist," Kaz said.

If Kaz had recruited T'Chura to have a little fun at my expense, they were doing a convincing job of it. They both looked worried, especially T'Chura. The Sasquatch's big eyes drew down in a calm expression of concern, and he looked as if he didn't want to alarm me.

Something cold settled into the pit of my stomach. I

glanced down at Larry, who seemed immune to the change of mood in the corridor. He stepped toward T'Chura without glancing up at him and disappeared, only to reappear farther down the corridor. He became still, as if he wasn't sure how he'd gotten there. Then he turned toward me and there was something off about his gaze. It wasn't menacing, just peculiar, as if he knew more than he let on, and a shiver crawled down my spine.

I looked at the others, grim-faced. "I think maybe you guys are right. I might've caught something back on that planet."

Kaz and T'Chura looked relieved to hear me say it.

The walk back to the elevator seemed to take forever. Along the way, Larry phased in and out of view. He stayed within our vicinity, and I tried not to look at him.

We got on the elevator, and I glanced at Kaz, looking for some indication that this was an elaborate prank. God knows I didn't make it easy on him. They could've recruited Crim to project an image of Larry. That would explain how he seemed to disappear for short bursts.

I frowned in thought. Crim couldn't have been in on it. He'd told me that the problem with the unusual energy detections began while the rest of us were off the ship. I hadn't imagined the corridor plunging to subzero temperatures. I recalled how the frost patterns formed in concentric patterns, and if someone had been manipulating the environmental controls in the area. I didn't think they could do that. I might be wrong, but if I wasn't, then something could seriously be wrong with me, and it was affecting my brain.

We walked toward the med bay and entered the lounge area just inside. It was empty. Kaz took the lead while T'Chura stayed behind me. Did they expect me to run away?

I inhaled a deep breath and looked down at the ground.

Larry walked gingerly by my side. He moved like a feline, half stalking and always ready for action. Was I just imagining him?

We went into the nearest open room, and Kaz gestured for me to go to the circular platform. I stepped onto it.

Kaz stood by a nearby workstation. "I'm going to initiate a scan and we'll take it from there."

Larry walked over to the platform, and I grimaced when he hopped up next to me.

A red light from the ceiling came on, lighting up the area. It felt warm against my skin. The light began pulsing and I closed my eyes. I kept trying to determine whether I was feeling ill, but I didn't. I felt fine. I thought if I kept looking for something to be wrong with me, I'd start imagining there was.

A cool breeze blew over the top of me, startling me a little. I opened my eyes and the lighting overhead had become an emerald-green color. It flashed a few times and then it was done. The platform lowered to the ground. I looked down at the ground and Larry was gone. I glanced around the room, and he was nowhere to be found.

"According to the scans, you're in perfect health."

I stepped off the platform. "That's a relief, I guess. It's either that or I'm going crazy."

Kaz regarded me for a second. "Do you still see it?"

I shook my head. "No, but he did follow us in here. He was on the platform with me."

T'Chura frowned. "He? How could you tell its gender?"

I arched an eyebrow. "Do I need to review how biology works?"

T'Chura chuckled and shook his head.

"I call him Larry."

Kaz frowned. "Larry?"

I nodded. "It's a good name. I'll let you know if I see him again."

I wasn't sure I was actually going to do that, but I knew it was what they wanted to hear. If I kept telling them I was seeing something they couldn't, I could imagine them offloading me to the alien equivalent of the loony bin. I imagined some kind of weird aliens experimenting on me and locking me in a padded room.

I rolled my eyes at the thought. I was starting to think like Ben had when we'd first come aboard the ship—paranoid, with a bunch of conspiracy theories swirling around in his brain.

I walked toward the door and both T'Chura and Kaz blocked my way. I stopped and regarded them each for a second. "I thought we were done here."

"We're concerned," T'Chura said.

"I appreciate it, big guy, you know I do, but if the scans didn't show anything wrong with me, there's no reason for whatever this is," I said, gesturing at them both.

Kaz stepped out of the way.

I walked through the door and saw Ben sitting alone in the lounge area. The ladies must've kicked him out for some reason.

I looked at Kaz and T'Chura. "Since I'm not crazy yet, we've got other things we need to focus on."

"What do you need us to do?" T'Chura asked.

"We need to know whether there are any other Humans roaming around the orbital station. Is there anything you can do to check on that without drawing attention?"

T'Chura shared a glance with Kaz.

"There is," Kaz said.

"Good, get started on that and come find me later with an update."

"What do you want me to do if I find others?"

I considered that for a few seconds while I glanced at Ben. "We go after them."

Kaz frowned. "No plan, just go out and abduct them?"

"Isn't that what you did to us?" I asked, gesturing toward Ben. Kaz didn't respond. "If you want to get technical, we'll do some reconnaissance and the like. Then we'll get them."

T'Chura nodded. "We'll get to it."

They left the med bay, and I wandered over to where Ben sat.

"Is this seat taken?" I asked as I plopped down in the chair across from him.

Ben frowned. "What were you doing in the autodoc?"

I shrugged. "It was time for my checkup," I said, not wanting to talk about the real reason I was there.

He rubbed his eyebrow for a second, looking distracted.

"How's our guest? What was her name again?"

"Lanaya. She's more responsive now, but there's something not right about her."

I raised my eyebrows. "Still searching for the perfect woman, kid?"

He chuckled and it chased away the worry on his face. "No, geez Nate, come on."

I grinned. "So, what have you learned about her?"

"Her responses are conditioned, as if she's been trained with a certain script in mind and she can't deviate from it. It's a little strange. Also, her physiology is different. Raylin is working on that now."

I frowned a little. "Won't the scans detect it and the autodoc give an analysis?"

"It can, but it operates from a database of known species. When it encounters something new, it gives estimates that need to be verified," Ben said.

"She looks Human."

He nodded and I caught the somewhat dreamy look on his face. "Well, she's not entirely Human."

"Why did they chase you out of there?"

He arched an eyebrow. "What makes you think they chased me out?"

I stared at him. "Kid, there's a pretty girl in there you found on the station who seems to have been some kind of prisoner, and she seems to trust you a little bit. And you're telling me you're out here to get some air? Is that what you're trying to tell me?"

Ben blinked, looking a little uncomfortable. He sighed. "Once they got her to settle down, they thought it would be better if I waited outside."

"They?"

"Serena."

"Oh, I see. Well, she would know."

He nodded. "Yeah."

We were quiet for a minute.

"How are you doing, Ben?"

"I'm fine…Nate."

I chuckled and he rolled his eyes, smiling.

"I don't know what to do."

"About what?"

He shifted in his seat, leaning to the other side and sighing. "What if there are other people out in the galaxy?"

"I guess it depends. We'll figure it out."

"I hope so."

"I've got a question, and I don't want you to read into it or anything."

Ben narrowed his gaze in thought. "Okay, I guess."

"Are you all right with this? You know, being on the ship? What we're doing out here?"

Ben inhaled and considered it for a few seconds. "Yeah, I mean it's the opportunity of a lifetime."

"You're not lonely?"

He shrugged. "Sometimes. I get along fine with everyone here, but it's just the three of us," he said and paused, considering. "Sometimes I feel like a third wheel."

I blinked.

"Come on, Nate. Any idiot can tell there's something going on between you and Serena."

"I can assure you that nothing is going on."

He shook his head. "Sometimes it would be nice to see other people once in a while."

"Want us to swing by Earth and pick some up?"

We were nowhere near Earth.

Ben laughed. "I don't know."

"I'm serious. We've kinda gotten so wrapped up doing things out here that maybe we've overlooked something. Plus, you're full of youthful vigor."

Ben eyed me wryly. "I'm surprised you still remember, old man."

I'd walked right into that one. Alien aphrodisiac aside, I'd been flying solo for a lot longer than I would've liked, but I decided to let his quip slide. I'd come to regard Ben as a younger brother. Sometimes that meant giving him some tough love, and others not so much.

"I'm going to let that slide," I said judiciously. "Once."

Ben wasn't as lanky as he'd been when I'd first met him. A good diet and some regular exercise had put some much-needed muscle on his frame.

"I do think about going back to Earth one day. Not anytime soon. I'm learning too much. I want to return someday and give humanity a leg up."

"Are you sure we're ready for that?"

"We'll need to be. I'm not just going to hand things over, but I think things can be nudged here and there to put people on the right path."

I arched an eyebrow toward him. "I had no idea you were so manipulative."

Ben grinned and shook his head. "I haven't worked out all the details. I've talked about it with Crim."

"Oh yeah? What'd he say about it?"

"He wished me luck."

I chuckled. "Crim is a smart man."

He frowned. "You don't think I should?"

"No, I wouldn't say that, but challenge aside, it could be a thankless endeavor, and there are ethical arguments to be made about it."

"I was looking into studying theoretical physics before all this happened."

I knew he'd taken a year off of college to earn money, but now Ben didn't need money, at least not for a long time.

"And now?"

"It sucks. The theories being studied have stagnated and all physicists do is devote all their time to performing complex calculations that are flawed. I don't just mean a little bit. There's missing the mark and then there's trying to swim with both hands tied behind your back."

"I never gave it much thought."

Ben leaned forward. "Okay, think of it this way. Computers aside, if we took all that away, have things really changed since the 1970s?"

"Sure, they have. Heck, I don't know."

"How?"

"I just said I didn't know," I replied and thought about it.

"You don't even carry a smartphone. You said they were trackers, and you're right. The current model of internet sucks, and it's stacked against us."

"So, you want to create a better internet?"

"Better everything. That's just one thing. If we hadn't been so preoccupied with chasing theories that have no practical application and are unproven, we could've been exploring the galaxy right now."

I knew very little about what he was talking about, and he sensed this.

"I'm sorry. I've been thinking about it a lot. Crim has been teaching me things he says are basic but would turn everything upside down back home. The way we use energy is laughable, Nate. And it seems like it's been stagnated to keep things as they are."

I sighed. "That much I do understand, but before you go blowing the roof off how the world works, remember that there are people involved in it."

He frowned. "I don't understand."

"I don't want to get too philosophical here, okay?" He nodded. "Any change that you propose or implement…Never mind that. Let's say you go back to Earth, and you've got a way to revolutionize how we create energy. Suddenly, it's super cheap and we abandon the old tech that's been around for the past hundred or so years. What happens to everyone who works in those industries? What do they do?"

"They can be trained in the new tech."

"True, maybe that takes care of some of them. You're talking about affecting people's livelihoods, and all I'm saying is that you should be strategic. As in, don't just do it because you think that's the way it should be done. It's okay to start off, but you need to think it through. Build a team because no one is smart enough to do it all."

Ben considered it for a few moments and then shrugged. "I see your point."

"That's my lesson for today. Get yourself a juice box."

He shook his head and laughed.

"Seriously, it's good that you want to improve things. Go for it but be careful about it."

He nodded. "I will."

Kierenbot sent me a message asking that I come to the bridge.

I stood up. "Want to take a walk?"

"Where?" he asked, rising to his feet.

"To the bridge. I had Kierenbot working on something for me, and he's got an update. If anything, it'll take your mind off how you're going to rule Earth one day."

Ben blinked. "I don't want to rule Earth!"

I grinned and shook my head. Sometimes it was just too easy to get his goat.

CHAPTER 13

We left the med bay and headed toward the bridge. As we climbed onto the elevator, Ben eyed me. "So, you and Serena."

I grimaced and said in my best radio personality voice, "On tonight's episode of Gossip Boys, Ben wants to know if Nate and Serena are ever going to hook up."

The elevator doors opened, and Ben's laugh echoed down the corridor. He took the hint and stopped pestering me about it.

We walked onto the bridge. There were several large holoscreens active, and Kierenbot stood off to the side, waiting to present his findings.

Ben turned toward me. "What did you say he was working on again?"

Some of the images on the holoscreen had been captured from my recordings of the ruins, and there were others I'd never seen before. They looked like they were from somewhere entirely different.

"Thanks for coming so quickly," Kierenbot said and waved us over excitedly.

"Looks like you were able to find something," I said.

"I've found a lot, actually, about the artifact, the recordings you brought back, and some of the residual particles on your combat suit."

"Residual?"

Kierenbot nodded. "Yes. Each part of these things reveals only snippets of knowledge, but together it's something else. Uh, together it elevates their worth."

"Okay, you've piqued my interest. What's this about?" Ben asked.

I gestured toward a nearby holoscreen. "Those are some of the recordings I took while exploring the ruins I found near the crash site."

Ben nodded, peering at them for a few moments.

"Captain, you've stumbled onto something quite remarkable," Kierenbot began but stopped when the door to the bridge opened. Kaz and T'Chura walked in.

"What's going on?" Kaz asked.

"Kierenbot was telling me how remarkable I am—Wait a minute. That's not right. How the ruins I found are remarkable," I said with a shrug.

"Indeed," Kierenbot said, and I nodded for him to continue. "The ruins are quite old."

He put an estimated age on one of the holoscreens.

"That's preposterous," Kaz said. "That can't be right."

"I assure you that the number is accurate. I triple tested my results and also compared them with the particles from the captain's combat suit."

"But these are almost as old as the galaxy itself," Kaz said and frowned. He stared at Kierenbot, considering, and then shook his head. "No. It's not what you think."

"I'm afraid it is. There is no other explanation," Kierenbot replied.

Kaz sneered as his eyes swept over the holoscreens in disgust.

I cleared my throat. "Hey guys, remember the rest of us," I said, waving at them.

Kaz sat down in a nearby chair. He crossed his arms, looking annoyed.

Kierenbot turned toward me. "Evidence has been found in almost random places in the galaxy of a civilization that existed at the time when the galaxy was newly formed."

I frowned and glanced at Kaz. He was still stewing. "Really?"

The robot nodded. "I'm afraid so. I've cross-referenced what you discovered with some records I was able to pull off the orbital station archives."

I blinked. "Are you sure about that? That's," I glanced at Ben for a second, "billions of years old. It looked old inside the ruins but not that old. Exposed as it was, it should've decomposed, turned to dust, that sort of thing."

"I can see why you'd believe that, and in many instances it's true, but it goes back to the particles from the materials used when those ruins were built."

I glanced at Kaz, and he still looked angry. "Is that why—"

He scowled. "Yes, that's why Griff Tarken was there. He's still trying to find the Asherah Empire." He swallowed hard, then inhaled sharply. "The Forgotten Empire."

My eyebrows knitted together in a thoughtful frown. "If you know the name of it, then how is it forgotten?"

Kaz rolled his eyes. "That's the name associated with it. No one really knows who they were or what they were actually called."

I eyed him for a few seconds. "What's the matter with you? Why are you so mad about this?"

Kaz took a steadying breath, looking more tired than angry. "Griff Tarken, my mentor, made claims that were proven to be fraudulent. His reputation was ruined, which included anyone associated with him."

Kaz looked as if it still hurt him to talk about, as if he was admitting some enormous, life-altering regret. It didn't make any sense.

"That's nonsense. You were his apprentice. It's not like you helped him to…"

Kaz just stared at me. "I didn't know that's what I was doing."

It was an old wound that had been reopened because of our encounter with Griff. It also explained some of Kaz's behavior.

"All right, fine, I'm not going to dredge up the past for you."

Kaz chuckled bitterly. "Isn't that what you do? Dredge up the past?"

I thought about it for a second. "Well, yeah, but not yours." I gestured toward the holoscreens nearby. "This sounds interesting. I want to know more about it."

"You and everyone else who's gone on this fool's errand," Kaz said.

I arched an eyebrow. "Does that mean you don't want to find this lost empire?"

Kaz stood up and sneered. "You'll never find it. No one has because it's just a myth based on some unexplained civilization that used materials almost as old as the galaxy to build things, but nothing was around when the galaxy first came into being. That's an undeniable fact."

He stormed off the bridge.

Ben cleared his throat. "He might be right. It's not like things were stable across the galaxy after the Big Bang."

"Not you, too," I replied.

"What?"

"Do you know how many extinction-level events have happened on Earth since the planet started bobbing around the sun?"

Ben shook his head.

I held up my hand. "At least five that we know of. Five that we've found evidence for, and that doesn't even account for the entire history of our planet. Guess how long Humans have been around."

Ben shrugged and didn't reply.

"Just under two hundred thousand years, and look how far we've come. Ten thousand years ago, we started farming more and building cities. If you go back a hundred years before now, we were just starting to figure out how to fly and build cars. It doesn't take as long as you might think for a civilization to rise, and in this case, fall," I said, gesturing toward the holo-screens.

Ben shrugged. "You know more about it than I do."

T'Chura cleared his throat. Sometimes the Sasquatch was so quiet that you could forget he was there, but when he made his presence known, there was no mistaking it.

"Nate is right. Some intelligent species emerge quicker than others."

I smiled, appreciating someone backing me up instead of challenging me on every little thing.

"However," T'Chura continued, "there has to be some kind of flaw in the dating methodology used because no matter the material, there should've been some kind of breakdown over time."

I considered this for a few seconds and looked at Kierenbot with raised eyebrows.

"I can only relay the data I've found. I cannot offer you an explanation of how the material came to be at that particular location in the first place."

"And this dating methodology you used is reliable?" I asked.

"The analysis I did utilized multiple standard methodologies used by corporations and academics. They're standard because their reliability has been proven millions of times over for longer than your species has been farming."

I chuckled and tipped my head to the side. "Okay, so instead of focusing on whether or not Kierenbot's analysis is accurate, let's focus on coming up with explanations of how it came to be there in the first place."

T'Chura looked at Kierenbot. "Did you match these results against the Nasarian archives?"

"I did. I used their findings as the foundation from which to base the results I found."

"I don't understand," Ben said.

"It means that, shockingly, not everyone agrees on the data extracted from the archeological findings," I said.

Ben pressed his lips together a little and then looked at Kierenbot. "Is that right?"

"An astute observation," Kierenbot replied.

The robot was being way too complimentary, and it was getting a little embarrassing. That needed to change.

"I don't understand why Kaz is so bothered by this. I mean, so what if his old mentor was a fraud? How long has it been since Kaz escaped all that?" I asked, looking pointedly at T'Chura.

He considered it for a few seconds. "Reputations are hard to build and easy to destroy. Kaz has had to deal with the fallout of being associated with such a prominent figure. But the relationships between mentor and mentee—Gabris and Nabris—is a deeper bond, akin to the bond that comes from a familial relationship. It runs very deep, and even if the bond is severed, you're never really free of it."

I glanced at Ben for a second. He shrugged.

"Okay, there's a bond, so Kaz still feels like he owes Griff something?"

"You'd have to discuss that with him. I don't know. If you choose to pursue this," T'Chura said, lifting his chin toward the holoscreens, "then it will be difficult for him to cope. He might even leave the ship if it proves too much for him."

My eyes widened in surprise. I hadn't expected that. "What about you? How do you feel about this?"

"I'm contractually obligated to protect you and the other members of the crew for the duration that we agreed on."

"But."

"Pursuing the Asherah has fallen out of fashion to the point that if you admit it to anyone they will treat you with derision. This will affect the viability of any other enterprise you choose to take on in the future," T'Chura replied.

I nodded. "I won't win any popularity contests. So what?"

"It's more than that, Nate. Armed conflict is assured. Wars have been fought that stemmed from a finding associated with the Asherah."

"That confirms that there is value in what the Asherah left behind." I looked at Kierenbot. "What makes them so popular?"

"Some technological advancements came from recovering Asherah artifacts."

A bit of bronze reflected off something beneath one of the holoscreens. Larry slunk underneath it and peered up at the holoscreens. I blinked a few times and blew out a breath to cover up my surprise. I looked at the others, but no one noticed that Larry was in the room.

Not good.

Either Larry was real and I was the only one who could see him, or I was going crazy. I knew which I preferred, but I didn't know how to fix it.

Larry turned away from the holoscreen and settled his gaze on me. My stomach tightened, as if I was about to be punched.

I tore my eyes away from the phantom meerkat and addressed the others. "So, the reason everyone was so interested in the Asherah was because they had a technological edge."

Kierenbot looked at T'Chura, and the Sasquatch sighed. "Raylin is better at discussing these things than I am."

"I'm sure you'll do fine."

T'Chura chuckled a little. Then he regarded me for a few moments. "There is a technological edge and then there is a technological leap. Usually, leaps are built upon many steps in the march of innovation. *Then* breakthroughs occur." He paused for a moment, pressing his lips together while he considered what he would say next. "From what I can remember learning about them, no one really understands the artifacts that have been recovered. There is a lot of speculation and contradictions about what and who the Asherah were and what ultimately happened to their civilization. I'm afraid that's all I really know about them."

"It's something," I said and gave T'Chura an appreciative nod. Then I looked at Kierenbot. "What's in the archives?"

The bright red orb in the robot's head flashed, and I quickly held up my hand. "I don't want you to recite the archive, but can you confirm what T'Chura has said?"

"There have been technological...leaps that appear to stem from discoveries tied to Asherah artifacts. It's nothing all-encompassing. They had what was considered peculiar ways of doing things—galactic travel for one. They seemed to be focused on speed and observation," Kierenbot said and updated some of the images on the holoscreen.

"I can't make sense out of any of this," Ben said and looked at me. "Can you?"

I peered at the holoscreen. There were images of different types of chambers that displayed strange symbols I didn't understand. I stepped toward one of the screens and made a swiping motion with my hand, and the images advanced to another set.

"Not really," I admitted. I crossed my arms and rubbed my chin while I stared at the images.

Larry walked toward me, and I tried not to react at all.

"This is probably going to take awhile to go through," I said.

"What about the anomalies? The strange energy detections?" Ben asked.

"I'm monitoring for them," Kierenbot said. "However, none have occurred since the large-scale anomaly observed by the captain."

Larry sat on the floor a short distance away. I must've been staring because Ben was calling out to me.

"Nate," Ben said, "what's the matter? You look like you've seen a ghost."

I grinned. *You have no idea, Ben.* "I'm fine," I said.

T'Chura turned toward me. "The autodoc didn't find any kind of infection."

"That's right. I'm fit as a fiddle."

Ben frowned, and I rolled my eyes. "What am I missing?"

"I saw something the others didn't."

"What did you see?"

"Something like the creatures I'd encountered in the ruins, but no one else could see it."

Ben glanced at T'Chura, who nodded.

"I believe that you believe it," T'Chura said.

I considered a snarky reply, but in the end I didn't think it was worth it. "Thanks."

Ben looked at me and then his gaze sank toward the ground. Larry stared up at him. Then Ben looked at me. "That's gotta be weird."

I nodded. "Pretty much. Look, you guys don't have to stay here. I'm going to look over some of these images and check out the archives. Think about stuff alone for a bit."

"Oh, all right. I'll head back to the med bay and check on Lanaya," Ben said.

I arched an eyebrow, and his cheeks reddened a little. Then he shook his head and left the bridge.

"I think I'll make another sweep of the ship," T'Chura said.

"Kierenbot, why don't you go with him," I said.

"I thought I'd serve best by reviewing the data I've compiled for you."

"You've done a great job with this, and I just want to look it over myself for a while. Absorb it. I'll contact you if I have questions, and we'll discuss it when you get back. Sound good?"

Kierenbot considered this for a few moments and then nodded. "Very well, Captain."

They turned to go, and I said, "Let me know if you find anything."

They left the bridge, and I looked down at Larry.

"I guess it's just you and me," I said and sighed.

Larry glanced up at me and looked as if he were puzzling something out. He gave me an inquisitive look.

"Look sharp. I expect you to let me know if you recognize any of this stuff," I said, gesturing at the holoscreens. Then I began reviewing the data Kierenbot had pulled together for me.

CHAPTER 14

The hours went by in a blur of holoscreens and absorbing snippets of information about the Asherah gathered over thousands of years. Many different species had sought out information that led to the discovery of the origins of the mysterious race. I'd recognized a few species that had taken up the search. Many would-be experts who'd tried to predict where the lost empire would be found were wrong. Griff Tarken was by no means the first. Nasarians, Mesaklorens, Akacians, Ustrals, and many other species that I didn't recognize had taken up the search. It seemed to come and go like a fad that would periodically return.

T'Chura had been right. There'd beem no shortage of bloodshed when it came to searching for the lost empire. The last major push had occurred several hundred years ago. Some charismatic explorer had convinced several mega corporations to fund research efforts. He must have had some compelling evidence, but the records didn't indicate what kind of evidence had been found. In the end, the expeditions were lost, even after a staggering amount of resources had been devoted toward another expedition.

There were a few historical analyses that showed various narrative-driven efforts to convince many that the expeditions had been lost to a new and hostile galactic species, although they never found any trace of the lost expeditions or an undiscovered hostile galactic species. There'd been a few skirmishes over salvage rights, which I suspected was a coverup for being on the trail of the Asherah.

I sat at a workstation, leaning on my elbows and staring up at a holoscreen. My eyes kept tearing up and I yawned. I'd been at this too long. Kierenbot and T'Chura had left hours ago. They hadn't contacted me, so they hadn't found anything. I glanced down at Larry, who was curled up on the floor. There was a shimmer around him and sometimes a wave of distortion came over him from head to tail. In any other circumstance, he behaved like a lost puppy, but sometimes there was a look on his face that indicated a deeper intelligence that I didn't understand. I couldn't imagine why no one else could see him.

The door to the bridge opened and I didn't turn around.

"There you are," Serena said.

She carried a cup of coffee, along with a couple of ham, egg, and cheese croissants.

I turned toward her, saw the food, and smiled at her tiredly.

"You're a goddess among women."

She arched an eyebrow, feigning surprise. "These are mine. You'll have to get your own."

I glanced at both plates of food. "So, you're eating for two now?"

She shook her head and shoved one of the plates toward me with a grin. "No chance of that."

I picked up one of the coffees. She'd already added cream and sugar to it. I sipped it, tasting notes of chocolate and caramel. I sighed contentedly. "This is so good. French press?"

She nodded.

"Thank you."

"You're welcome."

She sat next to me and put her feet up on the workstation.

I bit into the buttery goodness of my croissant egg sandwich and enjoyed every bit of it.

"So good. I didn't realize how hungry I was," I said between bites.

She nodded and nibbled on her own sandwich. "I know. Kierenbot mentioned that you were still on the bridge."

"I guess he's giving me some space."

Serena looked at the holoscreens for a few seconds, but then her gaze sank toward where Larry lay on the floor.

I stopped chewing my food and watched her.

She frowned a little and turned back to her food.

We ate in companionable silence. When we were finished, I gathered her plate and stacked it on top of mine.

"So, this is it," she said, lifting her chin toward the holoscreens.

I sat up, feeling a new burst of vigor from the food and caffeine sustenance, and proceeded to tell her about the Asherah. After I was finished, she eyed me for a minute.

"Where is the artifact you found?" she asked.

I stood up and walked over to where Kierenbot had stored it. I brought it back over and set it on the workstation. The octagonal, dark-metal object floated above a small counter-grav display cube. There was a field around it that kept it isolated from the artificial atmosphere of the ship.

"And this is what Griff Tarken was searching for?"

I shrugged. "Who knows? Maybe. I guess so. One of his

drones was cutting into that chamber, but either something had disabled it, or it had the bad luck of being struck by a stalactite that fell from the ceiling with surprising accuracy."

"And you just went inside?"

"Nothing ventured, nothing gained," I replied and smirked.

"It *is* interesting," she said, and gestured toward the holoscreen. "All of it. I can see why it intrigues you."

"That's why I want to keep looking. I think we could really be onto something here."

She frowned for a second. "How do you even know where to search next?"

"There were symbols in the chamber, and some were spotted on the artifact. Kierenbot believes they might be a key or a set of coordinates."

Serena looked away for a few seconds. "I don't know, Nate. Are you sure that's all this is? This could just be a red herring."

I leaned forward to catch her eye, and she looked at me. "What do you mean?"

She sighed and gestured toward the holoscreen and artifact. "This."

I frowned, not understanding. "What about it? It's an artifact from a long-lost empire. Serena, according to a lot of other species, it predates everything else in the entire galaxy."

"Or it could be someone's idea of a joke. When is it enough, Nate? When do you move on from the next big thing?"

"If you're concerned about the value proposition, I can assure you that it'll be worth it."

She shook her head. "You don't know that. The history of this hunt is that a lot of people died searching for it. And Griff Tarken isn't above attacking us."

I leaned away from her. "This isn't my first rodeo."

Standing up and walking away from me, she crossed her

arms and turned around. "So, what happens if you find it. Then what?"

I blinked. "Then we would've solved one of the most pervasive mysteries in the galaxy, not to mention receiving all the bounties available for it."

"If anyone will still honor them. Those bounties you showed me are hundreds of years old."

I shrugged. "Delos could help with that."

"Then what?" she asked in a sharp tone

I shrugged. "I don't know. Something else will come along."

She stepped toward me with a sneer. "Of course, it will. Another legend, another search, and on and on it goes."

I gritted my teeth for a second, feeling like I was being attacked. "What's wrong with that?"

Larry stirred from his slumber and hopped up onto a nearby workstation.

"Everything! It'll never be enough, Nate. First it'll be this, and then it'll be something else in an endless cycle, each riskier than the last."

"You make that sound like a bad thing."

"It is. It's the kind of thing people die for. It's the kind of thing that takes fathers away from their daughters," she snarled.

I blinked at that and took a deep breath. "I'm not Flynn," I said, trying to keep my tone as even as possible. "I'm not."

She blew out a breath. "No, you're not, Nate. But you're well on your way."

"That's not fair," I replied.

She stared at me for a long moment. "What about Lanaya?"

I frowned. "Who?"

She hissed. "You can remember countless references to ancient civilizations, but you can't remember the name of the woman Ben found on the station?"

I winced. "Oh yeah, I'm sorry. I just forgot her name for a second. That doesn't mean you have to bite my head off about it."

Serena didn't reply. Instead, she leaned against the workstation.

"What did you learn about Lanaya?" I asked.

Serena exhaled a long, slow breath. "I'm sorry I snapped at you."

"It wouldn't be right if someone didn't every now and then."

She glared at me, not ready for peaceful banter.

"Don't start again. Are you going to tell me about our wayward girl or not?"

"You can be so difficult sometimes," she said and paused for a moment. "She says she's not the only one on the station, but we can't find any trace of them. Raylin is particularly bothered by it."

"Why?"

"Well, you saw how Lanaya reacted to her. She recognized Raylin's species. The other thing is that Lanaya isn't entirely Human. She's been engineered."

"By whom?"

"I don't know. Neither does Raylin."

"And you want to find out."

"Don't you?"

I nodded. "Yeah, of course I do, but did you ever consider that this is someone's idea of a sick joke?"

Serena frowned and shook her head. "What? Who would do that? Why would they do it?"

"How would they do it?" I asked and grinned. She narrowed her gaze. "I was just making sure we covered it all. You know as well as I that there were certain groups of aliens that weren't happy about how things turned out."

"You think Kael Torsin had something to do with this?"

I shrugged. "I don't know. Doesn't seem like his style. I think if he was coming after us, it would be a more direct approach, but who knows?"

"I hadn't thought of that."

"How about this: What if people aren't being abducted from Earth and Lanaya is the product of some kind of DNA harvesting?"

Serena blinked a few times. "You've been spending too much time with Ben. He's the one who comes up with conspiracy theories."

I grinned a little. "Maybe. I just find the circumstances suspicious."

"You make a valid point. I think you should speak to Raylin."

"Why?"

"Because she thinks Lanaya could be part of something else."

I glanced up at the holoscreens for a second. The Asherah weren't going anywhere. I could take a break from it for a while and come at it fresh later on. I killed the work session and the holoscreens turned off. Then, I felt something cool brush past my leg. It was Larry. He'd walked by me.

"What's wrong?" Serena asked.

I gestured in front of me. "Do you see anything on the floor?"

Serena peered down and shook her head. "No, why?"

"Do me a favor and walk toward the door."

Serena frowned for a second and then did as I asked. She walked right by Larry. He stared up at her in wide-eyed amazement, as if he'd just noticed her.

Serena walked to the door and turned around, brown eyebrows raised. "Well?"

"You didn't feel anything?"

She narrowed her gaze. "Are you messing with me? Is this just an excuse for you to check out my ass?"

I laughed and shook my head. To be fair, I *had* done something like that in the past a few times. "No, not this time."

She regarded me for a few seconds, deciding whether I was telling her the truth.

"Look, I'd take any opportunity to admire you, but this time I wasn't doing that."

"Okay, what was I supposed to see?"

I considered not telling her. It would've been easier. "I've been seeing something that looks like one of those creatures from the planet, the ones in the recording I showed you, the meerkat-looking things. It's not quite like the others but close enough."

Serena's eyes widened and she glanced around her. "Right here?"

I nodded.

"I don't see anything," she said, searching the ground for a few seconds. "Do you see it now?"

I glanced down at Larry. "Yes."

She gave the area another once-over. "Where?"

"He's right there just a few feet away from you."

"He?"

I nodded. "I named him Larry."

She frowned. "You named him?"

I shrugged and bit my lower lip for a second. "Think I'm going crazy?"

She regarded me for a few seconds and shook her head. "No. At least not any more than usual."

I snorted. "Thanks."

"Can you touch him?"

I walked toward Larry, squatted down, and extended my

hand. He did the same. It felt like a cool draft on my skin, and it gave me goosebumps, but he didn't feel solid. My fingers only felt some kind of resistance like a heavy curtain.

Serena stepped over and did the same. She reached out her hand. "The air feels cooler here. Am I near him?"

I guided her hand toward Larry. His body phased out as if our hands were magnets that were repelling his presence somehow.

"I don't know why, but we can't touch him."

Serena looked at me with concern. That worried me even more than Kaz and T'Chura insisting that the autodoc scan me for parasites.

CHAPTER 15

Serena tossed me a few thoughtful frowns while we walked toward the elevator in silence. I let her go through her own inner monologue about whether I was hallucinating.

She sighed. "If this was the ER, I'd recommend a psych consult to come down to evaluate you, but given where we are, I don't think it would help."

I smiled a little. "You, at least, are one other person who doesn't think I'm crazy."

"You were the only one who went down into the ruins. Larry…" she rolled her eyes at the name. "He's drawn to you, and it must have to do with that."

"And the autodoc didn't detect anything wrong with me." She giggled, and I stared at her. "Laugh it up. T'Chura and Kaz basically strong-armed me into getting scanned."

She pursed her lips. "Poor baby."

I gave up.

"They're just looking out for you."

I looked down at Larry, considering. What if I tried to pick him up?

Serena stepped onto the elevator and looked at me expectantly. I joined her.

"I'd like you to speak with Lanaya."

My eyebrows peaked. "Me? Why?"

The elevator doors opened to H-Deck.

"Because, Nate, sometimes you're really good with people."

"Ouch, did that hurt?"

She jabbed her fist into my arm. I gave it a cursory scan and ignored it. She rolled her eyes. "Not as much as that all-too-proud-of-myself look you've got right now."

I shrugged. "I've learned to celebrate my accomplishments. Even the small ones."

"I bet."

"So why do you want me to talk to her?"

"Geez, Nate. I just want you to speak to her. Listen to what she has to say. Get her to open up a little and give us your opinion about what she says."

I frowned in thought. "She wouldn't talk to you?"

"A little. We were able to get her to allow the autodoc to scan her, but she couldn't quite settle down while Raylin was around. Having Ben nearby helped. I even had Raylin leave the room."

I considered this for a few seconds. "Does she still think 'the masters' are coming to collect her?"

Serena looked worried. "That's what she says."

"And you think I can get her to loosen up and give us more information?"

She gave me a furtive look and nodded a little.

"All right, I'll see what I can do."

"Put some of that *charm* to work toward a good cause for a change."

I nodded a little and then frowned. "What?"

Her eyes gleamed and she grinned.

"Just so you know, you're asking the guy who might be hallucinating to speak to a girl who might be suffering from severe PTSD and some kind of behavioral conditioning for which I have no technical term."

Serena placed her hand on my arm, and we stopped walking. She looked up at me with those big brown eyes of hers. "And a good man," she said.

Heat spread across my chest for a second, and I smiled. "We're really hard to come by."

She removed her hand from my arm and sighed. "You really know how to ruin the moment there, cowboy."

I regarded her for a few seconds. She was only mildly annoyed. "It's so hard being this good all the time. You know what I mean?"

She looked away from me, her shoulders shaking as she chuckled.

We walked inside the med bay and Serena gestured toward one of the rooms down the hall.

"Ambush the terrified girl alone in the room. Got it," I said and lengthened my stride.

Serena jogged to catch up. She beat me to the door and gave me an irritated look. "Be nice."

I nodded and winked.

Serena palmed the controls. There was a soft chime from inside and the doors dematerialized.

The room was furnished with a bed and a couple of chairs near the wall. The wallscreen showed a live video feed of the orbital station from our docking slip.

Lanaya stood facing the wallscreen, her hands resting on the small sill underneath it. She wore a dark-blue jumpsuit, and her long, Nordic-blonde hair was tied back in a loose ponytail.

Lanaya turned toward us, and her big blue eyes widened. The shade of blue was similar to Raylin's. They didn't look quite Human, or perhaps something more than Human. Her pale skin had swirling patches of opal on one side of her face and below her neckline.

"Lanaya," Serena said, "this is Nathan. I thought it would be a good idea if you two were to meet and talk for a little while."

Lanaya looked at me with a guarded expression.

I put on my friendliest smile that had caught the attention of a few women from time to time. Then, I looked away from her and stared at the wallscreen for a minute. I glanced at Lanaya, and she returned my gaze shyly. "There's only so long I can look at a docking station. Ships coming and going. Some lifeless red planet below. It can get old really quick. What do you think?" I asked her.

Lanaya turned toward the wallscreen, considering. "There's a pattern to the comings and goings of the ships arriving at the station."

I saw Serena's eyes widen, and I waved her back with a quick motion of my hand.

I stared at the video feed for a few seconds. "I haven't been out here that long. Only a few months, if you can believe that."

Lanaya frowned but didn't reply.

"I've been to a couple of space ports since then. I've even visited a couple of planets. Have you been on this station before?"

Lanaya frowned and looked away, shaking her head a little.

I glanced at Serena, and she nodded toward me encouragingly.

I stepped closer to Lanaya, expecting her to flinch or move away, but she didn't.

"Where were you before the station?" I asked.

"The academy," she replied.

"What kind of academy?"

"Training. We trained every day, sometimes without rest."

"Who else was there with you?"

Lanaya frowned as if she were having competing thoughts, warring for how to reply to me.

"Were there other people like you at the academy?"

She frowned. "Like me?"

I nodded. "Yeah, did they look like you?"

She nodded. "Some, but not that many. They disappeared. But one day they did come to train with our cohort." Her expression became haunted, and she shivered.

I almost reached out to comfort her but knew better than that. "It's okay. No one is going to hurt you here." She looked at me. "I promise. We'd like to help you."

"Help…Yes, return to the master. I must return. I must report in, or my cohorts will suffer. They'll be punished if I don't return. Do you know where the academy is?"

I blinked a few times. She'd spoken so fast. I glanced at Serena.

"She doesn't know," Lanaya said. "The others didn't know. Do you know?"

I considered answering her honestly, but I thought if I did, she'd shut down and stop talking. "Do you want to get out of here? Want to take a walk with me? I could show you around the ship."

Lanaya frowned and glanced at the wallscreen. Then she looked at me.

I smiled. "I always feel better if I move around a little bit. We've got food if you're hungry. If not, then that's fine as well."

I moved toward the door and gestured for her to follow. She did. Lanaya walked past Serena and I led her out of the room.

As I walked through the lounge area, I looked around for Larry, but he wasn't there. I didn't know what to think about that. Kierenbot was monitoring the ship sensors. He'd let me know if there were any more environmental anomalies.

We left the med bay, and I took her on a walk of the ship, giving her the nickel tour, as it were. Serena followed us but kept her distance.

I told Lanaya about the ship and the different sections. She asked a few questions but was also quiet. She did seem to relax.

"Do you remember Earth?" I asked.

Lanaya frowned and shook her head. "What's that?"

I almost sighed, disappointed. "It's a planet where people like us live. You look like us, so I thought you might have heard of it."

Lanaya stopped walking, looking troubled.

"I can show you a picture of it. Maybe that'll jog your…"

Lanaya stared at me. "This is a test. You're testing me. See if I will give something away." She shook her head vehemently. "I won't. I won't. I won't."

I shook my head. "I'm not testing you. We're talking. I'm trying to learn about you while telling you about me and the ship."

She considered this for a few moments and the tension seemed to drain from her shoulders as she relaxed. We started walking again.

"We weren't supposed to think about where we came from before. None of us were," she said.

I stopped moving, unable to keep the surprise from my face.

She noticed, and I cleared my throat. I saw Serena's wide-eyed gaze from behind us. I looked at Lanaya. "Well, here you can think whatever you want. No one is going to hurt you."

"I believe you."

"Good. Now can you tell me about what you remember from before the academy?"

She looked away from me as if she was staring at something that wasn't there. She closed her eyes, her face becoming serene. "Cinnamon. Apple pie cooling on the windowsill. Muffet barking in the yard. My Dad, busy fixing the fence, is trying to get him to quiet down, but Muffet won't. He keeps barking at something in the woods nearby. My Dad sees me watching from the window and tells me to stay inside the house. He does that sometimes when certain people come around."

I stared at her. She blinked a few times, as if suddenly coming out of a deep memory.

"That's when they came. That's when they took me away. Muffet tried to stop them, but he's just a little dog. I can still hear him whimpering when they hurt him." Her eyes became watery.

There was a special place in hell reserved for people who hurt dogs. Hearing about it was different than witnessing it, and I had done both. My throat became dry. I cleared it and said, "Who took you away?"

"The masters from the academy. I'd been chosen."

"Chosen to do what?"

"I don't know. That's why I need to get back there. I haven't finished my training."

"Did they bring your father with you?"

Lanaya's eyes sank and she shook her head.

"What about your mother?"

She swallowed hard and gave a slight shake of her head.

I waited a few seconds before I asked, "How did you arrive at the station?"

She considered that for a moment. "I don't know. I was with my cohorts and then I was walking around the station."

I nodded. "When Ben found you."

She smiled a little. "Yes, Ben found me. He didn't know who the masters were."

"Your cohorts were at the station?"

She flinched, biting her lip a little. "No, they weren't."

She said it as if she hadn't realized it before.

"Does Raylin know who the masters are?"

Lanaya shook her head. "No."

Her shoulders slumped and she moved toward the wall of the corridor, leaning against it.

"Maybe we should go back to the med bay. She can rest there," Serena said.

"One second," I said and looked at Lanaya. "Does Raylin look like one of the masters?"

Her chin quivered for a second, and she swallowed hard. "She looks like an enforcer," she said softly.

The door to the bridge opened and Raylin stood just inside, speaking with Kierenbot.

Larry sauntered by the open doorway and Lanaya gasped. I glanced at her, and she was staring right at Larry. My eyes widened. "Do you see it?"

She blinked and then looked at me.

"I see it, too."

Larry peered in our direction. We were a short distance from the door.

Lanaya gave a small nod, and then she backed away, looking frightened.

"Captain," Kierenbot called out to me from the bridge. "Captain, I need you."

I turned back to Lanaya, who was standing next to Serena.

"It's all right, Nate. I'll look after her."

She'd seen Larry. It happened so fast that I'd almost missed it.

"I'd like to see Ben. Can you take me to him?" Lanaya asked.

"Okay, I'll take you to see Ben. We'll go right now," Serena replied.

"He'll be in the workshop," I said.

Serena nodded at me and then they went back down the corridor.

I turned around and walked onto the bridge. Larry watched them go until the door rematerialized.

Kierenbot looked as if he were about to burst.

I looked at Raylin. "What did you do to the poor girl?"

Raylin looked at me impassively. "I've done nothing to her."

"Well, someone who looks like you has done something to her. She said you look like an 'enforcer.' I'm not sure what that means. Do you know?"

Raylin shook her head. "I'm afraid not. What do you think of her now that you've had a chance to spend some time with her?"

I looked at Kierenbot. "One minute," I said and went back to Raylin. "I'm not sure. On the one hand, if her responses are conditioned, she could just be saying the things someone taught her to say. On the other, she could be telling the truth, and someone has been abducting children from Earth."

"Children?" Kierenbot said.

"Why do you think it's children?" Raylin asked.

"She told me about her home, and it was through the eyes of a child. Now, I'm not up on current brainwashing trends, but that's what it reminded me of. What about you?"

Raylin could sometimes be taciturn and other times show a dry sense of humor, but right then she looked worried. "Her origin story could be a conditioned response as well. I don't know what to think of this, although the timing is suspicious. Lanaya suddenly shows up on the station and Ben happens to find her? Why would someone bring her here?"

"I was hoping you might know."

Her gaze narrowed. "Why would you think that?"

"Well, she recognized you—someone who resembles you. And, I don't know all that much about your past, but I've been around you long enough to recognize a certain tradecraft. I'd guess a former intelligence operative, or whatever passes for that out here."

She regarded me for a minute. "I wish I knew. I can tell you that there is no one else who looks like her or any of you on the station. I checked."

I tilted my head to the side. "How did you check?"

"Monitoring stations track the different species that come to the station. According to the logs, Lanaya arrived shortly after we did."

"Did you see from where?"

Raylin shook her head. "No, she just appeared on one of the monitoring stations inside the station."

"Do you think her captors are here?"

"No. If she was put here so we could find her, they would've already left. There is also the possibility that she escaped."

I frowned. "If she escaped, why does she act so lost?"

Raylin leveled her gaze at me. "That can happen after a long incarceration. The subject shuts down and can appear to be in a daze."

She said it so matter-of-factly that it caught me by surprise.

"Do you have a lot of experience with that?" I asked, not sure if I wanted to know the answer.

"No, I've never been held captive, nor have I held anyone else captive. At least not for long and not for reasons of torture," she said in a tone that lulled my imagination into thinking all kinds of things. "Nate, it's in my line of work to understand certain psychological profiles to assist me assuming a particular identity."

Raylin could change her appearance. She could shape-shift into an entirely different-looking species. She was a specialist, and the ability wasn't shared by every member of her species. Sometimes she made an offhanded comment that hinted at her past. I didn't know how she came to be traveling with Kaz, but her contract with the ship had passed to me when I, along with Serena and Ben, bought the ship.

"I'll take your word for it."

"Good, now I need us to leave immediately and bring me to Wonfiner Space Port," Raylin said.

"Now isn't really a good time for that."

Raylin looked amused. "I'm afraid I must insist."

"Okay, insist."

Raylin looked at Kierenbot.

I didn't know a robot could appear sheepish, but somehow Kierenbot pulled it off.

"I'm afraid she can, Captain. It's part of her contract with the ship that she be allowed to request transport to select destinations," Kierenbot said.

I felt my mouth hang open for a second, and then I looked at Raylin. "Is that so? I'm going to have to review this contract of yours."

"At your own discretion, but in the meantime I need to go to Wonfiner Space Port."

"Well, we're in the middle of a maintenance cycle, and there are a couple of things I need to do here on the station."

Raylin's lips parted into an alluring smile. She grinned. "Nate, you're so adorable I could just eat you right up, but we both know you can't get out of this. The maintenance cycle has already completed, and the local officials have requested that we leave this station."

I sighed and looked at Kierenbot. He nodded. "All right then, I guess we're going to…"

"Wonfiner Space Port," Raylin said.

"Kierenbot, set a course for Wonfiner, best speed."

"Of course, Captain," he replied.

Kierenbot walked over to the navigation station and began initiating the decoupling sequence from the docking platform.

I looked at Raylin. "As you requested."

"Thank you."

"Kierenbot, the contract with Raylin. Do these transportation requests have some kind of limit?"

"Yes, Captain. Six per yearly cycle, and it's up to the captain's discretion as to whether compliance is required after one of the slotted segments is used."

I smiled at Raylin. "Thank you, Kierenbot. So, why are we going to Wonfiner Space Port?"

CHAPTER 16

Traveling among the stars didn't take as much time as I thought it would. I'd never really given it much thought before because it wasn't something I ever thought I'd be doing. Just when you think you've gotten things figured out, the universe laughs at you.

The journey to Wonfiner Space Port would take us a little over a day, which was just as well because I needed to catch up on some sleep. I woke up in my bed and got myself cleaned up before going out into the commons area.

I left my room (Cabin? Berth? I could never get the nautical terms straight in my head) and glanced at the kitchen. Ben had tried calling things by those nautical terms but didn't stick with it for long. I'd been on my fair share of ships, but the habits weren't ingrained in me.

I approached the food processing unit and requested a cup of coffee. Our food choices had become much more sophisticated since we'd first come aboard the ship. Some things it could do very well, but more often than not, preparing the food ourselves tasted better than what the processor could produce. But the processor could make one hell of a French press coffee. I selected a medium roast blend with hints of chocolate and cherries, and the smell wafted throughout the area.

Serena left her room and inhaled deeply. She sighed, looking at me with a smile. "That coffee smells amazing. Can you get me a cup, too?"

"Absolutely," I said and prepared another one.

Brewing didn't require the average five minutes it would normally take. I used boiling water, but the actual brewing took just under twenty seconds. I had no idea how it worked, and all I really cared about was how good my coffee tasted.

I carried both cups to a nearby table. "Not babysitting today?"

Serena stifled a yawn and shook her head. "Lanaya is a little more relaxed. She's with Ben in the workshop. Seems like she's familiar with the equipment."

I slid a cup toward her, and she took it gratefully.

I blew on mine before taking a sip and let out a long, contented sigh. "I can't help it."

Serena frowned. "What?"

"Making that sound after the first sip of my coffee."

She snorted and then tasted hers. She made the same sound. "Hits the spot, doesn't it?"

I wasn't much for big breakfasts when I first woke up, but I did like my coffee. We raised our cups in a companionable salute and drank.

Serena set her cup down and looked at me. "I'm going to contact Delos about Lanaya's origin."

Despite Lanaya being more forthcoming about certain things, we really weren't sure if we could trust what she told us.

I sighed.

Serena eyed me. "What was that?"

I arched an eyebrow. "I'm breathing."

She simply stared at me with those big, honey-brown eyes of hers. Sometimes I could almost feel the jab from them.

"Delos might be able to help, but it's always going to have some kind of cost," I said.

"So what?"

"It adds up after a while, and before you know it, we're at his beck and call."

Serena cradled her mug in her hands and took another sip. "It doesn't have to be one or the other."

"It will be, though. Mark my words."

"I know you want to maintain your freedom, Nate, but this is a bit much."

I blinked. Was she telling me that I was paranoid?

"I just want to ask for some help."

I finished my coffee. "I'm not stopping you."

She regarded me intently for a few moments. "But you don't approve."

I stood up and put my cup in the washer. "You're going to do whatever you want anyway. Why listen to me?"

She finished her coffee and joined me at the washer. "Because we're partners. I don't think using our network is a bad thing. Delos isn't so bad."

"No, he's not, but he is what he is."

"What does that mean?"

I sighed. "It means he'll use us as much as he can get away with until we're in so deep that we can't get out. I thought you would've been more aware of that."

She frowned, considering what I'd said. "Maybe, but we need help with this."

She wasn't wrong about that, and there were worse things than getting help from Delos. I could see it going south, though, because it wasn't just Delos; it would be whoever he tapped in his own network to get us the information we needed.

I didn't think I could convince Serena not to contact Delos. There were some things you had to learn on your own. I might be wrong about Delos, but I didn't think I was. My experience carried its own bias, but it didn't offer any other solutions either.

We'd left the orbital station behind and would soon be on Wonfiner. Just then, Kierenbot made a broadcast over the ship's intercom announcing that we'd arrived.

I looked at Serena. "I'm going to the bridge."

"I'll go with you."

I wanted some space, and she must've seen it in my expression. She frowned.

Just then Raylin came out of her room, dressed in some kind of spacer garb. She spotted us and walked over.

"I'll be heading out now. I'll check in with the ship later," Raylin said and regarded both of us for a second as if she sensed the tension between us. She looked at Serena. "Do you feel like stretching your legs?"

Serena considered it for a moment and shook her head. "I have some things I need to get done first."

Raylin nodded. "Maybe next time."

A message buzzed on my omnitool. I read it. "Looks like you're not the only one going ashore."

"Where are you going?" Serena asked.

"Kierenbot just informed me that Wonfiner has a special one-of-a-kind archive and museum display about the history of this sector."

She blinked. "You're going to a *museum?*"

I nodded. "You'd be surprised by what you can learn there. Lots of history and artifacts. Maybe a few other things."

Serena looked as if she wanted to say something, but she didn't reply. It was probably better that way. I couldn't dissuade her from contacting Delos, and she wasn't going to convince me to abandon my search for the Asherah.

CHAPTER 17

I met up with Kierenbot at the airlock. T'Chura joined us.

I looked at him. "Kaz?"

"He's remaining aboard," T'Chura replied.

I rolled my eyes a little as we exited the airlock. Kaz was still in some kind of funk because of our run-in with his old mentor. And Serena was annoyed because I didn't want to run to Delos for help with every problem we came across. That might not have been fair, but I didn't want to think about it.

"Thank you for allowing me to come," Kierenbot said.

"We wouldn't have known about this place if it weren't for you, and I think you'll be a big help."

"I will endeavor to deliver, Captain."

We walked through an automated registration terminal that logged our entry onto the space port. The welcome area had information terminals with holographic displays of the Jupiter-sized planet that the space port orbited. Wonfiner was built on one of the many moons that orbited a Jovian planet. There was no telltale sign of the giant red eye; the bands of gaseous clouds tilted toward greens and mustard yellows. The welcome area had enough activity that we could get our bearings, but it wasn't a place where anyone would spend a lot of time. It reminded me of a large airport terminal.

Kierenbot led us toward an automated tram area that would take us into the actual space port.

I saw T'Chura glance at the ground ahead of us, and I raised an eyebrow. Larry had stayed near me since I'd first seen him, although I couldn't always see him when he phased out. He was never gone for long, and I had no idea what he did while I slept. I'd been so exhausted that I didn't care if the alien watched me sleep. I was fairly certain he wouldn't do anything to me.

T'Chura leaned down toward me. "Is he there?"

I nodded. "Can you see him?"

T'Chura shook his head. "No, it's strange."

"Like seeing something out of the corner of your eye."

T'Chura frowned. "More like being in a dark room and sensing something moving nearby."

I glanced at Kierenbot and he gave a small shake of his head. The robot, with all his highly acute sensors, couldn't detect any trace of Larry, but he didn't question that I was able to see him. He probably didn't want to offend me, but at this point I had to take whatever support I could get. The only other person on the ship who'd actually seen Larry was Lanaya. I didn't know why, but it had happened. Either she was the best actress I'd ever seen, or she'd somehow been able to see Larry when everyone else on the ship couldn't. I couldn't decide which.

T'Chura was making an effort to see Larry.

We climbed onto a tram that didn't have a roof on it. It was one long platform that had various kinds of seating and standing areas for the different kinds of species that came here.

Kierenbot cleared his throat. "There's something I've been

meaning to bring up with you, Captain."

"What is it?"

"You've made several statements about the fragility of my current body. It serves well enough for everyday use, but for more specialized use, it is not equipped to handle extreme circumstances. I'd like to address this shortcoming so I could be of more use to you and the other members of the crew."

It took me a few seconds to unravel what he'd said, and I tried to remember what off-handed comment I'd made that had stuck with him.

"What are you talking about?"

Kierenbot swung his head from side to side and then leaned toward me. The tram began to move, and I hardly felt a thing but braced myself in anticipation of movement all the same. "If I'd been with you when you encountered those battlebots, I could have assisted in a more direct manner."

I frowned. "The what?"

Kierenbot's orb flashed. "The battlebots. Griff Tarken's assault troops."

I nodded and considered what Kierenbot was saying. "Well, if you had been with me, you'd have been armed."

"I've analyzed the encounter from the data you provided through the recordings from your combat suit. Your assessment is correct, but taking it a step further, my analysis reveals that I would've been overwhelmed. My services could therefore be insufficient to the task at hand."

I thought about the battlebots for a few seconds and shook my head. "*I* was overwhelmed. Any one of us could've been overwhelmed with the sheer number of battlebots Griff used against me."

T'Chura raised his big bushy eyebrows. I'd seen him take on a platoon of Mesakloren elite soldiers. He'd gotten banged up pretty badly, but let's just say I was glad to have him watching my back. He'd certainly have given the battlebots a good fight.

"Be that as it may, I'd like to rectify the situation by acquiring a new body that is more combat-capable than my current form," Kierenbot said.

I tried to keep the surprise from my face and failed. "You want a new body?" I asked and looked at T'Chura. "Can he do that?"

"No need to ask him, Captain. I'm capable of migrating my consciousness into a new body. I can also remote pilot another body, so I could maintain this form if you prefer but use the other as the situation called for it."

It took me a few seconds to pick my jaw up off the floor. As captain of the *Spacehog* I encountered all kinds of requests, but the one Kierenbot had just made left me speechless.

Kierenbot glanced at T'Chura.

"I think he's processing your request," T'Chura replied quietly.

"I used simple language. His intelligence should have no issues with grasping the concepts. Perhaps I should try again using even more simplified language. I should also use the hand gestures that they seem so overly fond of," Kierenbot said.

I shook my head. "I understood you just fine."

"Then will you approve the request?" Kierenbot asked hopefully.

"How much is this going to cost?" I asked and could hear echoes of my father sticking me with that question more than once during my life. It was the prelude to either a maybe or an outright no.

Kierenbot enabled his personal holoscreen, which showed what amounted to an online storefront. There were several robotic models queued up and ready for me to review.

"They all have specialties that I think could be useful," Kierenbot said.

I almost asked which one was cheapest, but I stopped myself. I was not my father.

I looked at the data on the holoscreen and eventually found the prices listed at the bottom. I blinked and my eyes widened.

"Now, I realize the cost is quite high, but think of the value you'd gain if we had this at our disposal," Kierenbot said.

He was pulling out all the stops, using terms like *we*, *you*, and *our*, along with the concept that this was all in my best interest. I tore my eyes away from the staggering amount of the retail price of a new body for Kierenbot and smoothed my features.

I cleared my throat and pulled another phrase from my past, which parents far and wide used to put off a request they didn't want to fulfill. "I'll need to think about it."

Kierenbot's orb froze, and I continued. "I need to see if the ship has the budget for something like this. I'll talk about it with the others."

"Oh, do you want me to present this to Serena and Ben?"

I shook my head. "No," I said quickly. "I'll look into it. I promise."

Kierenbot nodded.

I was glad he couldn't read my mind because I didn't know if I'd ever be able to deliver on that promise. Sure, I'd look into it, but with the recent setback, I wasn't eager to dip back into the proverbial cookie jar. He'd have to wait.

The tram took us down to the ground level, and I hadn't even felt the descent. The automated doors opened, and we climbed out. Wonfiner looked like a small city that had been carved out of the moon. The tram had taken us to a crater whose walls looked to be miles away from where I stood.

I pulled up my hood and followed Kierenbot as he led the

way. There were quite a few Akacians in the area. Kaz would've blended right in with his own species here. After spending so much time on the ship, I was a little surprised he didn't want to come out and be with his own kind for a while. Ben wasn't the only one who missed seeing other people. It hit me at the strangest times and then was gone just as suddenly. There were plenty of species that had a humanoid shape, but the proportions might be a bit off from what I was used to. What was normal to them still appeared strange to me. I thought I'd get used to it the more time I spent out here.

Like most cities I'd been to, there was a museum that celebrated the area with its history. Whoever was in charge of the Wonfiner Space Port must have felt the same way, or maybe there was some attribute of sentient species that found value in knowing the past.

Kierenbot led us to the entrance, but when it came time to pay for our entry he looked at me expectantly. I transferred the credits using my omnitool. Galactic credits were used for currency but had different values attributed to them, depending on where we were. I tried to think of it as just another currency, which helped, but I still found some of the pricing schemes a bit odd. Food and general entertainment didn't cost that much. The museum cost a good bit more. Maybe Kierenbot had selected the VIP tour or something.

We went inside and Kierenbot took the lead. He must have downloaded the layout and was following a path he'd already selected.

"So, there are archive consoles and exhibits?" I asked.

"Yes. The consoles aren't accessible from outside, which is why we had to come here. I'm not sure what's in the exhibits, but it might be worth our time to study them for a while."

Larry maintained his distance of a few feet in front of me. He occasionally stopped to look up at me. The bronze-colored particles seemed to shuffle and reform as he moved. If I hadn't brought the artifact with me, would Larry have come?

Once inside we walked through an atrium that had several exhibits showing looping holographic depictions of how the sector had been explored. I couldn't understand the reference to time, so I wasn't sure how long ago this had happened.

The farther we went inside, the smaller the rooms became. Kierenbot led us to a closed door and entered a special-access code. The door opened to a narrow tunnel. T'Chura had to duck his head to fit inside.

"We'll only have about a half hour with the exhibit," Kierenbot said.

"Why?" I asked.

"Because I didn't think you wanted to pay for a longer duration," Kierenbot said, and then pointed his finger at me. "I was joking. Those are the rules."

I glanced around. No one else was there, and it didn't look like anyone had been here in a long time. We came out of the tunnel onto a path. A short distance in, the first exhibit lit up. It was a partial wall about seven feet tall and maybe twelve feet wide. The air around it shimmered.

"The exhibits are shielded so the artifacts can be maintained in a vacuum," Kierenbot said.

"Doesn't look anything like what I found. Is this all there is?"

"No, there is more," Kierenbot said.

"Were the artifacts moved here?"

Kierenbot's orb flashed for a moment. "No, this is the original location where the artifacts were found."

My eyes widened a little in surprise. "They built this place around the artifacts?"

"It was the best way to preserve them."

I glanced up at T'Chura for a second and then down at Larry. He'd moved beyond the clearly marked boundary meant to keep us away from the exhibit, peering intently at the wall for a few moments. He then rejoined us.

The other exhibits lit up and it appeared as if we were standing inside some kind of inner chamber. Several holographic displays projected into the air where it was believed the original pieces of the exhibit had been located. It wasn't until the exhibits all came online that it made any sense to me. No doubt the original curator had set it up this way.

I lifted my gaze, trying to imagine what this extensive chamber looked like when it was whole.

"What happened to the rest of it?" I asked.

"They did an extensive excavation of the area, and this was all that was found. If the place was abandoned, there could be any number of scenarios that could account for its destruction. What it comes down to is that no one really knows what happened here."

As I looked at each exhibit, which was way more conjecture of what the alien archeologist believed than any facts deduced over time, I looked for some kind of indication of advanced technology that was referred to in the data Kierenbot showed me on the ship. There wasn't anything like it. I didn't understand why this place was important at all, except that it existed and had somehow survived for so long.

"These artifacts led to an extensive search of not only this star system but the surrounding star systems within the vicinity," Kierenbot said. He was reciting the relevant information from the exhibit for us, which I appreciated since it saved time.

"Does any of this look familiar to you?" T'Chura asked me.

"Hard to say. Not exactly. Certain things maybe, but they

could just as easily be something else. I'm having trouble making sense of it."

As I was speaking, one of the exhibits caught my eye. It held a series of small, metallic, triangle-shaped columns coming up from the ground. They were frameworks and not solid. Several pieces lay scattered on the ground in a seemingly haphazard form. I walked over to the exhibit and stared.

After a few moments, I cleared my throat and gestured for the others to join me. When they got closer to me, I asked. "Are we being monitored?"

"Of course," Kierenbot replied.

"Can you get us some privacy?"

"Not a good idea, Nate," T'Chura said.

"I'm just asking the question. We haven't done anything yet."

"I don't think tampering with the security measures here is a good idea," T'Chura replied.

"Look at this place. No one comes in here anymore," I replied and looked at Kierenbot. "Can you do it?"

He regarded me for a few moments. "What do you want to do?"

"I brought the artifact with me," I said quietly, tapping the satchel hidden under my long coat. "It looks like it goes with that stuff right over there. I just want to see if it reacts."

"How would it react?" T'Chura asked.

I shrugged. "I'm not sure. It has some kind of low-lying power to it." I shook my head. "I'm not an engineer. I just know that when Crim scanned it, he detected a few things that didn't make sense."

"Those areas have sensors. They'd report your presence to the monitoring station and then we could be in trouble," Kierenbot said.

"So can you block the signal?"

"How do you suggest I do that?"

"Intercept the alert and stop it or delay it if you can," I replied.

Kierenbot hesitated for a few seconds.

"I doubt many people come in here. How reliable do you think the alarm system could be here?"

T'Chura eyed us for a second. "I'll go wait by the door."

He left us and I looked at Kierenbot. "You wanted more time out in the field."

"Captain, I must advise against this. The security measures could lock us in here."

"Do you know that for sure?"

Kierenbot looked around the chamber, likely scanning the area. "I don't detect anything."

I pulled out the artifact from my satchel. It was still within the protection field powered by the base Crim had given me.

Kierenbot's orb darted to it. "I'll do my best to delay the alert."

I waited for him to say something or go somewhere, but he didn't. "Don't you need to patch into the system or something?"

"Negative, Captain. I'm already in the system. I've inserted a virtual layer to the data communications node for this area. Unless there is some kind of dormant alarm system that only gets activated when certain conditions are met, we should be fine."

I nodded, following most of what he'd said. I assumed it was a technical way of saying he had it covered, which was good enough for me.

I took one last look around and crossed the barrier with the artifact. I paused for a second, expecting alarms to sound at any moment, but it was quiet.

"You're clear. Go on, Captain," Kierenbot said quietly.

I quickly covered the distance to the columns and saw a

subtle flash as Larry appeared nearby. His body seemed to bristle in anticipation as he watched me intently. I lifted my chin toward him and then powered off the protection field around the artifact.

It dropped into my hand, and I stuffed the base into the satchel. The artifact was cool to the touch but still had a field of energy around it that I could feel along my palms and forearms. I held out the artifact and felt a slight tug on it, as if some unseen force was guiding it to the center of the triangular columns. It lifted several inches above my hand and began to slowly spin.

I went to tap the recorder on my omnitool, mildly annoyed I hadn't done so sooner, and I couldn't move my hand. I tried to step back but I couldn't move; something was holding me in place. Since I could still move my head a little, I looked to the side. There was a bright aura around Larry, and he stepped closer to me. His gaze was focused on the artifact.

"Kierenbot?" I called.

There was no reply. My breath quickened and I tried to turn but couldn't. There was a stillness to the air that I hadn't noticed before. It was as if everything had slowed to a crawl, or time had stopped altogether.

Several of the metallic beams on the ground began to vibrate, breaking free of their rocky tombs. They lifted off the ground and darted above me. The beams began to bend, and the ends joined together as the artifact spun faster.

Larry sprung toward my outstretched arm, and I could barely feel the weight. What I did feel was intense cold, as if Larry was made of ice. He perched on the end of my arm and stretched his arms up, reaching toward the artifact. I heard a low subsonic thrum that came through my arms to my chest. I stared at the artifact, wide-eyed and mouth agape. Then Larry stood, balancing precariously on the edge of my hand while the area above flashed. The ceiling was simply gone, and in its place was a network of glowing azure lines. These lines stretched to take up more of the area until they reached the ground. It looked like I was standing inside a star map. I looked around, awestruck. Some kind of deep bellow came from the glowing edges of the map, and the breath caught in my throat. I wanted to duck and crawl away, but I couldn't move. Larry turned toward me, his shifting bronze body shimmering and the particles tightening to form a smooth, almost reflective surface. His eyes drew down in a serene look, as if he held some kind of secret knowledge, and I felt my heart rate begin to slow.

The star map folded in on itself, collapsing into the artifact. The metallic shafts dropped to the ground, clanging loudly. At some point I must have fallen because when I finally became aware again, Kierenbot was standing over me, calling out my name.

I blinked slowly, coming out of a daze. My right hand hurt, and bands of pain raced up my arm. I gritted my teeth, and a groan escaped my lips.

"We'll have to carry him," Kierenbot said.

"Let's get him on his feet," T'Chura said. He leaned down and lifted me up. I cradled my right hand to my chest.

"What's wrong with his arm?" T'Chura asked.

"It was closest to the artifact."

"Where is the artifact?"

"I think he's holding it."

"Nate, can you walk?" T'Chura asked.

I winced from the pain in my arm and nodded. I started to move forward, and my feet marched awkwardly.

"Guide him," T'Chura said.

We moved through the museum. It seemed to take a long

time, but I couldn't be sure. My brain felt like a fog had settled around it. I kept shaking my head, trying to clear it.

"What the hell happened?" I asked.

"You activated Asherah technology."

I frowned in thought for a few seconds. T'Chura changed course a few times so we blended in with other groups.

Kierenbot leaned toward me and spoke quietly. "Security forces are inbound. I managed to divert the alerts, sending them to another part of the museum, which should buy us some time to get out of here."

"What happened to the artifact?" I asked.

"You have it."

I tried to feel the weight of it in the satchel, but it wasn't there. "Where is it?"

"It's attached to your hand."

I frowned and looked down. A flexible metallic glove covered my hand and went up my arm, which felt cooler than my other hand. I flexed my fingers and watched them move. The metallic glove faded away and it felt like a weight had been lifted off me. The pain subsided to a dull ache, and I was able to move my arm.

I started walking on my own. "I'm all right," I said.

Kierenbot let go. His orb flashed and he turned back toward the way we'd come. Then he quickened his pace. I kept up with him as he started going faster, and we quickly caught up to T'Chura. We hurried to the exit, moving at a fast pace but not an all-out run. I kept expecting some kind of lockdown or klaxon alarms to sound, but they didn't.

Once we were outside, Kierenbot ushered us toward the nearest taxi. We climbed inside and the aircar left the area.

I looked at Kierenbot. "What is it?"

"A broadcast was sent about the Asherah exhibit."

"An alarm?"

Kierenbot shook his head. "No, it was a tracer." I frowned. "A latent protocol, but it's not associated with the museum's security systems."

I nodded, finally understanding. Someone was going to find out what I'd done. "We're going to need to cut our visit here short," I said.

"You should alert the others," T'Chura said.

"I'll take care of it," Kierenbot said.

I hoped Raylin didn't need more time.

"What happened to you?" T'Chura asked.

"I saw something. I think it's a map…a star map. Didn't you guys see it?"

T'Chura shook his head. "I was monitoring the entrance."

"I observed a flash of light from the artifact and then you collapsed to the ground," Kierenbot said.

I felt my shoulders slump. Once again something miraculous had happened and I was the only one to witness it. They were going to think I was crazy for sure. I glanced toward the empty seat near T'Chura, and Larry appeared as if emerging from an invisible curtain.

T'Chura flinched and grasped his elbow. My gaze darted between him and Larry. The Sasquatch eyed me for a second. "He's next to me, isn't he?"

I nodded. "Just appeared."

T'Chura leaned away from the seat and peered down. He reached one of his dinner-plate-sized hands toward Larry. Larry regarded it curiously and then moved away.

T'Chura glanced at me, and I shook my head. "I don't get it either. He moved away from you."

It wasn't often that T'Chura looked troubled, but this was definitely one of those times.

CHAPTER 18

I was beginning to wonder if there was a limit to how many times the autodoc could be used on a person. Was there some kind of side effect that I wasn't aware of? The designers certainly hadn't had Humans in mind when they created it. But these arguments fell on deaf ears, and I was getting tired of having the argument about being fit for duty thrown in my face.

Don't sit there!

Why not?

Because you're not fit for duty. Our machines must poke and prod you until we're satisfied.

But I'm the captain of the ship.

Doesn't matter. Safety of the crew circumvents your authority.

I blew out a long breath as the autodoc scanned me. It was a deep scan, which apparently required that I strip to my derrière. I hadn't realized just how drafty the examination rooms were. At least I didn't have an audience.

I frowned and glanced at the control panel by the door, imagining Kaz orchestrating a little payback for my treatment of him. I couldn't tell if there was a video feed active or if anyone was watching me. I slapped my own top-round posterior for good measure just in case anyone *was* watching.

The deep scan finished, and a metallic snake-looking appendage rose from the base of the platform. Words appeared on a small holoscreen in front of me.

Sample required.

I frowned and started to consider either running away or whether I could subdue the mechanical snake probe. There were some lines I refused to cross. Nothing goes in the exits, so to speak.

I grimaced and leaned away from it. "What kind of sample?"

Skin sample.

I looked at the snake and then back at the holoscreen. "From where?"

The holoscreen flashed and a linear image of my body appeared on it. The area by my right arm highlighted, and I blew out a quick breath, relieved it didn't need a skin sample from somewhere else.

Bullet dodged, I regarded the snake thoughtfully, then stuck out my right arm. There was a pattern of semitranslucent lines on my arm that shimmered very faintly. I'd thought I was imagining it, but then it kept happening.

The snake head opened, separating into a miniature hydra with five smaller heads. They looked delicate as they gently brushed against the skin of my forearm. I winced in anticipation of them tearing a piece of my skin off, but they didn't. Tiny pin pricks of warmth came from the heads, and the snake retracted back into the platform.

Processing sample.

I'd gotten so used to an instant response from it, that when it didn't happen, I found myself leaning toward it as if I was going to miss it.

Minor skin abrasion, right arm. No medical intervention required.

Cleared for duty.

I grinned and stepped off the platform. One thing I could say about the alien who designed this system was that it definitely took patient confidentiality into consideration. It was gratifying to learn that privacy wasn't unheard of and taken quite a bit more seriously than back home. The only bit of information my crew was privy to was whether or not I was fit for duty.

I dressed and glided my fingers over my arm. I could trace the pattern of lines from the artifact. I'd felt Larry on my hand, which meant he wasn't just a figment of my imagination. I still didn't understand how he appeared and disappeared, but he'd done something to the artifact. It had shown me a star map, and all I needed to do was figure out where it led.

I left the med bay and headed to the bridge, opening a comlink to Kierenbot. "Are you on the bridge?"

"Yes, Captain," he replied.

I heard others speaking in the background.

"Who else is there?"

"The rest of the crew except for Raylin and our guest, Lanaya."

I blinked. The entire crew on the bridge meant they were meeting without me.

"Is there something else you needed, Captain?"

I shook my head. "No, I'll be there shortly."

I closed the comlink and double-timed it to the bridge. I kept looking around for Larry, but he hadn't shown himself. I didn't know where he'd gone, but I didn't think it was far.

I walked onto the bridge and a wave of silence swept across

my friends. Serena stood in the middle by a holoscreen and looked surprised to see me.

I raised my eyebrows and smiled. "Speak of the devil?"

Serene recovered quickly. "No… How are you feeling?"

"Cleared for duty," I said and let my gaze slide toward the others. I turned back toward Serena. "Please continue."

She considered it for a second. "I was just going over some potential contracts that have become available."

I looked up at the holoscreen, quickly reading the headings. My gaze settled back on her. Each of the contracts were associated with Mercania Limited, which was a subsidiary of the Zerian Omega Corporation. Delos Nadeau had controlling interests, which meant that this new list of potential contracts had come from him.

Serena noticed the irritation in my gaze and leveled hers at me in kind. "Each of these contracts has lower risk than we've seen recently, but they pay well. Each are also good candidates for us to take on while Delos checks into where Lanaya might have come from."

I glanced at the others, and Ben caught my eye for a second before he looked at Serena.

"Did he know anything about Human abductions going on?"

Serena shook her head. "No, he was surprised to hear it. He asked for our medical scan data of Lanaya, which I've sent."

"He just happened to give you this list of contracts to occupy us while he conducts his investigation?"

"No, I asked him if he knew of any work available in this quadrant."

I nodded. "Okay, do you mind if I add something to this list?"

She regarded me for a moment and then gestured for me to begin.

I cleared my throat and told the others about what T'Chura, Kierenbot, and I had discovered at the museum.

Kaz kept looking at Kierenbot and T'Chura.

I lifted my chin toward him. "What is it?"

"They said there was just a bright flash of light, and you passed out."

I glanced at them. "Did they now."

"It's what we saw," T'Chura said.

I nodded. "Well, the experience for me was different. The artifact I found somehow interfaced with one of the exhibits, and it revealed a star map."

Kaz frowned. "That leads where?"

"I don't know. All I do know is that it has to do with the Asherah."

Kaz narrowed his gaze. "Can we see this map?"

I smiled and brought up my omnitool. It had recorded the entire event, which I discovered while in the med bay. I thought I hadn't activated it, but I must've.

I opened a connection to the holoscreen and began playing the recorded video.

The others watched the video in silence. It went on for almost five minutes. I looked at Serena and she watched it intently.

"Is that Larry?" she asked.

I nodded.

The audio sounded distorted, and I didn't know why. The video had some interference as well, occasionally blotting everything out, but it did clear up.

"It's real," Kaz said, sounding a bit surprised. I looked at him. "I thought you were making it up."

"Appreciate the vote of confidence."

He blanched and then shrugged. "You have, on occasion, played practical jokes."

He had me there. "I wasn't making this up. Larry is for real, and he has something to do with the Asherah."

The last thirty seconds of the video showed the star map, how it expanded all around me. A basso bellow sounded moments before the whole thing collapsed and the video stopped.

"What was that noise?" Serena asked.

"I don't know. It was louder… more intense when I was actually there," I said and glanced at T'Chura. "It reminded me a little of that growl N'Jaka made."

"Subsonic roar. It's meant to intimidate," T'Chura replied.

N'Jaka was the same species as T'Chura, but whereas T'Chura was honorable, N'Jaka was psychotic.

"Well, this was worse than that. I don't know what it was."

Serena sighed. "And the artifact hurt your arm."

I waved it around. "It's fine. Scan said it was a minor abrasion." I looked at the others. "What do you say we go search for the Asherah? Has anyone found something like this before?"

"Negative Captain, at least not according to the records I've been able to search," Kierenbot said.

I smiled at the others. "See. We can't let this go, not when we're so close."

"Nate," Serena said slowly, as if she was building up to something. I heard Kaz mumble something, but I kept my eyes on her. "I don't think this is a good idea."

"Oh, come on. This is definitive proof that could lead us to them, learn what happened to them, and find that valuable tech everyone is so eager to have."

She inhaled and regarded me for a few seconds. "Have you

looked at the history of this search? A lot of species died. When they weren't killing each other to find whatever they could, what they did find was deadly," Serena said.

I'd learned the same thing. "Not all of it. We'll be careful. It's not like I want to die, or anyone else for that matter."

Kaz snickered. "Thanks for including us."

I tipped my head toward him and looked at Serena. She stepped toward me, and the bridge suddenly felt smaller.

"Nate, please."

I looked up at the recording and then back at her.

"Excuse me, Captain," Kierenbot said.

"What is it?"

"I was able to extract the star map from the recordings and I'm running an analysis to compare it against what we have in the navigation system."

I nodded. "Good, but it could require more than that. I don't think that's going to work."

"Why not?" Kaz asked.

"Because of the findings from the other ruins. The one from the artifact indicated that they're almost as old as the galaxy. You'd need to do quite a bit of regression to get an accurate comparison."

"Excellent point, Captain. I shall add that to my query," Kierenbot said.

"It's not my first time tracking old records." I turned back toward Serena and didn't like what I saw in her gaze. I stepped closer and spoke quietly. "You can't expect me to give this up. This is unparalleled."

"I don't expect anything, Nate," she half snarled, but then she smoothed her features. "I'm asking you not to pursue this until we know more."

I felt my jaw clench. "You want me to go to Delos about this?"

She nodded and I scowled. "You're in over your head. Just like the last time. Maybe you don't get to walk away this time."

"If it comes to betting on myself, I'll always take that bet."

Her eyebrows knitted together in resignation, and I saw something change, like the ice I'd been standing on had finally broken and what was below was much colder.

The door to the bridge opened and Raylin came in with a small gravity-storage crate trailing behind her. I recognized her field kit.

"Where are you going?" Kaz asked.

"I need to leave the ship for a while," Raylin said.

I looked at her in surprise. "Why?"

"Because there are things I need to pursue, and I don't need to drag you all with me."

"I don't like this," Kaz said.

"I'm sorry but it can't be helped. I just wanted to inform you before I left. I'll catch up to you later," Raylin said.

I frowned. "How are you going to find us? I have no idea where we'll be."

Raylin smiled knowingly. "I'll be able to find you. There's only one *Spacehog* after all."

"Does this have to do with Lanaya?" I asked.

Raylin pursed her full lips a little and nodded. "It might. That's what I need to find out. It's better if I pursue this my own way."

I frowned, trying to think of something I could say to get her to stay. Raylin was one of the more mysterious members of the crew. If we'd been back home, I would've assumed she was part of one of the three-letter agencies.

"Do you need help?" Serena said.

I looked at her and blinked. She was speaking to Raylin.

I was dumbfounded. "Wait a minute."

Serena ignored me and walked toward Raylin, repeating her question.

Raylin regarded Serena for a few moments and then gave her a small nod. "I'll meet you at the airlock. Pack light."

"I will," Serena said.

"Now hold on a second. You can't really mean you're going with her," I said, then looked at Raylin. "You're not taking her with you?"

Raylin gave me a sympathetic look and I turned toward Serena.

She stared at me for a long moment and swallowed hard. "What do you care? I'm going. Do whatever you want, Nate. That's what you've always done," she said and stormed off the bridge.

I stood there, mouth partially agape, watching her go.

"Nate," Ben said.

I watched the door to the bridge rematerialize, closing off my view of Serena darting down the hall at a fast pace.

"Nate, don't you think you should—"

I thrust up my hand and glared at him. "Later!" I snarled. Then I left the bridge.

CHAPTER 19

I lengthened my stride, eating up the corridor in a pace just below a run.

"Serena, hold on," I called out.

She was a lot farther away and she kept going, turning from view.

Why did women play the ignore game?

I quickened my pace and started jogging. I rounded the corner and the elevator was gone. Sighing, I palmed the controls and had to wait a few minutes for it to return. I went inside and slammed the controls.

I burst out of the elevator on H-Deck and saw Serena coming out of the commons area. How had she already gone to her quarters to pack up and be ready to leave? I looked at the backpack she carried as she slung it over her shoulders.

"We need to talk," I said.

She looked at me as she strode right toward me. "We already did. You don't want to listen. Now get out of my way. I don't need your permission to leave the ship."

She brushed by me, and I fell into step next to her. "Don't give me that. I'm not your keeper."

We stopped at the elevator, and she spun on me. "Aren't you?"

I frowned. "What's that supposed to mean?"

"You promised my father that you'd watch out for me. Remember?"

The doors opened and she made a beeline toward one side, arms crossed tightly while she stared intently at the controls.

I moved to the other side and took a steadying breath. "Of course, I do. I was there when he died."

Sometimes my mouth spewed words before I had a chance to really think about it. I had to live with the consequences, and I knew that what I'd said was exactly the wrong thing even as she glared at me.

"I didn't mean that."

"Yes you did," she snarled. "I'm not your responsibility. You don't have to look out for me anymore. You're free to do whatever you want. Enjoy it!"

She stormed out of the elevator, and I stood there in the wake of her fury. I hesitated for half a second before catching up to her.

"You think this is what I want?"

She shook her head. "You've been quite clear about what you want."

"Would you just stop for a second and talk to me?"

She stopped and spun toward me expectantly, eyes full of molten fury wrapped in an icy sheath of certainty.

I flinched.

"You don't even know where Raylin is going. Since you're so worried about danger, the safe bet is to stay on the ship."

Her eyes became hooded. "Is that all?"

I sighed explosively, my own patience slipping away. "We're supposed to watch each other's backs."

She didn't reply for a few seconds. "Are we done?"

It was like trying to talk to a teenager and about as useful when they refused to see reason.

I sighed. "Talk to me."

"I'm done talking," she said and resumed her trek toward the portside airlock.

I started to say something about three or four times during that long trek. She wasn't going at the breakneck speed she had been before, and I caught a few subtle jerks of her head as if she had some kind of internal monologue going.

I didn't want to believe she was really leaving the ship. She was just doing this to exercise control over me.

Some of the others had gathered outside the airlock, but they were too far away for me to hear what they were saying.

Serena slowed down and sighed. She lifted her gaze toward mine. "I...I need to get out of here for a while."

She meant away from him. They both knew it. The unspoken tension between them had been mounting for a while. If I tried to stop her, she would pull farther away. Was that what I wanted? I hated this. My emotions were flatlining and I could feel myself retreating from them as the walls went up.

I clenched my jaw for a second and then said quietly, "If that's what you think is best, then you should do it."

She looked away, and I started walking down the corridor. I thought I heard a slight hitch or the shaky inhaling of a breath.

Raylin eyed us as we came toward them. Her gravity trunk hovered nearby.

I walked over to her. "Take care of yourself," I said and then glanced at Serena. "Both of you."

Serena leaned toward Kaz, and he lowered his head to listen. He glanced at me and then gave her a small nod.

A wave of silence settled over everyone outside the airlock.

Ben went over to Serena. "What are you doing? You shouldn't leave."

"I have to. This is something I need to do."

"But you don't know…" he started to say and stopped.

"We all need someone to watch our backs. Raylin is no different," Serena said.

My mouth became dry, and my eyes tightened. Then I walked over and slapped the airlock controls a little harder than I should have. The door swung open on perfectly balanced hinges.

Raylin walked toward the airlock and stopped, staring at me. "Good luck, Captain. We'll catch up with you."

"Good hunting."

Raylin walked into the airlock.

Serena walked by, and I considered reaching out to her. I wanted to tell her that we were both being stupid. We probably were, but nothing I could say would change what was going to happen.

She lingered in the frame.

"Be careful," I said quietly.

Her chin quaked a little and then stopped. She swallowed hard. "You too, Nate."

I watched her go, and T'Chura started to close the door. I had stepped out of the way but kept watching them through the small window.

When they were out of sight, I turned around. Kaz frowned at me.

"Are you sure you're not a mated pair?" he asked.

Sometimes Kaz liked to play with the language. Every now and then, he made a comment that Serena and I sometimes behaved like a married couple. If we were, then a separation was in order and just as final as the indomitable seal of the airlock.

I looked at Kierenbot. "Get us ready to depart. I want to be underway as soon as possible."

"Understood, Captain," Kierenbot said and wormed his way past the others, heading to the bridge.

"Wait," Ben said.

I'd started walking down the corridor. I stopped but didn't turn around. "I'm done waiting," I said and continued down the corridor.

I didn't have a destination in mind. I needed to get away from that damn airlock, but the image of Serena going through it refused to fade in my mind as I went.

CHAPTER 20

Finding myself standing outside the armory, I palmed the pad and the door opened. Racks of weapons in storage mode stood along the walls. There were a couple of workbenches across the room.

I heard the door rematerialize as I walked along the racks, passing a section of T'Chura's storage area. Everything in there was suitable for the Sasquatch, and there was quite a stash, the function of which I didn't have a clue. They all looked as if they could deliver untold amounts of damage.

I found that I really wanted to hit something, or punch something, more like it. I surveyed the armory and knew I wasn't about to tear the place up in a rage, so I walked toward my own locker and opened it.

There was a metal case about a foot long inside with a note from Crim.

I thought this might suit you on future excursions.

I lifted the case off the shelf in my locker and brought it to the workbench. Crim had a 'learn by doing' method of teaching. I recalled the first time he'd instructed me about combat suit capabilities. He'd done it by shooting me with his hand blaster.

I stared at the case for a few seconds, working up the nerve to open it, then blew out a breath and thumbed the lock. The metallic case opened. Inside was a black rod about an inch thick. As I moved to reach inside, some kind of mechanism lifted the rod up for me to easily grasp. As I glided my fingertips across it, it felt like the same material used for my combat suit. It was somewhat malleable and could take on different shapes, very strong and durable.

The surface of the rod was textured for ease of grip, and I lifted it out of the case. I held it loosely and felt it shift beneath my palm. Something morphed into view from across the room and Larry stood there on all four of his legs, peering at me curiously.

A small holoscreen became active on my omnitool.

Adaptable handheld multipurpose tool.

Beneath it were several rows of icons showing the different shapes it could take. They all looked familiar to me, and I realized that Crim must have set it up this way. I selected the option for a tactical Tomahawk. The rod quickly stretched, forming a sharp, wedge-shaped axe head with a spike on the opposite end. The weight hadn't changed at all. I lifted the edge up and it looked sharper than any axe head I'd ever seen. I glanced around, looking for something to test it on, and then shook my head. I wasn't about to go chopping anything.

I lifted the omnitool and selected another shape. The axe quickly morphed into a four-foot-long stick. I squeezed it and it felt solid in my hands. I spun and slammed it down on the open workbench. I had expected a loud and satisfying clang, but what I got was a thundering shockwave and the bench folded in from the crushing blow. I felt my eyebrows stretch toward my hairline as I stared at the stick.

I hadn't become super strong. I wasn't Superman, no matter how many times throughout my life I had wanted to become the best superhero ever.

Frowning, I held the stick away from me and lifted the omnitool on my other arm. I read the bullet points beneath the mode I'd selected, which said something about vibrations and sonic shockwaves.

My gaze darted toward the broken workbench, and then I looked at Larry. "Effective test," I said and sighed. Crim wasn't going to be happy about fixing the workbench, but what did he expect?

I scanned the different modes on my omnitool and selected the one for storage. The stick became flexible, like a well-worn leather belt. I stared at it for a second and shook the belt. It became smaller and went back to rod shape about a foot in length. I attached it to a small holder at my lower back, then picked up the metallic case off the floor and tossed it into my locker. When I turned around, Larry was gone.

"Where did you go?" I asked. I called out to Larry, and he reappeared near the door. A few seconds later he disappeared again.

I left the armory and headed toward the bridge.

"There you are," Ben said. His tone was somewhat accusatory.

I really wasn't in the mood for this.

I turned toward him. "You're looking for me?"

"What the hell, Nate. How could you let her go?"

"What do you suggest I do, Ben? Throw her over my shoulder and lock her in her room?"

Ben blinked and then shook his head. "No, of course not."

"I'm glad we can agree on that," I said and walked toward the bridge.

Ben followed.

"That's it? That's all you're gonna say?" he asked as we walked onto the bridge.

I glared at him. "What do you want me to say?"

Kaz, T'Chura, Lanaya, and Kierenbot turned toward them.

Ben glanced at them and then locked gazes with me. "She wouldn't have left if you hadn't insisted on going to find the Asherah."

"For Chrissake, you too!"

"She just wanted you to wait before going after it. Why couldn't you have done that? Why—"

I balled my hands into fists and gritted my teeth. "Just stop," I snarled.

Ben's eyes widened for a moment before narrowing. "No, I'm not going to stop."

The kid had picked a heck of a time to grow a backbone. I should've seen it coming.

"You don't like it that Serena left the ship. Well, neither do I," I said and rounded on the others. "What about you guys? Do you like it?" I asked and didn't wait for an answer. I turned back toward Ben. "No one likes it, Ben. Not one of us likes it."

Ben inhaled a breath and blew it out. "Yeah, but *you* pushed her to do this."

"She doesn't know what she wants. Big surprise," I said, staring daggers at him. "Neither do you."

Ben winced, and like a predator sensing weakness, I stormed over to him and flung my arm toward the bridge doors. "You're welcome to join them if you want. I won't stop you. You, like Serena or anyone else aboard this damn ship, can leave at any time."

Ben clenched his teeth and glared at me.

T'Chura was by my side. I hadn't even heard him come over. How could anyone so big move so silently?

"Why don't we all take a breath?" T'Chura said, his voice calm and without challenge.

I glared up at him and saw a reflection of myself in his serene, saucer-shaped eyes. As I felt the anger and frustration begin to loosen its hold on me, I almost snatched it back, but I didn't.

I lowered my gaze and sighed. Closing my eyes, I did as T'Chura wisely suggested and took a breath, a lot of them. I wasn't sure how many minutes had passed. I leaned against the workstation, not looking at anyone.

I lifted my gaze and found Ben staring at me. He looked concerned.

"I don't want you to go, Ben."

He nodded, looking relieved. "I was outta line. Serena," he said and paused for a few seconds. "She hasn't been…she's been restless for a while now."

I considered it for a few moments and nodded. "I know. I can't do anything about that now."

Kaz cleared his throat. "Raylin won't let anything happen to her. We'll see them both again."

"But how are they going to find us?" Ben asked.

Kaz smirked and then tipped his head toward me. "We don't exactly keep a low profile."

I chuckled and the others joined in. It felt good, even if we were all still tense.

Larry sauntered between us, appearing out of nowhere, and Lanaya gasped. She pointed right at Larry.

Ben walked over to her. "What's the matter?"

"She sees him. She sees Larry," I said.

The others peered at the place where Larry stood, but I didn't think they could see him.

Kierenbot cleared his throat. "Uh, Captain, Wonfiner Security would like to come aboard. They're heading to our slip now."

I frowned and shook my head. "That's not going to work."

"Just to confirm: you want me to deny the request?"

"No, just get us out of here."

"Yes, Captain," Kierenbot said and went toward the navigation workstation.

Lanaya sat on the floor, trying to get Larry to come to her.

Ben looked at me. "Why does Wonfiner Security want to come aboard?"

I shrugged. "I'm not sure, to be honest. It could be a couple of things, but I don't want to find out."

"Don't you think we should tell them thanks but no thanks?" he asked.

"If I don't acknowledge receipt of their message, I can deny ever getting the request."

Kaz shook his head. "That's probably not going to work."

"Well then, they can chase me down. I don't have time to get tied up here. We were already cleared to leave," I said.

"We've cleared the docking clamps," Kierenbot said.

I let out a slow breath. "Good."

Lanaya looked up at me. "He looks strange."

I nodded. "I know. He disappears sometimes, like he has trouble keeping that shape."

The others stared at me. Kaz and T'Chura exchanged glances.

I clenched my jaw. "I swear, if I hear either one of you breathe the word 'autodoc,' we're going to have a problem."

T'Chura, being over nine feet tall, towered over me. Yes, he could probably make short work of me, but I did have the multipurpose tool. I could give T'Chura a challenge for a few seconds if I took him by surprise.

T'Chura moved to a location across from Lanaya. He peered at the area where Larry sat, but I could tell that he couldn't see him.

"I still can't detect him at all," he said.

"Try not to take it personally," I replied, and he chuckled.

I felt a strange tingling sensation on my right arm and pushed up my sleeve to see an intricate pattern of darkened lines. They were the same as what had been on the artifact. I rubbed the area, and the lines didn't react at all.

Kaz peered at me, his gaze sinking toward my arm. "Is that from the artifact?"

I'd hoped it would've just gone away, but it hadn't. I nodded and then looked down at Larry. "I think things are more complicated than we originally thought."

CHAPTER 21

T'Chura leaned toward me, and it was like a solid wall of boulders leaning in. I tried not to flinch, and he frowned.

"Sorry, gut reaction. We don't make them big like you back home."

T'Chura sniffed and peered at my arm. "It's changed."

"How can you tell?"

"Because it's moving."

I looked at my arm, and since the intricate patterns on it made it look like an impressive sleeve of tattoos, I couldn't see it moving. I tentatively rubbed the skin of my forearm with my other hand.

Kaz sighed. "You're not going to be able to rub it off."

I scowled. "I was just seeing if I could feel something on my skin."

He rolled his eyes. "Maybe next time you shouldn't stick your hand where it doesn't belong."

My gaze narrowed. "You should have been there instead of sulking in your room."

"This isn't helping," Ben said in an effort to lower the temperature in the room a little.

Kaz leaned against the nearby workstation and watched me impassively.

I looked up at T'Chura. "I don't see it moving. What do you see, exactly?"

"My species can see across several spectrums of light and energy."

My eyebrows raised. "That explains it," I said with a grin.

He smiled with half his mouth. "The artifact has transferred to your skin."

I considered that for a few moments and frowned. "I never actually touched it once it was activated." I tipped my head toward Larry. "Larry was the one who touched it."

"While standing on your hand."

Kaz shook his head with a derisive snort.

"I couldn't move," I sneered toward him.

He frowned. "Why not?"

"I don't know. I lifted the artifact toward a group of metallic columns, and they powered on or something."

Kaz looked at T'Chura, who shrugged.

"The captain's account is accurate. I witnessed it," Kierenbot said.

Kaz sighed. "There had to be a power source then. Why weren't you able to detect it?" he said and leveled his gaze toward mine. "You didn't scan for power sources, right?"

I considered several responses before looking at Kierenbot. "Can you check Kaz's vitals? I don't think he's feeling well. Escort him to the autodoc for me, please."

Kierenbot's red orb darted between me and Kaz, and then he stepped toward Kaz.

Kaz lifted his gaze toward him. "Consider your next action carefully."

Kierenbot froze and then looked at me.

"Geez, calm down, Spanky," I said. "Yes, we scanned the area for power sources, security measures, and anything else Kierenbot was capable of detecting."

Kaz frowned toward me. "Spanky?"

I rolled my eyes a little. "It's not important."

"It was important enough for you to say."

"Now that I know you enjoy it, I'll say it more often, Spanky."

Kaz glared at me, and I didn't care if he was upset. I'd had enough of his sulking attitude.

"Right," Ben said. "So, no detectable power source, but something happened anyway. Where did the power come from?"

Kaz and I stopped glaring at each other, and I sighed. "Okay, I don't have the technical vernacular for what I'm going to say, so I'm just going to say it. What if the power source wasn't…" I paused for a few moments.

Ben leaned forward. "Wasn't?"

I glanced at the others, wondering if I'd be ridiculed for the ignorance of my next statement. I shrugged. Scold away. "From this reality, or universe, or plane of existence, or whatever you'd like to use to fill in the blank for something like that."

The others seemed to consider this until Kaz broke the silence.

"Kierenbot, prepare the autodoc for Nate, please."

I don't know what it was, but we all started laughing. First, a snicker bubbled up from my chest and then Ben snorted. Suddenly, the rest of us fell like dominos, giving in to the absurdity of the moment—that is, except for Lanaya. She smiled in a companionable sort of way, but I didn't think she'd understood. Not that I thought she was less intelligent than the rest of us, but it didn't seem like she'd been around a lot of people…regular people…non-captive-type beings. It was exhausting just thinking about it.

Once we all settled down, I asked, "So, am I right, or is it as crazy as it sounds?"

"The idea has merit," T'Chura said.

"One of the things I've noticed about Larry is that he disappears sometimes. Sometimes he comes back right where he'd been a moment before and others he appears in a different place entirely. I don't know if teleportation is possible and I'm not sure if that's what he's doing, but I figured I'd mention it."

Kaz and T'Chura shared a look. "It's not as crazy as it sounds," T'Chura said.

"Indeed," Kierenbot added. "Teleportation is not only possible but has been used before."

Kaz cleared his throat. "Let's not get ahead of ourselves."

I looked at him with raised eyebrows.

"Yes, it is possible, but that doesn't make it practical or safe. Otherwise, why would we need a spaceship?"

I nodded. "Okay, so how do we explain Larry? I can see him, and Lanaya can see him now," I glanced at her, and she nodded. "T'Chura can sense him a little bit, but the rest of you can't."

I covered up a sigh with a slight shake of my head, thinking about how Serena could also sense Larry.

T'Chura stared intently at the ground, frown lines deepening.

"What are you doing?" I asked.

He didn't look at me. "Trying to see him. I can't. I should be able to."

He extended his hand toward where he thought Larry was, and I guided him near, only for Larry to lean away.

I gave him a look. "He's not going to hurt you."

T'Chura frowned.

"He backed away. He doesn't want to be touched."

"That's just it. I don't think I *can* touch him," T'Chura said.

I considered that for a few seconds and then sat on the ground and lifted my hand toward Larry. After a few moments, he extended one of his paws toward me. I felt a cool, subtle vibration on my fingertips.

"Look at that," Kaz said. He lifted his chin and I looked at my arm.

The bronze-colored lines began to glow faintly. My eyes widened as I stared at it. "Tell me you guys see it too?"

They did.

"What does it mean?" I asked, looking at them.

"You're reacting to being touched by Larry," Ben said with a thoughtful frown. "Does it hurt?"

I shook my head. "No, but it feels a little strange and cold."

"Cold," Kaz said, pressing his lips together in thought.

"Yeah, cold."

"Typically, energy has a heat signature," Kaz said.

"Not necessarily," Ben replied. "Cold fusion does exist. Room-temperature energy is used by this ship."

I nodded, impressed. "All that time with Crim is paying off."

"You're right, Ben," Kaz said. "But high-energy output generates a lot of heat. The fact that Nate feels something cold, which he also mentioned when the artifact activated, is a clue. Now all we have to do is figure out what it means."

I stared at Larry for a few seconds. His gaze looked insistent, as if he was trying to communicate something to me. I had no idea what that could be, and it was anyone's guess at that point.

He'd seemed more interactive after the incident with the artifact.

I gestured with my other hand toward T'Chura, and Larry's gaze slid in T'Chura's direction, but he gave no indication that he was aware of him being there at all.

T'Chura regarded me questioningly.

"I was trying to get him to interact with you."

Larry pulled his hand back and slunk away.

T'Chura sighed, disappointed.

"Don't take it personally," I said, feeling bad for him. He wanted to see Larry so much.

I stood and looked at Kierenbot. "You said earlier that you were able to use the star map we saw at the museum? Do we have a heading?"

"I'll work on it at once, Captain," Kierenbot said and moved toward the other side of the bridge.

The lines on my forearm began to fade, which I found comforting for some reason.

I regarded the others for a few moments. "We're going after the Asherah."

"Are you sure that's smart?" Ben asked.

Kaz was stone-faced and quiet.

T'Chura looked as if he was quietly contemplating the meaning of life for all his face gave anything away.

Lanaya watched Ben and then looked at me. "Who are the Asherah? Is that where the masters are?"

I glanced at Ben, and he winced a little. Then I shook my head. "No, I don't think the masters are there."

Lanaya considered this for a few moments. "Who are they?"

"No one really knows," I said, looking pointedly at Kaz.

"It's amazing how you can dismiss thousands of years of searching for them," Kaz said.

"I'm not dismissing it. In fact, I acknowledge it, but there's been no new developments for how long?" I asked and then shook my head. "Never mind. It's been a while, but it looks like the trail to the Asherah isn't as cold as everyone thought."

I gestured with my right arm and Kaz glanced at it before nodding.

"I have a heading, Captain," Kierenbot said. "On the main holoscreen."

A holoscreen appeared that showed a star map. I didn't know what the scale of the map was, but the distance that we had to travel looked pretty vast. The waypoint blinked to draw our attention to it.

I watched as the others peered at the destination and waited for some kind of reaction from them.

Kaz walked toward the map and studied it for a minute.

I joined him. "Not where you expected?"

The Milky Way was a spiral galaxy, but something that had been drilled into my head since coming aboard the ship was that our galaxy had plenty of depth to it. The waypoint on the map took us toward a more central region but also quite low on the ecliptic disk. I supposed it might be considered the edge of the galaxy, but nowhere near the rim, just way down low.

"It's not exactly the most hospitable sector," Kaz said and turned toward Kierenbot. "Are you sure about these coordinates?"

"This star system has the highest probability for the Asherah's homeworld, as indicated in the map Nate discovered," Kierenbot replied.

I lifted my hands. "What is it?"

"It's not habitable."

I shrugged. "So what?"

"It's never been habitable."

I frowned. "You lost me."

"Like your own system of planets, there is a habitable area for carbon-based life," Kaz said.

I had a slight urge to make the Spock gesture and say something like 'fascinating.'

"I understand. Go on," I said.

"The galaxy has similar principles that govern it for habitable worlds."

"But," Ben said, "that assumes all life in the galaxy is carbon based."

I gave Ben an approving nod and looked at Kaz.

"It is widely believed that the Asherah were carbon based like we are. You'd find the presence of non-carbon-based life a bit unsettling," Kaz said.

I looked at T'Chura and he bobbed his head once.

"Unsettling? Do you mean disturbing?"

Kaz considered it for a few seconds. "Unsettling, disturbing, terrifying. I can use any expression you'd like."

"You sound like you're speaking from personal experience."

Kaz shook his head. "There are quadrants associated with them, but I've never been there."

I glanced at the star map. "Is that where the map is telling us to go? One of those places?"

"Possibly."

"You don't know?"

Kaz rolled his eyes and gave me an impatient look. "I've never claimed to have seen the entire galaxy, Nate."

"I think we're missing a very important point," Ben said. I looked at him and waited. "The dating method associated with the artifact indicated that those ruins were around when the galaxy was barely formed. So, the region that's not habitable now might have been before."

I nodded. "Good point, kid."

I looked at Kaz. He shrugged.

"Possibly."

"Do you think we'll be attacked if we go there?"

Kaz seemed amused by my question, and after I considered it for a few seconds I could see his point.

"Fine," I said. "Do you think we'll be killed outright for even showing up there?"

"Not if we're careful."

I waited for him to continue, but he didn't. "Are you going to make me drag it out of you?"

Kaz smiled with half his mouth. "You could try."

"Kaz," T'Chura said, "we've moved past these pitiful displays."

Kaz eyed me. "Have we?"

I sighed. "I'm sorry I hurt your feelings. Now tell me before I throw your ass into the nearest escape pod and make you ride the whole way to that waypoint by yourself."

Kaz chuckled.

Old jokes.

"On our way there, we'll stop at certain intervals to do a scanning sweep. It'll allow us to determine whether that star system is safe to approach," Kaz said.

"What do you think, Kierenbot?"

"His suggestion is logical, Captain."

I arched an eyebrow, wondering if the robot had been watching a few episodes of Star Trek.

"Okay, let's do that. Plot our journey there in stages and then we'll take it from there," I said.

Sometimes, traveling among the stars was much quicker than I would've expected. I'm sure if I asked Ben, he could tell me all about how fast the ship could travel by folding space or some such concept like that. All I really cared about was that we arrived okay. I could input a destination in the ship's navigation system and tell the computer to take us there, but I'd rather leave it to the professional—in this case, Kierenbot. He could double check that we didn't end up somewhere we hadn't intended to go. While I wasn't opposed to occasionally risking my life, I had no intention of throwing my life away.

In the end, it took us several days to reach our destination. Kaz remained insistent that we weren't going to reach the Asherah homeworld, and he might have been right about that. However, I was certain that our destination did have *something* to do with the Asherah. Our path was written in the stars.

More often than not, I thought about Serena. I tried not to, but I couldn't help it. Flynn had wanted me to look out for her, and instead I might've driven her away. Maybe she wasn't cut out for life on a spaceship. I doubted she even knew, and that was part of the problem. But that didn't stop me from wondering and hoping she was safe.

I glanced at the star map, which I'd brought up at my workstation on the bridge, and regarded the distance we'd traveled. It was staggering to think about. How would Raylin ever find a way to catch up with us? How would she even know where to find us?

Of course, once we finally arrived at our destination, all those thoughts were thrust from my mind. No apparent dangers had been detected during our trek here, but that didn't mean there wasn't any danger ahead of us.

CHAPTER 22

I sat at a workstation on the bridge. My arms were folded, and I waited for the main holoscreen to update. One of the surprising things about the bridge of the ship was that there was no captain's chair or command center or anything like that. There were select workstations, but they were pretty generic. Whoever sat at those workstations determined its capabilities. If Kierenbot had sat here, this workstation could perform any number of functions from navigation to engineering to weapons systems. For me, there was basic system access to the ship with enough safeguards in place to ensure I'd never fly us into the middle of a star.

Ben was the first to arrive on the bridge after my general announcement that we'd be arriving soon. His hair was disheveled, and he looked like someone had stolen his favorite toy on Christmas morning.

"What's the matter?"

He plopped down into the chair next to me and blew out a breath. "Crim was just telling me that…" He frowned for a second and blinked. "That a lot of the things we thought we knew were wrong."

Crim was training Ben in the ways of all things advanced tech beyond theoretical physics, as the kid liked to refer to it. Sometimes I think Crim took a lot of satisfaction in blowing Ben's mind.

"What did you learn this time?" I asked.

"The universe isn't thirteen billion years old."

I eyed him for a long moment. "Sound serious."

"You don't understand. This is unbelievable."

I frowned. "How old is it?"

I couldn't bring myself to say 'universe' because I didn't like thinking about such weighty matters in my mind. I existed in the universe, and I didn't need to question it…not that much anyway.

"About nine billion years."

"Doesn't sound so bad."

"I knew our estimates could be incorrect, but not by that much."

I shrugged. "Maybe we didn't have all the information."

Ben stared at me for a while, his mouth agape. He leaned toward me. "How the heck do you do that?"

I frowned. "Do what?"

He gestured toward me. "That. What you just did. 'Maybe we didn't have all the information,'" he said, mimicking me a little bit. "You just find what might be the most plausible explanation that, honestly, is usually the right one."

I smiled. "I guess some of us are just lucky."

Ben shook his head. "I've seen you do this before, and I don't understand how you do it."

"I question things, Ben. It's kinda my thing. Solving mysteries…seeking out mysteries is more like it."

"Yeah, but you're not even interested in all this stuff."

"What stuff?"

"The concepts behind all of this," he said, gesturing toward the entire bridge.

"I just use it; I don't need to know how it works."

Ben shook his head. "What if you need to fix it?"

"That's what Crim is for."

"What if he can't because he slipped and fell or something."

I arched an eyebrow. "That's the best you could come up with? Of anyone on the crew, Crim is never going to slip and fall. He's got six legs, kid."

Ben waved away the comment. I shrugged. "Kierenbot could fix it?"

"What if—"

I held up my hand to stop him. "Look, I know what you're saying. The thing about me is that I know my limits. I'll learn what I need to know the more time we spend here. You're the one who wants to condense a few hundred years of advanced scientific theory into your head to elevate the rest of humanity."

Ben considered this for a minute, and I continued. "Look, I'm not against what you're doing. In fact, I think it's a good thing, but don't get upset because I'm not interested in learning how the ship's engines work. I just care about how fast they can get us from here to there—point A to point B."

Ben stared at me for a few seconds. "Bullshit."

I laughed and looked around. "Where's Lanaya?"

"She's helping Crim. He said they'll be coming along in a few minutes."

"Something to keep in mind regarding what you're planning. All science without philosophy is bad. It's short-sighted. That's why you'll need a good team that can challenge the overall vision and keep you on a solid path."

Ben pursed his lips in thought for a few seconds, then smiled wryly. "I'll probably need a good lawyer."

I laughed. "You couldn't afford me."

He grinned.

Kaz and T'Chura joined us on the bridge. Even though it had been a few days, I still expected Serena and Raylin to suddenly appear. We'd all spent months aboard the ship together.

"What's taking so long, Kierenbot?" I asked.

"Apologies, Captain. I've had to adjust our scanners to clear up the data we've received."

I looked at Kaz.

"Probably some kind of interference."

"What do you mean 'probably'?" I said and smiled.

Kaz bobbed his head.

"Okay, I've filtered out most of the interference," Kierenbot said.

A live video feed appeared on the main holoscreen that showed a distant view of something that took my brain a few seconds to make sense of, and even then I wasn't sure if I trusted what I'd seen. In the distance was a red dwarf star that had multiple asteroid belts around it. I peered at the image, trying to see if those belts covered the entire area around the star. They didn't, not entirely.

"What the hell happened here?" I asked no one in particular.

"That's a very interesting question," Kaz said, staring at the holoscreen.

Kierenbot cleared his throat. "Our sensors have detected another ship in the star system."

"Does it have an ID?" I asked.

"It's not broadcasting. What I've detected is the remains of its entry into the star system. They came on a similar trajectory as we did."

"That means they came from the same place we did," I said, frowning. I looked at Kaz. "Looks like your old mentor beat us here."

Kaz blinked.

"Griff Tarken?" Ben asked. "How can you be sure of that?"

"Unless someone else you know is searching for the Asherah, he's the only one who makes sense."

"How'd he arrive before us?" Ben asked.

Kaz's mouth became flat as he thinned his lips.

"Because he probably came right here. He didn't stop along the way to make sure everything was copacetic."

Ben frowned. "Copa-what?"

I sighed. Kids these days—so damn smart in some ways and lacking in others. "Good order. Safe for us to come."

Ben nodded. He gave me a wry look, probably deciding on some kind of age-related comment, but he didn't say anything.

Kaz cleared his throat. "I guess it's safe to say that no one has been alive here for either a very long time or never."

He was right. If the Asherah's homeworld was here, it could very well be one of the few rings of asteroids orbiting the old star here.

"Doesn't have to be a planet," T'Chura said.

I stared at the holoscreen and rubbed my artifact-stenciled arm. It didn't ache, but the fact that no one knew what it was had been on everyone's minds. Larry still only appeared for me and Lanaya, but he seemed to only interact with me, which must have been due to my charming personality.

Larry hopped up onto my workstation and peered at the holoscreen.

T'Chura frowned. "He's there, isn't he?"

I nodded and then looked at Kierenbot. "Can you trace Griff Tarken's ship?"

Kaz blew out a breath. "You don't even know if it's him."

"Fine. Kierenbot, can you trace the other ship that in all likelihood is Griff Tarken's but we don't know for sure— You know what, never mind. Can you trace it or not?"

"I'm afraid not, Captain. I know the trajectory of the unidentified ship as it entered the star system." He winked at me and Kaz shook his head. "But it could be anywhere in the star system now."

I was about to speak when Larry perked up. A semitranslucent amber glow surrounded his body, and I felt something cold twinge inside my artifact-covered arm. I hissed and rubbed it vigorously.

"What's wrong?" Kaz asked.

I clutched my arm close to my chest and noticed that there was a small swirling mass on the holoscreen. It phased in and out like Larry's skin. I stood and moved away from him, hoping that some distance would alleviate some of the cold.

It did, but not by much.

"Larry's given us a heading," I said.

"I see it," Kierenbot said.

All eyes went toward the robot. "I can see the distortion. Right here," he said and highlighted an area on the holoscreen. It was right where Larry's beacon was located.

I nodded, more than a little relieved that someone else besides Lanaya could detect Larry's handiwork. "Can anyone else see it?"

Ben peered at the spot and shook his head. T'Chura did the same. Kaz narrowed his gaze and looked uncomfortable for half a second. Then he shook his head.

I stared at him for a second, eyes narrowing in suspicion. "Are you sure, Kaz?"

He looked away and clenched his jaw. I waited him out.

"Fine, I see your little pet."

"Why didn't you say anything?"

"Because it just happened now," Kaz admitted, somewhat grudgingly.

"Captain, I'm able to detect increased metallicity in that region of space," Kierenbot said, tilting his head toward the star map.

I frowned. "Increased what?"

"Apologies, there is a greater chance of ships in that area, but I don't detect any power signatures. Essentially, I just detect a lot of metal in that area," Kierenbot replied.

I considered that for a few seconds. "All right, then take us in. We didn't come all the way here just to turn around and go home."

"Very well, Captain," Kierenbot replied.

The door to the bridge opened and Crim entered, with Lanaya following him. He surveyed the room for a second or two and looked at me.

"What did I miss?" he asked.

I quickly filled him in, and Crim looked at Kaz. "You can see it now too?"

Kaz nodded. I almost suggested that he have the autodoc scan him just in case but decided against it. I needed cohesion and not adversity.

The ship traveled fast, and the closer we came to our waypoint, the more the video feed updated with greater detail of the area we were traveling to.

A cluster of large asteroids was ahead. Kierenbot put a scan plot on a sub window on the main holoscreen.

"These look like other ships, but they're not flying. They look abandoned," Kierenbot said.

Crim hastened over to a workstation and brought it online. "Shipwrecks. We're not the first ones to come here."

The glow around Larry diminished and went out, and so did the waypoint he'd created. We had our heading. The intense cold on my arm subsided.

"Any way to determine how old those shipwrecks are?" I asked.

"I'm working on it," Crim said.

The icons for the shipwrecks were located very close to our destination.

"The ship's computer systems do recognize some of their designs. They're older models."

"How old?"

"Older than when your species started farming."

I blinked.

"How old is that exactly?" Ben asked.

"Over ten thousand years old," I replied.

Crim had studied Earth as a hobby before we'd been abducted by Kaz. He was particularly fond of automobile designs from the nineteen-fifties and sixties. I shared that particular taste with him. His fondness for it was one of the reasons he had neon lights in his workshop, along with chrome accents, giving the workshop a mid-century-diner feel. It was quite retro.

"The ships are from a number of elder species designs—Nasarians, Ustrals, and more than a few species that aren't around anymore," Crim said. He considered his audience for a second. "I doubt we have time for a history lesson right now. There were wars between some species and they're not here anymore."

"Maybe they fought over this," I said, gesturing toward the holoscreen.

"Possibly, but these wrecks aren't from any fleet engagements.

They're exploration ships. They have a lighter armament than a warship design," Crim replied.

I knew Crim had been some kind of soldier and he was also several hundred years old.

"So, we're not the first to come here," Ben said.

"Evidently not," I said and looked at the others. "The map led us here. Is there any chance that these exploration ships never reported this place to anyone?"

Crim gave a mirthless chuckle. "That's a safe assumption. They knew what they were coming here for. Another race to find the Asherah, and look what happened to them."

I stared at the holoscreen for a few moments. "I don't like assumptions. Is there any way to tell if these ships killed each other, or were they victims of some kind of defensive battery or system they encountered?"

Crim's craggy face deepened in appreciation. "Are you sure you weren't a soldier?"

Both Kaz and T'Chura stared at me, waiting for my reply. I kept my gaze on Crim, eyebrows raised.

"We'll need to take a closer look, which would expose us to whatever defenses might be active there. It's your decision, Captain," Crim replied.

I considered it for a minute. There was no way to eliminate the risk in its entirety, but if there was some kind of defensive measure, it would've gotten the ship that arrived before us. Kierenbot would've detected it.

"Take us in," I said to Kierenbot.

"Aye, aye, Captain," he replied.

Ben gave me an amused look and I shrugged.

We flew toward our destination, and I tried not to stare at Crim. He was focused on his workstation holoscreen and navigating the interface.

"Damaged sections are old. This was not recent. The blast points are from weapons those ships would've carried. Since we can't detect any power cores active on the ships, it's safe to assume they're depleted."

"Or they're shielded," Kaz said.

I arched an eyebrow. "For thousands of years?"

I knew the power core on our ship could last a long time but not thousands of years. Not even close.

Kaz frowned and shook his head.

"Okay, so we're relatively safe to explore the area. Kierenbot, take us in for a closer look."

We all watched the main holoscreen as Kierenbot guided the ship toward a large cluster of asteroids. I didn't know if that was the proper term. They looked like a huge chunk of the planet that had been there. Could planet-sized rocks still be asteroids?

"I'm detecting a power source ahead," Kierenbot said. "It's from a ship. Yes, there it is."

Kierenbot zoomed in and we saw the ship.

"That looks familiar," I said. "Looks like it has a few more bells and whistles than we've got."

"It's docked with an outpost, Captain," Kierenbot said.

Built into the rock was a long docking station that only hinted at a deeper installation. Our angle to it was off, and Kierenbot righted the ship. The docking station was just above a deep crevice where some kind of structure disappeared inside.

The ship in the dock was Griff Tarken's.

I looked at Kaz and he sighed with a nod.

"Let's look for a place to park," I said.

CHAPTER 23

Crim closed down his workstation and came over to me. "I have a suggestion."

I smiled. "I love suggestions, especially yours, Crim."

He didn't quite preen from it, but I could tell he liked it. Crim was sometimes a wildcard in that I never knew how he was going to react. Granted, we were separate species that had evolved on completely different worlds, but something had changed in him, at least according to Kaz. Crim used to keep to himself in his workshop. He performed his engineering duties but had kept his distance. I told Kaz it was his leadership style, which he didn't appreciate but had to acknowledge. Kaz had run his ship operations into the ground and lost everything. I was determined to do better, but with Serena and Raylin on a temporary reprieve from the ship, I wasn't sure if I was any more successful than Kaz had been.

"I wouldn't dock the ship at all," Crim said.

I tightened my shoulders for a second in a stretch before looking at him. I'd been standing for a while. "Why not?"

Crim gestured toward the outpost. "We're looking at the docking station, but given the layout, there must be other access points. If we don't tie the ship down to a particular docking port, that will give us some flexibility in case we need it."

I considered it for a few seconds. "Someone will have to remain aboard the ship."

Kierenbot shifted on his feet and turned toward me. "Captain?"

I knew he wanted to be more active on the away teams. I think he was afraid I'd kick him off the ship, which I had no intention of doing.

"Crim makes a very good point, and right now you're all I've got," I said.

"There are others who could fly the ship. I'd rather support you and the rest while exploring the outpost."

I moved so I stood in front of him. "You will. If we get into trouble, it'll be you who comes to our rescue. It's one of the most important jobs, and I need you to do this."

Kierenbot's orb tracked from side to side while he considered it. "I will, of course, obey, Captain. However, I should point out that if you had acquired that battle-ready body for me, I could accompany you on this expedition. You'll need me to watch your back."

"I appreciate that, but we all watch each other's backs out there."

Kierenbot looked at the others. "I meant all of you," he said and turned back to me. His head tilted a little, and I couldn't help but think that he looked disappointed. After a few seconds, Kierenbot straightened. "I have your back. I'll continue to monitor the area and see what I can learn from here. Permission to patrol the area for surveying purposes."

"Granted," I said and looked at Crim, twitching my eyebrows. "Looks like we'll need a ride down there."

Crim regarded me for a second. "The XG8 Javelin is at your service."

I smiled and leaned toward him. "Doesn't exactly roll off the tongue, does it?"

Crim stared at me, and then sighed. "I'll ready the *battlewagon*."

I grinned and gave him a companionable slap on the shoulder.

Ben caught my eye. "I guess I'll stay aboard with Lanaya."

I shook my head. "Negative kid, you're coming along."

"But Nate, we shouldn't bring her into possible danger."

Time for Ben to learn another lesson. I looked at Lanaya, who'd been speaking to T'Chura. He protected us, and he seemed to look after all of us in his own way. He'd done the same thing when we'd first come aboard the ship. I felt a tinge of anger and guilt, thinking of Serena, and it was tied to Flynn. I wasn't about to change my mind about what we were doing, especially now, but I missed her. I missed Flynn too, that old sea dog. I sighed inwardly. I'd hated him for what he'd done to me but had come to forgive him as I learned the truth. Most important things were simple, but not all the time.

"Nate?" Ben asked.

I gestured for him to wait a second. "Lanaya, would you come here, please?"

T'Chura lifted his chin toward me, and Lanaya saw us waiting for her. She glided over to us. Ben moved to stand by her side, wanting to protect her, and I understood the impulse. It was a good one, but sometimes it needed to be reined in.

"We need to leave the ship," I said.

Lanaya nodded. Her long, Nordic-blonde hair shifted with the movement, and she regarded me with her almost alien eyes. "I've been listening. You're going to explore the outpost."

"You're a guest on this ship, but we're a bit short-handed," I said.

"This isn't right," Ben said.

I spared a glance at him and looked back at Lanaya.

"I don't have a lot of time, but do you think you can come with us and lend a hand? We'll do everything we can to ensure your safety, but I can't guarantee it."

Lanaya considered it and Ben looked at her. "You don't have do this. In fact, it's better if you stay here on the ship."

Lanaya frowned. "But *you're* going with them."

Ben winced a little and threw an accusing look my way. "I have to go."

"Then I would like to come with you," she said and looked at me, her head tilted to the side a little. "I'm familiar with the battlewagon's systems. Crim has shown them to me. I'm assuming we'll be wearing envirosuits. If you have equipment for me to use, then I'd like to help."

She'd been scared and disoriented when Ben found her on that station, but she seemed much better. I wouldn't put a weapon in her hands, but the battlewagon needed a minimum of two people to fly it effectively—probably three people, I thought as I glanced at Ben. He stood with his shoulders slumped a little.

I smiled at Lanaya. "Let's find you a suit then."

Lanaya nodded enthusiastically, and Ben just stood there, shocked and bewildered.

I lifted my chin toward Ben and said to Lanaya. "Give us a second."

She moved toward the door and T'Chura joined her.

Ben looked away from me and shook his head. "I can't believe you're bringing her along."

I arched an eyebrow toward him. "Technically, she's here because of you." Ben narrowed his gaze. "Look kid, either she's with us or she's not. I don't want her roaming the ship without us here. Kierenbot needs to focus on us. You and Crim have been spending time with her in the workshop." He frowned and I leaned toward him and spoke quietly. "We're all we've got. We're all she has. If she really didn't want to come, she would've said so."

Ben's gaze sank toward the ground while he considered it. Then he let out the breath he'd been holding. "I think she's been through a lot. She still says she wants to find the 'masters,' Nate. It's strange. It's not going to be safe down there. Bringing her is a mistake. It's a distraction."

I stared at him, feeling my gaze harden. "A distraction for whom? Get your head out of the clouds, kid. I get it. She's a beautiful girl, a damsel in distress. And she was put *right* in your path for a reason. You want to help her. So do I, but until I learn more about her, we have to be careful. Like it or not, she's going with us. Maybe we'll learn something about her along the way." Ben shook his head and looked away. "And she can see Larry. She might spot something the Asherah left behind."

Ben blinked in surprise as if he hadn't considered that. Then some of the frustration left his face. "All right, I get it. I don't like it, but I get it."

I nodded. "Good, now stop being a pain in the ass and make sure that girl has an envirosuit on."

He sighed. "I think you're letting this 'captain' thing go to your head."

I made a pirate 'Arrr' sound and we grinned. Ben was a good

kid, just young and a little isolated—mostly the type of self-imposed isolation I'd seen consume a lot of people.

I started to walk toward the door but noticed Kaz speaking with Kierenbot. I did an about-face and walked over to them.

"It'll alert them," Kierenbot said.

Kaz nodded. "I know, but it's worth the risk."

"What's worth the risk?" I asked.

Kaz regarded me for a moment. "I think we should contact the other ship."

"Give them a heads-up and let them know we're coming?" I asked with a straight face.

"They haven't contacted us yet."

"That's because they don't know we're here."

"I'd like to avoid a conflict if we can."

I chewed on my lower lip for a few seconds. "Do we have a problem, Kaz?"

It was an innocent enough question, but it carried enough weight to drag us all down.

Kaz locked his gaze with me. "No."

I nodded. "I hope not, because your head needs to be screwed on right if you're coming with us."

Kaz blinked and he glanced at Kierenbot before turning back to me. "Are you going to lock me on the ship?"

"Do I need to?"

"I just said we didn't have a problem."

"Is that what you were doing? Because I'm confused. You sounded like you wanted to hail the other ship."

Kaz clenched his jaw.

T'Chura walked over to us, his loud footfalls announcing his presence. "What's going on here?"

I kept my gaze on Kaz and waited for him to reply to me.

"It was a suggestion."

"Right," I replied. "Why don't you meet Crim at the battlewagon."

Kaz sighed and left the bridge.

T'Chura looked at me questioningly.

"Come on. I'll tell you about it on the way," I said.

We left the bridge and I told T'Chura what had just happened.

"It might not have been as devious as you think it is," T'Chura said.

"Maybe, but Kaz is conflicted about this."

"The apprentice bond with their mentor is strong. However, I don't believe Kaz would go against us."

I shook my head. "I disagree. We're crew mates, but family is different. Sooner or later, Kaz might have to pick a side, and I have no idea what end of the equation we'll end up on."

After a quick stop at the armory, I put on my combat suit and hand blasters, then activated the weapon Crim had given me. The adaptable multipurpose tool expanded to its short-staff mode, and I attached it to my back so it would be out of the way. I glanced at myself in the mirror and thought I looked strange with what could have been mistaken for a sword hilt poking over my shoulder.

Tallyho!

T'Chura glanced at it and didn't comment.

We met the others in Crim's workshop. The battlewagon had been moved to the adjacent hangar bay.

The battlewagon had a kind of symmetry to it. Its smooth lines projected a certain measure of sleekness, but there was power to it too. It had forward-facing mag cannons, with several blisters on top for energy weapons. Crim had upgraded the armor plating so we'd have better protection than the old battlewagon.

We climbed through the rear hatch and into the ship. Crim took the pilot's seat and Ben joined him in the co-pilot's seat. Kaz, Lanaya, and I each took a seat along the side, and T'Chura heaved his bulk down to an area designed for someone his size.

Kaz wouldn't look at me.

I had considered whether we should try to hail Griff Tarken's ship. If I had and he decided to take a shot at us, we would've wasted an opportunity to reach the outpost undetected. But there was no reason why scanners on that ship couldn't detect us.

I sighed a little and stuck to the decision I'd made earlier. A comlink was already open to the bridge. "Kierenbot, keep us clear of the other ship. We're going to let sleeping dogs lie for now."

"Understood, Captain," Kierenbot replied.

The hangar bay doors opened, and the ship's alerted course brought the dark, craggy surface into view.

Crim cleared his throat. "Preparing for departure in three, two, one."

The battlewagon's engines engaged, and we flew out of the hangar. "We're away," Crim said.

"Happy hunting. I'll begin my survey of the area," Kierenbot replied.

Crim flew the ship toward the docking station. He kept his speed steady and didn't rush to the site at all.

"Looks like they used a shuttle to explore the outpost," Crim said.

I directed my gaze toward a nearby holoscreen, which mimicked the one at the front of the ship. The hangar bay doors were open.

We flew toward the docking area and over it. Crim guided the ship down the deep fissure and the craggy walls of the planetary chunk seemed to swallow us up. I was a pilot myself and I didn't relish the thought of flying so close to such an unpredictable surface. It wasn't a straight shot down, but we were able to glimpse a structure that looked like a long shaft connecting the docking station to the rest of the outpost.

We reached the bottom of the chasm and found several landing pads. One held a familiar-looking shuttle. I recognized it from my last encounter with Griff Tarken.

Crim flew us over and we saw that dozens of battlebots had been torn apart and were scattered on the surface.

"Looks like we missed a fight," Crim said.

"Yeah, but with whom? I only see robots down there."

There was a scattering of lighter-colored rock or dirt near the battlebots' skeletons. "Did whoever attack them get on the shuttle?" I asked.

Crim circled the area and the shuttle looked intact.

"That's something at least," I said, peering at the area near the shuttle. I glanced at Kaz. "He could be in trouble."

He nodded and looked a little relieved to hear me say it. "We should take a look. There appears to be a hatch to enter the outpost."

He gestured at the holoscreen and saw what he was referring to. I nodded. "Crim, set us down nearby. T'Chura, Kaz, and I are going into the outpost. Mind guarding the way home for a bit?"

Ben twisted around in his seat to look at me. "I want you to stay here and help Crim."

He looked as if he was going to argue, but then he nodded.

Crim cleared his throat. "I'm going to deploy some recon drones. Ben, bring up the weapons systems. I don't want to get caught off guard like these bots were."

Ben brought the weapons systems online and several small turrets poked out of the hull of the ship.

Crim set us down and I stood up. "We'll try to stay in contact, but if something interferes, we'll go to the timer and return when it expires."

"Understood," Crim said.

We moved to the back of the battlewagon and the containment shield became active, cutting off the rest of the cabin from us. I waited for the atmosphere to reduce and match the outside. I saw Kaz looking at my feet and glanced down. Larry sat there, waiting. When the doors opened, he sauntered down the ramp. The lack of atmosphere didn't appear to affect him.

I shook my head. I didn't understand what kind of being Larry was. Sometimes he behaved like a friendly dog, and others he was aloof but not quite. It was like he was aware of us, but at the same time he was watching things we couldn't see. I doubted this would be the strangest thing I was going to experience that day.

I looked at the others. "Time to go."

CHAPTER 24

We stepped out of the battlewagon, and Crim flew it a short distance away. I watched as several oval-shaped recon drones popped out of a hidden panel on the bottom. They sped away and I quickly lost sight of them.

"Suit cameras on," Ben said over their shared team channel.

"That's right. We want to record as much as we can," I said and began recording with the cameras hidden in my helmet. They were forward-facing, so they'd capture everything I looked at.

"Too bad we don't have any smaller recon drones to take with us," I said.

T'Chura grunted a snort. He cradled his large assault rifle and surveyed the area.

We moved toward the nearby access hatch to the outpost. We were well away from where the battlebots and Griff's ship were located, and whatever had attacked them must've moved on.

"I'll add it to our resupply order next time we're at a station," Kierenbot said.

"Thanks. Is there anything to report from your scans?" I asked.

"Negative, Captain. I'll continue my sweep of the area."

Outside the hatch, Kaz set up a team comlink just for the three of us. "He continues to try to impress you."

"We had a rocky start when he worked for you."

"Yes, but it's been months."

"I'd rather he continues to be proactive and supportive than indifferent and sulking," I replied.

Kaz became quiet. Maybe he'd snap out of his mood from my not-so-subtle reprimand.

The access hatch was easily the size of the bank vault door I imagined being in Fort Knox. It was round and looked to be made from some kind of metallic alloy. It was partially open, and T'Chura pushed it the rest of the way while Kaz and I covered him with our weapons. When nothing terrifying burst from the darkened interior, we went inside.

We moved down a dark corridor, and beams of light pierced the darkness. My HUD enhanced the image so I could see the area clearly. At the end of the corridor was another hatch, which was also opened. It was easily twelve feet tall. Even T'Chura could walk through it with plenty of room to spare.

"Anyone know what the Asherah looked like?" I asked.

"By the look of these doors, my guess is that they were quite tall," Kaz replied, sounding more like his old self. I chuckled, and he said, "It's debatable."

"I bet."

"There's a species you haven't met yet called Screkvils, who are just a few feet tall, but their architecture is designed for someone three or four times their height. It stems from their religion."

"Interesting. Maybe they prefer building things this way, but on a planet full of short species, why would they have a complex about their height?"

"They need a reason? Sometimes groups just latch onto a belief system, even if it makes little sense to the casual observer. If you want, I can arrange a meeting and you can ask them yourself."

"If they had white sandy beaches, clear blue waters, and a few beers, I could be convinced."

"In that case, you'd enjoy Akacia-7. It's a prime colony world."

T'Chura cleared his throat. "I don't think their physiology could take the environment."

"Why not?" I asked.

"Atmosphere is too acidic, and heavy metals in the crust would likely kill you if you were there without an envirosuit for too long."

I looked at Kaz, and he shrugged. "My species loves it."

We walked through the hatch and there was a wide path that had been carved out of rock. I peered at it, and the HUD updated with a preliminary analysis.

"Is this right? The analysis says that the walls and the ground have been compressed."

"It is; it's a method that's still used. They deconstructed the rock and dirt and then used heat to form these tunnels. It's a quick way to make a mining installation that will support an artificial atmosphere for a time," Kaz replied.

I looked around and saw how the ceiling had opened up with a great big crack. We walked past several rocky mounds that looked to have collapsed from the ceiling. The walls up ahead glowed a deep green and rounded out of view. We moved toward it and saw there were large splotches along the walls above us that glowed green.

"What are they?" I asked.

"Some kind of bioluminescence," T'Chura replied.

I frowned.

"There isn't any atmosphere here," Kaz said and checked his omnitool, frowning.

Ahead of us I noticed a slight shimmer and it tugged at my memory. "I think there's some kind of shield up ahead. Maybe there's an artificial atmosphere?"

T'Chura swung his weapon ahead.

Kaz lifted something off his belt that looked like a flashlight, but it didn't emit any light. "I think you're right."

We moved ahead and Kaz nodded. "It's a weak containment shield."

"Weak?"

"We can move through it," Kaz said and strode forward confidently.

I followed, and my HUD updated with a very faint artificial atmosphere detection—nothing that could keep us alive if we took off our helmets, but it was enough for whatever that growth was on the cavern walls.

I walked over to the wall and peered up at the growth. It had the textured consistency of moss, and I thought it would just smear off the wall if I could reach it. The pale glow seemed to pulse lazily, and I had to wonder how something like this could still be alive. It wasn't as if this was the most hospitable place I'd ever seen.

I walked back over to rejoin the others and we continued. As we made our way through the cavern, I couldn't get a feel for the design. Usually, a structure was made for a purpose, and that was what made it stand out from a natural landscape. This outpost, if that was even what it really was, didn't seem to have a purpose. More likely that I couldn't figure out what the purpose was. Why build this place? Even if it was truly ancient, as in the dawn of the galaxy ancient, there should've been a purpose for it. Otherwise, why take the time to build it?

T'Chura scouted ahead of us a little and Kaz walked next to me.

"You're pretty quiet," he said.

"I'm just taking it all in," I said and shrugged a little. "It's really not that impressive."

Kaz turned toward me with a frown. "Not impressive?"

"So someone carved out an asteroid, or whatever this chunk of rock was billions of years ago. Does this really look like the place where technological marvels are found? Something that would make whoever found said marvels rich and powerful?" I frowned, thinking of the shipwrecks we'd seen earlier. "Or kill for?"

"I didn't expect this kind of skepticism from you."

"How about objectivity?"

Kaz snorted and was quiet. He looked toward Larry. "I don't understand why he follows you around."

"Me either. I mean, I could say it's my charm or I have a magnetic personality, but I'd really just be feeding my ego."

"I think you just happened to be at the right place at the right time, and for whatever reason he's attached to you."

I nodded. "Probably," I said but thought there was more to it than that. I couldn't pinpoint it to something specific. It was more like a little itch that hadn't quite annoyed me enough to really dig into.

We rounded a rocky mound and found T'Chura standing in the middle of the path. He stared ahead, and once I stood next to him, I could see what had stopped him in his tracks.

A wide cavern opened in front of us. More of the glowing green moss covered the walls but also moved between some kind of structures that were casting dark shadows. They looked like rounded rooftops to buildings, like a small village, but I wasn't sure that was correct. It couldn't be a village. Who would build a village on an asteroid? They had to be something else.

The farther we delved into this place, the more I wanted recon drones to scout the area for us.

"It doesn't look like anyone has been through here," I said.

"They probably went a different way. There were multiple hatches where we entered," Kaz replied.

Larry walked ahead of us and turned back to stare at me. He regarded the environment with a casual disinterest, almost like it was familiar to him. The thought didn't make sense, but I couldn't help it. The question remained as to where Larry was leading us, and why.

We walked toward the area, careful to avoid the moss-covered ground, pausing by the first building to peer in. The only thing inside was a giant dark metallic sphere that had sunk through the floor. It tilted to the side so we could only see part of it. I stepped inside and walked toward the center. The ground sloped inward until it appeared as if it had fused with the sphere.

"I doubt even T'Chura could lift this thing, but what I don't understand is what held it up in the first place," I said.

Kaz and T'Chura joined me. There were no walls, just columns that supported the domed-shaped roof. I looked up and saw that there was a gaping hole in the ceiling.

The comlink to the others clicked because someone had come off mute.

"Nate," Crim said, "look up through that opening in the ceiling. Is there something above it?"

I walked to the edge of the slope and peered up through the hole in the ceiling. Some kind of bronze metallic framework reflected off the lights from my helmet. I frowned.

"That looks like the artifact you found. The shape is similar," Crim said. He paused for a second. "Looks like the dimensions are the same, even though the scale is bigger."

I glanced down at my arm and frowned. The artifact had activated in the presence of those triangular columns at the museum.

"I think we should get out of this building," I said.

We quickly backed away and were out.

"What do you think it is?" Kaz asked.

We kept moving through the area, and I glanced at the rooftops of the different buildings. They all had a similar metallic structure on top. The direction of the buildings seemed to urge us forward, as if there was an implied direction in the architecture.

T'Chura cleared his throat. "This reminds me of an energy matrix. The flow is directed toward the structure on top, and then it's sent this way."

"So, this place is some kind of power core?" I asked.

"I'm not sure about that. Not all energy is meant for accumulating power. This could all be part of a larger network."

I frowned. "Why direct energy anywhere if they weren't going to use it?"

"I'm not sure. We're only seeing part of the puzzle."

We moved through the area, and all the buildings we passed were in the same state as the first one we'd explored. Whatever had happened here seemed to be the same across the area.

We found another path that was a straight shot to another cavern. I frowned. It wasn't a cavern, not really. Someone, the Asherah or whoever, had built this place.

Crim agreed with T'Chura that the design of the rooms was to direct some kind of energy and the destruction we'd seen could have occurred by some kind of overload or backlash. His advice to us was to keep going toward a central chamber.

We quickly moved through the chambers and found that there were others adjacent to the path we were on. I saw Kaz looking at his personal holoscreen.

"I was just looking for other communication signals," he said.

He was looking for a comlink signal from Griff. "Find any?"

He shook his head.

We kept going and found a different kind of chamber. Multiple paths led here, and it reminded me of some kind of central hub. If this place was a power plant, the energy from it would have been routed here, but this wasn't where it ended.

This chamber was more intact than the others. A large central sphere, easily the size of the battlewagon, rested in a huge central cradle that had been designed for it. Surrounding it were mounds of rocks. They looked out of place with everything else. I glanced at the ceiling high above us and saw the jagged edges of some kind of growth. There was still a partial artificial atmosphere here.

We weaved our way around the mounds until we reached the central platform. It had been purposely built, but there was no discernible control panel of any kind. We circled around it, and I saw very faint and intricate patterns akin to the artifact I'd found. There were no levers, buttons, or anything else that could be construed as some kind of interface.

I walked up a ramp to the top of the platform. It felt solid beneath my feet. Little eddies of dust swirled into the air. There were large patches of glowing moss that cast a greenish glow around the dark metallic sphere.

I stood there staring at it for a minute. Half of it was inside the platform I'd just climbed, about thirty feet down to the ground. Larry continued, occasionally pausing to peer at something, only to keep going. I wasn't sure if thinking of him as our canary in the coal mine was smart, but it did set my mind at ease, even if something about this place made me uncomfortable. If Larry suddenly let out a screech with his hackles raised, I'd know we were in danger.

I leaned toward the gigantic sphere and rapped my knuckles against it. A gong sounded from it. The sphere was hollow, and the vibrations seemed to gather in intensity as waves of it traversed the surface of the sphere. The glowing moss shuddered and began sliding down, smearing the side of the sphere like trails of blood. I heard the echo of a high-pitched whine, but it sounded distorted or choppy. I looked down at Larry, and the metallic particles were moving chaotically, as if something had disrupted whatever frequency kept him whole. Then, I felt something cold grip my arm, as if the markings on it had suddenly become rigid. My arm thrust out toward the sphere, slamming it, and another gong sounded even louder and more intense than the first.

The sphere started to slide in the cradle, breaking the hold of whatever had kept it in place. It started to spin, slowly at first, like a leviathan rousing from its slumber. I backed away from it, eyes wide. Colonies of smeared glowing moss moved out of view, revealing a pristine bronze half that had been concealed inside the platform. There was a distant rough spot that screeched as if the sphere was out of balance as part of it rubbed against the cradle.

I heard a choppy moan and saw Larry's distorted form appear as if it was coming apart. He disappeared from view for a second and then reappeared in the same spot. He sounded like he was in pain. I hastened toward him and scooped him up. The distortion field around him kept pushing my arms away, even as I clutched him toward my body. He almost squirmed from my grasp, and I leaped off the platform.

The combat suit controlled my landing with precise muscle augmentation that prevented me from breaking anything, but it wasn't a soft landing. Larry slipped from my grasp, and I stumbled.

"Nate, we've got company!" Kaz shouted.

I spun toward him and saw the mounds of rock beginning to shudder violently. Smaller pieces broke off, and sharp cracks split the rocks as they dissolved.

T'Chura pointed his weapon toward the two nearest moving piles.

"That's our cue to leave!" I said.

We circled around the platform, intending to go back the way we'd come, but all the rock mounds were moving as if something were coming alive inside them.

"Back up. Back up!" Kaz shouted.

I turned and began running in the opposite direction. Kaz was on my heels. I activated both my hand blasters, ready to start shooting at the slightest provocation.

As I came around the platform, one of the mounds rose in front of me. Its mass had reformed into some kind of alien stone Golem that barely held itself together. I raised my weapons and fired on instinct. Twin red plasma bolts belched forth, knocking the stone Golem back. It was strange to see, because the bolts were somewhat absorbed into the mass, but they also breathed new life into it.

The bottom of the Golem was still anchored to the ground, but it lunged toward me with startling speed. I dodged out of the way, firing my weapons at it, but the plasma bolts had no effect. They didn't plunge into it. The thing didn't absorb the blasts that I could see. They simply disappeared.

Kaz pulled me away just as the Golem was lunging toward me again. One of its newly formed legs broke free from the ground.

I heard T'Chura bellow, and he brought his weapon to bear. He aimed at the ground where the Golem was still attached. The ground blew apart and the Golem came undone as if something had cut off the umbilicus that gave life to the thing.

We ran without any sense of where to go, and that was dangerous.

I tried to get my bearings and spotted the large sphere spinning above the platform. I turned toward it.

"I hope you know where you're going," Kaz said.

"So do I."

We ran past a few smaller buildings, and I noticed that there were Golems coming to life just outside of them. Everywhere I looked there was movement, and our options for escape were narrowing.

The Golems moved like heaving masses on all fours, but could rear up, swiping toward us with their long arms.

Larry ran in front of us, suddenly appearing. Whatever had been hurting him had stopped. He was heading toward the opening area on the far side of the chamber. It was a lot closer than the entry point we'd used to come in here.

Several Golems pulled free of the ground before we could shoot out the base and immobilize them. I fired my weapon at them, and it had no effect.

Larry darted ahead, weaving his way through a bunch of Golems who, for some reason, wanted to get us and ignored him. I ran by the remains of a mound and something grabbed at my arm, pulling me off to the side. I tumbled to the ground and more slithering tentacles slid toward me. I shot at the ground, knocking the tentacles back. I fired another blast at the ground near them and the tentacles were thrust to the side.

They lashed side to side as if they were disoriented. Then something grabbed me from behind. Shocking cold swept down my arm, sucking a startled gasp from my mouth. I felt something large and heavy surround me, as if I was being absorbed into it.

T'Chura bellowed as he ran toward us. He couldn't fire his weapon without hurting me, so he came at me full tilt. He thrust the butt of his rifle out and slammed it into the Golem's head. It lurched to the side from the blow, dragging me with it. I thrust one of my arms down and fired a barrage of plasma bolts at its feet.

I slipped forward awkwardly and collapsed to the ground, but when I tried to roll to the side, the Golem grabbed my outstretched hand. I tried firing my hand blaster, but it didn't work.

T'Chura roared as he slammed the butt of his rifle onto the Golem's outstretched arm. The force of the blow made it loosen its grip on me, but not entirely. I saw T'Chura get pushed back by something, shock registering on his face, and the breath caught in my throat.

The Golem turned its amorphous head toward me, and I snatched at the hilt of the weapon Crim had given me. The adaptable handheld multipurpose tool was in its short-staff mode with sonic augmentation. As soon as my hand grasped the hilt, the weapon powered up. I slammed the stick forward and made contact with the thick, malleable rock substance. A sonic blast came from the length of the stick, and the Golem shattered, its particles flying apart.

Rocky debris was strewn across the way and some kind of glowing energy dissipated before my eyes. I stared at my weapon in wide-eyed amazement. T'Chura stared up at me from the ground. I hastened over to him and helped him to his feet.

"Good shot, Nate," he said.

He lifted his rifle and switched configurations. More Golems were lumbering toward us. Kaz fired his hand cannons at them, but the plasma bolts were useless.

"Step aside," T'Chura said, and Kaz hastened out of the way.

He fired his weapon, and the Golems looked as if something had sawed them in half. T'Chura swung his weapon in a controlled arc, back and forth, mowing the Golems down. Parts of them slithered along the ground, racing toward us, and Kaz and I fired our weapons at the ground, throwing them into disarray.

I saw that the gigantic sphere was still spinning. "Shoot it!" I shouted at T'Chura, gesturing toward the sphere.

T'Chura aimed his weapons and unleashed a powerful shot. The sphere shattered into thousands of pieces, and the stone Golems began to collapse into piles. They still moved, as if the energy inside of them hadn't completely dissipated.

We stood there, each of us catching our breath.

"How'd you figure it out?" Kaz asked.

"They didn't start moving until that giant globe thing started spinning."

"How'd it start spinning in the first place?"

I was feeling proud of myself now that we weren't going to die. Then Kaz's question finally registered in my brain, and I winced.

Kaz frowned. "Nate?" His gaze narrowed. "What did you do?"

I could feel both Kaz and T'Chura's gazes weighing down on me. I sighed. "I rapped my knuckles on the globe. It started to vibrate."

T'Chura blinked and then frowned in understanding. Kaz glared at me.

"I didn't know that was going to happen. I was just seeing how solid it was."

"It's a resonance sphere. Harmonics. Doesn't take much to get them going, and they can maintain the output for a long time without stimulation," T'Chura said.

Kaz shook his head. "But I heard a gong like you slammed your fist on it. There was also some kind of weird screeching."

I cleared my throat, feeling foolish, but then drew myself up because why sound uncertain in the face of uncertainty? "The harmonic resonance was hurting Larry somehow. And it made the artifact stenciled on my arm react as well. I really couldn't control it."

Kaz considered this for a few seconds. Then, the venom slipped from his gaze and he nodded. "Well, we managed to learn something else."

I frowned, feeling my eyebrows join together over my nose. "What?"

"Those things…"

"Golems," I said and shrugged. It was as good a name for them as any.

"Well, they were drawn to you."

I glanced at T'Chura, and he nodded. I looked down at my arm. "Not me. This," I said, lifting my right arm. "How the heck could they even tell I had it?"

We were all wearing combat suits and using our own life support. If Kaz was right, those things could somehow see through my suit and sense the artifact marks on my arm.

"At least T'Chura and I can get away," Kaz said wryly.

I lifted my gaze toward his. "I thought we'd have each other's backs."

"To a point, Nate. I'm not willing to die for you."

I hadn't expected that from him or T'Chura. "I'm glad you can be so pragmatic about it."

Kaz tipped his head to the side, looking amused.

"We should probably get out of here. Who knows what else could wake those things up?" I said.

One of my blasters was twisted and broken, so I only had one left, but seeing how it had limited effectiveness, I was inclined to keep using my sonic stick if we encountered any more of those Golems.

CHAPTER 25

We stood at the far end of the chamber with an entire crop of twitchy mounds that were eager for a piece of yours truly. T'Chura insisted that we wait around for the dangerous mounds of alien-specter-infused Golems to stop twitching.

As the minutes went by, I looked at the chamber in its entirety. The mounds were of a lighter color than the dark rock of the asteroid. Reconstituted asteroid was probably a more accurate way to think of it, since the Asherah had built this place.

I lifted my chin toward T'Chura's rifle. "Slugs?"

He frowned. "Oh, you mean the type of ammunition I'm using? Yes, these are high-density darts. I prefer kinetic weapons over energy ones in situations where I'm not sure what I'll be dealing with."

I frowned for a moment. "I understood most of that, but that last shot, the one that made…" I made an explosion gesture with both my hands. "That looked more powerful than the ones you used to cut down the Golems."

T'Chura nodded at me while keeping his eye on the mounds nearby. We were somewhat surrounded, with many of them between us and the entrance we'd used to find this chamber across the way.

"I can tweak the ammo's configuration, adjusting the density and range."

"That was more of an artillery strike."

"Good to have on hand sometimes."

"How many of those shots do you have?"

"Not an endless supply. Considering how many of those beings attacked us, I was concerned with running out of ammo. We could have easily been overwhelmed," T'Chura replied. He gestured toward the stick in my hand. "Crim give you that?"

I nodded. "It can change shape. Adaptable handheld multi-purpose tool." I shook my head. "AHMT."

T'Chura arched a dark eyebrow. "That explains the broken workbench in the armory."

I chuckled. "I was testing it. Crim has a more direct teaching method that I'd like to avoid."

T'Chura laughed.

"I'm unable to reach the others," Kaz said.

I frowned and brought up my omnitool. Kaz was right. Our team comlink session with both the ship and the battlewagon had been cut off.

"I can't establish a link to them either," I said.

"We should get moving," T'Chura said.

"Are we just going to head back?" Kaz asked.

"I'd rather keep going and maybe find a way to circle back. Find a place less active. What do you guys think?" I asked.

They agreed.

Kaz took point, with me in the middle. T'Chura covered our six with the big gun.

There were less suspicious-looking mounds toward the edge of the chamber, but we couldn't avoid them entirely. Kaz went by first. He was tall and lean and could move quickly.

I approached the pair of mounds with my stick held high. I might have looked foolish, but if either one of those things so much as twitched, I was going to bring down the hammer.

"Go on, Nate, I've got you covered," T'Chura said from behind me.

I did a quick shuffle that was not at all unmanly, but I managed to scamper by unscathed.

The outer edges of the chamber were free of anything dangerous, but I still felt as if something was about to pounce.

"Next time, don't touch anything," Kaz said over his shoulder.

"Everyone loves a Monday-morning quarterback," I muttered.

"What?" Kaz asked.

"Nothing, I was just appreciating your sage advice," I replied.

We left the chamber and the Golems of death behind, and not a moment too soon as far as I was concerned. I really couldn't blame anyone else but myself. I'd insisted on going to the museum and using the artifact to unlock the star map that had brought us here. And why did I have to knock on that damn sphere? Everything else was dead around here, but not that. If I kept this up, I was going to be in the fast lane of a long line of explorers who died while searching for the forgotten empire.

"If that place we just came from was a central chamber, then where are we going?" I asked.

"It's probably not central," Kaz said.

"Oh, that's just great."

"Sorry you came?"

I shook my head. "No, but I'm a little out of my depth here."

"We all are," T'Chura said.

I looked up at him.

"Then there's got to be an actual central chamber or something ahead of us. Since this is not the Asherah homeworld, what kind of place is this? Thoughts?" I asked.

They were quiet, each considering it for a minute. We had plenty of time because it was a straight shot toward whatever was ahead of us in the distance.

"My guess," T'Chura said, "is that this is some kind of outpost."

"I agree," Kaz said.

I glanced at the sheer walls of the tunnel we were walking in. The ceiling of it was high above us. Some kind of mineral reflected the lights from my helmet that gave the tunnel a sparkly brilliance, which was broken up by more glowing moss.

"This is probably my own bias, but aren't outposts small things? Just something where a few people kinda keep an eye on things?" I said.

Kaz regarded me with a bit of disdain, and then said, "You need to think bigger."

I rolled my eyes. Over the past few months, I'd stumbled my way through other discussions like this. It wasn't pretty. "Yeah, all right, fine. My planet doesn't have all the great stuff that you guys enjoy… yet." I gave a special emphasis to that last bit. After meeting quite a few different alien species, I was convinced that Humans definitely had a place and a role to play in this galaxy of ours. "Still, even if this is just an outpost—call it whatever you want—what's its purpose? Harmonic resonant spheres that channel some kind of energy and animates Golems? All that makes me think that calling this place an *outpost* is a huge oversimplification of what this place actually is."

They both stared at me, as if they were shocked. Clearly, I'd just robbed both of them of the powers of speech with my massive intellect. *Go me.*

I smiled. "Oops, did I just shatter your big brains?"

A deep chuckle rumbled from T'Chura until it became a full-on laugh. "Impressive, Nate."

I gave him a wave of my hand and a small bow.

Kaz sighed. "Yeah, that wasn't half bad."

I snickered. "I'm very glad you guys have finally seen the light and appreciate me, but let's take it a step further. You're an Asherah. This is the beginning of the galaxy shortly after the big bang, and—"

"I'm sorry, what?"

"The big bang," I replied. "The beginning of all things. How the universe got started."

Kaz arched an eyebrow and smirked with half his mouth.

"Look, Ben can explain it better than I can. That's as much as I know, but that's the theory, right?"

Kaz shook his head. "Not exactly. They predate us for sure, and there are some explorers who believed the Asherah were much older than most thought possible."

"Yeah, and in the ruins, Kierenbot's analysis indicated that they were from shortly after the dawn of creation," I said.

Kaz laughed at me. "It's so funny to hear the Human theory for how the universe came into being."

"You're just mad because someone didn't say, 'And then there was light.' But you know what? We're a very accepting species. We'd love to have you on our team," I said.

T'Chura gave me an amused look and I shrugged. I wasn't about to submit to anyone's professed superiority.

"Okay, back to my thought. We're the Asherah. We're here and we need to build this place. Why? What are we doing here? Why do people build outposts?"

"There are any number of reasons to build an outpost," T'Chura said. "We do it to observe something. Many colony settlements build outposts in a star system to monitor ship traffic going to and from the system."

"Observation," I said and nodded. "That makes sense."

"It does," Kaz agreed. "But this is an old star and has almost destroyed all the evidence of what the Asherah may have been doing here."

Something flashed on his omnitool and he looked at it. A small holoscreen appeared and he frowned.

"What is it?"

Kaz closed the holoscreen and looked at us. "I've been scanning for comlink signals, and I just got a return."

"Oh, was it the ship?" T'Chura asked.

I felt my gaze narrow while Kaz looked uncomfortable. "It's Griff, isn't it? Your Nubis or Nablis, or whatever you call it."

He thinned his lips. "Gabris. Really Nate, if you're going to interact with other species you should really pay more attention to the important terms."

"I'll review it in the next Akacian societal journal I read. So, is it him?"

Kaz stared at me for a second and then nodded.

"Great, so he knows we're coming then," I said.

"No, it's just a sniffer that listens for comlink traffic."

I considered that for a few moments. "Does it give us his location?"

Kaz lifted his chin toward the end of the long corridor.

"Okay, let's go see what Kaz's Gabris has in store for us," I said and quickened my pace.

We covered the rest of the distance in silence, and as we got closer to the end we heard the sounds of a fight going on.

I glanced at Kaz. "Let's survey what's going on. Don't—" Kaz started running, "go running ahead," I finished.

I shared a look with T'Chura and we both hastened to catch up with Kaz.

Kaz was a fast runner. I don't know if it was the combat suit or just his species in general, but it took me a while to catch up, even with my combat suit augmenting my movements. I was sure that T'Chura could have covered the distance much quicker, but he wouldn't leave me behind. T'Chura was good people. I liked him.

Kaz stopped at the entrance to a vast chamber much bigger than the one we'd come from. There were several large globes on elevated platforms in the room, all of which were in line with a long corridor similar to the one we'd just traversed. Several of the globes were spinning, and there were stone Golems marching toward the center of the chamber. Bright flashes of light came from that area, and I spotted several hammerhead battlebots leaping into the air and using suit thrusters to hover while they shot their weapons at the Golems.

These Golems moved differently than the ones we'd just encountered. They had smaller arms and more of them. Wings ran down their backs like long shields, similar to a cockroach, and they were almost the size of T'Chura.

The battlebots had established a perimeter around Griff Tarken, whose white armor reflected the light like a beacon in the darkness. It also made him a target. The battlebots used kinetic weapons, which were more effective against the stone roaches.

"They're being pushed back," Kaz said. "We've got to help them."

"If we sneak up, we can take out those spinning globes. That should stop them," I replied.

A huge Golem emerged behind Griff and lunged for him. Battlebots moved in to defend him, but the Golem swept them aside with a giant paw. I could only see half of its body as it pulled itself out of the platform where Griff had been taking his stand.

Kaz growled a battle cry and leaped into the air, his suit jets bursting. I called out to him, but he ignored me.

I swore, and T'Chura looked at me. "Stick to the plan," he said.

I nodded and we ran forward, closing the distance to one of the spinning globes. The Golems were already concentrated near Griff and his battlebot platoon, so we were able to get into position unnoticed.

"Nate," T'Chura said quietly, "use your hand cannon to weaken the platform."

I glanced at the metallic platform doubtfully. "It's not strong enough for that."

"Harmonic resonance. We just need to disrupt it and the field should come apart," T'Chura said.

I nodded and together we aimed our weapons. I lined up the target on my HUD and shot a burst of plasma bolts at maximum power output, while T'Chura shot the globe with smaller high-density darts.

The sphere wobbled at the impact, and T'Chura fired his weapon in controlled bursts. I copied his firing method with my hand cannons, shooting toward the rim of the platform. The sphere shuddered violently, and multiple ripples darted across the surface as it pushed against the edges of the invisible forces that held it in place, then slowly lumbered across the precipice to the point of no return, slamming into the ground. Its spin caused it to jerk to the side, crushing the Golems nearby as it ping-ponged off the nearest building and rolled away.

"Come on," T'Chura said, and we started moving toward the next target.

"Why don't we try shooting the others from here?"

"The angle is off. We'd just hit the top, and that's not going to finish the job."

He was right. There was a dip in the chamber, which put the platforms up higher from our location.

T'Chura was more of a soldier than I would ever be, so I took my direction from him. He picked a place that gave us a clear vantage point to the platform and sphere. We were ground level with a straight shot between two rows of the open-air buildings.

We made quick work of the giant sphere, but this time it actually began rolling toward us. It bounced and jostled to the side, and each time it did we heard a gong sound. There were pits and holes in the sphere, exposing the hollow inside of it as it rolled past us.

We emerged from cover and saw a few dozen Golems racing toward us. T'Chura grabbed me and leaped to the rooftop of the nearest building. We landed and he told me to use my suit jets. Any chance to fly like Iron Man was fine with me.

The Golems followed us like a ravenous horde, throwing themselves over obstacles and racing across rooftops.

"Go on ahead. I'll keep them busy," I said.

"No, Nate, wait!"

I didn't wait. I swung to the side, flying back toward our pursuers. They banked to the side like a flock of birds avoiding a predator, except they were the hunters, and they were flocking right toward me.

I glanced back at T'Chura, who didn't waste any time moving toward the third remaining sphere.

One of the limitations of flying like Iron Man on a low-gravity asteroid was that it was much too easy to fly way too fast. I had to adjust my speed so I didn't overshoot where I wanted to go.

The artifact tattoo on my arm began to cool off. It might have been doing it before, but I hadn't noticed. I flew up higher and saw that several of the roach Golems were using their wings to fly after me. My eyes stretched wide as Golem after Golem leaped into the air.

All my thoughts about flying safely and keeping my speed low were thrown right out the airlock. I hit the jets and zipped downward, banking hard. I saw battlebots staring up at me, along with Griff Tarken, as if they couldn't quite figure out what I was doing. At least I wasn't alone on that front. I thought I'd distract the Golems so T'Chura had time to destroy the last sphere. I spun in the air and watched as the sphere exploded. Twisting back around, I saw the roach Golems tumble out of the air as the energy that gave them life was cut off.

A wave of relief swept over me, and I flew toward T'Chura. He was making his way to the central platform. I saw that Kaz had made it there and was speaking to Griff Tarken.

With so many battlebots still standing, I decided to arrive at the platform at the same time T'Chura did. Safety in numbers. I landed on the platform and Griff Tarken scowled at me.

"Just what the hell do you think you're doing!" Griff said.

I blinked, utterly shocked by the outburst. It took me a few moments to recover. "We just saved your ass is what I was doing."

"Saving me? Is that what you call it?"

"They were about to overrun your position."

Griff shook his head, and his clear faceplate allowed me to see the disgust he felt. He turned toward Kaz. "This is who leads?"

"We thought you were about to get killed," Kaz said.

"Then I would've died. That's the extent to which I'm dedicated to finding the Asherah."

"Overzealous much?" I asked, and he turned toward me. "You might like to know that the battlebots you had guarding your ship have all been destroyed."

"What! You destroyed my ship!"

Dozens of hammerhead battlebots aimed their weapons at us. The movement was so sudden and precise that if I hadn't been so startled by it, I would've been impressed.

"Do you only register every other word I say?" I asked, snapping my fingers to get his attention. "I said that the bots you had guarding your ship have been destroyed, *not* that we destroyed your ship or even the bots you had guarding your damn ship."

Griff blinked and turned toward Kaz, considering.

"It's true. We found it like that," Kaz replied.

The battlebots were still pointing their weapons at us, and I didn't like it. "I didn't come here to fight with you. Now, order them to lower their weapons, or my big friend isn't going to take too kindly to that," I said, lifting my chin toward T'Chura.

He had a fierce protective instinct that was particular to his species. It was one of the reasons they were often contracted to protect newly established colonies. They were more than mercenaries because of their code of honor.

Griff turned toward T'Chura and then ordered the bots to lower their weapons. He looked at Kaz. "How the Nablis has fallen."

Kaz actually looked ashamed, and that made me angrier than anything else right then.

"What the hell is the matter with you! Ever since we saw your ship and that destruction of the bots, he's been concerned about you, and all you've got to give in return is judgement and derision?" I said. Griff scowled at me. "I know you were his mentor, but that doesn't give you the right to be such a dick."

Griff blinked in confusion, and I knew something had been lost in translation. He considered it, and some of what I'd said made him smooth his features and calm down. He looked at Kaz. "I appreciate your assistance."

Kaz inclined his head.

Griff turned toward me. "I knew you'd come here eventually." I frowned and he continued. "Who do you think monitors Asherah artifacts in every quadrant?"

"The tracer we detected. That was you."

"And I still beat you here anyway. If this was a race, you just lost."

"I'm here, aren't I?"

"Why did you come here? What were you hoping to find?"

Griff's questions were earnest; otherwise, I might've given him a snarky reply. Dozens of armed robots aside, I still wanted to.

"The map led us here," I said. Griff waited for me to continue. "I hoped it was the Asherah homeworld."

Griff laughed. It was mostly friendly but a bit offbeat. I wondered if all the years searching for the Asherah had taken a toll on his sanity. I'd seen it before with treasure hunters back home.

"Maybe you're not as foolish as I thought because I hoped for the same thing."

"How did you find this place?"

Griff regarded me for a few seconds. "Did you think you found the only artifact in those ruins?"

I blinked and almost admitted to finding an artifact. "Still think I stole it from you?"

Griff snorted and dismissed my question. "I found something better, or rather it found us." He turned toward Kaz. "Not everyone abandons their Gabris."

"My term was up," Kaz replied coolly.

Griff exhaled through his teeth. "That is true. Just when the predators were closing in."

"You had me committing fraudulent acts to cover up your own lies."

Griff narrowed his gaze. "You wouldn't have been— Doesn't matter now." He looked at me. "Nate, right?"

"Only to my friends."

Griff chuckled. "That's it right there. That's why Kaz follows you. He reminds you of me, doesn't he?"

I glanced at Kaz, and he wouldn't look anywhere near me.

"Tell me, Nate, have you figured out what the Asherah were doing here?"

"You want me to do all the work?" I asked.

Griff waved over one of the robots. Then he whispered something to it that didn't make any sense to me, and the robot walked away. It left the platform with two more following after it. They went farther into the chamber.

"I'd be curious to hear what a Human might make of this place," Griff said. "We have some time to kill, and you haven't given me any reason to keep this conversation going."

Veiled threats were something I understood quite well. They came in many different shapes and sizes, but they always promised violence. We were outnumbered, but I hadn't come here to fight Griff Tarken, so talking was better than fighting right now.

"I'm not sure. We thought it might've been some kind of outpost, but given these chambers, I don't think that's correct at all. These things," I said, gesturing lazily behind us, "channel or focus some kind of energy. I don't know why, but whenever those spheres are activated, those damn Golems come to life and attack us."

"Strange by every sense of the word."

"So you don't know what they are either?"

Griff glanced at Kaz, considering, and then turned back to me. "Not exactly. I think they're a byproduct of the work that was being done here."

I considered that. "You think this place was some kind of research center?"

Griff smiled and gave me an approving nod. "The Asherah struggled to understand the universe. It's one of the reasons they're so fascinating, not just to me, but for all species who've been lucky enough to study them."

"I've been told that not a lot of people are looking for them anymore," I said.

"Short-sighted bureaucrats have limited interest in expanding our understanding of the universe. They believe we've achieved the pinnacle and that the advancements we continue to make are better taken in small developmental steps. But it's all a lie," Griff said.

I waited for him to continue, but he turned away from me and stepped toward the edge of the platform. I moved over to the side so I could see what he was looking at. The battlebots nearby didn't so much as twitch.

Someone stood just outside another large corridor.

"Is that Osira?" Kaz asked.

"You didn't think I left her behind?" Griff said.

I looked at Kaz, eyebrows raised.

"Osira Daklan is his wife," Kaz said.

"My most loyal companion, and every bit the hunter I am," Griff said.

I saw some kind of flash nearby and Larry appeared on a

rooftop. His head was craned toward Osira, as if he was assessing the danger she posed. The particles along his back expanded in ripples that somewhat distorted his body.

I found Griff staring at me with a thoughtful frown.

The battlebots spun around facing an area near Osira.

"Something's wrong," T'Chura said.

"No, something is right," Griff said and clapped his hands excitedly.

I watched Osira turn to the side, looking alarmed. I couldn't see what she did, but I couldn't imagine what was right about any of this.

A silver flickering light shot out from the side, casting a strobing effect in the surrounding area. It seemed to pull in the light and darken the area around it. The battlebots, along with Osira, fired their weapons at something just beyond our view.

Griff ordered his bots to attack. They leaped off the platform and ran toward her. Griff followed, along with his personal guards. I glanced at Kaz and T'Chura for a few seconds before following Griff.

Larry, from atop the roof he was perched on, made a jumping movement but disappeared as if he'd stepped through an invisible portal and then reappeared on the ground. He looked up at me, his feline mouth open and tense, like he was making some kind of sound, but it wasn't anything I could hear.

Somehow realizing that I couldn't understand what he wanted, he darted toward me, occupying a space in front of me, then Kaz, and even T'Chura.

"I see it!" T'Chura said. "It's blurry, but I see it."

"What's he doing?" Kaz asked.

Larry phased in front of me, then to the side, and then behind us. I turned toward him, and he even went farther down the path between buildings.

"Something's ahead. The bots have engaged more Golems, maybe," T'Chura said.

Kaz continued forward, but I slowed down. I thought Larry was trying to get us to follow him.

I heard Griff bellow as he fired his rifle at the strobing light out of view.

Then I saw it, and it stopped me right in my tracks, my mouth agape as I tried to make sense of what it was. It wasn't more stone Golems; it was something else—something large and lumbering, and the battlebots closest to it had been torn apart.

A pulsating dark sphere with a silvery nimbus seemed to bend things around it, as if drawing everything in like a black hole. It was ten feet wide, surrounded by a storm of loose rock and debris that flew around it in a swirling mass of destruction. Then another one emerged from a smaller chamber to our right. We had another fight on our hands, and as I watched the battlebots getting torn apart, I didn't think it was a fight we could survive.

CHAPTER 26

T'Chura fired his weapon at the black sphere of death. Parts of the sphere shifted, as if moving around the high-velocity darts blazing a path toward it.

I fired a plasma bolt at it, and the floating sphere barely registered that molten plasma had come into contact with it. The plasma bolt just sort of fizzled out into a shower of tiny particles raining toward the ground, ultimately disappearing before they hit.

I'd seen my share of weird ever since Kaz plucked me off Earth, and this was the new reigning champion. The high heat of the molten plasma couldn't stop these things, and T'Chura's powerful darts couldn't even connect with it.

The sphere lumbered toward the wide-open path, bending the buildings it went by, slowly pulling them apart.

I looked ahead and saw the first sphere had blocked Griff and his battlebots from reaching Osira. The sphere was moving away from us, herding Osira down a path.

Griff tried to circle around the sphere, and bright blue arcs of lightning raced all around it, striking the walls, bots, and anything nearby. Kaz had caught up to him and pulled him back, even as the lightning scorched a nearby bot.

"You can't reach her," Kaz shouted.

Griff tried to jerk his arm free from Kaz's grip. "I need to go with her. You don't understand. Take your hands off me!"

Kaz heaved Griff back, dragging him away from the sphere. The sphere seemed to elongate, becoming a spike with a rounded top.

Bright light lit up the corridor where Osira had fled.

T'Chura was at my side, ushering me away from the second spike.

"Kaz is going to get himself killed. We need to get out of here," I said.

T'Chura's gaze darted to the spike, then to Kaz and Griff as they struggled against each other while the battlebots still tried to fight the spikes. They'd changed their tactics a few times, but nothing stopped the spikes from slowly moving forward.

The bright blue flashing light from farther down the corridor abruptly stopped, plunging it into darkness, and Griff howled.

I raced toward them and grabbed Griff. "Hey! Look at me! Do you want to die here? We're leaving. Together, we've got a chance, but we're not going to die for you."

I looked at Kaz, including him, and he gave me a grudging nod.

Griff stared at me as if he didn't recognize me.

I flung my arm toward the spike. The one that had forced Osira down the corridor was coming back toward us.

"These things are going to kill us! Now, knock it off," I said and looked at Kaz. "Let him go."

Kaz hesitated for a few seconds and then released Griff.

Griff sank to the ground, gasping. "You don't understand. I was supposed to go with her."

The battle bots circled around us but didn't engage the two spikes. Even they had determined that the fight was hopeless.

I looked at Kaz, who seemed conflicted. Common sense was at war with a much older obligation within him. I extended my hand toward Griff, and he stared up at me. "You can find her, but that won't happen if you stay here."

Griff blinked a few times and then grabbed my hand, and I hauled him to his feet.

The nearest sphere quivered in the air as it drew nearer to us. Then it stretched toward us, elongating to form a spike before it disappeared.

"Move!" I shouted and started running.

T'Chura was at my side, and I had no idea if Kaz or Griff followed.

I heard the spike reappear behind us and turned toward it. Kaz and Griff had just barely gotten clear. Some of the battlebots had made it too.

I turned around and kept running.

"Nate, use the flight system," T'Chura said, and I heard him engage his.

I glanced up and saw Kaz and Griff flying overhead, several battlebots with them.

I peered ahead and spotted Larry. He appeared frozen in place, and I could see his form resolve to something more solid. Gritting my teeth, I scooped him up and engaged my suit jets.

As I flew into the air, I saw the two spikes phase in and out as they teleported short distances in a vain attempt to follow us. They were restricted to the ground, and I wasn't about to question that particular gift horse. They shifted on the ground, changing from a sphere to a spike form.

For the moment we'd escaped the Shifter Spikes, but we couldn't stop them, and they weren't going to give up.

CHAPTER 27

The one thing I could say about my experiences of the next few months was that just when I thought I had a basis for understanding the world I'd been pulled into, something happened to turn all that upside down. I didn't pretend to understand the laws of physics beyond some of the more obvious things—mass and gravity go together, and that light speed was constant but there were variables that could slow it down.

We quickly flew out of the central chamber of the research station and picked the corridor we'd used to find this place. Griff had put up a brief argument about knowing a different way, but I ignored him. Kaz must have spoken to him on a private channel because Griff relented.

T'Chura flew on point, with the rest of us following him. Griff's remaining battlebots followed. There were significantly fewer of them, and I wondered how many robots Griff had at his disposal.

I watched the ground as we flew, searching for any sign of

stone Golems or even those strange Shifter Spikes. Griff had been trying to activate the devices the Asherah had left behind. He had to know more about this place, and I made it a point to take that matter up with him later. My gut instinct insisted that this place had a purpose, but even after witnessing some of it, I still had no idea what that could be. Osira had disappeared, and Griff didn't believe she'd been killed. His reaction indicated that she'd been teleported somewhere.

A comlink alert appeared on my HUD.

"Captain," Kierenbot said, "I'm relieved to finally be able to make contact with you."

"Yeah, Kierenbot, there's something here that interferes with comms."

"Indeed, I wonder what that could be. Subspace comms occurs—"

"Focus, Kierenbot," I said, stopping a lengthy explanation about technology I could use but didn't understand how it worked.

"Uh, yes, Captain. Sorry about that," he said. "Aside from re-establishing contact, there have been new developments. Griff Tarken's ship is under attack."

"Is it the Golems?"

"Golems," he repeated. "Ah yes, a mysteriously animated object. An apt description for them. A group of them arrived a short while ago and are swarming over the hull. They're trying to get inside the ship for some reason."

"Is the *Spacehog* in danger?"

"Negative, Captain, I'm far enough away that they can't reach the ship, and I don't think they're aware of the ship in any case."

"Good, maintain your location. We're on our way to you."

"Acknowledged, Captain," Kierenbot said and severed the comlink.

I quickly informed the others about the attack on Griff's ship. "What do you have on your ship that they want?"

"I'm not exactly sure," Griff replied.

"Really," I said, becoming a little annoyed. "Any artifacts that they might be drawn to?"

"Some, but none that are active. It's just reference materials."

I still didn't believe him, but belaboring the point wasn't going to help.

"Can't your ship do something to help?" Griff asked.

"I'm no weapons expert, but I'm thinking that firing our weapons at your ship would also damage the hull."

"Are they attacking your ship?"

"Not yet."

"They might have limited range."

We arrived at the battlewagon to find that it, too, was under siege. Hordes of Golems scrambled to reach it. The battlewagon's weapons unleashed a powerful barrage of kinetic attacks that stalled the Golems' push, but they still inched forward.

"There you are," Crim said. "We were about to leave you behind."

The battlewagon launched into the air.

"Nice to see you, too. We've got company with us," I replied.

The battlewagon spun around in the air and began flying away from us. The rear hatch began to open.

I glanced at the ground where the horde of Golems had been left behind, but then several of *them* launched into the air. At first I thought they were merely jumping up in a desperate attempt to reach the ship. Gravity was low on the asteroid, and they could certainly jump high. We were beyond any artificial atmosphere maintained by the facility, so if there were any winged Golems, they wouldn't be able to do much but flap their wings awkwardly and not get very far. That was why it was still surprising to see the Golems leaping into the air in an attempt to reach us. Without any means of propulsion I could see, they rose into the air but were unable to break free of the asteroid's gravity.

Crim maintained a constant velocity as we flew toward the open hatch. The combat suit computers took control of my flight system and guided me toward the opening. I could override the control, but my goal was to get aboard the safety of the battlewagon, not to collide with it.

T'Chura closed the hatch once we were aboard. There wasn't room for Griff's battlebots, and they clung to the hull as Crim increased our velocity. The battlewagon could fly much faster than our individual flight systems. We were limited by size and capacity.

The inside of the battlewagon wasn't spacious to begin with, and we all had to cozy up. Lanaya joined Ben on his bench at the copilot's seat. I didn't think he minded being in close proximity to the beautiful young woman.

We were all quiet for a few moments as we processed the recent events in our own ways.

Griff turned toward me. "Captain," he said, formally, "if it's not too much trouble, I'd appreciate your assistance with returning to my ship."

I still couldn't make up my mind about Griff. Sometimes I didn't like him at all, and others I couldn't help but have a grudging respect. Maybe he reminded me a little bit of Flynn. But like Griff or not, at odds or not, his wife was missing. There were limits to my own single-minded tendencies when it came to finding something like a lost civilization—call it compassion or whatever soft-hearted sympathy made me somewhat empathetic to Griff's predicament. I was raised in a household where my parents loved each other. I didn't want to imagine their reaction if one of them was in danger, and I didn't want to be the man who stood by and did nothing when I could've helped. It didn't matter that Griff had been a giant pain in my ass and had tried to stop me on more than one occasion. I wasn't going to leave him stranded on some rock while his wife, or whatever the Akacian equivalent was for a life partner, was in danger.

"Why don't we get there and assess the damage, then take it from there," I replied.

Griff glanced at Kaz for a second and they regarded one another, then he looked at me. "Very well."

It didn't take us long to make it back to the ship, lending credence to the old adage that it was quicker to return home than it was to reach one's destination.

Crim flew us toward a location about halfway between the *Spacehog* and Griff's ship. It was crawling with Golems. I couldn't tell whether they had breached the hull yet, but they were doing their utmost.

I looked at Griff. "I don't see how you can return to your ship."

Griff stared at the holoscreen. "I'm not going to leave it behind."

"Well, how are you going to get back aboard? You only have about a dozen bots left. That's not enough to retake the ship."

Griff lowered his chin, looking determined. "This isn't your problem," he said, standing.

"Wait," Kaz said.

Griff looked at him.

"Nate's right, you're not going to retake the ship like this. You know it."

Griff clenched his jaw for a second. "I can't track where Osira went without my equipment on that ship."

"Okay, but a suicide run isn't going to help her," I said.

"Actually, I've got a plan," Kaz said and looked at me. "But it's going to require the *Spacehog*."

Kaz rarely used the name I'd given the ship. He found it distasteful. Perhaps using it was his way of showing some kind of compromise or deference.

I sighed and looked at Griff. "If I allow you onto my ship, I can't have your battlebots tearing up the place. They're to be shut down."

"Done."

I held up my finger. "I wasn't finished."

He sighed. "Go on."

"Control of the bots will be temporarily passed to me."

"So you can use them to double-cross me as soon as we're aboard? I don't think so."

I gestured toward the rear hatch. "You're welcome to take your chances, but there's no way I'm allowing armed battlebots on my ship."

"Nate, one second," Kaz said. I shifted my gaze toward him. "We could shut them down and ensure they remain that way."

"How?" I asked.

Kaz looked at Griff. "Give him temporary access to them that has a specific expiration. It's the best option you're going to get."

Griff's eyes narrowed and then he looked at me. "I have very little choice. I accept your terms, Captain Briggs."

CHAPTER 28

I looked at Kaz. "What's the plan?"

"Get the ship away from the dock and see what happens with the Golems," Kaz replied.

I nodded.

Kaz opened a holoscreen and initiated a data connection to the ship's systems. He looked at Griff. "I need access."

Griff brought up his own holoscreen and then made a passing motion to Kaz. "Use this."

A new sub window appeared on Kaz's holoscreen, and he navigated the interface for a minute. "Initiating maneuvering thrusters now."

I looked at a video feed that showed Griff's ship. It didn't look like anything was happening, but then I saw that the kickers had pushed the ship away from the dock. Several Golems tried to jump the distance, but their trajectory was off, and they were eventually pulled back toward the large asteroid.

Once the ship was far enough away, I ordered Crim to take us in for a closer look.

The battlewagon wasn't a long-range ship, but it could handle this type of reconnaissance work with ease.

"Keep the weapons systems active," I said.

Crim chuckled. "As if I'd take them offline."

We flew toward Griff's ship, and the closer we got, the more I was convinced that significant damage had been done.

I looked at Kaz. "Are you able to get a damage report?"

He nodded and put it up on his holoscreen.

Griff leaned toward it and began reading. A few moments later he scowled.

I stopped reading after I saw the alert for the ship's main engines. They only had partial maneuvering thrusters available.

I blew out a long breath and glanced at Griff.

"It can be repaired," Griff said.

I nodded, but the fact of the matter was that the ship wasn't going anywhere anytime soon.

"Can you bring us around to the portside airlock?" Griff asked.

Crim flew the battlewagon around the hull. The Golems were still active, crawling over the ship.

Ben cleared his throat. "I think we can start picking them off. We don't need to destroy them, just knock them off the hull."

I peered at the holoscreen for a few seconds and looked at Kaz. "Can you disable the artificial gravity on the ship?"

Kaz looked at Griff.

"I can do it," Griff said.

A few seconds later he gave me a nod.

"All right, Ben. Show us what you can do," I said.

Ben had the combat systems interface up and selected one of the options. Then he began targeting Golems and picking them off, one by one. A quick burst from the mag cannon sent the Golems cartwheeling off the hull.

I chuckled at the sight, and the others looked at me. I shrugged a shoulder. "They look funny."

Griff frowned and looked at Kaz.

"He finds humor in a lot of situations."

"Learn to enjoy the moment when you can. It wasn't that long ago we were running from those things," I said.

Ben was able to quickly clear the hull. Kaz had put the ship on a trajectory that increased the distance from the asteroid, and the Golems eventually stopped moving.

"I didn't think they'd remain active for this long," Kaz said.

I had no idea what animated the Golems but didn't want to get distracted by that right now.

I looked at Griff. "How do you want to proceed?"

Griff considered it for a few moments. "Leave my ship here and use yours to rescue Osira."

"How do you know where she is?" I asked.

"I have a good idea. It's why we came here in the first place."

"Where is she?"

"The Asherah homeworld."

I frowned and glanced at Kaz for a second before settling back on Griff. "You know this for sure?"

Griff regarded me for a few seconds. "Not yet. I'll need your help for that, but first I need to retrieve a few things from my ship."

He ordered the battlebots to the ship. They'd hitched a ride on the hull of the battlewagon, and they used their flight systems to cover the short distance to the ship. While they retrieved the equipment that Griff insisted was essential for finding Osira, Kierenbot flew the *Spacehog* to our location.

"Space is vast" was the biggest understatement I'd ever heard, but seeing the hull of the *Spacehog* reach our location set my mind at ease. The ship had become home, our refuge in the vastness of space.

We didn't wait for Griff's robots to return to the battlewagon. Crim flew us to the main hangar bay on the *Spacehog* and we climbed out of the cramped quarters.

I watched T'Chura step off the loading ramp onto the hangar bay, stretch his arms overhead, and exhale a long, satisfying breath. He noticed me watching him.

"Maybe we need to upgrade so you're not quite so cramped in there," I said.

"It's fine for temporary voyages," T'Chura replied.

Griff's battlebots flew through the atmospheric shield and landed on the hangar bay floor. They carried a few storage crates with them. It impressed me that they landed in a perfect line, as if they were showing off. Since I'd learned to fly like Iron Man, I knew that doing that was much harder than it appeared.

Griff looked at me. "Where should I put them?"

It took me a few seconds to realize that he meant the battlebots. They were each as tall as T'Chura. I gestured toward the far side of the hangar bay.

"Line them up over there," I said.

Griff gestured toward the side of the hangar bay, and the battlebots marched over. The dull thump of their heavy footfalls sounded on the floor until they were lined up and had taken a parade-rest pose. Then they went into standby.

Griff made a passing gesture to me, and I had temporary control of the battlebots.

The hangar bay doors closed, sealing us off from our view of space.

We gathered near the entrance to the ship where T'Chura blocked entry.

Griff turned toward me, eyes narrowed in suspicion. "What's going on here?"

"I think we need to talk," I said.

"I've done as you asked."

"I realize that, but before we go any farther, you need to tell me a few things."

Griff glanced at Kaz, then stared at me for a long moment. "What do you want to know?"

"I want to know more about that base. Your reaction to Osira's disappearance wasn't about being concerned for her. No, you were upset that you didn't get to go as well. What happened back there?"

Griff blinked and glanced at the others. They all waited for his reply.

He regarded me for a few seconds. "You're young. You haven't spent a lifetime pursuing the greatest mystery of *any* time. You want to know about that base, then I'll tell you. It's an Asherah research base."

"What were they researching?"

"The universe."

I sighed, unimpressed. When people wanted to distract you from important questions, they tended to use high-concept, lofty replies. "That might work for gullible people, but you're going to have to do better than that."

Griff bobbed his head once in acknowledgement. "The Asherah were experimenting with many different things, but they were most concerned with traveling vast distances."

I frowned. "I thought they could already travel vast distances. The galaxy is pretty damn vast. What else were they after?"

"A way to increase their understanding of the universe. They were a lost species."

"How were they lost?"

"That's the real question—the piece that holds everything we've learned about them together. You see, they weren't from our galaxy."

I blinked, feeling my eyebrows race up my forehead as I considered that for a few moments. Then I sighed. "I'm not beyond the occasional stretch of the imagination, but this is too much. Where were they from then?"

Griff gestured toward the hangar bay doors. "Somewhere beyond our galaxy."

He didn't know. He'd become so wrapped up in seeking the Asherah that he was selectively picking theories and believing they were facts. Serena had said something similar about me, so did that make me the pot calling the kettle black?

I pushed those thoughts from my mind and decided to see just how far this rabbit hole went.

"But the relics. They were dated to when the galaxy was first formed."

Griff nodded, looking excited. "Yes, that's been proven multiple times wherever they were found, but there are records that indicate something about an emergence. I'll show you."

Kierenbot entered the hangar and strode toward us, but before he reached us, his head jerked toward the battlebots lined up at the far wall. His red orb flashed in recognition and his head cocked a little to the side. Then he looked at me, and I nodded for him to join us.

"Captain," Kierenbot said, "there is some kind of activity from the neighboring ship."

I frowned and looked at Griff.

"That's my repair drones. I've set them to the task of restoring full flight capabilities to the ship," Griff said.

"Will that work? I thought the main engines had sustained heavy damage."

"I'm well aware of the damage to my ship, *Captain*," he said in a reply that sounded more like an admonishment.

He activated his personal holoscreen and several different holoscreens appeared. "The search for the Asherah origins has been ongoing for thousands of years. Different species have stumbled onto their ruins while exploring the galaxy. At some point, someone recognized that the different remnant civilizations were similar somehow."

"What about their language?" I asked.

"There are translations, but it's difficult to trust them."

I frowned. I'd been to a few space stations filled with a large variety of spacefaring species. They were all able to communicate on a basic level. "Why not?"

"I don't know that the Asherah actually spoke. They had different ways of communicating, but all the findings share a similarity. They sought to travel incredible distances and they were trying to increase their understanding of the universe."

I shook my head. "You mentioned that before, but I don't know what you mean."

"He's not the only one," Crim said, chiming in before Griff could reply.

I was glad to have his support. Crim was one of the smartest beings I'd ever met. At least my confusion was in good company.

"I thought we were going to find the Asherah homeworld here," I said.

Griff nodded a little. "I...thought so as well, but if we didn't, I knew we'd find something to continue our search." He eyed me for a few seconds.

"I did find an artifact on the planet. You know I did. I used it to find a way here."

Griff regarded me for a few moments. "Indeed. However, I believe you found more than an artifact." He paused for a moment. "Tell me, has there been another being following you around?"

He meant Larry. The others looked at me, giving it away, so there was no point denying it. "Yes, it first appeared as strange energy occurrences on our internal sensors."

Griff nodded. "Extreme cold?"

My eyes widened a little. "Yes."

"It did for us as well," he said with a nod.

"You've seen it? Where is yours? Is he here now?"

Griff gave a frustrated shake of his head. "No, it appeared for Osira."

"Well, Larry looks a lot like the creatures I encountered on that world where we first met, but he's…"

"Somewhat amorphous?" Griff asked.

I nodded. "It seems like he has trouble holding his form sometimes, and he gets distracted. It's almost like…" I glanced at the others for a second. "It's like he occupies two planes of existence. He's here but he's also somewhere else."

I half-expected Griff to ridicule me for that, but he didn't. Instead, he clapped his hands excitedly.

"That's it! That's exactly it. Is it here now?"

I nodded and gestured toward the battlewagon. Larry sat perched on top, watching us intently.

"I can't see him," Griff said and turned to the others. "Can all of you see it?"

"Him," I corrected.

Griff shook his head. "It's not alive, not in the sense of you or I, for that matter."

"What is he then?" I asked.

Larry had shown all the hallmarks of being alive as far as I was concerned. He'd shown concern and fear, and he'd also interacted with his environment in a meaningful way. I was sure there were more extensive tests, but I was of the mind that if something walked and quacked like a duck, then it was a duck.

"It's the key to finding the Asherah homeworld."

"That's it?" Crim asked.

Griff frowned.

"There has to be more to it than that," I said.

"Of course. I was keeping the discussion on a high level so it wouldn't take as much time," Griff replied.

"Okay, well then indulge us a little because there is a lot I don't understand. Larry is just one of those things."

Griff considered it for a few moments. "I think beings like… Larry only appear with the discovery of certain artifacts. Think of them as markers."

"So they wanted to be found?"

Griff nodded.

"By whom?"

He smiled. "Another good question that has troubled anyone who's searched for them. I personally believe it was just for the Asherah. Why else make them so complicated?"

I glanced at the others and noticed Ben looking as if he had something to say.

"Go on, Ben. If you've got some kind of insight, this is the time to share it."

He cleared his throat. "I was just thinking that they might not have made the markers complicated to conceal it from someone else but because it's a reflection of how they viewed the world around them."

I blinked, more than once.

Crim gave him an approving nod.

"I like that," I said, gesturing toward Ben, and he smiled sheepishly. "That's good."

"A very astute observation," Griff said.

"Okay, so the Asherah made these markers," I said. "Why would they do that? You leave markers so you can find your way back to something. That doesn't answer why they're so scattered to begin with. I mean, if they traveled to different places across the galaxy, wouldn't they know how they got there?"

The moment I raised the question, I made a mental leap to the answer. My eyes widened and I looked at Griff. "They didn't know."

He nodded enthusiastically. "That's what I think. They were experimenting with some kind of instantaneous travel system that they couldn't quite predict."

"That's absurd," Crim groused. "The loss of life pursuing this would be unimaginable. That's even before they developed better methods of testing to minimize their losses."

I looked at Crim and then at Griff. "He's got a good point. There has to be more to it, especially given what we encountered on that asteroid."

"Of course there's more to the Asherah than instantaneous travel. That's just one explanation for why they appear in so many different parts of the galaxy."

"So, we're ruling out a galaxy-spanning empire?" I asked. I could hear the echoes of the Imperial March in my head.

"That was ruled out a long time ago," Griff said and frowned. "Oh, I see now. You were not being serious."

I shrugged. "So the Asherah had experiments, but how do you explain the Golems and that Shifter Spike?"

Griff frowned. "Golems? Spikes?"

I shook my head. "You know, those stone things that were held together by some kind of force, similar to Larry. And the Shifter Spike. Starts as a sphere until it shifts from place to place. It's that thing we couldn't stop. You know, the thing that herded Osira into that other machine."

Griff scowled. "I'm well aware."

"I'm glad you're aware. If you know something about those things, you should tell us. Start with the Shifter Spike."

"Primitive naming conventions aside, I don't have a good explanation for it," Griff replied.

I looked at the others and some of them looked confused.

Crim looked at T'Chura.

"It began as a black sphere," T'Chura said. "It seemed to gather things around it. It absorbed our attacks."

I nodded. "The energy just merged into the surface with barely any reaction at all. The kinetic, it somehow avoided or…" I frowned trying to remember exactly what I'd seen.

"The darts didn't pass through it, but didn't seem to penetrate it either," T'Chura said.

"They were like small storm systems, and they phased in and out of places like I've seen Larry do, but they stayed hovering over the ground for some reason. Doesn't make any sense, but that's what I saw."

I was quiet for a few seconds while the others stared at me. "There's one more thing. They didn't want us there."

"You can't know that," Griff said.

"Really? Those things attacked us. Kinda big signal that the Asherah didn't want us poking around their stuff."

I didn't like the look Griff was giving me, like he was superior to everyone on the hangar deck, or maybe it was just me. I knew my limits—some of the important ones anyway—and there was something about Griff that I didn't like, something that warned me not to trust him.

"It's common for beings to have a suspicious response to the unknown. For all we know they were trying to prevent us from being hurt."

"Bullshit. They tore apart your battlebots."

"All I'm saying is that we don't completely understand the nature of the Golems or the Spikes."

T'Chura cleared his throat. "They're dangerous and they've demonstrated hostile intent."

"And they don't obey the fundamental laws of the universe," Ben said.

Griff arched an eyebrow. "Only according to us. The Asherah were vastly superior in intellect and highly capable of developing technology well beyond our current understanding." He turned toward me. "That's what makes them so important."

"Where is Osira?" Kaz asked.

Griff regarded his former protégé for a few seconds. "That's what I was hoping your captain could help me with."

Now we were finally getting to it. I'd been expecting the "ask" for more than a few minutes now. He'd been priming us all with teaching us how awesome the Asherah were, but while they were impressive, I knew for damn sure that they might be more than anyone had bargained for.

"What do you need from me?" I asked.

"I need you to use Larry to find the Asherah homeworld."

CHAPTER 29

Larry walked on top of the battlewagon, seemingly aloof to what was going on around him. He occasionally paused long enough to peer at us.

"How is Larry going to do that?" I asked.

"Because that's what he's meant to do. He's to guide us to their homeworld," Griff replied.

"He guided us here, and look what happened," I said, raising my hand to stop Griff from speaking. "Assuming that Larry can do this, how would this work? All the evidence of where Osira went is on that asteroid, and I'm not going back there. It's too dangerous."

The others nodded in agreement.

"You're right about that, but before you arrived, we were able to recover a few things."

I knew Griff had arrived before us, but I wasn't aware of how much of a head start he'd had. He might've had time to recover some things.

"We were trying to activate the machine when you arrived,"

Griff said. "They use some kind of harmonic resonance to project energy into it."

"Harmonics require sound, and the atmospheric readings were minimal. Not the best environment for what you're proposing," Ben said.

"And," Crim said, "how would any kind of resonance accumulate enough energy to teleport someone across time and space?"

Griff looked as if he was in on a secret that the rest of us weren't. I couldn't decide whether this was some kind of charade, or if he really did know something we didn't.

I looked at Kaz and he gave a fractional nod.

"Won't Osira be in danger?" he asked.

Griff regarded him. "Not likely. Not yet, I mean. We assumed that she'd arrive inside a chamber similar to what we found on the research base." He gave Kaz a measured look and said, "You always *were* fond of her."

Kaz grimaced a little but didn't reply.

"She could be anywhere," I said. "It'll take time for us to catch up with her if we can. Judging by everything you've told us, she could be anywhere in the galaxy by now."

Griff shook his head. "She's not. I expect her to be in a specific sector."

I leaned forward a little. "Where?"

"I'd rather not say. I'd rather you confirm it for me."

I narrowed my gaze. "Don't like guessing wrong?"

"I'd rather not influence the results. Now, Osira does have supplies with her, but I'd rather not keep her waiting any longer than necessary," he said and paused for a few seconds. "And I don't like being wrong."

He'd meant that last bit to be charming, and it might have been, but I still didn't trust him.

"Don't worry, we'll find out whether I'm right or not soon enough," Griff said and looked at the others. "I've dedicated my life to finding the Asherah. I'm the foremost expert about their—"

"All right, enough bragging about it," I glowered. "You said I needed to use Larry to find the Asherah homeworld. How?"

"Do you still have your artifact?"

I winced. "Sort of," I said, lifting my arm. "It's kinda melded to the skin on my arm."

"Let me see," Griff said.

I accessed the combat suit controls on my omnitool and exposed my right arm. It was covered with faded bronze lines that formed an intricate pattern.

Griff peered at it and then looked at me. "You touched the artifact?"

I gritted my teeth and suppressed the urge to punch Griff right in the face. "I'm a hands-on kind of person. I like to get right in there."

"Understood," he said. "This can work. I need a few minutes to set up the relics." He looked at Kaz. "I could use some help."

"Of course," Kaz said.

Crim stepped toward them with a challenging expression.

Griff didn't seem put off by this. "Anyone who wants to help is welcome."

They moved off to the side and I gestured for Ben and T'Chura to come over. Lanaya also joined us.

I waved for T'Chura to lean down, so I could speak quietly.

"I don't trust him. He's not telling us everything," I said.

"What should we do?" Ben asked.

"I think we need to help him but be on the lookout for some kind of double-cross."

Lanaya stared at me with a confused frown. "If you expect him to betray you, then why help him at all?"

T'Chura watched me intently and didn't say anything.

"His wife is in trouble. She's alone on some alien world. I don't think it's right to just go on our merry way knowing that." I sighed. "And it's important to Kaz."

She glanced at the other group with a frown. "But you're the captain. You're the leader. You will be obeyed."

I blinked, and a small chuckle came out of my mouth. "I *am* the captain, but this isn't the military. We're all volunteers here, and we watch out for each other."

"Even when there's evidence of a betrayal on the horizon?"

"Just because Kaz might be conflicted doesn't mean he'd sell us out."

T'Chura gave an approving nod.

"Interesting. I'm sorry if my questions are a bit off base," she said.

"How else are you going to learn about us? Anyway, keep an eye on Griff. I don't know what game he's playing, but I don't trust him."

"That makes two of us," T'Chura said.

I looked over at Griff and the others. They were unloading the crates that had been brought over from Griff's ship.

Eight small triangular columns were being set up on the deck. They were made of a dark metal that seemed to reflect the light in strange ways, similar to the ones I'd seen in the museum. I frowned and looked at Griff. "You stole the exhibit?"

Griff laughed. "No, but I've been piecing it together for the last few years. Though admittedly, your feats in the museum did shed some light on how to work it."

"You've used them?"

Griff shook his head. "No, Osira did. She figured it out and had similar markings on the envirosuit she wore."

"Do you have another artifact to make it work?" I asked, but had a feeling I already knew the answer.

Griff gave me a once-over. "You're all I've got."

Kaz walked over and pulled me aside. "Nate, please. I wouldn't ask this of you if it weren't important."

I stared at him as I inhaled a breath. "You're going to owe me big time for this." I walked over to where the columns had been set up. "Kierenbot, make sure you get a recording of this."

"Ready, Captain."

I glanced down at my arm and hesitated. Then I swallowed, hard.

"Why is he just standing there?" Griff asked.

"Nate, are you all right?" Kaz asked.

I waved away the comments and sighed. This was going to hurt. I knew it, but maybe they didn't... or maybe they did, and they enjoyed seeing me in pain. I imagined Serena telling me that I'd brought this on myself. Raylin would agree, of course. Heck, *I* had to agree with them.

I clenched my fist and the muscles in my arm tightened. Griff had a partial pedestal and I stared at it for a second. Then I turned toward Larry. He was perched atop the battlewagon. We locked eyes, and some kind of recognition took hold of him. He stood up and leaped into the air. His body phased out of sight, and he appeared atop the pedestal, staring at me with a curious expression. Then, his gaze sank toward my arm.

"Yeah, I know, but does it have to hurt so damn much?" I said quietly.

Larry's body gave off a shimmer that went down the length of his body. I lifted my hand and stretched it toward the pedestal. The metallic tattoo on my arm darkened in color, and it felt like

I'd stuck my arm in an ice-cold lake. It was painful, and the shock of it forced a gasp from my lungs. I clamped my mouth shut and forced my hand closer to the pedestal. It felt like I was pushing on a heavy, soaking-wet blanket that weighed a few hundred pounds too much. Larry reached out with one of his claw-like hands, and the lines of my relic-inscribed arm became rigid. The lighting in the hangar dimmed to where I could hardly see the others anymore.

Larry stood before me in a sparkly glistening brilliance, his gaze alight with recognition. He looked as if he was happy to see me, as if I were some kind of long-lost friend of his. It didn't make any sense, but I didn't care.

Larry turned away from me and gestured overhead. Shining points of a purplish haze formed above the columns, and something seemed to set my mind at ease. There was a strange and unsettling feeling in a handful of moments, but then came the certainty of knowledge that I finally understood what was happening to me. This was a map, and it would give us the coordinates. First, it showed a bright beacon on the asteroid research base. Then as my view of it retracted, the asteroid collided with others until a planet was formed. The red dwarf star expanded and collapsed in seconds, but the beacon remained. The shaft of a semitranslucent material shimmered as if it would disappear in the blink of an eye, but it held. I focused my attention on it, and it held together. My perception of the shaft raced along like some kind of celestial pathway, bringing me to another star system. There were three stars in what appeared to be a celestial tug of war. I understood the patterns of orbit and could see the eventual outcome and destruction that would occur as three separate star systems collided. But the celestial highway didn't lead directly to the stars themselves; it brought me to a place nearby—a place of chaos and destruction where planets smashed into one another in an endless cascade of obliteration and reordering. There was a pattern to it that I could easily spot, and amid the destruction was a place that boldly kept it at bay. It was a flickering beacon that pulsed daringly, as if defying what should've been its destruction. Massive planetary chunks of rock were held together in a way that defied gravity. They wouldn't attract or repel. They were simply stuck into place by some kind of unyielding force.

As I peered into the center of those colossal masses, I saw the core of something. It was small in comparison to the massive objects around it, but it shone like a newly formed star. There was a structure around it, and it appeared that someone had built it.

Larry released my hand, and I was back on the deck of the hangar. The others stared at me in stunned silence.

"Nate!" Ben gasped. "Your arm. Look at his arm!"

My gaze sank slowly toward it. A metallic glistening mass encased my entire arm. It pulsed like a heartbeat as it diminished, going back into the lines of the relic it had once been.

I stared at it, utterly shocked, and exhaled forcefully a few times, followed by a certainty that maybe I'd taken things too far.

CHAPTER 30

I wavered on my feet as the strength drained from my legs. I tried to steady myself but sank to my knees, clutching my arm to my chest.

"Steady," T'Chura said.

"Let go of me. He needs help," Ben said.

The muscles in my arm cramped terribly, and I gritted my teeth while I tried to relieve the pain. "Just give me a minute."

I glanced up, seeing T'Chura holding Ben back with one giant hand and Kaz whispering something about it being dangerous to touch my arm. They didn't understand what was happening to me.

My relic-infused arm hurt like something had triggered all the nerve endings, sending pain signals to my brain. Reflexively, I rubbed my arm, and after a few moments the pain and cramping began to subside.

Lanaya was somehow at my side. "Sit down," she urged, holding my elbows and easing me back down. She was a lot stronger than she looked, and I allowed myself to be guided back.

"Maybe just for a second."

There were worse things than looking up into her beautiful face, and it was enough to pull my attention away from my aching arm. She gently massaged my shoulder muscles, working her way down my arm.

I frowned in surprise and craned my neck to look at her. She applied the right amount of pressure that scattered the aches to oblivion.

"Is it helping?" she asked.

I nodded. The ache and weakness fled as my strength returned and my mind began to clear.

"Thank you," I said and stood up.

I felt her give me a bit of a boost and then she stood.

The others came over, and I looked at my arm. The lines had faded back to a dull tan that made it look more like scars than anything as vibrant as what it had been before.

"Are you all right, Nate?" Ben asked.

I nodded. "Yeah, I am now." I looked at Lanaya. "What did you do?"

"I just massaged your shoulder and arm a little. I saw that when you rubbed your arm the pain seemed to subside, so I thought it would help if I massaged the places you couldn't reach."

I stared at her for a few seconds, considering.

"Did that help?" Kaz asked.

I nodded. "Yeah, it did. Crazy, but it did."

"It's not that crazy," Lanaya said.

"She's right," T'Chura said.

"Care to elaborate, big guy?"

"Well," Lanaya said, and T'Chura nodded for her to

continue, "nerve signals can get confused and start firing all at once. Sometimes that happens with injuries. I don't know how it happened with your arm, but I recognized the remedy. By rubbing your arm, it helped to overwhelm the nerves and force them to reset. I did the same thing by massaging your shoulder."

I raked my teeth over my lower lip for a second while I considered what she'd said. Then I shrugged. "Sounds good to me. I'm not a doctor."

I wondered what Serena would've made of all this. Would she have done the same thing?

Lanaya's expression became serious. "Neither am I. I've just experienced it before. I've seen it done to others."

I didn't want to bring up "the masters" because she hadn't mentioned them in a while, and she was doing well, but I did share a look with Ben. I could tell he was thinking the same thing.

I smiled a little. "I appreciate your quick thinking. The others were too worried about catching whatever the hell is on my arm to help." I eyed them reproachfully. "Thanks guys."

T'Chura arched a thick, bushy eyebrow. "Like it or not, there is a risk, and I was—"

"Protecting the crew," I finished for him. I smiled to take the sting out of my interruption. I gestured with the arm in question. "I really don't think it works like that."

"But you don't know that for sure," Kaz said.

"Come here and let's shake hands and find out," I said, extending my hand toward him.

Kaz glanced at the proffered hand disdainfully. "Pass. You haven't washed your hands."

"That hurts my feelings. It really does."

"I'm sure you'll find a way to soldier on."

I grinned a little and lowered my hand. "So did you guys see another star map?"

The others glanced at each other.

"We did not," Griff said. "What did you see?"

I frowned. At the museum, the others had seen the star map, and I wondered why they hadn't this time.

"I think I know where she is. Osira," I said and told them about what I'd seen.

"Remarkable," Griff said, sounding impressed.

"We knew something was happening," Kaz said. "The area around the pedestal darkened, similar to how Larry phases out, but it lasted much longer."

"Are you saying I disappeared too?"

Kaz nodded. "Yes."

I glanced down at Larry, who was watching me intently. I couldn't be sure what he expected, but it was a little unsettling all the same.

"Please, we must hurry. The Asherah homeworld awaits!" Griff said excitedly. I frowned toward him. "Not a moment to waste, and there will be plenty of credit to go around for finding the Asherah homeworld at last. Our names will be preserved for thousands of years as the explorers who persevered on this hunt that others have long forgotten and abandoned."

Griff started walking toward the door. "Come on. To the bridge. Can't fly the ship from here."

Kierenbot looked at me and I gave him a nod. We left the hangar with Kierenbot leading the way.

Kaz lingered behind to walk next to me. "He hasn't forgotten about Osira."

I stared straight ahead. "If you say so."

He let out a grumbled sigh that might have been a small growl. Aliens make all kinds of sounds, and sometimes it was hard to keep track of what they meant. "He hasn't," Kaz insisted. "He's just been working toward this for a very long time."

I nodded a little and then looked at Kaz. "It's easy to lose sight of what's important when it's been that long."

Kaz glared at me. "Is that what you tell yourself when you think about Serena?"

It only takes a split second to snap. I snarled and shoved him into the wall, eyes ablaze with anger.

Kaz locked gazes with me, enjoying the rise he'd gotten. "No one likes it when you poke at things that are important to them," he said, deathly quiet. I made a show of looking down at my fists pushing against his chest. "Now take your hands off me."

I held him against the wall, fists clutching at his combat suit. I felt the others staring at us as the corridor went quiet. Giving him one last push, I moved away from him and stormed down the corridor.

I tried to dismiss what Kaz had said, but I couldn't. It was what happened when you were smacked in the face with the truth. It stung, and I hated it. Kaz was right; I had been poking at him. Why should I be angry when he poked back?

I hated that she'd left and blamed myself for making it happen, at least a little bit. There was enough responsibility to go around between Serena and me. She had some issues that she needed to work through, but sometimes I wondered if I could've handled things a bit better. She just needed a little bit of space to get some perspective, and maybe that was good for both of us.

Kierenbot had opened the door to the bridge and gone inside. He had a star map queued up and waiting. I walked over to the holographic interface and snatched at the controls. It didn't have any substance to it. The star map jerked around in response to my brusque handling of the controls.

I exhaled and steadied my hands, then navigated the interface much better than I'd done before.

The others arrived on the bridge, and much to my surprise, it was Crim who joined me at the star map.

Crim studied the map as I navigated the interface. "You've gotten better at this."

One of the first things I'd learned on the ship was how the nav system worked. Couldn't go anywhere if you didn't know how to plot a course.

"I had very effective teachers," I said wryly.

Crim chuckled.

I glanced around and saw Griff speaking to Kaz.

"Keep an eye on him," Crim said.

"Which one?" I asked but thought I knew the answer.

Crim considered it for a few seconds. "Both of them. But I meant Griff. Akacians can be single-minded about things."

The nav system froze as it tried to interpret my inputs and I frowned, raising both my hands. "Come on, don't be difficult."

"Pleading with a computer has never helped. I ought to know; I've done it enough," Crim said.

He brought up a secondary interface and looked over my work. "There it is. Should work now."

"What'd I do wrong?"

"Nothing. You did it right, but the system has safety checks in place and threw up a red flag on the destination."

I frowned. "I don't see any alerts."

Crim chuckled. "You wouldn't, but I do. I've updated your access to the system so it will alert you next time."

"It's about time the training wheels came off."

"Don't get cocky."

Griff and Kaz walked over to us.

"Is that where it is?" Griff asked, staring up at the holoscreen.

I nodded. "Kierenbot, can you analyze the plot?"

"At once, Captain," Kierenbot said. Then, barely a second later, "This could prove challenging, Captain."

"I thought so, but can you do it?"

Crim cleared his throat. "It takes a crew to fly a ship, Nate."

I frowned. "I know that, but Kierenbot usually pilots the ship."

"That's correct, Captain. However, long-range scans are insufficient. The data indicates a number of anomalies in the system. I believe I can overcome them, but since this is an unknown star system, I would advise that all systems be covered by qualified personnel."

I nodded and looked at the others. "All right, you heard him. Get to your stations."

Crim moved over to a workstation and was joined by Ben. Lanaya went over and sat next to Ben.

T'Chura and Kaz went to the weapons workstations.

Griff came to stand next to me. "Mind if I join you, Captain?"

"All right with me as long as you don't interfere" I replied, and he nodded. "All stations report in."

"Nav system ready," Kierenbot said.

"Tactical systems ready," Kaz said.

"Engines and power core systems ready. *Spacehog* is ready to fly," Crim said.

"Acknowledged, we're green across the board," I said. "Kierenbot, execute course."

The *Spacehog's* hyperdrive systems took the ship out of normal space to travel extremely fast. That was pretty much all I needed to know. The nav system readout indicated our speed as it was measured by the ship's systems. Ben obsessed over the ship's capabilities, and I was always impressed by it myself.

However, whereas I could accept that the hyperdrive system was doing exactly what it was designed to do, Ben was determined to learn all he could about it so he could one day return to Earth to give humanity a technological leg up. This usually led to me joking with him about being careful what he wished for. People had enough problems communicating with each other most times, and any kind of political debate—or as I like to think of them, a poor excuse for a circus act—did nothing but reinforce my doubts. If Humans didn't have their act together by the time they reached the stars, they'd just bring their problems out there with them.

I frowned a little and glanced around the bridge, looking at the different species who had made the journey to the stars before us. I didn't know their species' histories and how they'd come to be part of the greater galactic community. None of them were perfect by any stretch of the imagination. When I stopped to think about it, they reminded me of home. Somewhat similar issues were faced by the variety of species, so maybe Humans weren't so different from everyone else. But that didn't mean we were ready for the challenge. After all, I was just making this up as I went, stumbling as I tried to run, but maybe I'd gotten that wrong. I had to wonder if it was the galactic community that was so different, or if it was that similar species found their way to each other and decided that interacting and coexisting was better than warring with each other. I hadn't logged enough hours on the ship to really form an opinion on that. The best I could come up with was that Humans weren't so different from the aliens I'd encountered. There was plenty of room for improvement, but I couldn't discount the enormous strides made back home. While humanity wasn't perfect, present-day Earth was a much better place to live than it had been fifty years ago, and there was no reason to believe it wouldn't be even better a half a century from now.

The journey to the star system didn't take long. It wasn't days or hours. The *Spacehog* was a fast ship, and Kierenbot brought us out of hyperspace outside the star system.

We'd only entered N-Space for a few seconds when alarms began showing on the main holoscreen.

Getting to the star system had been the easy part. Navigating to the actual destination was going to be a challenge.

"What's your status, Kierenbot?" I asked.

"Stand by, Captain. I'm processing scan data," he replied.

Kierenbot was integrated with the ship's computing core and able to process untold amounts of data—Ben's term—at blazing-fast speeds. I liked to think of it as ludicrous speeds, but as the seconds became minutes I started to wonder if he'd finally had a breakdown.

I looked at him and cleared my throat. "Kierenbot, are you still with us?"

He didn't reply.

Griff leaned toward me. "I think your AI has frozen."

Kierenbot was an artificial intelligence that was designed to believe he was a sentient being who'd left his physical form behind so his mind could occupy a robot. I'd occasionally test the design to see if I could get Kierenbot to see that he was an AI and not some ascended being, but it never worked. He simply denied it in many different ways. On the one hand, his denial was rather impressive, but it made me a bit sympathetic toward him. He was effectively living the life of a lie. He wasn't a slave. He collected a share of whatever we found, and I checked the ship's records to see that Kaz had done the same. I didn't know if that was the same for every AI out there. And I wasn't sure if Kierenbot could leave the ship for any extended period of time, even if he wanted to. I hadn't had time to test it, but I had to admit I was curious.

Griff was about to speak, and I cut him off. "Just give him a minute."

Griff remained quiet, but he did shift in his seat a little.

"Apologies, Captain," Kierenbot said. "There are a number of anomalies in that star system. It's the most peculiar system I've ever analyzed."

I glanced at Kaz, and he gave a slight shake of his head.

"Okay, can we make it to the target?"

"Unknown, Captain. This star system behaves as if there are different rules applying to it."

"Different rules?" Ben asked. "Are you saying that physics are different here?"

"Precisely," Kierenbot replied. "There are a number of anomalies that plague this system. The trinary star systems have shorter elliptical orbits, and the system itself is on a trajectory to break free of the galaxy, but that won't happen anytime soon."

I looked at Ben. His mouth was partially open, and he turned toward Crim for guidance.

"Okay, that's... peculiar," I said. I didn't need them to launch into a theoretical discussion about the laws of the universe just then. "But will the other anomalies prevent us from reaching the Asherah homeworld?"

"It's better if I show you, Captain," Kierenbot replied.

The main holoscreen updated with the current sensor feed. I peered at the star system model and frowned.

"That can't be right," Ben said. "The stars are orbiting around the target. Is that where the Asherah homeworld is?"

"That's what I saw, but I didn't know about the layout of the star system itself. I'm guessing those huge rings are all that remain of the planets that used to be here."

"That's a fair assumption," Crim said.

I nodded, appreciating that Crim agreed with me. I looked at Kierenbot. "Can we get there?"

"I've been trying to plot a course to the destination you've programmed into the nav computer, and I'm unable to do so. In theory, I should be able to avoid the anomalies, but some of them interfere with our scanners, so I can't be sure of that. It's difficult to account for the risk to the ship when I can't predict the spatial anomalies."

I stared at the star map, peering at the different icons that appeared and disappeared throughout the entire system. I'd thought it was just interference, but it wasn't.

I looked at Kaz. "What do you think?"

"What is the nature of the anomalies, Kierenbot?" Kaz asked.

"Erratic spacetime energy signatures, as if there are multiple dwarf-sized blackholes scattered throughout the system. Their range is limited, so even that is difficult to predict, but the issues are compounded by the stars' trajectory."

Kierenbot had lost me somewhere after he mentioned a blackhole. I looked at Kaz with raised eyebrows.

"Think of this system as a container, and the stars are the heads of a giant mixer. They don't let anything settle and are constantly disturbing things," Kaz said.

I nodded slowly. "Now that I can understand." I turned toward Griff. "Why would the Asherah homeworld be here? Nothing could survive in that."

Griff peered at the holoscreen with a thoughtful frown. "You're right. As it appears now, nothing could survive here, but perhaps things weren't always as they are. What we're seeing is three star systems combined, but we don't know how they got that way."

I snickered in disbelief. "Are you implying that the Asherah did this?"

Griff smiled. "Perhaps, but tell me, now that you've considered it, does anything else make sense?"

I glanced at the main holoscreen. None of what the Asherah could do made sense to me, but Griff's words had the ring of truth to them.

He watched me and nodded. "You agree, don't you?"

I looked at the others, hoping that one of them had a better explanation. None of them did. Even Crim looked baffled.

"If that's right, then their experiments destroyed their homeworld and we're here to see what's left," I said.

"There's plenty left. You've seen it for yourself. There's something in there through all the anomalies we can't completely explain. And Osira is waiting there for us to arrive."

I sighed and considered it for a few moments. "Kierenbot, what do you need us to do so you can navigate through that mess?"

"Captain, I must warn you that our chances of success are extremely limited. I must also point out that there is a strong likelihood that Osira Daklan is deceased."

"Absolutely not!" Griff said. "The Asherah meant for their people to return to their real homeworld. That's what that machine does. They wouldn't have done that if it was going to kill them upon their return."

He stared at me.

"She might be dead. It's a possibility. Kierenbot isn't wrong for bringing it to our attention." Griff started to speak, but I spoke over him. "However, I'm not going to pack up and leave, assuming she's dead. We're going there, and we'll find out for ourselves."

Griff exhaled forcefully.

"Nate doesn't give up," Kaz said.

Griff nodded, looking relieved.

"Okay Kierenbot, back to my previous question. What do you need from us to navigate through that star system?" I asked.

"Be ready for anything. I can't predict what's happening, and it's worse the closer we get to our target. How anything is still intact there is beyond me, but you are my captain, and I believe in what you saw. However, I do think preventive measures are required to ensure our own survival."

I bobbed my head once. "Okay, we should strap ourselves in and go to individual life support."

I happened to be looking at Kaz and saw the frown on his face. "Don't look so damn surprised. I paid attention when you were teaching me about the ship."

We still wore our envirosuits and combat armor. I used my omnitool to engage my helmet and then activated the straps for my seat. Two straps launched over my shoulder and others sprang up from my seat. They met in the middle, merging into one solid piece in the blink of an eye. I looked around the bridge and saw that the others had done the same.

"This could be a bumpy ride," I said. "Kierenbot, take us in."

CHAPTER 31

"Aye, Captain. Taking us to the Asherah death world," Kierenbot said, then gave a nervous laugh. "Apologies, what I meant to say was the Asherah homeworld."

His red orb flashed at me in what I assumed was a conspiratorial wink. Sometimes Kierenbot's attempt at humor was a bit off.

Griff leaned toward me. "You should have that robot serviced."

I shook my head. "I like him just the way he is."

"Very well," Griff replied and watched the main holoscreen.

Kierenbot flew us in. A tactical plot became active on the main holoscreen. Active scans alerted us to the presence of spatial anomalies, and Kierenbot avoided them. The farther into the star system we went, the closer we had to fly through the remains of who knew how many planets that had once been here. Like the rings around Saturn, there were partially formed rings inside the star system. Many of them rippled as if they'd recently been disturbed by the hand of God.

The convergence point of this star system was exactly where the coordinates of the Asherah homeworld was supposed to be. I wasn't a physicist or an astronomer by any stretch of the imagination, but I'd had to learn a little bit about both while on the ship. Almost every grade school student learned that a planet was never the center of a star system, hence it being called a star system. The star is the head honcho and calls all the shots. The planets are just along for the ride. Except here. This system was different. The centermost point of the system was exactly where we needed to go *and* the most dangerous place we could be.

I looked at Griff. "Did the Asherah do this? Did they set this up?"

"Now you begin to understand who they were, the power at their disposal, and why they've been sought since we first started roaming the stars."

Throughout my life I'd occasionally picked a fight above my weight class, and shockingly, none of that was going to help me now. The power core on the ship generated more energy than anything we were capable of back on Earth, which was what allowed us to traverse the galaxy. Crim had always been adamant that it wasn't about the power; it was about understanding how the universe worked. He'd told me that Earth had the technology to leave its star system. The pieces were there for us to put together and had nothing to do with our current method of going into space. Our understanding of the universe needed to develop. I thought that for all Crim's abrasive behavior, for some reason, he had a soft spot when it came to Humans. Maybe he identified with us. But as I stared at the main holoscreen, awestruck from witnessing something that should've been impossible, I wasn't the only one on the bridge who felt that way.

Awestruck expressions could be found all around that bridge. At least I was in good company. Griff looked as if he'd expected it.

There were technological leaps, but the sheer power on the screen was enough to make me want to tuck tail and run. I'd had the occasional power fantasy where anything I could dream up became reality, and it seemed as if the Asherah had actually been successful, but what did that make us to them? Not even an interesting pet or a curious life form. We were flies pecking at the hide of a dinosaur about to be swatted by something bigger.

The ship lurched suddenly to the side, temporarily overwhelming the inertia dampeners. The straps held us in place, but it still hurt. My combat suit helped freeze my body in place from within the confines of the straps, so it felt like a sudden jerk and then a discomfort that bordered on nauseating.

Thick fields of asteroids filled the holoscreen, along with giant blotches of absolutely nothing. Large asteroids hurtled toward us, and then some unseen force caused them to break down and disintegrate. The giant pockets of nothing seemed to snap into existence randomly and then disappear.

Kierenbot guided the ship toward the center of the death storm. The *Spacehog* had multiple methods of propulsion that included manipulating gravity, hyperdrives, and even limited maneuvering thrusters. The gravity engines could stop our ship in an instant. I was something of a pilot myself, but there was no way I could have gotten us through that star system. I would've killed us soon after we started this crazy run, but Kierenbot was an artificial intelligence that could augment his capabilities with the ship's computer systems. He could make decisions and alter our course before my brain even indicated that we were in danger. It felt much like riding a rollercoaster without a seat belt. Our lives were in Kierenbot's hands, and it was times like these that made me want to whisper a prayer for us to survive the next few minutes.

Making our way toward the target was much like flying through a powerful hurricane the size of a star system, and even that wasn't enough to convey what I was seeing. We held on tight and hoped the ride would be over soon.

We eventually pierced the veil of chaos into a small field of open space where massive planetary chunks held a tight orbit around a tiny, shining, moon-sized object complete with its own atmosphere.

I peered at the holoscreen, seeing cloud cover over the small moon.

"Is that what you saw, Nate?" Ben asked.

Even from as far away as we were, I could see the structures built around it, making me think that this wasn't a moon at all but something else entirely.

"Yeah, that's exactly what I saw," I replied. "Kierenbot, how are those asteroids held in place? The ones that look like chunks of a planet."

"Scanners indicate that a highly focused gravitational field holds them in place."

"Will they interfere with our approach?" Griff asked.

"It doesn't appear that they will. There is plenty of space for us to fly between them," Kierenbot said.

Griff looked at me.

"It's a shield," I said.

Griff frowned. "*What's* a shield?"

I gestured toward the holoscreen. "The asteroids. They're a shield to protect the core."

Griff stared at the holoscreen, pressing his thin lips together.

"He's right," Crim said. "I noticed massive craters on the

outermost parts of the asteroids. Who knows how many impacts there have been over time?"

Griff nodded.

"Okay Kierenbot, take us in," I said.

He flew the ship between the massive asteroids that were protecting the core. I wondered if whatever was holding them in place could be manipulated to slam them together. There was nothing we could do if that happened. The ship would be destroyed, and we'd be dead.

I shook my head. When had I become so damn pessimistic?

"I've detected Osira's subspace comms," Kaz said.

"Can you establish a link?" I asked.

"Not yet, but I've got her location. Not precise, but close enough to get us within her vicinity."

"Altering course," Kierenbot said.

I looked at Griff. "This can't be their homeworld."

"It's where the search has led us. Maybe this is all that's left."

"Scans indicate that the entire place is artificial. It was constructed. There are massive energy sources down there," Crim said.

I nodded and then asked. "Hey, are they similar to what we encountered on the research base?"

"Can't detect that from here. Once we get to the surface, I can run a scan."

There was significant cloud cover of the planet that made it appear as if it were surrounded by storms, but not all of it. The clouds were moving fast, exposing clear views of the surface. There were bands of yellows and blues, and Osira's subspace beacon was located on the equator right on the border between two significant cloud systems. I didn't think that was a coincidence.

Kierenbot guided the ship through the atmosphere, and we

got our first closeup look at the surface. It was covered with vast cities and buildings that stretched high. Bands of pure blue raced across the continent right toward our destination.

The surface showed some kind of vegetation, and fields of golden tundra occupied the space between the gray-and-white structures. The buildings looked as if they'd been woven together as one enormous piece of architecture that stretched as far as I could see.

We flew over vast swaths of destruction. It appeared that the surface had suffered some kind of cataclysm by large asteroid impacts, but I couldn't see how that was possible with the shield that was in place.

Large pieces of woven architecture had been brutalized by some kind of extinction event that must've occurred a very long time ago. Something must have survived because whatever the Asherah had built was still operating.

Could they have been trapped here all this time?

I dismissed the question. We'd been able to reach this place, and anyone who could manipulate entire stars could've very well escaped this place if they'd wanted to.

There was a large, city-sized region where a mountain had either formed or was the result of some ancient asteroid crashing into this place. Kierenbot flew us toward it. As we neared the mountain, a bright flash seemed to encompass it, rising to its peak and then mushrooming out away from it.

Alarms sounded as multiple alerts appeared on the main holoscreen. The ship dropped toward the ground, and I felt as if I'd fallen off a tall building and was plummeting to my death. Then the video feed swung up and leveled off, lining up with the horizon.

"Apologies Captain, but it's not safe to fly the ship near the mountain," Kierenbot said.

"Understood," I said and looked at Crim. "Is that a defense system?"

He shook his head. "No, it's looks like an energy discharge of some kind."

"You don't sound sure of that."

"I'm not sure of that!" Crim snapped. Then he evened his tone. "If it was some kind of weapons system, it could have destroyed the ship. I think we were either in the wrong place at the wrong time, or it reacted to the ship, which caused the discharge."

"Oh, like static discharge?" Ben asked.

Crim pondered it for a second and then nodded. "Yes, but way more powerful."

"So we can't even fly to where Osira is? The area ahead looks the most intact of anywhere we've seen yet," I said and considered it for a few moments. "We can't risk the ship."

"There might be a way," Crim said. We all looked at him. "Use the recon skiff and battlewagon. The energy rises from the base of the mountain. When we detect a spike in energy, we can fly near the ground. The structures in the area don't appear to be affected, so we should be able to shelter from the discharge."

I nodded. "I understand. Let's do that. Head to the hangar. T'Chura, Crim, make sure we're armed appropriately. Plasma cannons weren't effective."

"Pulse rifles would be more effective. They have the ammunition options we need," T'Chura said.

The others started to leave, and Kaz paused by the door. "Nate?"

"I'll be right there. Just need to have a quick word with Kierenbot," I said.

Griff stood in the doorway, watching me, and I gave him a nod.

Kaz ushered him off the bridge, and I was alone with Kierenbot.

The robot turned his head toward me. "I know what you're going to say to me."

I nodded a little and then regarded him for a few seconds. "And you probably already know why it has to be that way."

He looked away from me, his red orb staring fixedly at the holoscreen in front of him.

"Kierenbot," I said and waited for him to look at me, "we wouldn't have made it here if not for you. What you just did was amazing. No one else could've flown the ship through all that to get us here. Unbelievable."

"There's more I can do."

"You have nothing to prove as far as I'm concerned."

His red orb locked onto me, and I wondered what he could be thinking. "Thank you, Captain. I will wait for your signal."

I chuckled. "So certain we're going to need a pickup?"

He shrugged. "Unless our luck changes."

I nodded. "Fair enough."

"Good hunting, Captain."

I left the bridge and headed directly to the hangar bay where the others waited. Larry kept pace with me. I looked down at him and stopped. He cocked his head to look up at me.

"You're not going to go crazy and kill us all, right?"

He seemed to regard me for a moment and then looked toward the door to the hangar.

I rolled my eyes and started walking. "Yeah, I get it. We'll get a move on."

I entered the bridge and saw the others checking their equipment. I checked the power level of my combat armor and then joined the others.

Ben walked over to me carrying two pulse rifles. T'Chura

had trained us in their use. They fired in four-round bursts and their ammunition could be configured with the use of a single explosive round per set.

Ben handed a rifle to me.

"Thanks."

"I'm going with you."

I glanced over at Crim. He scowled in my direction and then resumed his circuit around the battlewagon.

"Ben," I started to say, and he shook his head.

"You need someone to watch your back, Nate."

"I know, kid. You're better able to cover me on the battlewagon using the weapons systems there."

"Lanaya can do it. I've been showing her how to use the systems, and she used the secondary systems on the ship. Crim will be fine without me."

"T'Chura is going to watch my back. Trust me, you don't want to be anywhere down there."

He glared at me. "No, you don't understand. I'm not asking you for your permission to go with you. I'm telling you that I'm coming with you."

I blinked a few times and regarded him thoughtfully. Ben was a kid, barely twenty years old, and had his whole life ahead of him. But he'd grown up a lot over the past few months. I recognized the man he was becoming, and seeing the stubborn gleam in his eyes, I knew that short of tying him up I wasn't going to stop him from coming.

I bobbed my head to the side. "All right, you don't have to be so mean about it."

Ben blinked and frowned in surprise.

I started walking. "Come on, kid, we're on a timetable. You can come, but you can't hold us back."

The recon skiff could fly fast but didn't have much in the way of weapons systems. The battlewagon had the firepower but not the speed.

I walked over to Crim, and he stopped examining one of the mag cannons to glare at me. "It's a bitch when the kids grow up."

Crim scowled. "It's your fault, Nate. He wants to protect you, which he can do from inside there," he said, tilting his head toward the battlewagon.

"I'll look out for him."

"That's what I'm worried about," he said, giving me a stern look. "Go on, get out of here. I'll cover you from above and run some analysis on the area as we go. Maybe I'll find something to help."

"Are you going to be all right with Lanaya?"

"I don't really have a choice now, do I?"

I snickered a little. "You've always got a choice; you just might not like it."

He glared at me, and for a second I thought he might try to kick me with one of his legs. Instead, he quickly climbed inside the ship and the hatch clanged shut.

I hastened toward the skiff, and Griff turned toward me. He gestured toward the line of battlebots.

I nodded and used my omnitool to pass control back to him.

"Thank you," Griff said.

The battlebots came out of standby and immediately came toward the skiff. One of them lagged behind for a few seconds, and Griff narrowed his gaze thoughtfully.

"Looks like one of them needs some attention," I said.

Griff looked at his omnitool and then shook his head. "Nope, it checks out."

The battlebots' pale armor displayed blue highlights that had been amber-colored while they'd been in standby. They stomped toward us and waited.

We climbed inside the skiff, and I sat in front with Kaz.

The hangar bay doors opened, and I could see the semi-translucent atmospheric shield.

Crim flew out first. "Clear," he said.

"Acknowledged," Kaz replied.

The skiff lifted off the hangar deck and flew out of the ship. I glanced behind us and saw that the battlebots had followed. They were in pairs and scattered their formation so as not to make a clean line.

The waypoint on the skiff's holoscreen was set to Osira's comlink signal, but we still couldn't reach her.

We flew around the mountain, keeping as much distance as we could while maintaining our heading.

A bright blue flash lit up the sky and was gone in an instant.

"That's the discharge," Crim's voice said over comms.

"Glad you were right about it," I replied.

He chuckled. "Me too."

Kaz cleared his throat. "We should hurry."

I nodded. "Crim, we're going to scout ahead."

"Understood."

The skiff sped ahead, and the ground blurred by. I looked in the distance and saw huge triangular columns that had been constructed with a smooth, forty-five-degree angle on top. Hovering above them were large metallic spheres with bolts of lightning arcing from mid-sphere to the corresponding column below. There were rows of these columns, and Kaz kept his distance from them.

I peered ahead at several dome-covered areas that were the focal points of all the columns.

"That's it!" Griff said and brought up his omnitool. "Should be close enough to establish a link now." A few moments passed and he sighed heavily. "Having trouble with the link. It seems to catch but then drops. Something is interfering with it."

Kaz flew us over the dome-shaped buildings, but we couldn't see inside. They all had a large oval entrance that gave the domes a snout appearance from our vantage above them.

"I'm going to set us down," Kaz said and guided the skiff toward an open area between the buildings.

"Look how the metal is mixed with some kind of concrete," Ben said. I glanced at him, and he shrugged. "I know it's not concrete, but it reminds me of it."

I nodded.

When I told Crim what we were doing, he said he would keep scouting the area.

We climbed out of the skiff, and the battlebots formed a defensive perimeter around us.

"I've got a connection!" Griff said. "Osira, can you hear me? We're here. We made it. We're coming to you."

The reply was garbled, but I thought I heard her voice.

I looked at Kaz.

"I heard it too. She's here. Let's get in there," Kaz said.

Griff gave up on the comlink and looked at me.

"One step at a time. We'll get in there, figure out where she is, and then work on getting her out of there," I said.

Griff nodded.

I saw Ben kneeling on the ground for a second. "What have you got, kid?"

"Quick sample, similar to what we found at the other site. This place is old. I mean really old."

Griff laughed. "This is it. This is where the Asherah kept their secrets from the dawn of creation itself, or damn well close enough."

He raced ahead and several of his battlebots moved to keep

up with him. The rest of us followed him toward the entrance of the dome.

There was no door, just a short entryway into the building.

Griff stopped and gestured for a pair of battlebots to scout ahead. Two of them walked through the small tunnel and went inside. They disappeared from view for a few minutes.

I looked at Griff and he shook his head. He was about to bring up his omnitool when one of the battlebots appeared at the end of the tunnel and gestured for us to come inside.

Griff charged ahead and we followed.

I lifted my rifle and switched the ammunition configuration to explosive round intervals. Ben glanced at me, and I showed him how to do the same. I hoped we wouldn't need the additional destructive boost, but I'd rather be prepared in case things spiraled out of control.

I came out of the tunnel into the biggest industrial warehouse I'd ever seen. At least, that's what it reminded me of. We hadn't entered a single dome-shaped building but an interconnection of all of them. I stood just inside the entrance, wide-eyed as my brain struggled to make sense of what I saw.

Griff looked at me. "Impressive. Most impressive. This is beyond anything ever discovered before."

A rolling wave of azure-colored energy sped high above us.

"There's an artificial atmosphere in here," Ben said.

"Don't take off your helmet." He gave me an exasperated look and I shrugged. "Just in case."

I looked to the side and saw a long row of entryways similar to the one we'd used.

"Looks like a lot of them came through here," Kaz said.

"Where'd they all go?" I asked.

We walked toward some kind of reception area that accommodated a wide path with kiosks that were designed for even taller beings than T'Chura.

I walked over to one of them and peered around the corner. The kiosks were dead. No power came from them, and they looked to be encased in a kind of crusty buildup of a yellowish substance.

I glanced at Larry, and he just walked by them as if they were inconsequential.

Farther inside there were lines of dark metallic walls that reflected the amber-colored light from the ceiling. Waves of blue from the mountain's discharge reflected off the smooth, mirror-like surface.

The walls looked to be about ten feet tall and curved away from the path.

I walked over to one of the walls, and a humming sound resonated from it. We stopped moving, and I brought my rifle up. This wasn't like the outposts. There were no suspicious mounds of rocky debris to come to life and attack us, but that only made me feel a little bit better. There was a bleakness to it that I couldn't quite figure out.

Griff peered at the walls, and I glanced at Kaz. "Still can't reach her?"

He shook his head. "No, but the signal is getting stronger."

I looked up at T'Chura. "What do you think?"

"Reminds me of a place for mass gathering. These could be information displays or decontamination scanners."

I chuckled. "Any chance they'll regard us as foreign contaminants?"

The others froze and turned toward me in alarm.

Griff shook his head. "Not you. You've got the artifact. Why don't you take a closer look? Maybe it'll trigger something."

"Why don't you do it?"

"Because I'm not the one with an Asherah artifact fused to my skin," Griff replied.

Half the times I found myself in trouble, it was because of something I'd done on a whim. Now it was time to fish or cut bait.

Griff was about to speak again, and I waved him to silence. "Give me a second here," I said and looked at Ben. "You said there's an atmosphere in here. Is it harmful?"

Kaz shook his head. "It wouldn't be fun to breathe, but it's not going to melt your skin off."

I stared at him. Kaz's skin could withstand a harsh atmosphere that would make me wish I'd never been born. He liked to boast about it, as if coming from a world with a more acidic atmosphere was something to be proud of.

"Why don't you go touch it then, if you're so sure about it?"

"Nate, come on. Stop screwing around," Kaz said. "We need to know if those things are dangerous, or we'll never reach Osira. I'll go up there with you, and if it looks like it's going to hurt, I'll pull you out of there. I promise."

I sighed and started walking toward the wall. "Why would they need to maintain an atmosphere in here anyway? If this place is as old as it appears, then answer me that."

"I don't know," he said and looked as if he regretted saying it.

I walked over toward the wall and lifted my right hand. The combat suit covered me from head to toe, but the material was a nanorobotic metallic alloy and could change shape, including exposing my hand and arm if I wanted it to.

Larry had disappeared, which didn't fill me with a whole lot of confidence. I'd come to rely on his reactions to our environment. It was probably foolish, because I didn't understand what Larry was, exactly, but sometimes I had to work with what I had. Larry had chosen this moment to disappear.

I used my omnitool to order my combat suit to expose my right hand all the way to the elbow. The air was cold—not a frigid, instant frostbite kind of cold, but cold nonetheless. It also felt a bit humid, which was a surprise. I moved my hand toward the wall and touched it. The cold, smooth surface didn't do anything. I moved my hand a little bit, letting my palm glide over the surface. Nothing happened. Then I did the only thing I could think of. I banged my fist on it in the time-honored tradition of would-be mechanics and weekend warriors doing a home remodeling project.

It worked.

The humming wobbled quicker until it was almost a whine, and then the metallic walls began glowing with a silvery light.

I stepped away from the wall and my combat suit covered my hand back up. The light flickered for a few moments and then seemed to even out as it settled into a kind of rhythm.

Huge holographic images began to show over the walls as Kaz and I rejoined the others.

There was no sound, at least nothing I could hear. The images showed immensely tall creatures that were vaguely squid-like, with long tentacles on powerfully built bodies. Something scampered at their feet, and we peered at it, but part of the image was distorted at the bottom and prevented us from seeing it clearly. The squid-like creatures lumbered ahead, and several smaller feline-like creatures climbed onto their backs.

I stared at them and blinked, squinting my eyes and trying to see past the distortion. Then it cleared up and my eyes widened. The smaller feline creatures looked exactly like Larry. There were hundreds of them. They all had the same metallic bronze skin that shifted as if the particles could realign to become something else at any moment.

The squids seemed dull and almost lumbering, as if they bore a heavy weight, but the metallic meerkats moved rapidly. They phased in and out of sight, as if they were playing some kind of game.

No one spoke. We walked along the walls, staring up at the holographic images on display above, as if they were playing from an old-style movie reel. The lumbering squids moved toward an inner chamber with a jade-colored forcefield. The meerkats darted ahead, leaping toward them. Their bodies appeared to scatter as the particles came apart and the forcefield disappeared. The lumbering squids moved toward the opening and were through it before the forcefield reappeared and the process started again.

The images changed to show the squids entering an inner chamber and stepping onto some kind of platform. Their bodies changed as they shape-shifted into more of a humanoid shape. Their skin took on a metallic sheen that reflected the light, which formed a halo around their wide, wedged-shaped heads. I'd seen quite a few species of aliens in my short time roaming the galaxy —some of them terrifying—but they all paled in comparison to the Asherah. Maybe it was the pale metallic skin, the black eyes, and a face with disproportionately small mouths, as if evolution had decided to add them as an afterthought. Their torsos were covered with a familiar dark framework of shapes that decorated their entire bodies. Something cold and dark with a deadly promise made my stomach clench. The beings…the Asherah? They were covered with the same shapes that covered the artifact I'd found, the very same that was now infused with the skin of my arm.

"Oh my God, Nate!" Ben said, tapping my arm.

I nearly jumped and didn't quite yelp, but it was close. I glared at Ben. "What!"

Ben lifted his chin behind me.

I turned around and saw that the walls had shifted, and a large structure had risen out of the ground. It was a chamber, exactly the same as what had been shown on the holoscreen.

Blue light raced over our heads, and part of it sank toward the ground in front of us. It didn't disappear as the energy discharge left the area. Instead, it seemed to ebb and flow like light streaming through shallow water.

Griff was nearest and touched it with his armored hand. He met some kind of resistance and pushed harder against it, but it wouldn't budge. He turned toward me, and his gaze flicked toward the chamber.

"You're going to have to enter there. Use that creature to gain entry," Griff said. He frowned. "I can see him now."

I turned toward the chamber and saw that Larry was sitting, watching me with a single-minded intensity.

I looked back toward the holoscreen, which replayed the images we'd already seen. I watched as creatures similar to Larry ran into the forcefield and did not come out on the other side. They were simply gone.

"What are you waiting for?" Griff asked.

I gritted my teeth, ready to snap a reply at him when Kaz let out a triumphant yell.

"I've got her!" Kaz said.

He stood off to the side and peered at his omnitool. "I know where Osira is."

CHAPTER 32

Kaz frowned at me and then looked over the newly formed shield that was shimmering nearby. He'd been so absorbed with what he'd been doing that he hadn't realized what was happening around him.

"Where is she?" Griff asked.

Kaz spun around with his omnitool active and came to a stop facing away from us. "Farther inside."

T'Chura gestured away from them. "It doesn't look like this shield runs the entire length of the area. We might be able to go around it."

"Yeah, but look over there. The Asherah used that chamber, and it transformed them," Griff said.

I almost lifted my rifle but didn't. "I'm not interested in transforming into anything else."

"It's probably not going to do anything to you. They used the chamber in there to become what they needed to be. Maybe that's their true form and they'd merely adopted the other like we would wear a combat suit and the like."

I looked at Larry for a second, unable to decide. There were times when he seemed so lifelike. He'd shown fear of the machines at the outpost, but now he seemed to be waiting for my cue.

I shook my head. "I'm not going to sacrifice anyone to get inside that chamber so you can learn about the Asherah."

Griff blew out a frustrated breath. "It's a chamber of enlightenment. It'll elevate anyone who enters. We already know it works. Look at this place. Look at what the Asherah accomplished. Stop being so damn afraid and be willing to take a leap of faith once in a while."

"Really?" I snarled through clenched teeth. "Is that what you told Osira before she explored that machine? Take a blind leap of faith and hope for the best?"

Griff shook his head. "She explored the machine while I held off the attack. Are you going to accuse me of being a coward?"

"You're too willing to sacrifice other people to get what you want."

Griff jabbed his fist toward me with a snarl. "You don't get to judge me!"

I looked at Kaz.

"You don't even know if Larry is alive, Nate. The evidence indicates that this is what he was designed for. He's a tool to be used."

An exasperated burst of air cleared my throat, and I shook my head. "I'm not doing it. Let's try going around this shield and find Osira that way."

"You're wrong, Nate," Griff said. "You *are* going to do it."

The battlebots could move so damn fast that I could barely keep up with their movement, much less lift my rifle to defend myself.

I heard T'Chura let out a startled grunt, and I watched as he went down, covered in some kind of webbing. It pinched around his body, preventing him from moving. T'Chura strained against the webbing, but it only seemed to squeeze him tighter. T'Chura was the strongest being I'd ever seen. I'd watched him take on an entire platoon of Mesakloren soldiers. His strength and battle prowess were beyond measure, but he'd been taken by surprise. We all were.

One of the battlebots snatched the rifle from my hands while another grabbed me from behind, lifting me off the ground. I was about to use my flight systems, but I saw two battlebots holding Ben down on the ground. One of them had their weapon pointed at him.

"You son of a bitch!" I growled, trying to twist free, anger demanding its due, but the damn battlebots were strong, and my attempts withered as if I'd been poisoned.

Griff stomped toward me. "It doesn't have to be this hard. No one has to get hurt."

I gritted my teeth and snarled at him. "Bastard!"

Griff turned toward Ben. The battlebot's weapon shifted toward his head.

"Get away from him. I'll kill you. I swear to God, I'll rip you apart myself."

Griff turned toward me. "Just open the damn chamber, and we'll all go inside. The Asherah meant for this place to be found."

I blew out a breath. "Sure, everything is linked to this place, but they're gone. The Asherah are gone. Why did they leave?"

"I don't know! That's why you'll open that door and find out."

Kaz was somehow behind Griff and aimed his weapon at him. "You've gone too far. Let them go."

Griff froze.

"Don't turn around. I said let them go."

"You disappoint me, Kaz. I thought you were above these petty attachments. You know what's at stake. Osira will die if we don't get into that chamber."

"You don't know that. You just want inside. We can do this without hurting anybody. Let them go."

Griff slowly turned around to face Kaz. "You don't suffer from their delusions. They are easily manipulated, but you know better. You wouldn't hesitate to use that weapon if it meant defending yourself. You wouldn't stop to consider how your weapon feels about what it was designed to do. Don't let their idealistic natures contaminate your mind. In that chamber is the vehicle that will increase our understanding of the universe a thousand-fold. It'll elevate our species above all others."

"This isn't the way. Please don't make me do this," Kaz said, pushing the end of his rifle toward Griff's chest.

Something burst from Griff's forearm compartment, and Kaz was pushed back, covered in the same webbing that had been used on T'Chura. Griff regarded Kaz as he thrashed on the floor, but his escape attempts were no more successful than T'Chura's had been.

Griff turned toward me with contempt. "You've lost this fight. I'm getting in that chamber and you're going to open the way for me. How that happens is up to you. Does your friend have to die for you to realize this, or can you concede that you have no other choice?"

My gaze flicked toward Ben and then toward Kaz.

Griff leaned so he was in my line of sight, and I wouldn't look at him.

The battlebots carried me forward, immune to my struggling. I needed to calm down and think of a way out of this. Maybe I was wrong, and Larry just happened to look like the creatures from the relic site but was simply a machine fulfilling its primary purpose. *He.* I shrieked the denial inside my head. When I'd gotten in trouble, Larry had intervened. He'd done it at the museum with the Asherah relics and he'd done it at the outpost.

I looked toward him, but he didn't appear to be afraid at all. He walked next to the battlebots as if he had nowhere else to go, behaving as if our being here was inevitable.

"Tell them to put me down," I said.

Griff didn't reply, and the battlebots kept ahold of me.

"I'll do it. I'll open the damn chamber."

One of the battlebots paused, and the other carried me forward for a second before he stopped.

"I didn't tell you to stop. Keep going," Griff said.

The battlebots resumed their pace and brought me right to the chamber where the silvery door waited.

The battlebots dropped me onto the ground and I pushed myself up onto my feet. I turned back toward the others. T'Chura was farthest away on the ground, tangled in the webbing and unable to move, and Kaz was a short distance from him, but the robots carried Ben over.

Griff gave me a get-on-with-it look.

I didn't have a choice, not really. Sure, I could try to run away, but I couldn't rescue the others. They would be killed. Griff wouldn't hesitate. I didn't need a demonstration to know that he was a killer. In his mind, he was probably showing an enormous amount of restraint. Maybe it was because of Kaz, but I could tell Griff's patience was running out.

I exposed my right arm and stretched out my hand toward the door. Larry looked up at me for a few seconds, then leaped toward it. There was a flash of light as Larry seemed to dissolve into the door, and then it disintegrated, leaving the way open. One of the battlebots shoved me inside, and I stumbled.

The others quickly joined me inside the chamber. The edge

of the darkened chamber began to glow, lighting up the room. There were several metallic platforms with a pedestal in the center.

Griff pushed past me to get a closer look at them.

I followed him. The bots would make me do it anyway, so why give them another Nate-stumbling-ahead show? Plus, there was freedom in taking action on my own—freedom like climbing onto one of the platforms first and letting it activate.

Several things seemed to happen at the same time, and none of them were at all what I expected.

CHAPTER 33

I wasn't in the chamber anymore, at least not like I had been before. I saw the battlebots clutching Ben's arms, but they were absurdly still, as if time had frozen around them. An amber veil covered them like peering at a light through a tightly knit shirt. I glanced to the side and saw Griff reaching toward me, but he was frozen like everyone else. The lighting from the floor at the edge of the room pulsed a little, as if whatever was powering it was being disrupted. It became dimmer, and a few moments later it brightened. I looked down and saw my hands clutching the metallic ring that went around the top of the pedestal. It didn't hurt. I couldn't feel anything. The detached realization made me want to snatch my hands away, and I almost did, but there was a sudden shifting of the light, and the dark ceiling overhead burst outward, revealing a starlit sky. A foreign galaxy stretched across it, and I marveled at the sight. Then the image above me changed. It dissolved into millions of pieces, only to reform showing the landscape of a planet. I saw a nearby mountain, and the area was desolate. Then I saw the Asherah.

Thousands of them appeared, and with each blink of my eyes a city formed around them, all ivory-colored buildings with splashes of maroon. Something about it looked out of place. I cocked my head to the side and saw that one half of the city had sunk into the ground, making it appear somewhat lopsided. Asherah ran from the city as if it were a death trap.

I couldn't control what I was seeing. The machine must've had some kind of pre-programmed info-dump meant for someone else. There was a flash, and the city appeared to be in a partial state of decay. I looked to the side and saw a new city being built from material salvaged from the old. I felt like I was watching a time-lapse video that showed things in spurts that could've been years going by. None of it made sense to me. Why would an ancient alien terminal show me these things? Was this what had happened to the Asherah before they disappeared?

As if sensing my confusion, the images changed once again. One side was a star map that I didn't recognize, and the other side was of a chamber similar to the one I was in. An Asherah stood with his hands on the pedestal, just like I'd done. Then an Asherah appeared in front of me. His entire body was semi-translucent, as if I was seeing a ghost or an echo. The Asherah's wide head tilted to the side and his black eyes stared at me. He looked surprised to see me...He *saw* me. What the hell was this place? I wanted to let the pedestal go and stop whatever it was doing to me, but I couldn't. I looked down at my hands, and one was covered with the pulsating bronze of the Asherah artifact. I tried to pull my hand away, but it had somehow attached to the pedestal and held me in place.

Multiple flashes of light occurred, and different Asherah appeared at the pedestal, some of them overlapping. They were there for only a few seconds. Some didn't notice me at all, while others did, and a sudden realization took hold of my mind and wouldn't let go. I was seeing this chamber across time, and it was happening faster, as if I could see events of an entire timeline all at once. I stood with one hand attached to the machine and even saw echoes of my own body standing in the same place.

At some point it stopped. No one was in the chamber, and then the chamber itself was gone. Nothing was in its place—not the chamber, not this ancient relic that the Asherah had built—it was simply gone. I felt like my brain was racing toward realizations and knowledge faster than I could work them out as coherent thoughts. I also felt like I was falling, adrift among a sea of stars. I squeezed my eyes shut, wanting to return to the chamber, *needing* to return. Suddenly, the drifting feeling was gone, and I felt solid ground beneath my feet. I opened my eyes, and I was back in the chamber at the exact moment I'd first touched the pedestal.

Larry sat in front of me. His feline body glowed with an otherworldly light as if his essence had been captured, and I'd finally achieved the awareness to see him as he truly was—not from this universe. I stared at him, wide-eyed and speechless. His head tilted to the side and looked at something behind me. I didn't need to turn around to see it. I could see around the entire chamber all at once, as if every action I could take was happening at the same time and I was aware of it all.

An Asherah stood behind me, watching as if contemplating something he had never encountered but might've expected. Pale skin reflected the light, giving him an ethereal look. He towered over me, and I recoiled from him. I imagined his face twisting with a primal fury at my intrusion into what the Asherah had left behind, but it was only my imagination. Fearful, intense dreams stripped away from me, revealing a pensive being in front of me. He stared at me with a curious look that reminded me of Ben as Crim explained some technological wonder to him.

The Asherah lifted one of his arms with a wide palm upward, and Larry leaped over my head. Instead of phasing out of existence, as I expected he would, he sailed through the area in a gravity-defying leap. Landing on the Asherah's palm, Larry dissolved to form a pattern up his outstretched arm—the same as the relic that appeared on my own arm and the key to understanding the purpose of this place.

Image-laced thoughts passed between us unspoken, and my understanding of the Asherah increased beyond what any ancient relic could convey. I knew how they first arrived here and what had driven the survivors to push the boundaries of their understanding of the universe. They were beings out of time from another galaxy, a place they yearned to return to, as if being here was the price of some kind of galactic mistake they never completely understood. The being with me in the chamber was a scientist, an unraveller of mysteries, an explorer of the universe, and the being I'd brazenly named Larry was an extension of himself, a relic comprised of the Asherah and their exploits beyond our universe.

These thoughts or lessons of understanding swirled around in my brain, stretching my mind to the brink. It was too much too fast, but the Asherah didn't understand or care. He had his own mission to achieve. He showed me the true purpose of this place and why it was doomed to failure. The Asherah were a race of beings who were never going to return home. Each failure had driven wedges among them, giving way to factions when they'd built the machines to help increase their understanding of the universe. Knowledge trapped and forever denied, but still, they pushed on until they'd triggered a response from a place beyond.

I gasped, watching, and finally understanding what the spikes that attacked us were, how the Golems were echoes of beings trapped in a place between universes brought forth through Asherah experiments that later spiraled out of control. The spikes had two forms—a sphere that slowly moved from place to place, consuming everything in its path. They'd been brought to this universe because the Asherah wanted to ascend to achieve knowledge and understanding beyond the constraints of time. The resonance inside this chamber would summon them. As the Asherah attempted to return to their homeworld in some other galaxy, they were willing to risk the spikes pouring in through their machine. With the machine offline, the spikes had become dormant, but once activated they returned. They were the cause of the destruction here. The Asherah never escaped. This was where they had perished, victims of their own imperfect understanding that knowledge was meant to be earned by taking smaller, incremental steps that might lead to a leap but could never be circumvented entirely.

I looked up at the scientist, the explorer, the traveler, an echo of a race gone from this galaxy, and finally realized that I'd led an expedition here to a place better left forgotten.

I saw Griff and the others again, all artificially still like a living photograph. Griff was reaching toward the pedestal, about to begin his own journey of Asherah design, except I knew exactly what he would do. He'd use the knowledge here, like a child in a roomful of explosives. Not only would they destroy the child but the house he lived in and the street where his neighbors lived, triggering a cascade of nightmares that would spiral out of control.

I had to stop Griff.

I needed to destroy this place.

The echo of the Asherah scientist seemed satisfied at last that I had the knowledge I needed to do what he'd failed to do countless eons ago, or was it happening right at this very moment? The thought threatened to scatter my focus and I'd be unable to fulfill my mission.

I frowned at the thought.

Not *my* mission. Destroying this place was *their* mission.

I looked down at my hand, encased in a living bronze material, and knew there was only one way I could be rid of it completely. I let go of the pedestal and time remained frozen in place. The process of starting the machine had already begun and I didn't need the pedestal anymore. I could move into a space between moments. This was how Larry seemed to phase in and out as if he was teleporting across space.

I reached over my head and drew the multipurpose weapon Crim had given me. The rod expanded into a stick, and I swung it toward the other pedestal. The sonic emitters burst forth, shattering the ancient pedestal to dust.

Crim screamed, eyes wide in shock.

I turned and swung the stick toward the pedestal that I'd used, destroying it, too.

Then the battlebots lunged toward me. I flinched backward and my back slammed against the far wall. The force of it jolted my concentration, startling me, and I shook my head to clear it.

A cascade of images appeared in front of me, all of them actions I could take and their outcomes, some of which were difficult to see as the images overlapped. Instead of attacking Griff, I moved toward Ben, seeking to strike the battlebots that held him.

I almost made it.

A battlebot blindsided me and dozens of images flooded my mind, some with us inside the chamber and what was outside of it, and it was the outside that gave me pause. What I saw stopped me from doing anything, even as the battlebots seized both my arms. Griff spoke, but I couldn't hear him. Outside the chamber, making their way here, were thousands of spikes. Otherworldly metallic spheres that worked outside the laws of physics were seeking me out. They weren't after the machine or the others. I was the person with a connection to the Asherah machine. It attracted them toward me, and nothing could stop them.

CHAPTER 34

"What have you done!" Griff screamed.

My head spun with the possibilities of so many actions, timelines, and outcomes. It made it almost impossible to stay focused on the moment I was in. I was both disoriented and focused at almost the same time, with everything jumbled together like I was tumbling through space. I clenched my teeth, squeezing my eyes shut in an attempt to block everything out.

I felt myself get lifted and my feet dangled above the ground. Inhaling a long, steadying breath, I opened my eyes. Griff stood where the pedestal had been. He spun toward me.

"You destroyed it. The knowledge here, countless years beyond measure gone because of your pathetic whim," Griff said.

He looked around the chamber as if he couldn't believe what had happened.

"There are other chambers," Griff said walking toward the back of the chamber. "I see something better."

My perspective shifted outside the chamber, and I saw the

vast openness filled with other chambers, most of which had been destroyed. Griff didn't realize it yet, but there were only some like this one that might have escaped destruction.

I extended my connection to what must be the Asherah central core. It was a hub where millions of Asherah had perished. I saw them all there, launching a futile attempt to traverse the universe to their home galaxy even as the Spikes raced toward them. I watched them die and I turned away from it, but I couldn't escape the knowledge of all the death that had occurred here. The machine was what mattered. It had to be stopped.

Among the Spikes and Golems racing toward us even now were the servants—some kind of bridge species that had been made to take a form similar to a meerkat. It was as if I had an army of Larrys at my command. They emerged from the metallic Golems, able to stand apart from them, and I ordered them to destroy the machine. They threw themselves at the central core in a suicidal attempt to overwhelm what the Asherah had created with knowledge that was beyond them.

"No. No. No!" Griff screamed and turned toward me. "Kill him. Kill him. Kill! Him!"

I watched myself be killed. Timelines of possibilities stretched before me. I died. I fought. I begged. I stumbled. I screamed.

Imagining dying could startle me awake sometimes, gasping from a nightmare with only a glimmer of what was going to kill me, except I couldn't wake from this nightmare. I faced it because I couldn't put a limit on seeing across time, and I hated it. I hated the inevitability of it all. It leeched hope from my soul and promised that no matter what I did, I was going to die here. Griff was going to kill me, or his damn battlebots would do it.

I became so fixated on my imminent demise, that I nearly

forgot to observe my entire surroundings. Too many things going on at once made things blurry around me but also presented possibilities—things I hadn't considered. Just as taking action was important to influencing the outcome of events beyond our control, sometimes not doing anything was an important option. Knowing when to act was just as important as when not to act.

A battlebot reached a long arm in front of me, firing his weapon at the bot that held me, taking it by complete surprise. The battlebot's head exploded and it released me. My would-be rescuer pulled me behind it, firing his weapon at the bots holding Ben prisoner.

Kaz used the distraction to break free of one of his captors, but I saw that it wasn't enough. I pulled my rescuer's arm to the side and fired its weapon.

"Captain," Kierenbot said, his voice coming from the head of the battlebot. He had his weapon pointed at Griff. "Shall I dispatch him for you?"

Gritting my teeth, I wanted to let him do it. It would only take a second and Griff would be gone, but seconds wasted could be the difference between escape and dying here. There were too many timelines where Kierenbot failed to kill Griff.

And I wasn't about to die here.

"We have to leave. Free T'Chura," I said, stooping down to retrieve my rifle.

The battlebot that Kierenbot had taken over ran from the chamber.

Griff scrambled out of the chamber, and Kaz moved to follow him.

"Wait," I said.

"Osira's down there. She's that way. I've got a clear signal. I can't leave her here," Kaz said.

"You won't have to. Go on ahead, we're right behind you."

Kaz was about to leave and paused. "Nate, I'm sorry."

"Apologies later. Run now. The Shifter Spikes are coming."

Kaz's eyes widened, and he ran out of the chamber.

Ben stared at me for a second, then his gaze went to my arm.

"Get ready to run," I said and looked through the door to see a battlebot helping T'Chura to his feet.

Beyond, a wave of Shifter Spikes moved toward them. The space between them was filled with metallic Golems that galloped on all fours like some kind of vicious alien primate.

The few remaining battlebots outside the chamber fired their weapons at the oncoming horde. Lacking any other instruction, they were going to be overwhelmed. At least they'd buy us the seconds we needed to escape.

"Come on!" I said, trying to ignore the various echoes of timelines that hadn't happened.

T'Chura ran toward us in a limping trot while Kierenbot urged him forward. Griff's battlebots ignored him and maintained the last line of defense.

T'Chura swung an arm around Kierenbot, and they began to move faster. Soon, they were inside the chamber, and I waved them through to the other side.

I quickly darted ahead of them.

"Come on, we can't fight them here. If they surround us, we'll die," I said.

We raced down a path outside, and I looked to the side. A rising wave of Shifter Spikes moved toward us. They altered course to chase us down. I was the one they wanted. As long as I remained connected to the central core, they'd hunt me down. I had to get there to destroy it.

As we ran, multiple options appeared in front of me, and I could take the time to see what all the outcomes would be.

Anything that kept us away from the Shifter Spikes was the path I took.

I glanced back to see that the others were only a few steps behind. A group of metallic Golems hurtled over the structures nearby and I swung my weapon up and fired. Explosive rounds pushed them back a little. I slowed down to lay suppressing fire, which didn't work. The Golems were mindless machines and didn't exercise anything like rational thought. Where others might've taken cover against superior firepower, they kept coming, trusting their sheer numbers to get the job done. They weren't wrong.

Ben ran ahead and I saw the timeline diverge with terrible possibilities. I raced ahead and pulled him a different way. We both stumbled a little but quickly got moving as more metallic Golems appeared. They were hot on our heels, followed by a chaotic swirling mass, as if multiple tornados were wreaking havoc in the area.

We ran onward and Ben turned toward me.

"I've got Crim!" he said.

"Tell him we need help. He needs to get here asap."

CHAPTER 35

By the time we reached the central core, I'd come to realize that the Golems and the Shifter Spikes didn't play well together. They were like a pack of rabid dogs fixated on a solitary target. Neither cared what got in their way, including each other. The Spikes gained momentum, tearing through Golems as if they were a minor inconvenience, and the Golems hardly reacted at all.

Over the course of my life, I'd pushed a fair number of people to the breaking point with frustration and perhaps rage. I always thought most of them took themselves entirely too seriously. This wasn't the first mob to chase yours truly, but as we finally made it to the central core and saw what waited for us there, I had to laugh.

Kierenbot all but carried T'Chura and had no problem keeping up with Ben and me. Our combat suits helped us move with a speed that would impress any sports car enthusiast.

The central core was much like a giant colosseum. The ground sloped toward a massive black sphere that spun as waves of energy raced across the ceiling and were drawn into it, giving it a surrounding nimbus of ethereal glow.

Griff was already near it, about to reach one of the access points similar to what had been in the chamber. I wasn't going to be able to stop him from reaching it. Kaz was more than halfway there, but what had stolen an absurd laugh from me was the storm of Shifter Spikes and metallic Golems on the edges of the colosseum. It was a deadly gathering and we'd made it just in time to the party.

Without looking at the others, I said. "We've got a straight shot to the core. Go. Go. Go!"

I started running and saw Kierenbot jump past me in a high arc. T'Chura was on his back. Kierenbot was using the battle-bot's thrusters to take exceptionally long jumps toward the core.

Multiple possibilities opened before me. I hadn't used my flight system because I didn't want the torrents of high energy waves to instantly kill me as if I'd suddenly became Icarus and flown too close to the sun. But since the central core was at a lower elevation, Kierenbot had correctly surmised that the risk was worth it.

I realized that the timelines I saw were limited to my own perceptions and biases for what was possible. Simply put, if I couldn't think it, then I'd remain ignorant of the possibilities.

I engaged my suit's flight systems and sped ahead, calling for Ben to do the same. As he ran, he called back to me that his suit didn't have flight capabilities. I swooped down and did a controlled tackle-and-fly, carrying him into the air.

"Thanks, Nate."

"No problem, kid."

"I think I'll take you up on your offer to learn how to use the flight systems."

I grinned a little and sped toward the core.

It wasn't that long ago that Ben would've been paralyzed by fear. The fear was there. We both felt it, but it didn't keep us from moving forward. Being frozen in terror was how we died.

As I flew toward the center, I saw thousands of Shifter Spikes surge forward in a deadly wave of darkness. They reminded me of mighty flood waters, and we were scrambling toward the highest peak to escape them, but we were only delaying the inevitable.

I had to stop the machine. It was the only way we'd escape and send the aberrations back to where they'd come from.

Griff was there now, opening the floodgates of the Asherah archives, and I needed to stop him before it was too late.

I sped toward the core and reached it just as Kaz arrived. Osira was sprawled on the ground. She was alive, but her eyes were bulging and her chin trembled. She looked as if she was about to scream, but only soft moaning and whimpering escaped her lips, and I thought that was worse.

I dropped Ben near Kaz and continued toward Griff. A silvery nimbus surrounded him, and I flew toward it like a moth to a flame.

Contact.

I was part of the machine. This place was where millions of Asherah had come in an effort to return home. For all they'd accomplished, they'd been unable to give up on the one thing that had ultimately destroyed them. That was what the scientist had shown me. If the Asherah had chosen a slower path of development, they might've survived and figured out another way for their descendants to return to their home galaxy. But they couldn't let it go. They'd latched onto the idea so completely that letting go simply wasn't an option.

As I watched Griff use the machine, attached to the knowledge of the universe, I saw him absorb the possibilities with a thirst that could never be quenched. Then I had the sudden awareness of a third person attached to the machine.

A barrage of possibilities surrounded me, but I was also participating in them. They swept me off in their wake like a powerful river that I couldn't overcome.

Me, stuck in the exact moment that I finally reached Griff, and Griff bringing the machine completely online, greedily seeking to acquire knowledge he couldn't comprehend while legions of Shifter Spikes poured through in a deluge of unstoppable force that would unravel everything.

Then there was Osira. She'd touched the machine and had a Larry-type servant of her own.

I focused my attention on her and saw a swirling mass of emotions, actions, and despair trapping her in a terrible loop. She remained fixated on her own death until she couldn't consider anything else, as if the thought of surviving was beyond her comprehension. The machine had broken her, just as surely as it would break all of us.

"Griff," I said.

He turned toward me. We were in a place outside of time that was no longer linear.

He was awestruck, and I saw new possibilities swirling around him.

"Nate, isn't this wonderful? Not only all the knowledge of the Asherah right here for us to find, but a way to push the fringe of technology beyond everything the great thinkers of the past ever conceived. The entire galaxy will pay homage to what we will give them. The entire universe is at our fingertips."

The thing about megalomaniacs was that they were often too far gone to let go of the very thing they believed made them powerful. But I had to try.

"Look at Osira, Griff. She's in pain. She won't survive this."

Griff frowned as if the possibility had never occurred to him. He hadn't even known she'd already touched the machine.

He turned toward where she lay on the ground. Kaz and Ben leaned over her, frozen in a moment of time.

"She's confused. I'll help her understand."

I shook my head. "It's too much, Griff. Too much for anyone. We need to turn it off. You have to let this go."

Griff stared at me. Divergent echoes of his emotions played out for me.

Denial.

Anger.

Arrogance.

Derision.

And the cycle began again. None of the reactions held any inkling of wisdom, as if the possibility of letting the archives go had never occurred to him. Then he arrived at another echo of thought, the one I knew had to come to him.

Threat.

"There was a group of Asherah scientists that tried to stop them from using the machine. None of this is what we thought it was. You have to stop before it's too late."

Griff leaned away from me with a half-formed snarl. "Short-sighted fools. The Asherah found a way to extract knowledge from the universe. They elevated themselves beyond anything we can imagine, and we can do the same. We can do it better!"

I shook my head. "No, we can't. They killed themselves doing exactly what you intend."

"No, they succeeded. They…"

Griff's tenuous connection to the machine wasn't as strong as mine, but he more than made up for it with sheer will and intent. Whether he realized it or not, his finger was on the trigger, and the stakes were our lives, but beyond that, if this machine was replicated, it would lead to hordes of unstoppable Shifter Spikes. They had a purpose, even if I would never understand it. They didn't belong here, and I was more than willing to help them leave.

Griff turned toward me with a scathing look of betrayal.

The edges of my lips lifted. "Time never really stops, Griff. Even when we see entire lines of possibilities."

He snarled, seeking to activate the core and do what the Asherah had failed to do billions of years ago. They'd somehow stumbled across time and space, unable to return home. Griff was going to do the same and damn the cost. This was what the galaxy owed him for a lifetime of fallen grace.

I grabbed Griff and pulled him away from the core, but he was still connected to it with his mind. I didn't know how it worked, so I did the only thing I could think of. I threw Griff into the horde of Shifter Spikes.

Griff, distracted by multiple timelines of possibilities arrayed around him, as well as the threat that I was going to destroy the core, was paralyzed long enough for him to reach the devastating embrace of an anathema to life. The Shifter Spikes were the negative to our positive. They were the antimatter to our matter, and when Griff collided with them, they split his every atom apart in seconds. It was as if a lynchpin held us together and the Shifter Spikes caused it to cease to exist, and we fell apart.

I spun in the air, and the battlewagon blew a hole through the side of the building. A comlink immediately registered with me.

"Destroy it now, Crim!"

The battlewagon's cannons swung toward the core, unleashing a powerful barrage. For all the power that was part of the core, it was also built upon precision and a delicate balance that created the perfect conditions allowing the Asherah to tap into the brain of the universe and also traverse the universe. The slightest disruption from the battlewagon's powerful weapons were enough to interrupt it.

We just had to escape before the backlash of energy killed us all.

CHAPTER 36

I saw Ben helping Kaz lift Osira off the ground.

The kinetic strike from the battlewagon's mag cannon slammed into the spinning globe, causing it to wobble. Crim was a veteran soldier. He knew better than to become trigger happy to the exclusion of everything else. A disruption would give them the time they needed to escape.

The battlewagon dove toward where the others were on the ground.

T'Chura and Kierenbot fired their weapons at a small army of metallic Golems, which barely slowed them down. They were completely animated, and the only thing that would stop them was the destruction of this entire place.

I lunged toward them, traveling at breakneck speeds. The machine couldn't simply be turned on and off; most complicated things didn't work like that. I saw the disruption that the battlewagon's weapons caused, and it seemed to increase the Golems' fervor to reach the others.

The battlewagon hovered above the ground, its weapons

firing at the enemy, pushing them back toward the Shifter Spikes that tore them apart while the Spikes moved toward them with the intensity of a gathering storm.

The rear hatch opened just as I joined the others. Osira screamed, and tried to pull away from Kaz and Ben. I swooped in behind her and shoved her into? the ship. The others climbed in?.

Kaz turned toward me. "Come on, Nate. What are you waiting for?"

"Go. I have to stop this." Kaz stepped toward the edge of the hatch, determined to come with me. I backed away, hovering in the air, and his eyes widened in shock. "You can't help with this. Go on. I'll be right behind you."

I didn't wait for his reply but spun around and launched myself toward the wobbling sphere. The battlewagon launched into the air, just barely out of range of the oncoming enemy.

I exposed my relic-infused arm. It was completely encased in that bronze material and had taken a life all its own. Balling my hand into a fist, I thrust my arm in front of me and flew toward the sphere with all the force I could muster.

What had begun as a disruption to a perfectly balanced machine was exacerbated by me. If I'd had the time to actually think this through, I would've gotten my ass aboard the battlewagon and gotten the hell out of here. But with all the possible timelines converging in my head, I was focused on how to stop the machine. The battlewagon's weapons, while powerful, weren't enough to stop what had already been set into motion.

The sphere stopped spinning, as if my hand had the power of God to make it so. The relic on my arm was the same material as the sphere. I became part of the core, and the Asherah scientist had given me the knowledge I'd needed to stop it once and for all.

There were still forces at work trying to keep the core going—energy provided with some kind of tap into three stars—but what dwarfed that was the energy pulled from elsewhere. It was the same place that the Shifter Spikes had come from. It was also what animated the Golems and was a core component of the servants.

I saw the Asherah scientist with a brief flash of Larry at his side. They'd stored the necessary instructions in the relic on my arm. I was the key, and the core was the lock.

The skin on my arm felt like I'd dipped it into a boiling acid bath, and I screamed. The pain took all of my attention until it blocked out everything else. I watched as the relic tore away from my arm, taking my skin with it.

The pain.

My God, it hurt...

With the relic gone, my combat suit surged over my arm. I felt my consciousness begin to slip and I fought to stay alert. The Shifter Spikes clustered together at the bottom of the core, clamoring to get at me. I stared at them with the slow realization that I was about to die, but somehow I was moving away from them. They pushed up like large black globules of consuming death, but somehow I managed to stay just ahead of them.

The power-draw of the flight systems in my combat suit maximized and pushed me away from the core.

Violent ripples of living bronze caused the surface of the core to bend in forceful spikes. Then it collapsed onto itself, becoming a quivering mass until some threshold had been achieved, and then expanded at blurring speeds. I tried to watch it, my head moving slowly as I craned my neck to gaze at the destruction of the Asherah stronghold, the last remnant of a doomed civilization.

I couldn't move my arms or legs. They were locked in the

rigid formation necessary for fast flight. My thruster output was at maximum. The core seemed to expand in slow motion as echoes of timelines began to strip away from me. My connection to the machine was gone.

I looked away from the rapidly expanding core and a dark shadow loomed directly in front of me. It took me a few seconds to realize that I'd somehow flown right into the hangar of the *Spacehog*.

My arms moved as the flight systems brought me in to land on the deck where I collapsed onto the floor.

"Out of the way!" Kierenbot shouted.

He lifted me into the air. After all that had happened, I was having trouble keeping up with events. I went from having too many thoughts in my head to the point where some part of my brain—probably the smart part—had put on the brakes to save the core that is me.

The walls of the ship's corridors went by in a blur, and Kierenbot might've handed me off to someone. All I knew was that they put me into the autodoc…again. It was like someone was playing some kind of cosmic joke that made the aliens aboard the ship need to stick me into the damn autodoc.

When I finally emerged from my stupor, I learned they hadn't had any other choice.

The autodoc was really a multipurpose trauma unit. For serious injuries, like mine, it became a medical capsule.

I woke with the silver canopy over my body. I had just enough room to look down at myself and saw a thick yellow cast covering my entire right arm and about half of my chest. I couldn't feel my arm at all.

The canopy opened and Crim's dark-eyed, craggy face peered down at me.

I winced and looked away. "No offense, Crim, but I never want to wake up to see your face."

He chuckled and gave me a once-over. "My responsibilities have expanded from keeping the ship operational to keeping you alive. I want to renegotiate my contract."

The walls of the capsule sank down to become just an ordinary bed. The air was cooler than it had been inside.

I sighed, still a little groggy. "Not even awake for thirty seconds and you're complaining about all the work you'll have to do."

His face twitched with amusement, but I became somber.

I cleared my throat. "How bad is it?"

He was quiet for a few moments before he spoke. "It's quite serious. Losing your arm would've been bad enough, but it was your cognitive functions I was most concerned about."

I blinked and looked at my arm, heart beginning to race.

"Now don't get too upset. I said *almost*."

I frowned, trying to remember what he'd just said, and shook my head. "No, you didn't. You said I lost my arm. 'Losing your arm would've been bad enough…'"

Crim considered it for a moment, then made a flicking motion with his hand, as if whether or not I lost my arm was inconsequential. "Maybe I did. Sorry about that. Your arm will eventually be fine, unless your body rejects the muscular regrowth matrix the autodoc put together. It's just going to take a little while."

My eyes narrowed. "Just so I'm clear, I didn't lose my arm, but you had to regrow my muscles?"

Crim gestured toward it. "Obviously, Nate. Your arm is right there. Oh, and not *all* your muscles. Just some bits here and there. Chunks actually. Anyway, I'm surprised you're not more concerned about the other thing I said."

Chunks?

I inhaled a deep breath, then lifted my gaze toward his. "God, you really suck at this."

He frowned. "Technically, this was Raylin's role. She had a good feel for this. Serena too."

I looked away from him and nodded. The ship felt empty without them on it, as if we were incomplete.

"So, you don't want to discuss the other thing I mentioned?"

I rolled my eyes. "If there was something wrong with my brain, I'd know it…" I paused for a second, staring at him, eyes narrowed. "You're testing me. This is some kind of cognitive-performance thing."

Crim nodded, dark eyes gleaming. I was glad he was having fun with it.

I arched an eyebrow at him. "So, did I pass?"

He nodded. "With flying colors, Nate. I'm actually impressed by your resilience."

I wasn't. I hadn't even begun to wrap my mind around what had happened. I lifted my chin toward my arm. "No alien miracle paste to regrow the skin?"

He shook his head. "Skin is easy. It's the muscles that take a little bit of time."

"Muscles?"

"You forgot already?"

I shook my head. "No, I'm still just waking up."

He considered that for a few moments and then nodded. "Yes. We think that when the relic finally detached from your skin, it took some of your…" He frowned for a few seconds. "Musculature. Flesh. Yes, that's the reference. A pound of flesh."

I pinched my lips together and blinked. Then I shook my

head. "No, that's got nothing to do with it. The Asherah weren't some Shylock from a Shakespearian play. Dammit Crim, this isn't the time for that kind of stuff."

He looked away from me and yawned, as if I was the one overreacting.

"You know what, your bedside manner sucks."

"I'm better with vehicles."

I nodded. "Anything else I should know?"

He sighed. "Where to begin."

"Why don't you start with the ship. I'm assuming we escaped. Did we take any damage?"

Crim started to speak a few times and stopped himself. "I'll keep this high level. Yes, Kierenbot managed to get us to a safe distance, but we did sustain some damage. We're working on the repairs, but honestly, what he did was really quite remarkable."

"What did he do?"

Crim's eyebrows raised. "He hacked into one of Griff's battle-bots for one. He remote-piloted your combat suit, saving your life, and he was able to fly the ship out of that mess."

I pursed my lips in thought. "I should probably give him your share of the profit we made off this trip."

Crim frowned in surprise and crossed his arms. "We didn't make a profit off this. We have nothing to show for this at all. In fact, this whole trip cost us credits. You know we lost the recon skiff."

I considered that for a few seconds and then smiled. "At least we didn't lose the battlewagon, right?"

He stared at me for a few seconds, shoulders slumping, and gave me a grudging nod. "I wouldn't say we escaped free of damage…"

"Crim, you need to start looking on the bright side of things.

We escaped with our lives. We almost didn't. Believe me, I saw too many times where we…"

My memories of so many different timelines were still in the forefront of my mind. All those times I watched us die, or some of us, was enough to make me clench my jaw.

Crim glanced at the holoscreen where my vital signs were on display for the whole world to see. Then he looked at me with concern. "Nate, it's all right. You did it. I don't know how you did it, but I know that we owe our lives to you."

They wouldn't have been there if not for me. I'd pushed for it, and then it had become something Kaz couldn't walk away from.

I swallowed hard.

The worst thing about a non-linear perception of time was that I experienced the emotions of the moments I happened to focus on. It was enough to drive a person insane, being pulled in so many different directions, sometimes forgetting what was real and what wasn't.

I squeezed my eyes shut and pushed those false memories out of my mind. They hadn't happened, but they were almost memories, and they weren't pleasant.

I needed to distract myself. I looked at Crim. "So, my arm is going to be fine?"

Crim nodded. "It might take about six months of wearing that specialized cast."

I blinked. "Are you serious?"

He stared at me, deadpanned expression.

I sighed. "So, about a week then?"

He smiled and shrugged. "About that."

I let out a long breath and sat up. The cast completely immobilized my right arm. Crim helped me sit up all the way.

"It feels weird."

"It will. You're getting numbing medication to block the pain, otherwise you'd be screaming."

I looked down at the cast, trying to feel my arm. I tried to flex my fingers, but they wouldn't move.

Crim shook his head. "Why don't you listen to me? I just said that you shouldn't move your arm."

I frowned. It was becoming a habit. "No, you didn't. Stop helping me. Whatever you're doing, I want you stop it now. Just go back to treating me as you normally do. Got it?"

He nodded. "Okay. You really need to… the rest of the crew is in the commons area. We have a lot questions, but I need to warn you about Kaz."

"What's wrong with Kaz?" I asked.

I'd killed his mentor, but he had to understand that I didn't have a choice about that.

"Osira didn't make it."

"Didn't make it? She got on the battlewagon. I pushed her in? the ship. What do you mean she didn't make it? What happened to her?"

"It was the machine. She was too far gone. Most of her cognitive capabilities were impaired, but when she learned that Griff had died…" Crim said and became quiet.

"How did she die?"

Crim sighed. "She committed suicide by going out the airlock. Kaz tried to stop her, but she wouldn't listen to him. By the time anyone else learned what was happening, it was too late."

He looked as if he had more to say, so I nodded for him to keep going.

"She began to get more coherent, and with it, the loss of Griff was too much."

"So, you're saying that starting to heal was why she ended her life?"

Crim nodded a little. "I don't have a good answer, mostly because we don't know what that machine did to her, or to you."

I considered it for a minute. "That's why you were asking me all those questions, pretending to say things to test me. I think I understand now," I said and paused for a long moment. "Should I be concerned about Kaz?"

"He'll be fine, eventually."

I stared at him. "Crim, come on."

He rolled his eyes. "I don't know, Nate. I'm better with engines and power cores than I am with living things. There is a bond that Kaz shared with both Griff and Osira. How would you feel if someone you were close to suddenly died?"

I inhaled a breath and sighed. "I wouldn't like it. All right, I think I understand."

I moved to stand up and Crim shook his head.

"You should rest more."

"If you try to push me back into the autodoc, I'm going to swing my indestructible cast at your face. Now, I'm getting out of this bed," I said. Crim stared at me, and I added. "But if I start to fall, you'll need to catch me."

Crim backed up. "I think it'll be more fun to watch you fall. I've noticed that sometimes Humans—you, in particular—learn things the hard way."

I shrugged, or I tried to. Only one of my shoulders moved. "I've never been much of a follower."

Crim chuckled and shook his head.

I snickered. "Neither are you."

I stood and waited for a few seconds to see if I could handle it. Walking with this giant cast was not going to be fun.

"Don't we have a wheelchair or something I can use?"

"Oh, *now* you want help."

I nodded. "Yeah, I just don't want to lie down in a bed anymore. I don't even know how long you had me in that capsule."

Crim walked over to the wall and opened a holoscreen.

"Crim," I said.

He grunted a noncommittal reply.

"How long have I been out of commission?"

He closed the holoscreen and turned toward me. "Five days."

My eyes widened as my eyebrows attempted to invade my hairline. "What? Five days!"

"You were in bad shape."

"Gee, you think?"

Crim shrugged. "I'm glad you're feeling better."

A large panel opened, and a metallic block floated out. A seat back opened, along with two arms, making a space for me to sit.

"Your chariot awaits, Captain," Crim said.

I looked at the floating chair doubtfully.

"It'll support you. It's got a grav pallet that could even support T'Chura."

I moved away from the bed and the chair floated toward me. It moved behind me and I sat down. I expected the chair to sink a little, but it didn't. The comfort wasn't bad either.

"You can control it with your omnitool," Crim said.

I feigned disappointment. "And here I thought you were going to push me down the corridor."

CHAPTER 37

The others were delighted to see me. Even Kaz perked up, and despite missing the crewmembers who were absent, it felt good. They spent the next half hour bringing me up to speed about what had happened.

"The entire star system is destroyed?" I asked.

Ben nodded. "That's what we saw. The Asherah had somehow forced the three star systems together to power their machine. Once it was destroyed, there was nothing to keep them together."

"But wouldn't the stars merge or gobble each other up or something?"

"There'll be a realignment," Crim said. "They've collided, and the system won't settle down for a long time. Chances are they'll eventually combine, and new planets will form from the materials of the old."

Ben nodded, excitedly. "It's really something."

"Do you think anyone will notice?"

Ben frowned and looked at Crim. He probably knew the answer but still deferred to Crim's expertise.

"Yes, there are a number of monitoring stations that track anomalies," Crim said.

I chewed on my lower lip for a moment, considering. "Suggestions on what to do about that? Should we inform someone? Let them ponder it? Get Delos Nadeau to send a survey team there?"

"That might not be a bad idea," Kaz said. "The survey team, I mean."

Crim shrugged. "If you're concerned that there is some remnant Asherah tech left there, then don't be. Everything was destroyed."

I looked at Ben and he shrugged. Then I turned toward T'Chura.

"There is wisdom in both actions, but I think it would be better to know for sure. And Delos has the resources required for discretion."

Delos was a Nasarian, a species dedicated to peaceful exploration and scientific research.

I nodded and looked at Kierenbot.

His red orb flashed. "Me, Captain?"

"Yes. What do you think?"

"I agree with T'Chura, Captain. Better that we know for sure, but the counterargument to that is what would Delos's team do if they did find something?"

I pressed my lips together in thought, and then bobbed my head to the side. "We can tell him it's dangerous, but we'd just have to trust their judgement. Regardless, even if they did find something, it wouldn't be intact, and they would never have the complete picture of what happened there."

"That's something we were hoping you'd clear up for the rest of us. What exactly happened to you?" Kaz asked.

I told them then. I told them about meeting the Asherah scientist, what Larry actually was, and how the Asherah were responsible for bringing the Shifter Spikes in from some other place.

"What other place?" Ben asked.

"Your guess is as good as mine."

He cleared his throat, eyebrows drawing together. "Somehow, I doubt it."

Sometimes these high concepts went right over my head. I wasn't a physicist or an engineer, and I couldn't be sure that what I was about to say wouldn't sound crazy. Besides, I no longer had the ability to witness multiple timelines to decide what the best course of action would be.

"This will sound a little strange, but would it be crazy to say it was another universe?"

Ben's eyes lit up and he smiled. "I was thinking the same thing. It makes the most sense. You know, as in why we couldn't stop them. Like the laws of physics didn't apply to them."

"Doesn't explain why when we came into physical contact we just sort of unraveled," I said.

Kaz locked gazes with me. "Is that what happened to him?"

He meant Griff.

I nodded. "It was the only way I could stop him."

Kaz's eyes sank toward the table, and he let out a long, low sigh. "I understand, Nate."

I winced, and my own gaze sank. "I'm sorry."

We were all quiet for a minute but not in a silent tribute for Griff. God no, he'd gotten what he deserved. It was for Kaz.

I lifted my gaze and looked at him. There were times when we disagreed, sometimes vehemently, but he was a friend—a real friend and not some acquaintance pretending to be a friend.

We'd both put our lives on the line. It was the kind of bond that was forged through trying times and on battlefields.

Kaz met my gaze and gave me a singular nod.

Crim tapped his hand on the tabletop and cleared his throat. "What was Griff actually trying to do?"

"He thought he was going to use the machine to travel to a distant galaxy. Remember how the Asherah ruins appeared almost at random around this galaxy? They were trying to perfect the technology to travel back to their home galaxy. They arrived here accidentally. An whole research facility. It looked like an entire city."

"An accident," Crim said, frowning in thought. "You saw it?"

I nodded. "Yeah."

"But that doesn't match up," Ben said. "The dating of the ruins we found, as well as at the core, indicates it was from near the beginning of time."

I raised my eyebrows and nodded toward the others. "Don't get them started about all that. Like I said, according to the scientist, they arrived in this galaxy because of some kind of experiment. I don't know what they were doing exactly, but they couldn't reverse it to return home."

"So, they spent years trying to recreate it," Kaz said. "That's why they'd appear at random places throughout history. They were jumping across time as well as space."

I nodded. "There's more," I said, and they waited for me to continue. "The chamber that Griff forced me to open, that was an enhancement thing. It allowed me to see time non-linearly but also possibilities. They used it to… they referred to it as a way to extract universal knowledge or knowledge from the universe. It put them in some kind of mental state."

Ben frowned. "Flow state?"

I stared at him. "What?"

"You know, flow state. It's when you're in deep concentration. Sometimes it's achieved through meditation."

"Maybe," I replied and looked at the others. "Does this make sense to you guys?"

Kaz nodded. "Yes. All kinds of species have tried to augment their intelligence to push the limits of what is possible."

Crim nodded slowly. "And some methods were more barbaric than others."

T'Chura stared at me for a long moment. "Are you experiencing any lingering effects?"

"You mean, can I still see multiple timelines?" I asked and then shook my head. "I wouldn't recommend it."

"Why not?" Ben asked, eyes wide.

"Because it's not right. Or maybe I'm not the right person for it."

"But you could prevent any mistake you might have made. You'd have a life without regret."

I noticed that the others watched me intently, which meant they were thinking along similar lines. "It's not that simple. I wouldn't wish this on anyone. It's too easy to lose yourself. That's what happened to Osira, I think. She was overwhelmed, and it made her lose her grip on reality. None of us are meant to be able to do this."

Kaz peered at me. "Could you see what she saw?"

I shook my head. "No, but I wasn't just a witness. I experienced it, like a memory. Sometimes they were vivid, as if it was happening right now. Others were distant. And there were so damn many of them. The effects compounded."

"Remarkable," Crim said.

I leaned toward him across the table as if I hadn't heard him. "Come again?"

"You sometimes demonstrate a singular focus to the exclusion of everything else. While others get caught up analyzing all the variables, you ignore them. I think it's that tendency that made you able to resist the effects of the machine for so long."

"Griff would've never been able to do that," Kaz said. I looked at him. "You were able to let it go. You used it to see not only the effect it was capable of having on you and other people, but also the Asherah. Others might not have been able to do that."

I let out a forceful breath. "Look what it got us—all of us nearly getting killed. People we care about actually getting killed. When we first came across those ruins, I thought we'd find something amazing…valuable. Something to show for our efforts, but all we got… are scars and nightmares."

"That's not all we got," T'Chura said.

I arched an eyebrow toward him.

"We've all gained a little bit of wisdom. Valuable insight to broaden our horizons. Change doesn't occur in a vacuum."

I considered it for a few moments. "I'll keep that in mind."

Crim sighed. "We're still down a lot of credits. You don't have an endless supply of them."

I grinned and Crim frowned toward me. Then he looked at the others.

"Oh, don't look so scared," I said. "There's an open bounty on finding anything related to the Asherah. When I contact Delos, he'll pay us the bounty."

Ben's mouth hung open. "But there's nothing left for them to find."

"Delos doesn't know that. And the bounty doesn't state that something physical has to be retrieved. Anyway, before you start lecturing me on ethics, there's evidence of what the Asherah did there that *is* valuable."

Ben glanced at Crim, but he didn't show any reaction at all.

He looked at me. "So, you're turning in the data for the bounty."

I nodded. "Yes, I think Delos will find some value in it. Conceptual-type things. He can decide whether it's worth the bounty. I doubt he'd give us anything out of the goodness of his heart."

"I guess I never thought about it that way."

I looked at Crim. He'd become something of a teacher of Ben's.

"It's best if he figures things out for himself. He'll get there," Crim said.

Ben rolled his eyes and smiled.

"Don't worry, kid. He did the same thing to me earlier," I said. I looked around the commons area. "Where is Lanaya?"

Ben gestured toward one of the doors across the room. "She's resting."

I nodded and then stifled a yawn.

I expected Crim to make some comment about me needing to rest, but it was T'Chura.

"You've been through quite an ordeal. We'll keep the ship running while you rest," he said.

I yawned again. "All right, fine. But I'm going to my own bed. No more of this autodoc business."

I started heading toward my room and opened the door.

"Oh Nate, one more thing," Crim said. I navigated my chair to turn toward him. "The chair can help you get into bed."

"Captain, I'd be more than happy to assist you," Kierenbot said.

"No, thank you, that won't be necessary," I said quickly.

Kierenbot might've looked disappointed.

I hastened through the door but thought I heard a few chuckles as it rematerialized behind me.

Grinning to myself a little, I managed to get into my own

bed and drift off to sleep.

I woke up and looked at my watch. I'd slept for seven hours. Yawning, I stretched as best I could with part of my body immobilized.

I looked at my cast. I could feel my arm a little. It didn't hurt. I was pretty sure there was still some kind of numbing agent that was part of the cast, but I was able to move it a little bit. I hoped that was normal.

I climbed out of bed and dressed myself. The nice thing about my fabricated clothing was that they could easily adjust to compensate for the cast. The smart fabric quickly adapted to perfectly fit my body.

I looked at the chair I'd used earlier. The safe course of action would be to use the chair. I'd needed it before, and maybe I still did, but no one ever pushed their limits by always taking it easy. I'd rather walk on my own two feet. If for whatever reason I failed to make it to the bridge, I'd suffer the indignity of someone bringing the chair to help me.

I walked past the chair and out of my room.

The commons room was dimly lit. The others were likely asleep except for Kierenbot, who'd be on the bridge.

I walked onto the bridge, and Kierenbot turned toward me in surprise.

"Captain, I wasn't expecting to see you at this hour."

"There's only so much time I can sleep. I knew you'd be awake, so I came here."

"Crim and Lanaya are also awake. They're doing something in his workshop. Minor repairs for the battlewagon."

I walked toward him and sat at the nearby workstation. The

chair didn't have any arms, so I could sit comfortably with my injured arm.

"Crim told me you managed a few miracles, and you saved my life."

"I was able to remote-control your combat suit and fly you toward the ship."

I didn't know he could do that, but I probably should've realized he could. "Yeah, and before that by taking control of Griff's battlebot."

"I wasn't sure if I could maintain control of it. The onboard AI was quite stubborn. I had to let it think it was in control most of the time until I decided direct action was required."

I regarded him for a few seconds. "I don't know how to thank you, Kierenbot."

"You just did, Captain."

"Yeah, but it doesn't seem like enough. I know you wanted a new chassis with combat capabilities so you could come with us off the ship. Maybe it's time to move on that."

Kierenbot waved the comment away. "Oh, you don't have to worry about that anymore. I kept the battlebot chassis. I have a few upgrades planned for it that I think you'll approve. It's in Crim's workshop."

I chuckled a little. "Whatever you need. You deserve any help I can give you." Kierenbot stared at me, his red orb gleaming. "I'm serious. You've gone above and beyond what you signed on for."

The red orb disappeared and Kierenbot became perfectly still. I stared at him and started to stand. Had I overloaded his computing core? I could almost hear Crim complaining that I'd broken Kierenbot and that I should've been more careful. He'd probably keep going on about it, but by then I would've tuned him out or told him to be quiet.

Kierenbot's red orb flashed back on and expanded to take up his rectangular view port where his sensors were located.

"Alpha protocols updated," he said. His voice sounded monotone, like it wasn't him. "Human interaction project updated. Goals have been realigned with new data. Clearance to proceed to phase three."

I stood, eyebrows peaked above my eyes. "What's phase three?"

He didn't reply. Instead, he seemed to shut down again for a second and then he came back online. He peered at me and back at the seat I'd been sitting in as if he wasn't sure how I'd come to be standing in front of him.

"Apologies, Captain, I must've blanked out. What did you say?"

"You said something about phase three."

"I'm not sure what that means. Are you sure you heard correctly?"

I blinked. Kierenbot wasn't above pulling the occasional prank, but I didn't think this was one of those times. "I know what I heard."

"Hmm," Kierenbot said and brought up a holoscreen. A video feed came to prominence. It showed me sitting for a second and then I was standing in front of him. The entire event hadn't been recorded. "Looks like there was some kind of data corruption."

My shoulders slumped a little. "Come on, this is some kind of joke, right?"

Kierenbot shook his head. "I'm attempting no deception at this time, Captain."

I wasn't sure whether to believe him or not, but he seemed like he was telling the truth.

"Oh Captain, I'm actually glad you came. I pulled navigation and media updates, and there was something for Lanaya."

I frowned. "Lanaya?"

"Yes, she had some kind of public mailbox."

"What's in the message?"

"Captain, you of all people should know about the privacy protocols you made sure we adhere to."

I did, and interestingly enough, most aliens I'd met took the matter of personal privacy quite seriously. But it was something you had to ask for, so the assumption was that you were under some kind of surveillance unless you specified otherwise.

"Yeah, but this is different. Lanaya isn't an ordinary passenger. No one is supposed to know she's here."

Kierenbot considered it for a moment. "No one does know she's here. It's a public mailbox. It's just a generic message that contains some kind of image. Nothing that we should be worried about. Can I send it to her?"

I sighed and thought about it for a long moment. "Have her come to the bridge to get her message."

"Very well, Captain."

I turned to a workstation and checked my own messages. There was only one from Delos. It was a specialized comlink address to contact him directly. He'd been wanting me to contact him for a while now, and I'd managed to put it off for as long as I could. At this point, I had no other choice. We didn't know where Serena and Raylin had gone based on the data Delos had provided, and there was the Asherah bounty to collect. Beyond those things, Delos would likely want to know about whether I was interested in the occasional contract job to investigate things he needed to learn more about.

I opened the communications interface and initiated a connection. I had no idea where Delos was or if he was even awake.

Delos answered almost immediately. "Nathan Briggs, it's about time you responded to my message."

His pale-skinned head and neck appeared on my holoscreen. Jade-colored eyes seemed to stare right at me, and his mouth had a pleased tilt to it.

I glanced at the date of his original message and realized it was several days old. "Sorry about that. I was…honestly, I was injured and in recovery."

"Injured?"

I leaned to the side to show him the cast on my arm.

"Five days in the autodoc? That's serious. You should return to Vaois. I can arrange for one of our doctors to examine you."

I shook my head. "I appreciate it, but I think I'll be fine. While I've got you, there are some things you should know, but before we begin I need to confirm whether this comlink is secure."

"Always," Delos replied.

I proceeded to tell him about the Asherah, enough for him to consider sending a survey team to determine if fulfillment of existing bounties were appropriate.

"And you weren't able to retrieve any of the equipment you saw?" Delos asked.

I'd left out some of the details that would've led to some uncomfortable questions. I didn't need to become some kind of lab rat they studied.

"The place was in bad shape, and well, you'll see for yourself. I'll have Kierenbot create a report and send it over to you. Then you can let me know what you think."

Delos considered this and then leaned toward the camera. "You already know I'll move on this, or you wouldn't have brought it to my attention."

I smiled. "Pretty much. I knew you'd be interested."

He regarded me for a few moments, and the silence seemed to stretch out. "I'll send out a survey team, and we'll continue this discussion later. Have you been in contact with Raylin?"

I shook my head. "No, our next order of business was to go searching for her and Serena."

Delos frowned. "I didn't know they'd gone off together."

Something in his expression made me concerned. "What is it?"

"I haven't been in contact with them since I provided the data Raylin asked for, but I'd be lying if I said I wasn't concerned."

"What did you give them?"

"Raylin was concerned that the Human hybrid you encountered was the result of a clandestine operation that could've been backed by a number of organizations. They don't appreciate anyone poking around into their affairs."

"Well, they put Lanaya—or the Human hybrid—right in our path. It's probably an invitation of some kind to come look for them."

Delos considered it for a few moments, and then his gaze lifted to look away from the camera. "Perhaps."

"Is there anything else you can tell me? Something that will help me find them?"

"I'm afraid that's all I know, but I'll have my resources keep checking into it. I'll let you know as soon as I hear anything. I'll also make the data I provided Raylin available to you."

"Thanks, Delos."

"Of course."

"You know, this could come under that occasional contract work you spoke to Serena about."

He arched an eyebrow, amused. "You want to find your

friends, and you'd like me to pay you to do it? That's a bit of a stretch, isn't it?"

I shrugged. "I guess I figured I'd try."

"I'll tell you what: if you find out something that implicates any of our operations or represents a threat to developing species, I 'd like to know about it. Perhaps an arrangement can be reached between us."

I smiled. "That sounds fair. Thanks again for your help."

I closed the comlink and pondered the conversation. If Raylin had thought she'd be in danger, would she have allowed Serena to come with her? I guess that depended on whether Raylin thought Serena could handle the danger. I tried to make myself believe that they were probably okay, but a gnawing knot of worry began to tighten in my gut.

The door to the bridge opened and Lanaya walked in, followed by Crim.

She looked at me and smiled. "Crim told me you were out of the capsule. Are your injuries improving?"

"Yes," I replied. I tried not to regard her as some kind of sleeper agent or a grenade about to explode. Perhaps I was getting paranoid. "Kierenbot told me you had a message."

Lanaya frowned. "A message?"

Kierenbot turned toward us. "Yes, from a public mailbox. It had your identification associated with it."

"I don't have any identification."

I arched an eyebrow toward him. "Are you sure about this?"

"Positive. Our identifications are linked by our unique DNA sequences. This message is for you," Kierenbot replied.

She looked at me, and I shrugged. "Let's take a look at the message and then decide."

She nodded.

"I'll put it on the main holoscreen," Kierenbot said.

A series of images appeared. They were star maps with flashing sequence colors between them. It passed so quickly that I couldn't make sense of it.

I was about to ask Kierenbot to replay the message when I noticed Lanaya. She stood so still that I wasn't sure she was breathing. She stared off into space without blinking. Her head was tilted to the side.

I moved in front of her and called out her name.

She didn't respond right away. Her eyes began to glisten from not blinking. Then she frowned at me.

"Nathan Briggs," she said in an assertive tone, "I have them. If you want them back, you'll need to do something for me."

I glanced over at Crim, who looked just as confused as I was.

I looked back at Lanaya. "Who do you have?"

She blinked several times and looked as if she'd suddenly become aware of me. She smiled. "What was that?"

My mouth hung open. "You just said you have them, and if I wanted them back I needed to do something for you."

She frowned and bowed her head demurely. "I'm sorry, I don't remember," she said softly.

I looked at Kierenbot. "Replay the message."

He did, but this time Lanaya didn't lapse into some kind of trance. She hardly reacted at all.

"I'm really sorry I can't be of more assistance," she said.

I looked at Crim. "We need to figure this out. Kierenbot, find out where that message came from."

"At once, Captain," Kierenbot replied.

"Who do you think sent it?" Crim asked.

"I don't have any idea, but I'm going to find out."

If I had any doubts as to whether Serena and Raylin were in danger, they were gone now. "Get the others up here. We've got work to do."

AUTHOR NOTE

Thank you so much for reading. I hope you enjoyed the book and the series. *Space Raiders Forgotten Empire* is the second book in the series and there will be a third. I enjoy writing the stories that I write and this book was no different. The characters and their interactions are what invests me in the story and what I look for when I read books.

I'm not done with Nate or the crew of the Spacehog just yet. There is plenty of trouble for them to get into. I sincerely hope you enjoyed this book, and if you could help spread the word about it, I would be grateful. Reviews, ratings, and recommendations are ways to help.

Thanks again for reading my books. Space Raiders Forgotten Empire is my 30th book, and I'm looking forward to writing at least 30 more.

Thanks again for reading my books. Please consider leaving a review for *Space Raiders - Forgotten Empire*.

Space Raiders continues with book 3 - **Space Raiders - Dark Menace.**

If you're looking for another series to read check out one of the following:

First Colony Series: The Ark – humanity's valiant effort to reach beyond the confines of our solar system to establish the first interstellar colony on a distant star. For three hundred thousand colonists, the new colony brings the promise of a fresh start…a second chance. Escaping wrongful imprisonment wasn't something Connor had in mind, but being put into stasis aboard Earth's first interstellar colony ship was something he couldn't have prepared for. Connor might be the wrong man for the colony, but he's the right man to see that it survives what's coming.

Federation Chronicles: First came the development of a Personality Matrix Construct—PMC, transferring human consciousness into a machine. It changed the galaxy and the way wars were fought. Then something went wrong with PMCs and the Federation Wars toppled the galactic order. PMCs became a menace to be hunted and exterminated. Long after the Federation Wars, the galaxy limps on. Spacers carve out an existence upon the bones of the old worlds, but things are about to change. . .something has begun broadcasting signals to reactivate PMCs that were stored in secret.

Ascension Series: Join the crew of the spaceship Athena on an epic journey. Kept secret for 60 years, the discovery of an alien signal forces a NASA pilot and computer hacker to team up to investigate an alien structure discovered in the furthest reaches of the solar system.

ABOUT THE AUTHOR

I've written multiple science fiction and fantasy series. Books have been my way to escape everyday life since I was a teenager to my current ripe old(?) age. What started out as a love of stories has turned into a full-blown passion for writing them.

Overall, I'm just a fan of really good stories regardless of genre. I love the heroic tales, redemption stories, the last stand, or just a good old fashion adventure. Those are the types of stories I like to write. Stories with rich and interesting characters and then I put them into dangerous and sometimes morally gray situations.

My ultimate intent for writing stories is to provide fun escapism for readers. I write stories that I would like to read, and I hope you enjoy them as well.

If you have questions or comments about any of my works I would love to hear from you, even if it's only to drop by to say hello at KenLozito.com

Thanks again for reading *Space Raiders - Forgotten Empire*

Don't be shy about emails, I love getting them, and try to respond to everyone.

ALSO BY KEN LOZITO

SPACE RAIDERS SERIES

Space Raiders

Space Raiders - Forgotten Empire

Space Raiders - Dark Menace

FIRST COLONY SERIES

Genesis

Nemesis

Legacy

Sanctuary

Discovery

Emergence

Vigilance

Fracture

Harbinger

Insurgent

Invasion

Impulse

Infinity

Expedition Earth

FEDERATION CHRONICLES

Acheron Inheritance

Acheron Salvation

Acheron Redemption

Acheron Rising (Prequel Novella)

Ascension Series

Star Shroud

Star Divide

Star Alliance

Infinity's Edge

Rising Force

Ascension

Safanarion Order Series

Road to Shandara

Echoes of a Gloried Past

Amidst the Rising Shadows

Heir of Shandara

If you would like to be notified when my next book is released visit kenlozito.com

Printed in Great Britain
by Amazon